The Fourth Question

By James Arendorf

Inspired by true events and real people

Proudly made in Morocco.

The best school; the real Antman Bouvard.

The best motivation; the real Augustine Bouvard.

The best lesson; the real Richard Poirier.

1

Contents

Chapter 1

If

Tuesday, December 13th, 1892.

It was a beautiful winter day in Georgetown city. The snow embellished the streets, the sky was clear blue, the cold winds blew occasionally, a beautiful white layer covered the ground, the decorations in the streets and on the house facades announced the approach of the greatest holiday of the year; Christmas. Everyone was in a happy and festive mood. Almost everyone.

In one of the Law firm offices, the mood was tense. Lyor Laszlo was furious at the courier:

- I gave you the letter to legalize it and submit it to Court!

The young courier replied in a confused tone:

- I … yes, Monsieur Lyor … I legalized your signature; I myself included this letter in the folder, at the office of your father's Secretary, Mr. Ernest Laszlo. And I myself submitted the folder to Court. The letter was indeed submitted to Cou…

Lyor grew impatient:

- So, explain to me why I'm still Dalya Bouvard's legal guardian for another year?!

A few weeks ago, in a moment of anger and frustration, Lyor Laszlo had written a request to officially remove himself from the responsibility of the Late Governor Iskander Balthazar's Will, thus bequeathing the right of stewardship to his father Ernest Laszlo. This letter had to be legalized and submitted to Court, before the answer of the 3rd Challenge. Except that, until this day, Lyor Laszlo was still the little girl's legal guardian.

For several minutes, while Lyor Laszlo and the courier tried to understand the situation, the Lawyer Sloan Wilfrid was sitting comfortably in a chair, enjoying his cup of coffee, in an innocent calm. Sloan Wilfrid listened attentively to the conversation between Lyor and the courier. At one point, Sloan Wilfrid pronounced one single word:

- If.

In a furious mood that morning, Lyor paid no attention to the presence or the words of his mentor Sloan Wilfrid. With an insistent and upset tone, Lyor continued to reprimand the courier:

- You have been tasked with this procedure thousands of times! It's easy to do, just one letter to legalize and submit. Yet, according to the Court documents, I am still the legal guardian of Dalya Bouvard. I don't understand where is the mistake?! Submitting this letter to Court was sufficient to nullify my responsibility for this Will…

Sloan Wilfrid interrupted him in an amused tone:

- If.

The young courier was lost too; he tried to remember the details of that day:

- I... Monsieur Lyor... the same day, you told me not to come back without this letter legalized. I legalized your signature and then I immediately came back here. The Secretary was not in her office ... so I myself included this letter in the red folder. At the end of the day, I swear I took that folder myself, and I submitted it to the legal correspondence office. This letter has been submitted to Court. You cannot still be responsible for this Will. Surely there must be a mistake in the legal correspondence offi...

Sloan Wilfrid observed the two young men, trying in vain to find the error in the legal proceedings. And with a calm voice, Sloan Wilfrid interrupted the courier:

- If.

At that moment, Lyor could no longer repress his anger, he exploded:

- Wilfrid!! It's the 3rd time you say the word if!! If what? What do you mean? If what?

After finally having Lyor's attention, Sloan Wilfrid let out an innocent chuckle:

- I add only a little correction to your sentence... the word if. If the letter has been submitted to Court, you would have been released from this Will.

For a few long seconds, the young Lyor Laszlo thought aloud:

- If... If the letter has been submitted... If the letter has been submitted... so ...then ... I am still her legal guardian, because the letter has not been submitted to Court?!

At that moment, Sloan Wilfrid couldn't hold back his amused laugh any longer. Apparently, the Lawyer Sloan Wilfrid was the only one who knew that this letter had innocently disappeared from the red folder of the Secretary, when the young woman was absent from her office ... and therefore, this letter was never submitted to Court.

Lyor Laszlo and the courier exchanged a confused and surprised look. As he got up and walked out of the office, Sloan Wilfrid laughed heartily. Immediately, Lyor Laszlo followed him rapidly, and he screamed upset:

- Wilfrid!! But what have you done again?! Wilfrid !!

Chapter 2

The Christmas Gingerbread house

Wednesday, December 14th, 1892.

In the French neighbors' house, the Poirier, the atmosphere in the kitchen was warm and joyful.

- The icing is ready!! Mrs. Glorina declared, while quickly stirring a white cream in a large bowl.

The kitchen of the Poirier house was getting ready for the Christmas holidays. The stoves were well lit, the cake pans were all full, several bowls held treats of many colors and shapes; the large table in the center of the kitchen was fully occupied.

- I finished the cake polishing! Dalya Bouvard exclaimed in a proud voice.

Mrs. Glorina asked Dalya to refine the edges of the cake with a butter knife. Another person was comfortably sitting in a large armchair in front of the kitchen table. The great old woman, Mrs. Marianne Poirier was busy painting with caramelized sugar, the square cookies that would form the roof of the Gingerbread house.

- Now we need to put up the walls of the Gingerbread house and glue them together. Mrs. Glorina thought aloud.
- Glue the walls with the icing? Dalya wondered curiously.
- Yes, Mademoiselle. You will hold 2 cake walls, and I will put icing on the edges. Then, we glue the 2 pieces together. Mrs. Glorina explained to her.

It was the first time in her life that Dalya baked and created a Christmas Gingerbread house. To build a house of cakes, creams and sweets, Dalya was fascinated and curious about the final result.

- So, Mademoiselle, lift gently these two pieces of cake, with both hands, hold them vertically... yes... slowly... and I'm going to put icing on the edge... slowly...

Except that in a second, the 2 cakes in Dalya's hands broke. Her hands were too small, and the 2 cake walls were very fragile. It was very difficult to hold 2 cake walls vertically. Mrs. Glorina stifled an amused laugh:

- It's alright. Try another piece of cake ... gently... raise it ...yes, that's good. Try not to move... yes, toward u...

For the 2nd time, the 2 cake walls broke in Dalya's hands. Mrs. Marianne followed the construction of the Gingerbread house, with a curious and interested look. The great woman was delighted to participate in this activity; it occupied her mind and her days, from her illness.

- I thought it was easy to build! Dalya sighed, while looking surprised.

Mrs. Marianne and Mrs. Glorina laughed in an amused tone.

- Come on Mademoiselle, don't be discouraged! Mrs. Glorina replied. You just need a little practice. Once the first walls are built and settled, the rest of the house will be easy to achieve!

Dalya wiped her hands; she stretched her fingers for a second. Then, with a determined air, and for the 3rd time, Dalya took 2 pieces of cake, and she tried to lift them up, under the encouragements and directives of Mrs. Glorina:

- Yes, that's good... here you go... slowly... slowly... spread your fingers... up... lift... lift... li...

Suddenly, the kitchen door opened. This intrusion disturbed Dalya; the cake in her hands broke and fell on the kitchen table.

- Hello.

The intruder was Richard Poirier, the prodigy son of Mrs. Marianne. His elegant and sober suit and tie, indicated that he was returning from an important event at the Government Headquarters. Richard walked into the kitchen, and he greeted his mother first, placing a soft kiss on the great woman's hand. Mrs. Marianna smiled back at him, and she continued to paint the cookies. Richard Poirier was very happy to observe his mother busy and in good company.

Then, the young man turned toward the employee of the house, Mrs. Glorina:

- Is this the Christmas Gingerbread house you are preparing?
- Yes, Monsieur. And it will be a masterpiece! Mrs. Glorina exclaimed proudly.
- I don't doubt it, Mrs. Glorina.

Richard greeted Dalya with a discreet smile. And despite Dalya Bouvard's usual visits to the Poirier home, Richard always and still felt nervous by the presence of this strange little girl. The young Richard made a considerable effort to hide his nervousness; his throat tightened, his heart was beating at high speed, his hands were shaking, his words were lost ... and yet, Richard Poirier was happy by Dalya Bouvard's presence.

Dalya smiled back shyly. It is true that since always, Dalya thought that Richard was intimidating. With his elegant and sober suits, his calm face, his courteous and composed personality, Richard Poirier exuded an intimidating air. And despite that, Dalya was delighted to meet him on each visit.

- Would you like some tea, Monsieur Richard?

- No need to bother you, Mrs. Glorina. I will wait for dinner when you're done.

When Richard turned around to leave the kitchen, Dalya picked up 2 pieces of cake, for the 4th time, and she whispered:

- We won't be finishing this house any soon. It's almost impossible to raise both walls at the same time! My hands are too small; it slips in a second!

Mrs. Glorina laughed:

- We will try again, Mademoiselle. We have enough cake for the walls. It will take a few minutes to stick them, but we'll get there...

Suddenly, a voice interrupted Mrs. Glorina:

- I have a few free minutes.

The 3 women turned toward the origin of this voice. Richard Poirier was still present in the kitchen. Immediately, the 3 women stopped in their moves, and they looked at Richard Poirier, they were all surprised by his offer.

The young man cleared his tight throat, and he continued in a confident voice:

- You need another pair of hands; I suppose?

It is true that a pair of hands was needed to lift the walls of cake and fix them together. The great woman, Mrs. Marianne couldn't help, her hands were shaking. And Mrs. Glorina had to put icing on the edge of the cake and stick the walls. Only Dalya could hold the cake walls, but her hands were too small.

Mrs. Glorina asked again, with a confused tone:

- You ... help us ... build the ...

Richard Poirier answered, with a little smile:

- I will be happy to help.

The 3 women were surprised by Richard Poirier's offer. Mrs. Glorina was happy to have help with this complicated cake to build. Mrs. Marianne was very surprised by her son's offer; Richard had never helped in the kitchen before, in all his life. Mrs. Marianne tried to hide her proud smile, and she watched the construction of the Gingerbread house with an even more interested stare than before. Dalya Bouvard was as intimidated by the young man's offer, as by his presence in the kitchen.

Instantly, Richard Poirier took off his elegant jacket, he rolled up the sleeves of his white shirt, and he washed his hands. Mrs. Glorina ordered in a serious tone:

- So… Mademoiselle, raise one wall of cake, with both hands, gently. And Monsieur, please raise another wall of cake… yes, just like that… bring this wall closer to that of Mademoiselle… a little more… gently…

Dalya and Richard carried out Mrs. Glorina's orders to the letter. Mrs. Marianne observed the construction of the Gingerbread house with an amused and curious look; she never thought watching her son participate in the cooking. Richard himself was surprised to feel a pleasure in having his hands in the dough; he never thought one day of helping in the kitchen.

When Mrs. Glorina finished putting the icing all along the edges of the cake walls that Dalya and Richard were holding, she ordered:

- And now… pull the walls together gently, and stick the edges together… squeeze your fingers together, and don't let go of the cake… the icing needs a few moments to stick the two pieces together.

At this precise moment, a strange thing happened in the kitchen of the Poirier family. When Dalya and Richard brought their walls of cake together, they tightened the fingers of their hands to hold the 2 walls. As soon as their fingers touched and intertwined, a powerful sensation invaded Dalya and Richard, to the point that they jumped instantly. One would have thought that the two young people were struck by an electric shock. It was a strong, uncomfortable, and inexplicable feeling. Dalya turned very red, and Richard turned very pale. Their fingers intertwined and tight, the two young people did not dare to move and even less to undo their fingers from each other.

Mrs. Glorina was focused on her cake; she was finishing a few missed holes in the two walls of cake, not realizing what was going on in the kitchen, at that moment.

Only Mrs. Marianne Poirier noticed the reaction of her son and the little girl. The great woman had a precise eye. When the fingers of Dalya Bouvard and Richard Poirier touched, Mrs. Marianne noticed the electric shock which struck the two young people. And this electric shock… Mrs. Marianne understood it perfectly well. The great woman leaned back in her armchair, and she smiled, with an amused air, but above all delighted.

Mrs. Glorina announced in a confident voice:

- The walls should be well glued by now. Release the cake, gently and slowly.

When they untangled their fingers and pulled away from each other, Dalya and Richard were out of breath. Their throats were tight, their hearts beating rapidly, and their hands tense. They both didn't understand the origin of this electric shock which struck them. They didn't dare to look each other in the face. Mrs. Marianne Poirier observed Dalya and Richard, and she smiled discreetly. While Mrs. Glorina exclaimed in a proud and joyful tone:

- That's a great job! The walls are holding up perfectly! Let's restart a second time. Mademoiselle, Monsieur … raise the walls of cake, please… gently… slowly…

Several minutes later, and several walls of cake built later, the Gingerbread house was finally created. Richard Poirier left the kitchen and he headed toward his office. He watched his hands curiously. Never in his life had Richard felt such a sensation. Each time he touched Dalya Bouvard's fingers, Richard received an electric shock that invaded his entire body. Why and how, he had absolutely no idea. And the strangest thing was that it wasn't an unpleasant feeling... uncomfortable, yes... but not unpleasant. At a moment, Richard Poirier looked at his hands ... and he smiled.

Chapter 3

Cooking in the grand Mansion

Friday, December 16th, 1892.

This year, the Italian Cook of the grand Mansion, Mr. Ferrero Lutché, had also decided to build a Gingerbread house for the Christmas holiday. Except that, the building of this cake was not the same as at the house of the French neighbors. After several hours of work, the Gingerbread house of the French neighbors was very well built, delicious, nicely decorated, in a serene and joyful mood. In the kitchen of the grand Mansion, it was an entirely different scene...

-   LEAVE THE MARSHMALLOWS ARI!! DON'T TOUCH THE MERINGUES ADI!!

Dalya had both hands busy holding the wall of cake vertically, she couldn't move and chase her little twin sisters. Her friend and classmate Amira Mounier was holding the other wall of cake, trying her best to stifle her giggles. Meanwhile, the Cook was focused on gluing the icing to the edges of the two walls of cake, that the two girls were holding:

-   Alright... va bene... va bene... non muoverti... don't move... va bene, va bene... la glassa terrà...

The little twins were sitting in front of the large kitchen table. Dalya thought her little twin sisters would have a blast helping build this Christmas cake. And the little twins helped a lot... specially to eat the treats intended for the decoration of the cake!

At one moment the Cook asked:

-   Mesdemoiselles Dalya, Amira ... stick the two walls back together, per favore. The frosting is finito.

When Dalya brought her wall of cake closer, and she touched her friend Amira's fingers, Dalya felt no strong and intense sensation, no electric shock like the one she felt with Richard Poirier. Never before had Dalya felt such a strong feeling, with anyone else... except with Richard Poirier. Why and how, Dalya had absolutely no idea.

-   It's a good thing we didn't have a lot of homework for this holiday! Amira sighed in a reassured tone.

Standing still, squeezing her friend's fingers to glue the two walls of cake together, Dalya replied:

-   Yes, it is indeed a miracle, for once. I think the Teachers just forgot to fill us with homework.

Amira laughed:

- And luckily, they forgot! This week, we had to repair the roof of our house and do some renovations work, we had a lot of cleaning to do, my father and I. We covered all the furnitu...

Dalya interrupted her friend :

- PUT DOWN THE BOWL OF CHOCOLATE RAISINS, RIGHT NOW, ARI!! ... ADI, YES, I'M TALKING TO YOU TOO!! ... THE BOWL STAYS ON THE TABLE!! ARI !! ADI !!

The little twins defended themselves with all their might:

- We are zentilles! We just taste a little!
- One raisin Socolate! We took only one!

Her hands stuck and busy, Dalya barely held her anger:

- One chocolate raisin?! Put down the bowl immediately!! We need it to decorate the surroundings of the walls!! Put the bowl back down right now!!

Amira thought aloud:

- They are adorable...

Except that Dalya immediately corrected her:

- They are pests!

Ari and Adi instantly retaliated, while filling their mouths:

- We are zentilles!! We not pests!!
- We did nothing!! We very nice!!

The Cook asked:

- Mesdemoiselles... va bene... let go of the walls now... it should hold well by now.

When the two girls let go of the cake walls, Amira Mounier was the first to notice a strange thing in the cake:

- Mr. Cook, it seems to me that the two walls do not match perfectly, there is a gap.

Dalya tilted her head and stared at the cake for a long second:

- My wall is long rectangular... Amira's wall is a small trapezium...

At this moment the Cook jumped:

-   What a fool I am! Che vertigini sono! I gave to you a house wall, and to your friend the garden terrace!

Dalya and Amira exchanged an amused laugh. It is true that the Cook prepared excellent meals, however the architecture was not his strong point. Amira Mounier approached the Cook, and she took a paper from her bag:

-   I will help you review the house plans. So, we need 4 long rectangular walls, 8 small squares for the windows, a small rectangle for the door…
-   DON'T TOUCH THE CHERRIES!! ARI PUTS THE CHERRY BACK IN ITS PLACE!! ADI PUT DOWN THE CHERRY IMMEDIATELY !!

Now that her hands were free, Dalya came close to her little twin sisters, who justified themselves with one voice:

-   We just want to taste cherry!! Only one!!
-   We want to know if cherry sweet or bitter!! That's all!!
-   We zentilles, Dindin!! We adorable!!
-   We just taste!! We nice, Dindin!!

For a moment, Dalya stared confusedly at the decoration containers, she asked her little twin sisters:

-   Where are the chocolate raisins that filled the bowl? The bowl is empty!

Ari and Adi exchanged a curious look; they didn't understand their big sister's question. The little twins answered naturally with an innocent smile:

-   Dindin said put the bowl down…
-   Dindin didn't say put the Socolate raisins too…

Anger invaded Dalya in a second, she screamed:

-   YOU ATE ALL THE CHOCOLATE RAISINS?!

Immediately, the little twins escaped and they ran in opposite direction, in the kitchen of the grand Mansion, laughing heartily:

-   Sorry Dindin!! Sorry Dindin!!

While Dalya chased her little twin sisters in the kitchen, Amira Mounier and the Cook tried to rebuild the Christmas Gingerbread house. The kitchen of the grand Mansion was upside down; containers and bowls everywhere, the big table was filled with cakes and treats, a noise of escaped laughs and screams of anger could be heard until the outside.

One thing is for sure, this Christmas cake at the grand Mansion seemed far from being done!

Chapter 4

Determined to take back her right

Tuesday, December 20th, 1892.

All the houses in Georgetown city, were preparing for the Christmas holiday, in a good mood and joyful spirit. However, in the house of the Edelmen family, anger and worry occupied the minds. The Late Governor's nephew and niece had not foreseen this turn of events.

- So ... if I understand correctly ... this little vegetables and fruits seller, will succeed to answer all the Challenges of this Will, and have this fortune!

In the luxurious living room, the nephew Mr. Ferdinand Edelmen looked confused and anxious. His voice was shaking. His dark eyes circles and pale face, clearly indicated that he hadn't slept well for several days ... to be more exact, he hadn't slept well since 3 years. After the passing away of his uncle Iskander Balthazar, and the reading of the Will, the events were out of the control of Mr. Ferdinand Edelmen.

Sitting next, in an armchair, immobile and pale, his dear friend, the Lawyer Mr. Ernest Laszlo became more and more silent and less and less arrogant. Never in his entire career did he lose a case to...a poor little girl. The Lawyer Mr. Ernest Laszlo used all the tricks, the pressures, and the detours that he could to recover this fortune. He even tried to invalidate the Governor's Will and correct the right to inheritance. Except that the Lawyer Mr. Ernest Laszlo failed in all his attempts.

Mr. Ferdinand Edelmen whispered nervously, having almost lost his senses and reason:

- We will be ruined ... we will not inherit a penny ... we have lost this fortune.

For several long minutes, the niece Mrs. Honoré Edelmen was comfortably seated on a couch, watching the 2 men confused and crushed by their failures. Always sublime and of great beauty, Mrs. Honoré was wearing a long blood-red dress, and black precious stones around her neck. She sipped her tea in a refined manner and calm. Except that it was a strange calm.

After a long moment of heavy silence, Mrs. Honoré put down her cup of tea, and she announced in a confident voice:

- I will personally take care of it, this time.

Mr. Ferdinand Edelmen and Mr. Ernest Laszlo awoke from their confusion and worry. The two men exchanged a surprised look. Mrs. Honoré Edelmen never intervened in their affairs, being often of a calm and passive nature. Except that day, Mrs. Honoré's gaze showed a determined anger. Her beauty was no longer peaceful, but terrifying. Mrs. Honoré repeated in a defiant tone:

- I will personally take care of it, this time!

Where 2 men failed ... a woman will succeed. And this time, Mrs. Honoré Edelmen seemed determined to take back her fortune and her right ... at any price!

Chapter 5

The Snow Panther and the strange Box

Tuesday, December 27th, 1892. In the grand Mansion.

This year, the Christmas holiday went peacefully and joyfully at the grand Mansion. In the luxurious dining room, Dalya Bouvard was joined by all the employees for the Christmas feast. The Cook Mr. Ferrero Lutché had prepared a delicious and copious buffet. The help Cook, Océanie Shell had brought out the most precious plates and cutlery. The head of the grand Mansion, Mr. Benjamin Bûchebois decorated the luxurious dining room, to perfection and caring about the smallest details. The Gardener Mr. Weil Rosenwald installed the Christmas tree in the living room. The maid Cristelle helped Dalya's twin little sisters to decorate the tree. The server assistant Igor Richter complained as usual, having to reload the wood for all the fireplaces in the house.

And since Christmas never ends without nice surprises, Dalya was happy to receive a special gift from the Lawyer Mr. Sloan Wilfrid: a registration card at the National Library of Georgetown!

Dalya was always touched by the Lawyer's kindness and care toward her. Sloan Wilfrid understood the little girl's wishes, even before she speaks them. The City's National Library had several books and manuscripts that Dalya could not find elsewhere. Dalya didn't dare to ask the Lawyer how he convinced the young Lyor Laszlo to register her in the Library, and to remain her legal guardian. Dalya only thanked Mr. Sloan Wilfrid warmly, and she promised him a basket full of cinnamon apple muffins.

After the Christmas holidays, this last December day was busy both inside and outside the grand Mansion. The snow was falling in flakes. A white layer decorating the ground, became more and more thick. The trees suffered the cold of the season, without complaining. And the sky showed no other color but gray. Winter reigned as master of the place.

In the Library of the grand Mansion, Dalya and her best friend Amira Mounier were assiduously working on their last holiday homework. The Mathematics Teacher asked them to look up the definition of 20 arithmetic terms. Amira was coming down a ladder, carrying a large book in her hand:

- I found a word... hypotenuse!

Sitting in front of the desk, and writing down her definitions, Dalya exclaimed happily:

- This is the word before the last, in the list! We'll be done with this homework soon!

Amira put the book on the desk, and she sat down to copy the definition of the word. When a little noise was heard in the Library. The two girls turned around, and they watched the Snow Panther lying on a rug in front of the lit fireplace. Séraphine stuttered, half asleep. Amira Mounier laughed:

- A panther's life! I would have liked to take naps all day. Séraphine has not changed her habits; she spends her days eating, taking naps, and following you everywhere and all the time.

Dalya laughed at her friend's remark, while finishing her homework:

- Yes, it's very true; Séraphine follows me all the ti...

Except that at this moment, Dalya stopped writing and she turned around a second time toward the Snow Panther. While contemplating the magnificent and mysterious creature, a crazy idea crossed Dalya's mind, she thought aloud:

- Since my first days here, at the grand Mansion, the Panther followed me everywhere, in my bedroom, in the living room, in the Library. Séraphine waited for me to come home from school every day, in the garden.

Amira answered in a half-concentrated voice, while writing on a paper:

- Yes, I admit it's very strange; this Panther has always followed you like a shadow!

Dalya continued to think:

- Except, no... Séraphine didn't always follow me.

At this remark, Amira also stopped writing, and she turned toward her friend:

- What do you mean ?

Dalya straightened up on her chair:

- Do you remember the incident that happened before the 3rd Challenge? The disappearance of the Excelbox.
- Yes of course! We almost went crazy looking for this strange box!

For a long second, Dalya stared at the Snow Panther:

- When the box disappeared, the Panther stopped following me. Séraphine watched the annex house assiduously...because that's where the box was!

Amira's brain needed a long minute to understand her friend's idea:

- So... so, you think ... the box and the Panther ... are related?

The two girls turned around and they observed the magnificent Panther with a thousand mysteries. And with certainty, Dalya affirmed:

- Séraphine is linked to the Excelbox. I don't know how and why. But the Snow Panther and the strange box are linked to each other!

After several seconds of silence and thinking, Dalya thought aloud:

- I had previously sought to understand the mystery of this strange box, in all the books of the Library. But I never managed to find any information on the Excelbox. Maybe... maybe, I should have looked for informations on the Snow Panther ... maybe Séraphine will lead me to the origin of the Excelbox!

Suddenly and abruptly, Amira Mounier jumped up from her chair:

- I search in the left shelves! You search in the right shelves!

It is true that a link between the Snow Panther and the Excelbox was a strange and surprising idea. Nevertheless, one thing is for sure ... Dalya Bouvard was getting closer and closer to the truth.

Chapter 6

Iskander Balthazar and the great Master

Tuesday, April 8th, 1890. About 2 years and 9 months ago.

The grand Mansion sank into a peaceful silence. Seated in front of his desk, Governor Iskander Balthazar was working in the Library of his grand Mansion. Having only his Snow Panther for company, Séraphine was lying down in front of the fireplace. The file that the Governor was working on that evening, was about the water dam project a few kilometers away from Georgetown city. This construction would benefit the agricultural lands surrounding the city, the cattle farms and even the residents of Georgetown city. Iskander Balthazar wanted to validate this project and begin the construction of the water dam, before the disease prevail him.

At one moment, focused on his files, Iskander Balthazar was interrupted by the presence of the head of the grand Mansion, Mr. Benjamin Bûchebois.

- Sorry to bother you, Mr. Governor ... someone wants to meet you.

Without looking up from his files, Iskander Balthazar asked the employee of the Mansion:

- Who is this? What about?

The head of the grand Mansion hesitated for a few moments:

- The visitor... the visitor says it's about the Snow Panther.

With these words, Governor Iskander Balthazar stopped writing, and he exclaimed in a curious tone:

- About Séraphine?!

A few seconds later, the employee let a man into the Library of the grand Mansion. The visitor was a middle-aged man, of Asian origin, a calm and serene allure, a polite smile, he wore modest and simple clothes. When the employee withdrew, leaving the two men alone, the visitor greeted the Governor, bowing his head in a respectful way:

- Good evening, Mr. Governor.

Curious about the visit of this stranger, Iskander Balthazar asked in a courteous tone:

- Good evening, Sir ... may I know who you are?

The visitor approached the Governor's office with a slow step, and he smiled:

- Do you remember me, Mr. Governor?

Iskander Balthazar stared at the visitor for a long minute. The stranger had a foreign accent, and he was wearing unusual clothes. Without finding a clue or a memory in his mind, Iskander Balthazar replied in a certain tone:

-   No...sorry, Sir...I don't think we've met before.

The visitor ended the Governor's sentence with a certain tone too:

-   ...not in this Country, anyway.

At these words, suddenly, Governor Iskander Balthazar froze in his chair for long seconds. He couldn't believe his eyes and ears. Instantly, a small detail emerged from the distant memories of Iskander Balthazar:

-   The strange box... the traditional market, in the city of Bayannur, China... the shop seller, at the end of the Alley... you... you were the shop seller who gave a strange box to my wife Irea!

The visitor with Asian features smiled:

-   That's quite right, Mr. Governor... quite right.

And as unlikely as it was, Iskander Balthazar let out an innocent chuckle as he recalled a memory:

-   My wife had tried by all means to open this strange box, without succeeding. You gave her a box that won't open !

In a confident voice, the great Master affirmed:

-   The box will open, Mr. Governor... at the right time... at the right time.

These were strange words which the Governor did not understand. However, Iskander Balthazar was curious to know why a stranger met in a very distant Country, was in Georgetown city, why he asked to see the Governor, and why the Snow Panther was involved. Iskander Balthazar asked the visitor:

-   And what brings you here, Sir? May I know what you want from me and my Panther?

At that moment, the great Master answered in a calm tone:

-   The reason for my visit tonight, is an unusual move that the Snow Panther had made at the Toscana restaurant ... 3 days ago.

Iskander Balthazar's stare shifted toward the Snow Panther, still lying on a rug in front of the fireplace. And although he enjoyed Séraphine's company, the Governor still couldn't understand the behavior of this strange creature. The Snow Panther was a mystery to everyone. The Governor replied:

- It is quite correct. Séraphine made a sort of bow in front of a little girl ... a poor stranger who sells vegetables and fruits at the market in front of the Toscana restaurant. How do you know about this?

The great Master was expecting all these questions, and he was ready to answer them, but only at the right time. And before continuing, the great Master wanted to confirm one important thing:

- The bow of this Panther, at the Toscana restaurant... was it the same bow that a mother Panther had already made to your young wife, during your visit to China?

Stunned by this distant memory, the Governor was paralyzed in front of the man with Asian features. Iskander Balthazar had a feeling that he was about to discover something far greater than just a courtesy visit. The Governor asked in a serious and grave voice:

- What exactly is happening? Who are you?

The great Master displayed a calm and serene smile:

- It's a long story, Mr. Governor... an ancient Legend.

Lying back on his armchair, the Governor invited the visitor to sit down on one of the armchairs, in front of his work desk. The fireplace illuminated the Library with a soft but powerful fire. The Snow Panther stood up and approached the Governor; Séraphine sat down at his feet, resting her little head on the Governor's lap. In a curious voice, Iskander Balthazar addressed the visitor:

- I'm listening to you.

The great Master Fong Ka-Ho narrated, and Governor Iskander Balthazar listened. That night, in the grand Mansion, Iskander Balthazar heard a story, and he discovered an ancient Legend that will charm your imagination ... Dear readers.

Chapter 7

Back to school

Monday, January 2nd, 1893.

It was the first day of the new school year for the 2nd semester. The city of Georgetown was bustling with students returning to their schools, early in the morning. And the parents were all active and anxious to support well their children.

At the grand Mansion, when the maid Cristelle knocked on the bedroom door, she was surprised to find Dalya Bouvard already wide awake, wearing her school uniform, and busy arranging her school bag.

And despite all the explanations and arguments from the employees of the grand Mansion, the Heiress of the greatest fortune in the Country Dalya Bouvard insisted in tidying up her own bed, every morning. Seeing the tidy bed, the maid Cristelle smiled, and announced joyfully:

- Good morning, Mademoiselle! You are well ready, this morning!

Before the little girl answered, the help Cook Océanie also entered the bedroom. Océanie announced:

- Good morning, Mademoiselle Dalya! Here are your well-polished shoes. Monsieur Bûchebois insisted on cleaning your shoes, himself.

Dalya filled her school bag with books and notebooks, politely replying:

- Good morning, Cristelle ... good morning Océanie ... thank you for bringing me my polished shoes. It's nice of Monsieur Bûchebois to take care of it.

The maid Cristelle took care of drawing aside the large curtains of the bedroom, inviting the light of the day to come inside:

- Today, the Cook has prepared delicious apple and cinnamon muffins for you. The spicy sweet smell already fills my stomach. He added the caramelized sugar with a pinch of vanill...

When suddenly, the help Cook Océanie put Dalya's shoes on the floor, with a quick move, and she ran toward the bathroom, choking her mouth with both hands. Dalya was busy arranging her school bag, and Cristelle was busy opening the curtains; none of them noticed Océanie's reaction. The maid Cristelle continued in an enthusiastic voice:

- And it's your back to school this 2nd semester, isn't it? It's going to be a beautiful day, Mademoiselle!

Dalya was closing her school bag, while looking left and right, in every corner of the room, with a worried voice:

- It will be a beautiful day if I can find my Mathematics textbook. But where is it?! It was supposed to be on this work table. I might be late for my first day of school. I thought I put the textbook here.

Cristelle adjusted the cushions of the armchair, thinking aloud:

- Maybe you left it in the Library downstairs.

Kneeling and searching under the bed, Dalya replied:

- No, I'm sure it's here. I didn't leave it in the Libr...

When suddenly, the Snow Panther entered the bedroom. Séraphine emitted a little meow, which caught Dalya and Cristelle's attention and stare. And what the two girls discovered shocked them. The Snow Panther proudly held in its jaw... the Mathematics textbook! Why and where did Séraphine find this book? How did Séraphine guess that this book was wanted? No one could answer these questions. The Snow Panther wore a proud and a happy smile.

- The intelligence of this Panther fascinates me! Cristelle laughed.
- The intelligence of this Panther worries me! Dalya replied.

Moments later, Dalya entered the dining room. Breakfast was served and still hot. And for her first day of school, the Cook had spoiled Dalya very well; on the table there was coffee with milk, fresh orange juice, apple and cinnamon muffins, diced fruit, toasts, various cheeses, and many jams.

- Bonjour Mademoiselle. The head of the grand Mansion announced in a formal tone.
- Bonjour, Mr. Bûchebois!

The head of the grand Mansion repressed a smile on his lips. The little girl's courteous and spontaneous manners did not change. The employee poured orange juice into a glass, and he served it to the little girl:

- I guess Mademoiselle is ready for her back to school?

Dalya sat in her chair, and she quickly ate her breakfast, glancing anxiously at the large clock on the wall:

- I wouldn't have turned down some more vacation days. But I can't wait to find out the schedule that Professor Canfield will give me. Each semester, Professor Canfield registers me in new classes to take.

The head of the grand Mansion served Dalya a basket of crispy toasts:

- I understand that you are already taking 8 classes.

23

Dalya spread jam on a toast, and she looked at the clock:

- Yes, 8 classes already! I take almost all my friend Amira Mounier's classes. I have 3 classes left to be at exactly the same level… can I take 3 muffins with me on the way to school, please?

The head of the grand Mansion froze in his move. He stopped pouring milk into a cup. It must be admitted that it was a strange and ridiculous question coming from the owner of the grand Mansion. Except that even for a simple muffin, the little Dalya Bouvard always asked permission. Mr. Bûchebois pulled himself together, and he replied:

- Of course … certainly, Mademoiselle … take as many as you want.

Immediately, Dalya wrapped 3 muffins in a white napkin, glancing anxiously at the clock:

- Thank you, Monsieur. I must go out, right now, I can't be late!

Picking up her school bag, Dalya left the dining room, her mouth full of the last bits of bread:

- Thank you … for … the … breakfast … Monsieur … Bûchebois … and … the … muffins!!

The head of the grand Mansion watched the little girl leave the house, with a quick and hasty step. And as formal and serious as he was, Mr. Bûchebois smiled thoughtfully.

Barely out of the grand Mansion, two little silhouettes called Dalya, with joyful screams:

- Good morning Dindin! Good morning Dindin!

Dalya walked toward the annex house, and her little twin sisters joined her halfway, in the large garden. For the little twins to wake up so early in the morning, it must have been an important day for them.

- Good morning, Ari… good morning, Adi… so, are you ready for your first day at kindergarten?

By the way, this January day was the first day of school for the two little twins. Ari and Adi were ecstatic to start their education in a school. The little twins were wearing their uniforms; a pink apron, midnight blue pant and coat, a small pink hat, and black shoes.

The little twins welcomed their big sister, jumping joyfully:

- We going to school today!!
- We play with others!!
- We have Teacher like Dindin!!
- We have school bags like Dindin!!
- Looki!! Looki!! Zolie bag!!
- We school uniforms!! Zoli apron!!

Dalya Bouvard was happy that her little sisters started school, much earlier than her. Her father, Antman Bouvard had decided to register the twins in a little school, downtown, few streets from Dalya's College. Composed of only 3 classes, the little school welcomed children from 4 to 6 years old, teaching them many subjects and activities throughout the day.

Kneeling down, Dalya tightened the hats of her little twin sisters, and she ordered them in a serious tone:

- So listen to me! No fooleries. You must not upset the Teacher, you must be nice to your classmates, and you must follow all the Teacher's orders!
- Yes, Dindin!! We nice!!
- No fooleries!! We are zentilles!!

Dalya continued in a more considerate tone:

- Have fun. You will learn many things; drawing, counting, reading, calculating, playing, singing. You will love school, I'm sure of that!

Ari and Adi smiled proudly:

- Yes!! We happy to go to school!!
- We play in school!!

Dalya took 2 muffins out of her bag, and she put them in her sisters' little bags:

- Here are apple and cinnamon muffins … for your way to school.
- Mici Dindin!! Mici Dindin!!

After kissing their big sister, the little twins ran to the garage of the annex house, answering their father's call. Antman Bouvard had taken the carriage out and attached it to the horse he had bought a few weeks earlier. Antman took care to drop off his twin daughters at school each morning and bring them back each afternoon.

Antman Bouvard still pretended not to see or hear his eldest daughter, and Dalya had sadly grown used to her father ignoring her. Dalya waved to her little sisters. The twins immediately sat down on the carriage, jumping up and singing joyfully:

- We go to school!! We go to school!! We go to school !!

Dalya turned around; she resumed her way to school. And she was late!

Several minutes of walking later, Dalya finally arrived at the door of her Mathematics class. Out of breath from running, her legs no longer holding her, Dalya immediately sat down on the first chair she found in front of her. As soon as Dalya regained her normal breathing, a hand patted her back. Amira Mounier sat on a chair behind Dalya, she asked her:

- Good morning, Dalya. I waited for you in the school yard. Why are you late ?

Dalya opened her school bag, and she replied:

- Good morning, Amira. I had to see my little sisters this morning; it's their first day at kindergarten today.

Amira took a few books out of her bag, and she sighed:

- Oh! Kindergarten! The good old times; coloring, songs, snacks, naps, games, nice Teachers ... the good old times!

Repressing an amused laugh, Dalya took a muffin out of her bag and she handed it to her friend. Immediately, Amira took it and she asked in a serious tone:

- Is it apple and cinnamon?

Dalya put books on her table:

- Yes, Monsieur the Cook prepared them fresh this morning. The smell of baking reached me to my bedroom upstairs! I thought you might like to taste it.

Amira tasted the muffin, affirming in a happy voice:

- ...and that's the reason why you are my best friend!

The two students laughed, as the Mathematics classroom was gradually filled with other students.

Later in the afternoon.

In his private office, Professor Canfield was sitting in front of his desk. He looked preoccupied and lost in his thoughts. Joyful and serene by nature, it was the first time that Professor Canfield seemed worried. The reopening of classes this semester went rather well; all the students received their new schedules, the Professors resumed their usual lessons, the employees of the College were busy with their work. The back to school this winter went off without a hitch. However, for several silent minutes, Professor Canfield observed a little paper placed on his desk. He had distributed all the schedules ... all but one.

At the sound of the bell, the halls of the school were filled with silhouettes and voices. Immediately, Professor Canfield came out of his office, and he waited for someone in the exit hall, while watching the students leave the school. At a moment, Professor Canfield walked toward a particular student, and he forced himself to put on his usual smile:

- Good afternoon, Mademoiselle Dalya Bouvard.

Dalya adjusted her bag, and she answered in a cheerful voice:

- Good afternoon, Professor! I have just finished my Mathematics class.

Professor Canfield asked:

- And I hope your first day this semester is going well?

Before Dalya could answer this question, the voice of her friend Amira Mounier appeared behind her:

- And how so?! First day of the semester and we already have homework! The Teachers who forgot to give us homework during the holidays, they are catching up now!

Professor Canfield and Dalya exchanged an amused chuckle. Amira adjusted her bag, and she addressed her friend Dalya:

- I'm going to drop off some borrowed books from the Library. Shall we meet outside, in the schoolyard?
- Alright.

When Amira left them, Professor Canfield cleared his throat; he tried to sound as natural as possible. While handing Dalya a paper, Professor Canfield announced to her:

- Mademoiselle, this is your schedule for this semester.

Dalya took back the paper and read it. The schedules indicated 2 classes. Delighted with this new addition, Dalya thought aloud:

- So, this semester, I will have 2 classes more with the 8 classes of the previous semester. That makes 10 classes in total for me to take. It seems doable to me. My friend Amira is already taking 10 classes too. Thank you for registering me Profess...

Professor Canfield interrupted Dalya in a strangely serious voice for once:

- You misunderstood your schedule, Mademoiselle. During this semester, you will not take 10 classes, but only 2 classes.

For a long minute, Dalya observed the Professor and the paper in her hand. Dalya asked in a determined voice:

- 2 classes only? But why? I followed 8 classes the previous semester, Professor. I can very well take 2 more classes.

Professor Canfield expected this confusion and these questions. Except that he couldn't reveal the reason for such an unusual schedule. Professor Canfield just smiled and affirmed in a decided voice:

- You did very well in the previous 8 classes, Mademoiselle. And I'm delighted. However, this semester is somewhat special. You will take only 2 classes. I will not keep you busy any longer, Mademoiselle. I let you join your classmate.

Moments later, Amira Mounier found her friend in the schoolyard.

- Guess what, Dalya! They have set up soft and comfortable chairs in a corner of the Library. It looks very nice. The Library assistant Miss Guendolyn informed me that they received them as a donation. A comfortable chair makes you want to read and spend the entire week at the Libr...

Dalya Bouvard didn't listen to a word her friend was saying. Her mind was occupied. And Amira Mounier realized it:

- Dalya, is everything alright? What did Professor Canfield want?

Pulling herself together with difficulty, Dalya answered in a confused voice:

- He... Professor Canfield handed me my schedule for this semester. I have... I have 2 classes.

Amira Mounier tried to relieve her friend's worry:

- I understand that it seems too full to you, in addition to the 8 classes of the previous semester, you have 10 classes now. But don't worry, we'll study together. And in the worst-case scenario, we will ask overtime hours from Teachers. 10 courses to pass this semester, it's not so worr...

Dalya turned toward her friend and she interrupted her:

- Amira... I don't have 10 classes to take this semester, I only have 2 classes!

Amira stopped walking, and she looked at her friend with a surprised stare:

- 2 classes? During the entire semester, you will have only 2 classes? Are you sure you understood correctly?

When reading Dalya's schedule paper, Amira froze.

- But... it's... Philosophy and Gymnastics, that's all? I have never seen such a schedule. I admit that 6 months studying only Philosophy and Gymnastics, is strange. You'll be bored; you won't have much to do. Did Professor Canfield explain to you why?

As they continued their walk, Dalya sighed:

- No, he gave no explanation. I didn't dare to insist on knowing.

Amira thought aloud:

- Professor Canfield is in charge of your education at the College. I think he lightened your schedule this semester in order to rest your brain. Maybe he is preparing you for the next semester. Perhaps you will receive classes of a higher level. Anyway, he has always watched over you, trust him. Surely, he must have a valid reason.

Dalya had no explanation for this special schedule. But Amira was right, Professor Canfield has always watched over Dalya. Therefore, she will just trust him.

After a minute of walking, Amira said in an embarrassed voice:

- Dalya, I'm sorry to inform you that for once, I can't help you with the Philosophy class. Although I myself do summaries, I take additional classes, and I learn by heart, I never get the average score ... fortunately, Professor Canfield understands that this class is difficult for all the students, he allows us to pass the class with 9 or 8 out of 20, a score below the average, as long as it is not a zero... the course is so difficult, no one gets it at all!

Dalya replied in a confident voice:

- If you are struggling in this Philosophy class, then a beginner like me has no chance of succeeding in it!

Dalya and Amira shared a giggle, continuing their way to their homes. With a carefree and innocent laugh, Dalya Bouvard had no idea of the Challenges and trials that lay ahead of her.

Chapter 8

Gymnastics

Tuesday, January 3rd, 1893. At the Royal Georgetown College.

Dalya followed the instructions of her friend Amira Mounier, in order to find the Gymnastics classroom. When arriving in front of the indicated door, Dalya paused for a moment. She breathed for a long minute, then she encouraged herself:

- Here we go!

Upon entering the room, Dalya discovered for the first time in her life what a Gymnasium is. It was a huge place, covered with a thin, puffy black carpet. The windows surrounding the room were large and transparent. In one corner stood a cupboard of several types of balloons. And in another corner were some several other strange objects.

Although the place was very intimidating, Dalya entered inside anyway. She noticed a little silhouette sitting on a bench. As soon as she noticed Dalya, the little silhouette stood up and greeted her with a kind smile:

- Welcome to your class... Mademoiselle Dalya Bouvard!

She was a young girl in her early twenties, beautiful almond eyes drawn in Asian features, a svelte shape, straight black hair and a pretty porcelain-pink skin, a smile and a softness imprinted on her face. The girl wore a pretty little cherry blossom on her hair. Dalya had the strange feeling of having met this girl before. But she couldn't remember where and when.

- I am your new Gymnastics Teacher. Call me Tudi.

The girl's accent and pronunciation clearly indicated that she was of foreign origin to the Country. And it was a very odd thing; because Amira Mounier informed Dalya that her Gymnastics Teacher would be Mr. Josh Williams; an old man in his sixties who slept almost two-thirds of the class time. Now, Dalya found herself face to face with a dynamic young girl of Asian origin. Not daring to ask about this change, Dalya quickly pulled herself together:

- I...yes...as you wish. Thank you for your help. Professor Canfield decided that I take this Gymnastics course 5 times a week, for the entire next semester.

At this moment, the young girl bowed her head greatly, and she affirmed in an admiring tone:

- ... And it would be a great honor for me to train the Nature's Chosen One, Mademoiselle.

Dalya remained frozen in her place, understanding neither the words of the young Professor, nor her reverence move toward her. Dalya just smiled nervously.

The young Tudi offered an object to Dalya:

\- This is your Gymnastics suit. The locker rooms are on this side. Change, please. And don't forget to wear these special socks. They are important for your workouts.

Dalya obeyed at the directives of her new Gymnastics Teacher. The uniform consisted of a tailored sweater and pants, in dark gray color. The fabric was soft and stretchy. Dalya observed the socks the young girl asked her to wear. Black, a flexible fabric, the socks were long to the calves.

When she came out of the locker room, the young Professor walked toward Dalya and explained to her:

\- At each session, we will start with an hour of breathing. Then, we will continue with an hour of stretching and warming up. The muscles must be warmed up and stretched, so as not to injure ourselves. At 10:00 AM, we will begin the kicking trainings. And after your lunch break, we will continue with other movements. Each month, we will study a specific exercice.

Dalya followed the young Professor toward a corner of the Gymnasium Hall. Sitting down on a thick carpet on the floor, Tudi showed Dalya:

\- Sit down in front of me. Keep your back straight. Cross your legs like that. Relax your arms. Raise your head. Remain still in this position. Close your eyes. Breathe in and out, as slowly as possible...

Dalya complied. Tudi took a deep breath, closing her eyes and repeating in a calm, gentle voice:

\- Breathe in ... exhale ... slowly ... recharge your body ... relax ...

The exercise seemed easy to do. And even though it was the first time in her life that Dalya had attended a physical class in a school, Dalya thought that after all, Gymnastics was a rather easy and pleasant class.

Chapter 9

Very special lessons

Sunday, January 15th, 1893. In the grand Mansion.

The back to classes went smoothly for all students at the Royal Georgetown College. Except for Dalya Bouvard. Her friend Amira was right about the Philosophy class. It was an indecipherable course. The Professor was an old man over 70 years old; always in an elegant black-tie suit, a calm attitude, and slow moves. The Professor had a monotonous, sleepy, and hypnotizing tone of voice. The students had to make a considerable effort to stay awake. Dalya and Amira tried as best as they could to follow the class and take notes. But it seemed like the Philosophy was a foreign language to planet earth.

Dalya and Amira often stifled their giggles with difficulty, wondering how they were going to pass the Philosophy exams. Philosophy classes and lunch breaks were the only times Dalya met with her friend Amira. The other days of the week, Dalya spent them alone in Gymnastics class with the young Professor Tudi.

On this Sunday, Dalya had as homework, to argue a text of Philosophy. In the Library of the grand Mansion, Dalya got busy looking for vocabulary dictionaries, in order to help her understand this text a little more. Several books and several hours later, Dalya still could not understand the subject of her assignment. Usually persistent and determined, Dalya leaned back on her chair and she gave up her search, for once.

Although the cold covered the city of Georgetown, the sun was shining bright in an azure blue sky, no clouds were present, the birds ventured outside singing a merry song, and the squirrels cleaned their habitats of infiltrating snow. It was a beautiful winter day.

Dalya decided to take a walk in the garden of the grand Mansion, in order to breathe some fresh air, and clear her mind. She found the Gardener, Mr. Weil Rosenwald, near some trees. The big man was hanging on a ladder, and he was picking fruits from a tree.

- Hello Mr. Gardener.

The old man smiled at her, stretching out his arm to pick up a fruit:

- Hello Mademoiselle.

For a long minute, Dalya observed with admiration the big tree:

- The apples are very big and so many this year.

The Gardener managed to reach an apple at the end of a distant branch, and he dropped it on the ground covered with a large tablecloth.

- And they are very delicious too, this year, Mademoiselle. I watered them with sugar water, on the advice of a farmer friend.

Dalya never hesitated to help with gardening work. She picked up the apples that had fallen on the tablecloth, and put them in a wooden crate. The Gardener had already filled 7 large crates from the other apple trees. Dalya asked:

- May I take some apples, Monsieur? For my little twin sisters.

The Gardener shook a large branch, he dropped a few apples on the tablecloth, and he answered immediately:

- Take as many as you want, Mademoiselle. We have a stock of apples for 5 months, and I haven't even finished picking yet! The Cook will have a hard time putting away all these crates. I did not foresee such a huge harvest. I'll leave you 2 crates of apples, give to whomever you want, Mademoiselle!

Dalya put the apples into the wooden crates, thinking aloud:

- I will drop off a crate of apples at the annex house, for my parents and my little sisters. Ari and Adi love applesauce and cinnamon. And I'll bring some for my friend Amira Mounier. Her father, Monsieur Jacob Mounier, loves making apple pies. And some also for the French neighbors, Madame will certainly love the caramelized apples...

Several minutes later, the apple picking was done. And the Gardener was right, the harvest was plentiful. 12 crates were filled with big delicious apples.

And stubborn as she was, Dalya insisted on driving a crate of apples herself on a cart, to the annex house, to offer it to her parents and little sisters. For a long minute, the Gardener watched the little girl pushing the cart of apples herself. And like most people, the Gardener was always and still confused by the spontaneous and hardworking moves of the little Heiress.

When Dalya finished her delivery to the annex house, she returned to the grand Mansion, and she decided to change her clothes, to bring some apples to the French neighbors. As soon as Dalya opened the door to her bedroom, two voices exclaimed simultaneously:

- My Goodness, Mademoiselle! Your clothes are dusty! What happened to you?
- I thought you were studying at the Library, doing your homework.

The employees of the house, Cristelle and Océanie were hanging up the new curtains in the little girl's bedroom. And as soon as they noticed Dalya's condition, Cristelle immediately came down from her ladder, and Océanie put the rest of the curtains on an armchair. The two young girls came close to Dalya, looking worried and curious. Dalya stifled a little amused laugh, while taking off her dusty shoes:

- I was studying my Philosophy homework in the Library. But I couldn't understand anything about the assignment. So, I decided to take a break, and help the Gardener to pick and gather the apples. This year's harvest is generous; he gave me 2 well-filled crates. I drove a crate on the cart to the annex house for my little sisters. And I still have a 2nd crate to distribute !

Cristelle thought in a confused voice:

- Picking apples ... driving a crate on the cart ... you still don't realize you are an Heiress to the Country's biggest fortune?

While taking off her stained sweater, Dalya laughed:

- No, not yet!

Océanie picked up the little girl's shoes to clean them later:

- Anyway, Mr. Gardener is very happy to have you as an assistant. He who never speaks! The other night, he was proud to tell me that you quickly learned the names of plants and flowe...

Cristelle exclaimed furiously:

- Océanie! She is not an assistant! She is an Heiress!

Stifling an amused laugh, Océanie turned around:

- Yes, that's true ... sorry, I forgot. I was just saying that Mr. Gardener was delighted to have you here at the grand Mansion, Mademoiselle. And so are we!

Dalya came out of the bathroom, after washing her hands and face. Cristelle handed her a towel to dry off:

- Would you like a hot chocolate, Mademoiselle? The Cook will add whipped cream.

Dalya opened the door of a closet, and she pulled out overalls:

- Thank you, Cristelle, but I'm going out to bring some apples to the French neighbors. I will have the hot chocolate when I get back. I admit that the last time, the whipped cream was very creamy and delicio...

At that precise moment, the employee Océanie ran toward the bathroom, choking her mouth with both hands. Cristelle was about to ask why Océanie rushed to the bathroom, when a detail caught Cristelle's attention:

- You will wear overalls again, Mademoiselle?!

Although Dalya had a vast, refined, and elegant wardrobe, she preferred to wear overalls and white shirts. Except that the maid Cristelle had a completely different opinion:

- You've never worn these dresses, Mademoiselle! You have pretty coats, beautiful hats, and magnificent outfits never worn before! It's such a waste!

Dalya laughed nervously:

- It's just that ... overalls are more practical and easier to wear. And it's just a quick visit to drop off the apples at the French neighbors' house, I won't stay for long.

Cristelle insisted, while taking out an outfit from the closet:

- Why not try one of these dresses, with this cute coat? It will look great on you, Mademoiselle. Please! Just for once, try on this dress, and these shoes too!

In front of Cristelle's insistence, Dalya put the overalls back in the closet, and she agreed to please Cristelle, by wearing a dress. Cristelle was happy to change the little girl's outfit, for once.

While Océanie remained busy in the bathroom, Cristelle helped Dalya put on a new outfit. After several minutes of trying on and combining colors, Dalya left her bedroom, and she headed toward the exit of the grand Mansion, carrying a basket full of apples.

And as always, the Snow Panther accompanied Dalya to the Iron Gate door of the large garden. Dalya offered an apple to the Panther, and she smiled at her:

- See you later, Séraphine !

For a moment, the Snow Panther bit into the apple, and watched the little girl walk down Dumbarton Oaks Park Road.

When Dalya arrived at the house of the French neighbors the Poirier, she went to the back door leading to the kitchen, and she rang the bell. Usually, it was the housekeeper Mrs. Glorina who opened the door for her, with her cheerful smile. Except that day... guess who welcomed her!

Richard Poirier himself! The young man opened the door with one hand, and he was holding a porcelain teapot in the other hand. A long second of silence and confusion settled between the two young people, at the threshold of the kitchen door. Richard pulled himself together first, and he smiled:

- Hello Mademoiselle Dalya Bouvard.

Dalya was surprised to meet Richard in the kitchen. She hesitated for a few seconds:

- Hello... I... I was... is Mrs. Glorina here?

And since a while now, at each of their meetings, Richard Poirier felt paradoxically anxious but happy by the presence of this strange little girl. The young man replied spontaneously:

-   Mrs. Glorina is in downtown for a few errands; she shouldn't be long. But ... I am here!

At this precise moment, Dalya Bouvard blushed, and Richard Poirier realized his hasty clumsiness. He tried to catch up:

-   And ... Mother is here too. I was trying to make her some tea, since half an hour.

Dalya looked at the teapot in the young man's hand, with a curious air:

-   Half an hour ... to prepare a tea?

Richard let out a little amused and embarrassed laugh:

-   I'm having trouble finding the tea. I looked everywhere in the kitchen. And sugar is not found too. I don't know where Mrs. Glorina keeps them.

Without hesitation, Dalya replied in a confident voice:

-   The tea is in a box in the cupboard on the left. And the sugar is in the bowl next to the flour one. I can prepare tea for Madame, if you allow me?

And without hesitation, Richard answered in a delighted voice:

-   Certainly, yes! That would be very nice of you, Mademoiselle. Come in, please.

When she entered the kitchen, Dalya put her basket on the central table:

-   I brought apples for Madame; I know she likes them very much. We had a good harvest this year, in the garden of the grand Mansion.

Richard placed the teapot he was holding on a small silver tray:

-   It's nice to spoil her, thank you. Mother love caramelized apples.

Having helped Mrs. Glorina in the kitchen several times, Dalya was familiarized with the locations of objects in the kitchens of the French neighbors. Dalya took a small box of herbal teas from a cupboard, and she moved a small bowl of sugar to the central table. Richard announced proudly:

-   I heated the water. It's the only thing I managed to do!

Dalya stifled an amused laugh:

-   It's essential.

Richard sat down on a chair in front of the central table, and he watched Dalya's moves as she made tea. That day, Richard noticed an unusual thing. Spontaneously, Richard thought aloud:

-   That's a very pretty dress you're wearing, Mademoiselle. This purple color suits you very well.

Dalya's hand trembled as she placed a cup of tea on the tray. She didn't expect this compliment. It is true that Dalya has always wore boys' clothes; white shirts, overalls, and work pants. Except for this day, and under the insistence of the employee Cristelle, Dalya wore a pretty knee-length dress, light purple color, a gray coat with silver buttons, and matching gray shoes. At that moment, although Dalya was surprised and intimidated by the presence and the remark of Richard Poirier, she was happy with the compliment the young man said to her.

Richard noticed Dalya's shaking moves and red cheeks; he understood that he had made Dalya uncomfortable for the 2nd time. Richard sat up from his chair, and he tried to ease the discomfort:

-   Can I have some tea too, please?

Immediately, Dalya took out a second cup from a cupboard:

-   Sure. Would you like to take it to your office?
-   Thank you, but I'll take it in the living room; I have a free day today. I was reading a book; I thought I'd take a break and make some tea for Mother.

Filling the teapot with hot water, Dalya asked:

-   What book were you reading?

Richard picked up a book from the kitchen counter and he showed it to Dalya:

-   The Biography of Aristotle.

At this moment, Dalya stopped in her move:

-   It's the same name mentioned in my homework for this weekend. Is it Aristotle, the Greek Philosopher?

Richard relaxed in his chair and slowly turned the pages:

-   Himself. It is a very interesting Biography on the life of the Philosopher, his influences, his mentors, his discoveries. He established the foundations of several sciences and fields. Aristotle was a great thinker, well ahead of his time.

Dalya was filling a plate with madeleines cakes, while listening attentively to Richard's explanations. Dalya dared to ask:

-   So ... you understand the ideas of the Philosopher Aristotle?

The young man smiled:

-   Yes, his thoughts are very clear and interesting to read. Mademoiselle is interested in Philosophy?

With an amused and anxious chuckle, Dalya replied:

-   Philosophy is a new class I have this semester. Except that I absolutely don't understand a single word. I have tried everything; lesson summaries, vocabulary dictionaries, learning by heart ... nothing helps me understand. And I must pass an exam in this subject in 5 months. I really don't know what it is talking about. I will fail this course if I get a zero. I must have at least a 9/20.

Instantly and without thinking, the words came out of Richard Poirier's mouth, without him being able to control them:

-   I can help you understand this class, Mademoiselle.

A long minute of silence settled in the kitchen. Although always courteous and polite to her, Dalya was surprised by Richard Poirier's offer. And as intimidating as the young man was, Dalya was delighted with his help:

-   If I can get close to the average score in this course, Professor Canfield would be happy and proud of me. I need to understand what this Philosopher Aristotle is talking about, in order to be able to answer the exam questions. You ... are you sure you want to help me in Philosophy? Your schedule seems a little busy.

Richard Poirier confirmed with a sure tone and a proud smile:

-   I will be happy to help you in Philosophy, Mademoiselle.

And it promised to be very special lessons between Richard Poirier and Dalya Bouvard.

Chapter 10

The delivery service

Saturday, January 21st, 1893. The Morning.

Dalya Bouvard got up early that weekend day. She arranged her bed and cleaned her bedroom. And as usual, she wore her habitual blue overalls and a large white sweater. Adjusting her hair in her black cap, Dalya smiled at the magnificent creature starring at her:

- Did you sleep well, Séraphine?

The Snow Panther was lying on the carpet, in front of the fireplace. Séraphine watched the little girl who was getting ready to go out. Looking for a winter scarf in her closet, Dalya thought aloud:

- It's a busy day for me. I must hurry so as not to be late.

Dalya came out of her bedroom, followed by the Snow Panther. In the dining room, she met the head of the grand Mansion.

- Bonjour, Mr. Bûchebois.

The grand man was always punctual and meticulous. He greeted the little girl:

- Bonjour Mademoiselle. Hot chocolate as usual?

The employees of the grand Mansion had enough time to learn the tastes and preferences of the little girl. Dalya smiled:

- Yes, thank you.

A silhouette entered the dining room, and she exclaimed in a joyful voice:

- Good morning, Mademoiselle. I brought you some hot croissants.
- Thank you, Océanie.

Putting down a basket in front of Dalya, Océanie asked in an amused voice:

- You are very early today. I thought you'll sleep a few more hours.

Dalya helped herself to the croissants:

- I must join my friends Alfie and Maurice, downtown. They are launching a new grocery shopping and delivery service, right to the customers' doorsteps. Amira and I will help them get started in their new business, until they recruit helpers.

Since a long time, the employees of the grand Mansion understood that the little girl will not change her spontaneous ways, and she will not stop doing manual labor, or working in the market, despite being an Heiress.

With a courteous smile, the head of the grand Mansion served her a glass of orange juice:

- It's very generous and kind of you to help your friends in their business. They are hard-working and dynamic young men. I have no doubt that they will succeed in life.

Océanie cut the Brie cheese into pieces, affirming:

- It's so true. Your friends are very polite. The other day, they refused to come into the living room with their ... their ... boots ... this smell of cheese ... is ... is ...

Suddenly, Océanie left the dining room, running and murmuring:

- Bathroom! Bathroom! Bathroom!

The head of the grand Mansion and Dalya exchanged an amused smile. Apparently, the smell of cheese affected Océanie. Quickly eating her breakfast, Dalya asked hesitantly:

- Mr. Bûchebois, it will be a long day of work, in downtown. And I was wondering, if you don't mind, if I can ... if I can ...

Having lived with the little girl for enough time now, the head of the grand Mansion guessed her request:

- I will put some sandwiches in a basket for you, Mademoiselle. For you and your friends.

Dalya thanked him with a grateful smile.

Several minutes later, Dalya arrived in downtown of Georgetown city. The kiosks in the Saturday market were already set up, the goods were spread out and plentiful, and the vendors were serving customers quickly. Dalya easily found her friends near the vegetable seller.

- Hello Alfie, Hello Maurice, Hello Amira.

Amira smiled, while continuing to write names on labels:

- Hello Dalya! I too, have just arrived 5 minutes ago.

Maurice emptied some potatoes into a sack:

- Hello Dalya! Glad to see you with us today!

Putting down a bag of zucchini, Alfie asked Dalya in a serious tone:

- Did you bring lunch with you?

His friend Maurice gave him a knock on the arm:

- And where did your good manners go?

Amira and Dalya stifled their amused laugh. Alfie justified himself:

- Dalya has a Chef Cook just for her! And he cooks delicious food. I was just curious to know what's for lunch today, that's all!

Lifting the towel covering her basket, Dalya showed her friends:

- On the menu today, there are duck pâté sandwiches with cherry tomatoes and pesto sauce, cheese and tuna lettuce sandwiches, fresh orange juice, hot chocolate, muffins freshly baked this morning, cubes of cheese with grapes.

Immediately, Alfie jumped:

- Can I taste?

Maurice exclaimed in an annoyed tone:

- We haven't even started our working day!! Pull yourself together!!

Amira arranged the labels, while laughing:

- I admit, the menu is appetizing. It makes us want to have lunch now.

Dalya took some food out of her basket:

- There's nothing better than starting our work day with muffins and hot chocolate.

Alfie didn't need to be invited; he immediately sat down on the bench opposite Dalya. Amira helped her friend pour the hot chocolate. Maurice sighed:

- It's already 9 AM and we're late for the deliv... cherry and white chocolate muffins?! Wow this is very very delicious! Can I have some more hot chocolate, please, Amira?

Amira filled his cup with drink, and Alfie smiled at him:

- You were saying, Maurice? What are we late for?

Dalya was happy to help her friends, bringing them delicious food and drinks, before the start of their working day. And while Alfie was teasing Maurice, Dalya whispered to Amira:

- I found someone who can help me in the Philosophy class.

This news made Amira jump off her chair:

- Seriously? Who?

Dalya informed her:

- He's a neighbor who lives near the grand Mansion. Apparently, he understands the ideas and books of the Philosopher Aristotle. He offered to help me understand the course.

With a suppliant smile, Amira exclaimed:

- And you will share his explanations with me, wouldn't you? This class is a headache; I understand absolutely nothing about it. I can't get a zero in Philosophy. You will explain to me later, won't you?
- Of course, yes, Amira! I will write down all the explanations that the neighbor gives me, and I will lend you my notebook to copy out. There are two of us who don't want a zero in this class!

Dalya and Amira exchanged a happy laugh. When suddenly, Maurice got up and he announced:

- It's time for work!

Immediately, Dalya put the cups back in her basket, Amira picked up her pen and her labels, and Alfie took some lists from his pocket. Maurice divided the tasks between them:

- We have 15 shopping orders, that's 15 bags to fill and deliver. Me and Alfie will take care of buying all the ingredients that are on these lists. Dalya, you will distribute the ingredients in each customer's bags. Amira, you will write the labels with the names of the customers, the ingredients purchased and the prices.

After filling up on muffins and hot chocolate, Alfie was full of energy:

- And we begin!

Chapter 11

Both embarrassed

The same day, Saturday, January 21ˢᵗ, 1893. In the afternoon, at the grand Mansion.

Dalya finished delivering the groceries, much earlier than expected. The customers were happy to get their groceries delivered to their homes. Alfie and Maurice were happy with the success of their new business, and especially the money earned. For having spent years alone, Amira Mounier was simply happy to have new friends with whom to spend her free time. And Dalya was happy to help her friends as best as she could.

This late January afternoon seemed to be peaceful and joyful, despite the winter cold. Dalya ran into the grand Mansion. It was already 3 PM, and she had to go somewhere else. She ran to her bedroom, and she quickly changed her clothes.

A few minutes later, Dalya hurried back down the stairs of the grand Mansion. When a voice interrupted her:

- You are very elegant, Mademoiselle!

The employee Océanie appeared in the hall of the grand Mansion, at the same time as Dalya came down the last step of the stairs. Dalya wore a black winter dress, a chic emerald green coat, a small brown hat, and matching brown shoes. Dalya smiled:

- Thank you, Océanie. I finished helping my friends with their new business, in downtown. We finished earlier than I thought. I had planned to visit the French neighbors, this late afternoon.

Immediately, Océanie asked in a curious voice:

- But ... the French neighbor's house was on your way back from downtown. Why did you take all this detour, Mademoiselle?

Dalya explained to her with a little embarrassed laugh:

- Because ... I ... I wanted to change my clothes before visiting the French neighbors. I didn't want to go there in my work clothes.

Océanie jumped:

- But of course! What a fool I am!

Coming close to the little girl, Océanie closed a button that Dalya forgot:

- And you did well to come back to change, Mademoiselle! You wear overalls and big sweaters too often. You have very pretty dresses and beautiful coats; you should try them on more frequently.

While wearing her black gloves, Dalya smiled at Océanie:

- I won't be late. I will be back on time for dinner.
- Understood, Mademoiselle. I will serve your dinner in your bedroom.
- Thank you, Océanie. See you soon!

The same day, Saturday January 21st, 1893. In the afternoon. In the house of the French Family Les Poirier.

- Good afternoon.

Dalya Bouvard smiled shyly, knocking on the office door. The young Richard Poirier was as always, sitting behind his desk table.

- Good afternoon, Mademoiselle. Come in, please.

Each time he met this girl, Richard Poirier felt an unexplained embarrassment. His throat was tenser and tighter, and his movements become awkward.

And each time she met this young man, Dalya Bouvard was intimidated. A burning fever invaded her body, and her cheeks often blushed.

- Have a seat, please.

Richard closed a folder and he pushed aside a few books, while Dalya sat down on a chair opposite to him.

- I was waiting for you.

These words escaped from Richard Poirier, without him being able to retain them. Strangely, each time they met, Richard lost control over his words and his moves. Immediately, Richard realized his clumsiness, and Dalya blushed.

- Thank you for helping me with the Philosophy class.

Richard drank his tea, to ease the pressure on his throat:

- It is with great pleasure, Mademoiselle. It's the least I can do for you.

Dalya took a book out of her bag, and she handed it to him:

- Here is the program of the class that we will study for the next few months.

Richard thought aloud, as he flips through the manual:

- Science … freedom … reason and reality ... The themes are simple. These are the basics of Philosophy. It is a basic program and easy to study, I assure you.

Immediately, Dalya pulled out a notebook and a pen:

- And I'm ready!

Richard smiled. It is true that Philosophy was a difficult subject to understand and to follow. And despite being from a modest background and only recently registered in a school, Dalya Bouvard was determined to pass this class and obtain the average score. Richard Poirier was fascinated by the determination of this strange girl.

At the end of the afternoon, in the house of the French family, the first Philosophy lesson between Richard Poirier and Dalya Bouvard went better than expected. Richard explained the subject of the class, simplifying the vocabulary and definitions of words. Dalya wrote down all the words spoken by the young man, without missing a beat.

After an hour of work, Richard relaxed in his chair:

- So … these are two principles of a different type: on one hand, the matter, the body, the brain. And on the other hand, the spirit, the soul, the conscience. Matter is everything you can see, touch, and feel. It is measurable. And the spirit is...

Dalya finished the sentence :

- The spirit is… from the Latin spiritus, it designates an immaterial reality, and not tangible.

With a proud smile, Richard replied:

- It is quite correct. I assume that you have understood the difference between the two principles?

Dalya happily exclaimed :

- This is the first time in weeks that I understand the subject of this class. Finally!

At that moment, Richard and Dalya shared an amused laugh. Closing her notebook, Dalya picked up her bag:

- I don't want to hold you back any longer than that. One hour of Philosophy on Saturday is enough for my brain. This class requires so much concentration, I feel like we worked for several hours.

Richard answered naturally:

- It's true. Time passes far too quickly with you, Mademoiselle.

Dalya was surprised by this unusual remark. Richard was surprised by his uncontrollable clumsiness. A long second of embarrassment settled between the two young people. Dalya felt her cheeks blush, and Richard felt his throat suffocate.

Putting on her gloves, Dalya avoided the young man's gaze:

- I ... I'll leave you, then. Thank you for today. See you next time!

Richard got up from his chair to greet her, and he smiled at her:

- Until next time, Mademoiselle Dalya.

That day, Richard Poirier and Dalya Bouvard were intimidated, clumsy, embarrassed... and above all, they were both happy to share this Philosophy class.

Chapter 12

Océanie

Saturday February 4th, 1893. At the end of the afternoon, in the grand Mansion.

February season was quiet and peaceful. The winter cold was about to pack up, the snow was about to disappear, and the sky was filled with gray clouds raining heavily.

The activity at the grand Mansion resumed to its usual routine. Immediately after the start of the school year, Dalya Bouvard was determined to pass her only class of the semester, Philosophy. Dalya almost lived in the Library of the grand Mansion, drowned among books and papers. The employees of the grand Mansion were also all busy with their usual work.

- Tomorrow, I must shorten the trees surrounding the large garden. Announced the Gardener, while entering the kitchen of the grand Mansion.
- And we also need to repair the cracks in a few chimneys on the roof. Do you think it will take much time? Asked the head of the grand Mansion, Mr. Bûchebois, who followed the Gardener inside the kitchen.

The Gardener sat down on a chair around the dining table:

- No, I don't think it will take a lot of time... 2-3 days... I'll go up to the roof with Igor, after I've finished cutting the stems of the trees.

The head of the grand Mansion also sat down:

- Excellent! Do you need materials for the roof? I'm going shopping tomorrow, in downtown.

While the Gardener and the Manager were discussing the renovations to be done in the grand Mansion, the Cook was working in front of his counter and he was thinking aloud:

- Salt and pepper... ginger... parsley... grated carrot... delizioso...

Dinner tonight consisted of an oats soup with grated vegetables, slices of bread buttered with garlic and fine herbs. The smell that hovered in the kitchen was exquisite.

- Again oats?! Igor exclaimed as he entered the kitchen.

The Cook exclaimed, pointing his wooden spoon toward Igor:

- Yes! Avena e grano! Again oats! Mademoiselle Dalya loves this soup, è delizioso! Non dirmi cosa cucinare! Don't tell me what to cook!

Igor put his basket of firewood in a corner, and he settled around the dining table:

- And not only her, Océanie also loves it! You would think that in this house, the menus are only made for Océanie and Madem...

Igor was hit on the head with a kitchen towel by the Cook. Igor didn't have time to answer Cristelle entered the kitchen:

- What a weather tonight! I can't wait to have dinner and get back under my covers! It hasn't stopped raining since this morning!

Océanie followed Cristelle inside the kitchen:

- Me, I want to sleep for days, not hours.

The two young women sat around the dining table. Cristelle said:

- I can't wait for spring. Only a few more weeks and we will enjoy the beautiful sun!

The Cook placed the large pot of soup on the dinner table. Océanie stretched out her neck to see the contents:

- What's for soup tonight ?

Igor placed a basket of bread slices buttered with fine herbs on the table, and he replied in an amused tone:

- His Royal Highness Océanie's favorite soup, oats with vegetables! Very creamy and velvety. There are also slices of bread with bu...

Suddenly, Océanie got up from her chair and she ran toward the kitchen exit:

- I ... I forgot to organize ... closet of clothes ... I ... I'm not hungry ... I have to ...

When Océanie disappeared from the kitchen, Cristelle and Igor exchanged a confused look:

- What is wrong with her?
- I don't have the faintest idea.
- Odd. She wants to tidy up the closet now, instead of having dinner?!
- She is always the first to help herself to her favorite soup.

All the employees were hungry after a long day of work. So, the empty dishes soon filled up. And the conversation continued its normal course:

- Is Mademoiselle's tray ready?
- Yes, I'll take it to her as soon as I'm done.
- Perfect. Mademoiselle is in the Library. She's been working in it, since this morning.
- I'm going to reload the wood at the Library tonight.
- It won't be necessary; I already did it this morning. Since Mademoiselle spends all her time there, I put aside the rest of the wood in a corner of the fireplace.
- It's an excellent soup, Mr. Ferrero!

- Yes, very very good! Can I have an extra slice of bread?

Several minutes later.

Cristelle entered Océanie's bedroom, holding a dinner tray:

- The Cook asked me to bring you a bowl of oatmeal soup, in case you get hungry later at night. It was delicio...

Except that before Cristelle finished her sentence, Océanie got up from the bed and she ran to the bathroom. Cristelle put the dinner tray on a small bedside table, and she rushed to Océanie who was vomiting:

- What's wrong with you ?!

After a few minutes, Océanie went back to sit on her bed, looking out of breath:

- The smell ... of this soup ... sickens me.

Cristelle handed her a little towel:

- But ... but, you adore this soup?! You even have it for breakfast!

Océanie took a perfume bottle, and she put a few drops on the towel to inhale it:

- I ... that smell of soup ... makes me vomit ... I can't stand it anymore!

Cristelle sat down on the bed, and she caressed Océanie's forehead:

- You are pale from vomiting. But you don't have a fever. Do you want me to ask for the Doctor now? It's strange that the smell of soup that you love, makes you vomit ... it's very strange.

In front of Océanie's silence, Cristelle continued to think aloud:

- And I've also noticed that you've been using the bathroom more and more often, since the past few weeks. You go there several times a day. You may have stomach trouble. We need to get a Doctor; he'll tell us more about what is w...

At this moment, Océanie interrupted Cristelle. With a pale face, terrified eyes, a trembling voice, Océanie Shell whispered:

- Cristelle ... I think that ... I think that ...

The next morning. Sunday, February 5th, 1893.

Dalya woke up a little late than usual. The research of the Philosophy course had exhausted her; she needed more hours of sleep and rest.

When Dalya went down to the dining room, she did not find breakfast there as usual.

- I was late waking up this morning. Cristelle surely left me a tray at the Library.

Upon entering the Library of the grand Mansion, Dalya found no meals there:

- Monsieur Bûchebois must have ordered her to wait for me to wake up.

The grand Mansion seemed oddly quiet that morning. Dalya thought that the employees must certainly be busy with their work. When Dalya entered the kitchen, she found it empty; none of the employees of the grand Mansion were there.

- Strange ... it's very strange. Where did they all go?

Dalya walked out the kitchen door into the large garden, looking for at least one of the employees.

- Nobody is here ... the grand Mansion is empty. Where can they be?

The last place Dalya thought of visiting was the employees' rooms. As soon as Dalya entered the corridor, several silhouettes appeared at the door of a bedroom. When Dalya came close to the employees of the grand Mansion, the little girl immediately felt that something serious had happened. In Océanie's bedroom, all the employees were standing leaning against the wall, looking shocked and serious. Océanie was sitting on her bed, her face pale, her gaze lost, and her lips trembling. A grave silence reigned in the room.

- Good morning.

None of the employees answered Dalya. No one dared to say a word or make a move. This was unusual coming from the employees. Dalya started to worry about the situation, she moved toward the bed:

- Is everything alright, Océanie? Are you in pain? We can call the Doctor.

Océanie did not move; arms crossed, body shaking, eyes terrified. At that moment, the head of the grand Mansion gathered up all his courage and he announced to Dalya, in a serious voice:

- There is an event coming ... Mademoiselle.

Dalya turned toward Mr. Bûchebois, trying to understand what could have put the employees of the grand Mansion in such a state of shock:

- What event? What's going on?

The news was not so easy to announce, for anyone. Mr. Bûchebois lost his words; he remained silent and looked worried. None of the other employees dared to look Dalya in the face, let alone speak a word. The silence has become more and more worrying for Dalya Bouvard. At one point, Cristelle tried to announce the news, in a trembling voice and with confused words:

- It turns out that ... Mademoiselle ... an incident happened ... a few months ago... and it turns out that ... in the next few months... there will be a... nothing is certain... we still need an opinion on this subject... I hope it's a false alarm... I hope so... it's that the next few mo...

Dalya grew impatient and worried:

- Cristelle... what's going on? I don't understand what you sa...
- I am carrying a child!

Océanie's voice was clear and her words were distinct. However, Dalya was shocked by this news:

- A ... a ... a child?

As simple as this announcement was, it took several long seconds for Dalya to understand what was really going on. Dalya remained standing for a few moments, motionless and shocked. Dalya pulled herself together with difficulty:

- You ... you are carrying ... a child?

Océanie didn't dare to move or make a sound, much less look up at Dalya or the other employees. Cristelle answered in her place, in a small voice:

- Yes, Mademoiselle. A ... a child.

Dalya trembled as she asked this next question:

- And ... and the father of this child ... is ...

Cristelle answered several other questions as well:

- Your aunt's husband, Mr. Henrik. During his stay at the annex house, a few months ago.

At that moment, Océanie Shell could no longer hold back her tears and her fear:

- I... I'm... sorry... please; I have nowhere... to go... please... I'm sorry...

All the employees of the grand Mansion lowered their faces, no one dared to say a word or make a move. A heavy silence and total shock invaded Océanie's room.

When finally, Dalya gathered her courage and her strength, and she announced in a calm but confident voice:

- Nobody should know about this child. Nobody but us.

The employees of the grand Mansion exchanged a surprised look. They did not know how to handle this situation, and no one expected this reaction from Dalya Bouvard. The head of the grand Mansion, Mr. Bûchebois asked in a curious tone:

- And the Lawyer? ... Mr. Ernest Laszlo?

Dalya explained in a clear voice:

- Having worked with the Lawyer Mr. Ernest Laszlo for 3 years now, I believe I know him well enough to assure you that he will not leave Océanie and her baby for a single second longer in the grand Mansion. Therefore, he must not be aware of this child... especially not him! This child must remain a secret. You must all hide it, at least until my 4th Challenge!

Mr. Bûchebois bowed his head in a respectful gesture:

- If that is your decision, Mademoiselle, then we will all keep this child a secret.

The Cook could not repress his reassured smile:

- Thank you for your kindness, Mademoiselle! Grazie Grazie!

Dalya smiled at him:

- You have all watched over me since I've been living at the grand Mansion. It's the least I can do for you.

The Gardener seemed relieved:

- It's a wise decision, Mademoiselle. To keep the child a secret, until your 4th Challenge. At least during the pregnancy and childbirth.

Cristelle affirmed in a determined tone:

- Exact! And by next December, until the 4th Challenge, we will see how the situation will be resolved.

Igor was delighted with this solution:

- Yes! We will keep this baby a total secret! No one will know!

Océanie trembled, weeping lots of tears:

- Thank you... thank you very much... I owe you my life... thank you... I owe you my life.

And as usual, Dalya disarmed the situation with her spontaneity and generosity. She approached Océanie and she hugged the employee:

- Don't worry, Océanie, as long as I am in the grand Mansion, no harm will happen to you ... neither to you, nor to this child. You will be safe here. We will protect your secret!

Chapter 13

An ordinary day

Wednesday, February 8th, 1893. In the Gymnasium of the Royal Georgetown College.

Dalya Bouvard had been taking Gymnastics lessons for almost a month now. The young Professor Tudi was polite and encouraging with her. Each session, Dalya wore her uniform in the locker room. And when she returned to the Gymnasium, the young Professor Tudi greeted her with the same usual smile:

- Good Morning, Mademoiselle Dalya.

And while putting her school bag in a corner, Dalya was always delighted to start this class:

- Good Morning, Professor Tudi.

Despite being asked to call her by her first name only, and despite her young age, Dalya preferred to address the young girl as Professor Tudi.

Gymnastics sessions proceeded almost at the same pace. First thing in the morning, Dalya and Tudi would sit down on a mat on the floor. In total calm, Dalya begins with slow and relaxing breathing exercises. Then, stretching and warming up of the muscles take place. Dalya performs jumps on a rope, repetitive movements, rolls on the mat, and she runs around the Gymnasium 10 times. Always under the supervision and instructions of the young Professor Tudi.

- Perfect, Mademoiselle. Sit down for a moment. Catch your breath. Slowly.

When Dalya finished her 10th round, Professor Tudi handed her a towel:

- You ran this distance in less time than the previous sessions. You are getting faster, and your legs are stronger. Excellent work, Mademoiselle.

Dalya dried herself off and she drank a glass of water:

- I admit that the stretches and warm-ups I do at the start of each class, help me run better.

Adjusting her gloves, Tudi smiled:

- That's right, Mademoiselle. These exercises prepare your body for the next physical efforts, and prevent you from injuries of wrong movements.

Dalya took the gloves that Tudi gave her. The young Professor continued her explanations:

- The previous month, we worked 4 special positions. You master them perfectly, today. In this month of February, we will work on a new movement.

Dalya put her gloves on, and she followed the young Professor toward the center of the Gymnasium.

- Take a good look at me. We stand straight. Your legs should be slightly apart. Your hands should be up like this. I will move slowly so you can clearly see my hands and legs. The new movement is divided into 3 steps ... look at me ... one... two... three, like this. I repeat. One... two... and three. Did you understand the movement correctly? It's in 3 steps only. Now it's up to you, Mademoiselle.

Tightening her gloves, Dalya held herself upright; she shifted her legs and raised her hands. Under the instructions of the young Professor Tudi, Dalya practiced the new movement of the Gymnastics class.

A few hours later.

At the end of her Gymnastics class, Dalya rushed out of the College. She had to visit her uncle Giorgi. After walking for a few minutes, Dalya arrived in front of her paternal uncle's house. Each year, this house filled with new gadgets, pieces, and tools. And to the delight of the little Dalya Bouvard, she always discovered new interesting things there.

- Hello Uncle Giorgi. It's me, Dalya.

Entering inside the house, Dalya heard a voice answer her:

- Hello Biggo! What a pleasure to see you! Come in, come in!

Dalya put her school bag on the floor, and she sat down on a large, worn armchair:

- I finished my class at school today. And before going home, I had to visit you. I needed something.

Uncle Giorgi's voice was heard:

- And you did very well to come and see me today. How can I help you?

The pains of the Gymnastics movements, began to be felt in the body of the little girl. Dalya relaxed in the armchair, and she asked him:

- A few months ago, you gave me a white powder to clean silver dishes. I don't know its name.

Immediately, the voice of Uncle Giorgi echoed in the workshop:

- It's called Blanc de Meudon. It is a powder for making silverware shine. It is a clay limestone mainly composed of calcium carbonate and clay.

Dalya repeated the name to remember it well:

- Blanc de Meudon... Blanc de Meudon... I gave it to the employee of the grand Mansion, Océanie. It was such an effective product that she asked me if you still had any. Do you have any left, Uncle Giorgi ?

Uncle Giorgi's voice affirmed with certainty:

- Sure! With great pleasure! I'm going to prepare this powder for you, right now... as soon as I get out of this machine.

It took a long second for Dalya to realize that her Uncle Giorgi hasn't appeared in the workshop yet, since her arrival. And the old man's last sentence was weird. Dalya straightened up from her chair, she searched right and left:

- What machine? Uncle Giorgi ... where are you?

A little amused laugh was heard:

- I'm... I'm stuck inside a machine.

The most bizarre experiences and adventures took place in Uncle Giorgi's workshop. Dalya stopped being surprised since a long time now. She stood up quickly, stifling an amused laugh:

- Alright. And how can I help you? Where is this machine?

After a few minutes and some directions, Dalya finally found the machine.

- What is that? What does it do?

Uncle Giorgi was proud to explain his new invention:

- It is a machine for drying clothes with steam. No need to iron them. For example, we introduce a shirt. The machine is activated. And in a quarter of an hour, the shirt is impeccably dried!

Dalya exclaimed :

- It will be a really efficient machine! Especially for shirts, aprons, uniforms. But... how did you get stuck inside? And since when?
- It's only a few minutes before you arrived. I had to adjust a steam pipe inside. As soon as I got in, the door of the machine closed behind me.

Thinking aloud, Dalya exclaimed :

- And luckily, I'm visiting you today! You would have been stuck in this machine for a long time.

Dalya and her uncle Giorgi shared a giggle.

- I'm in front of the door, but I don't see a wrist. How should I open it?
- Use a paintbrush to unlock the door. Look on my work table, there is an orange pencil case, including several brushes, in several sizes.

Dalya quickly complied. She used a small brush to unlock the steel door. As soon as she made a move, the brush broke in two.

- Use 2 brushes, Biggo. The door is in steel.

After several long minutes, several broken brushes, several strong pushes, several giggles, several attempts, and trying … Dalya finally succeeded in freeing her uncle Giorgi from inside this machine.

Nothing really new. It was an ordinary day for the little Dalya Bouvard.

Chapter 14

Giving him strength

Saturday, February 11th, 1893. The morning, in the grand Mansion.

This beautiful February day was calm and sunny. Winter ruled quietly over the city of Georgetown. After breakfast, all the employees went back to their usual jobs in the grand Mansion.

Océanie knocked on the bedroom door, before going inside.

- Good morning, Mademoiselle. I am bringing you, your hot chocolate.

Dalya raised her head, and she smiled:

- Thank you, Océanie.

As she walked inside the bedroom, Océanie noticed that all of the little girl's dresses, coats, hats and shawls were spread all over the bedroom furniture. Dalya was sitting on a small chair, focused on reading a large book, in the middle of all this mess.

Océanie didn't understand why all of Dalya's wardrobe was scattered over the armchairs and the bed. Without being able to restrain her curiosity, Océanie put the tray down on a small table and she asked:

- Can I help you with something, Mademoiselle?

Turning the page of her large book, Dalya sighed in confusion:

- I never thought that coordinating the colors of dresses and accessories could be so complicated! I've been trying to adjust the colors of a single outfit for an hour; I can't do it at all!

Océanie understood the reason for this disorder:

- So… you spread out your wardrobe on the bed and the furniture, in order to coordinate the colors of your outfits?

Dalya confirmed:

- Yes, that's right! And I borrowed a fashion book from the school Library. It was supposed to provide information on how to coordinate outfits.

Océanie was surprised by the idea of the little girl. Since her arrival at the grand Mansion, Dalya always wore blue overalls, white sweaters, and black shoes. Dalya never cared about her outfit … until that day.

Turning over a few pages, Dalya muttered in a confused tone:

- Helping Mr. Gardener with house renovations, was much easier than coordinating the colors of a dress. I don't even understand the fashion vocabulary… Bustier… Cardigan… drapé… what does that mean?! I need a dictionary to understand this fashion book!

Stifling a little amused laugh, Océanie approached the little girl:

- If you allow me, Mademoiselle, may I help you? I know a bit about fashion and style.

Immediately, Dalya exclaimed:

- Yes of course! please!

Océanie took the fashion book from Dalya, and she read some pages:

- It is well detailed in this book. Warm colors, cold colors, accessories, styles according to events. There is even a section on hairstyles. This is a great fashion book!

After a few seconds, Océanie decided:

- First of all, we will choose the dresses, and then we will choose the coats that will go with these dresses, according to seasons. And at the end, we will choose the accessories and the hats, according to the colors.

Instantly, Dalya quickly complied:

- I will spread all the dresses on the bed!

Throughout the morning of this Saturday, Dalya and Océanie were busy adjusting the wardrobe. Dalya was happy and relieved to have some help coordinating her outfits. And Océanie was delighted to assist the little girl, in order to look prettier and more refined.

The same day, Saturday, February 11th, 1893. In the afternoon, in the house of the French family, les Poirier.

For the first time in a long time, Richard Poirier hesitated to finish his work. In his office, and for hours, Richard had been sitting at his desk; he was rereading a few papers in front of him, for the 50th time.

- *This report is far from what the Congressman will expect to read. He will certainly not agree with the recommendations that I have proposed. However, I have studied the problem from all possible angles.*

After several minutes, Richard put the papers on his desk, and he sighed.

- *I don't know what to do. Should I continue to write this report which will certainly displease the Congressman. Or change the report and avoid upsetting the Congressman?*

Flipping through a book next to him, Richard Poirier looked for the slightest clue that would help him decide.

- *The Secretary to the Congressman warned me to avoid these recommendations. However, I can't find any other solution to the problem. This report could cost me my career.*

The report was due in 2 days. Richard was worried and he hesitated more and more. When suddenly, a little silhouette appeared at the office door.

- You seem busy. I can come back another day.

When Richard raised his head, he was pleasantly surprised:

- Good afternoon, Mademoiselle. I'm glad you came today. Come in, please.

Dalya took a few steps toward the office:

- I knocked on the door, but you didn't hear me. You were busy in your report.

With a worried chuckle, Richard replied:

- I was lost in my report, more precisely.

Without further explanation, Dalya sensed that Richard was stressed and worried. The young man closed his files and he moved a few books away from his desk:

- Sit down, please.

Dalya put her bag on a small table, and she sat down in front of the desk:

- Do you have a problem writing your report?

Richard relaxed on his chair, and he sighed:

- Yes, and it's a real headache. I've been trying to decide on a few points, for days. And I find myself at an impasse.

With a timid little voice, Dalya dared to ask:

- Does ... does your report have something to do with Mr. Grover Cleveland's Democratic Presidency?

At that moment, Richard Poirier smiled:

- Mademoiselle is still interested in politics?

Dalya smiled proudly:

- I read the newspapers every day on the way to school.

Richard Poirier observed the little girl in front of him with a fascinated gaze.

- Yes, indeed. My report is about the next Presidential elections which will begin in a few weeks. There is a problem to solve. And my recommendations will not be unanimously welcomed.

Dalya thought aloud:

- We don't always need people who agree with us. Whether they like it or not, if your recommendations are right, they will be good to apply.

Straightening up on his chair, Richard explained his concern:

- This report could cost me my career.

Without hesitation, Dalya replied:

- Or this report may make you more honest and set you apart from other false supporters. The goal is to solve the problem, not to avoid offending a politician.

This response stunned Richard Poirier. He never thought he was getting political advice from a little girl. Every day, the young man was more and more fascinated by the naturalness and quick wit of this strange little girl.

At that precise moment, and after days of hesitation, Richard Poirier decided on his report.

- Thank you for your opinion, Mademoiselle. You give me strength.

Suddenly, a long second of embarrassment settled between the two young people. Richard felt that his last sentence slipped away from him, his throat was choking. Dalya felt her cheeks blushing, and she couldn't stop it. In order to ease the discomfort of the moment, Richard attempted to change the subject:

- That's a very pretty outfit you're wearing, Mademoiselle. Yellow and green suit you very well.

For the first time ever, Dalya wore both colors; a yellow dress, and a green coat. Dalya exuded a joyful freshness. She was happy that Richard noticed her clothing efforts. And as always, Dalya was intimidated by the young man's stares and smile. Feeling a fever invading her, Dalya took a book out of her bag with a shaking hand, and she answered shyly:

- Thank you. Océanie helped me this morning to coordinate the colors of my outfit. And … about the Philosophy class, this week at school, we studied the definitions of body and soul. I didn't understand a single word from the Professor, after his Hello! For me, he was speaking a completely different language!

Suddenly, Richard Poirier let out an amused and sincere laugh. Just a few minutes ago, Richard was confused, worried, and hesitant. Except that, a strange little girl came into his office like an illuminating and joyful ray of sunshine. This strange little girl helped him decide, she made him laugh, and above all … she gave him strength.

Chapter 15

Useful arrogance

Friday, February 24th, 1893.

Sometimes, what we fear happens much faster than we hope it would...

Even at the end of the day, the activity in the Lawyer's office was lively. All the employees were busy with their files. The Lawyer, Mr. Ernest Laszlo came out of his office, adjusting his coat. His Secretary followed him, holding her employer's hat and gloves.

Since almost 2 months now, and precisely since the answer to the 3rd Question, Sloan Wilfrid has been intensely and eagerly watching every move, word, and movement of the Lawyer Ernest Laszlo. Wilfrid was convinced that the Lawyer will not stop preparing another conspiracy against Dalya Bouvard and against the Will. Wilfrid had asked for the help of an assistant and the driver, in order to better watch the visits and the schedule of the Lawyer.

That day, Sloan Wilfrid was busy writing his notes on a file, when the door to his office opened. A young girl whispered to him at the doorstep:

- He is leaving to the grand Mansion! Right now!

Immediately, Sloan Wilfrid jumped from his chair, he dropped his files, and he left his office:

- Thank you for letting me know, Juliette!

Sloan Wilfrid caught up with the Lawyer in the hall. Mr. Ernest Laszlo was wearing his gloves. With an innocent and natural smile, Sloan Wilfrid asked him:

- Sorry to interrupt you, Mr. Ernest. I wanted to have your opinion on the Dumont affair, if you have a few minutes to grant me.

The Lawyer took his hat from his Secretary's hands:

- When is the trial?

Wilfrid replied:

- Tomorrow at 11 AM, Monsieur.

Ernest Laszlo thought for a minute:

- Very well. Come with me, then. I have a quick visit to make. We'll discuss it on the way.

Sloan Wilfrid turned around to pick up his coat and hat. If Ernest Laszlo will visit the grand Mansion, Wilfrid insisted on being present, in order to protect Dalya Bouvard.

That very day, at the grand Mansion, Dalya and her friend Amira were working peacefully in the living room. And despite being studious and intelligent, the two students were stressed because of a difficult subject.

- I'm giving up! It is evident; I will fail this course of Philosophy! Amira announced, lying back on her chair.
- Come on … courage, courage! With the explanations that my neighbor gave me, we can obtain at least the average score. Dalya replied encouragingly.

Letting out an amused laugh, Amira said:

- I have 6 other courses to review, aside from Philosophy, and I'm not worried about any of them. Even the Latin class, I'm sure I will get a good score! The Philosophy course is simply impossible to pass… it's the 3rd time that I miss it!

Dalya laughed, even though the situation did not predict a success in the Philosophy exam. It is true that the private lessons and the explanations of Richard Poirier, allowed Dalya to understand some notions and texts. But, to get the average score in this class, Dalya and her friend had a lot of work to do. And the exams were approaching.

After a few seconds of silence, Amira thought aloud:

- We must share the tasks. At this rate, we won't be ready for the Philosophy exam in two months.

Dalya straightened up on her chair:

- What do you propose ?

Amira took a white paper, and she wrote while thinking aloud:

- Here is the new study plan. We must finish the list of words and the vocabulary of Philosophy imperatively today. Then, I will take care of the summaries of the first 2 lessons… and you will take care of the summaries of the last 2 lessons. This way, we'll finish faster.

Dalya jumped:

- It is an excellent idea! We will exchange our summaries afterwards!

The living room door opened before Amira answered, and Océanie entered with a delighted smile:

- Hello Mesdemoiselles!

Dalya and Amira greeted her with a smile. And while Océanie went toward the fireplace in the living room, Dalya asked her:

- Do you need any help Océanie? We can help you with the housework.

Océanie barely retained a laugh:

- And I didn't believe Cristelle when she told me that you love housework! Thank you, Mademoiselle. It's very nice of you to offer help. But you have exams to study and pass.

Amira straightened up on her chair:

- Is the baby banging today?

Since several weeks, Océanie no longer wore a belt around her waist, her belly had grown rapidly and she had even gained weight. At this question, Océanie smiled, caressing her big belly:

- The baby bumps every day, more and more. This baby can't wait to get out! And I admit me too. I'm starting to feel heavy and fat like a whale.

Dalya reassured Océanie:

- Of course not, you're not fat. You're carrying a child, it's normal to feel heavy.

Amira affirmed with a confident tone:

- I read in a natural science book that with breastfeeding, pregnancy weight decreases. I didn't quite understand how and why ... but that's what the book said. So, it is certain that you will lose the excess weight after breastfeeding.

Océanie replied cheerfully:

- Thank you for this good news, Miss Amira! I hope to return to my usual size. And by the way, how are your studies going, Mesdemoiselles?

Dalya and Amira stifled their laugh:

- We are trying not to fail our Philosophy class.
- We still don't understand what it is about.

Océanie put her bucket down in front of the fireplace in the living room. She took out a towel and a small broom, and she laughed:

- I'm sure you will succeed, Mesdemoiselles. The Cook is preparing a white chocolate and raspberry cake for you, its smell is delicious. With a good hot tea, it will help you work well!

Amira jumped from her chair:

- White chocolate and raspberry cake?! It will help us work very very well! When can we have a piece of this cake?

Dalya and Océanie exchanged an amused laugh. Océanie replied, kneeling in front of the fireplace:

\- I'll wipe the edges of the chimney, and I'll go and check the cake for y...

When all of a sudden, the door to the living room swung open. And an icy voice startled the employee and the two students:

\- Here you are at last! I don't have time to look for you all day!

The Lawyer Mr. Ernest Laszlo entered the living room, and immediately he settled on an armchair in front of the work table of Dalya and Amira. Mr. Sloan Wilfrid followed the Lawyer into the living room, and he greeted Dalya and Amira with a friendly smile. The two girls exchanged shocked stares at the sudden presence of the Lawyer in front of them. Dalya and Amira remained frozen in their places.

The employee Océanie tried to get up slowly to discreetly leave the living room. Except that she was interrupted by the Lawyer Ernest Laszlo, with the icy voice:

\- You can stay Océanie. No need to make me tea this time. I won't stay for long.

Immediately, Océanie lowered herself in front of the fireplace, and she tried as best she could to hide her rounded belly. Dalya was worried at the idea that Océanie remained in the presence of the Lawyer. Mr. Ernest Laszlo addressed Dalya in an angry tone:

\- Do I have to repeat my orders to you a hundred times?! Why didn't you let me know the clues of that strange box? I've been waiting for your visit to my office for almost 2 months! Are you having fun making me come all the way here? Don't you think I have other business more important than you?

Dalya replied in a courteous tone:

\- It's because... Mr. Ernest... I haven't yet asked for a clue from the Excelbox, for the 4th Question. I only ask for clues when needed. I had no necessary reaso...

Mr. Ernest interrupted her in a furious voice:

\- So what?! Should I wait for you to ask for clues at your leisure? That's stupid and silly! Why don't you ask for all 5 clues once and be done with it? Are you enjoying prolonging your stay here, at the grand Mansion?

At one moment, a ray of bright sunlight disturbed the Lawyer sitting on the armchair. Mr. Ernest Laszlo ordered:

\- Océanie ... adjust the curtains, this ray of sunshine bothers me!

When Mr. Ernest Laszlo made this request, Dalya, Amira and Océanie exchanged a terrified look. In this living room, and on that day, only the 3 young girls were aware that the slightest movement from Océanie, would reveal her secret.

Instantly, Dalya stood up to adjust the curtain herself, and thus prevent Océanie from having to get up and be exposed. Except that the second Dalya got up from her chair, the Lawyer ordered her with an angry voice:

- Sit down when I talk to you! What are these manners?! I guess I shouldn't expect too much from a vegetable seller like you, to have good manners!

A few chairs away, Sloan Wilfrid noticed the anxious looks between Dalya and her friend Amira. And being used to the obnoxious character of his employer, Sloan Wilfrid thought that Dalya was bothered by the words of the Lawyer. Except that, Sloan Wilfrid didn't know that Dalya wasn't even listening to what the Lawyer was saying! Dalya was thinking of a solution to get Océanie out of the living room, without the two men realizing her secret.

Mr. Ernest Laszlo turned round:

- Océanie! How many years does it take you to adjust the curtains?

No solution or way out was in sight. Océanie got up slowly and walked toward the curtains. The only idea that Océanie came up with at that moment was to hold the bucket of ash, high enough up to her chest to hide her belly.

Mr. Ernest Laszlo continued to shoot Dalya:

- Why do I have to wait 12 months to get the 5 clues? When will you ask for them all? It's silly to ask for a clue every 2 months! And anyway, you never understand these clues, so what's the point of asking for them separately? ... And Océanie, why do you carry the ash bucket toward the curtains?

This question, as natural and simple as it was, shocked the 3 young girls. Océanie became pale and motionless; she didn't know what to do to get out of this impasse. Amira straightened up on her chair, her throat choked. And Dalya trembled. They had to help Océanie get out of the living room, right away and at all costs!

The words hesitated to come out of Océanie's mouth:

- I... the curtains... yes... I... the bucket... is for ... I...

Suddenly, Dalya exclaimed in an angry tone:

- Océanie! I asked you to make us tea an hour ago! How many times do I have to tell you that?! Have you forgotten again?! How dizzy you are! Bring us tea right now!! And hurry up!!

Sloan Wilfrid was shocked by Dalya Bouvard's words and tone of voice. This is the first time since their meeting that Dalya Bouvard was ... arrogant!

Having understood her friend's idea, Amira followed her in the same haughty and angry tone:

- Yes, we've been waiting for our tea for an hour!! Why are you so slow? Did you forget again? How dizzy you are!! Bring us the tea right now!

Immediately, Océanie quickly pulled herself together:

- Sorry Mesdemoiselles... I... yes, your tea... immediately, Mesdemoiselles!

Dalya insisted urgently:

- Go now! Hurry up! Hurry up!

Amira also insisted:

- And don't forget the cake with it!

Océanie didn't need to be repeated twice; she quickly turned around and disappeared, answering in a relieved voice:

- Yes, right away, Mesdemoiselles!! Right away!!

Exasperated by this ray of sunshine which was blinding him and by the incompetence of the employee Océanie, the Lawyer Mr. Ernest Laszlo moved to another armchair. He sighed with an annoyed tone:

- What a dizzy this Océanie!!

Dalya and Amira exchanged a relieved and accomplice smile. They succeeded in getting Océanie away from the living room.

However, Lawyer Sloan Wilfrid's curiosity sparkled. He didn't understand Dalya Bouvard's odious attitude and arrogance. It was very unusual coming from the little girl.

Except that before Océanie closed the living room door, a tiny little detail caught Sloan Wilfrid's eye. And although surprised by his discovery at that moment, Sloan Wilfrid smiled and he understood this very useful arrogance!

Chapter 16

Never bored

Tuesday, March 7th, 1893. In the Royal Georgetown College.

Spring had gracefully settled in the city of Georgetown. The snow had melted, the greenery reappeared again, the sun became more and more present, the joyful and active mood of spring was contagious.

In the Gymnasium of the Royal Georgetown College, a little girl was actively training with a ball, under the supervision and instructions of a young Professor.

- Left... right... left... left... right... right... right... left...

Suddenly, Dalya Bouvard stumbled, and she fell on the carpet, for the 37th time since the beginning of the class. The young Professor Tudi picked up the ball, and she held out a hand to Dalya to help her get up:

- It's a difficult exercise, I understand. But with more practice, you will get there, Mademoiselle.

Dalya stood up and let out a little amused laugh:

- It's confusing. Between your instructions, my feet, and the ball... I don't know who to follow.

The training consisted of running while kicking the ball, with the foot indicated by the young Professor. When Dalya changed feet abruptly, she tripped over the ball. Fortunately, the young Professor Tudi was encouraging and patient with her.

- The key to this exercise is concentration. You need to focus on one thing only; my instructions. Your feet and the ball will naturally follow the rhythm of the instructions you hear. Focus on my voice only.

Dalya repeated aloud:

- Focus on your voice only... focus on your voice only.

The young Professor Tudi took a few steps back:

- We start again. Go slowly. Then we will pick up the pace. Ready, Mademoiselle? ... right ... left ... right ... right ... left ... left ...

A few hours later and a few falls later, the young Professor Tudi handed a towel to Dalya, with an encouraging smile:

- That will be enough for today. You have made good progress, compared to the beginning of this course.

Dalya stifled an amused laugh:

- Fortunately, I train on a soft carpet. I could not have finished the exercise, falling on the hard floor.

Professor Tudi laughed discreetly, before continuing:

- It would be good if you also practice at home. With a ball, on the lawn of the garden or on a carpet. Visualize my voice, focus. Your feet and the ball will keep pace.

After finishing her Gymnastics class, Dalya headed toward her favorite spot; the big College Library. In one of the corridors leading to the Library, her friend Amira Mounier had stopped halfway to adjust her bag full of books.

- Hello Amira. I was just thinking of meeting you at the Library.

Closing her filled bag with difficulty, Amira sighed:

- Hello Dalya! ...I was heading to the Library, to return some borrowed books, when my bag broke. I need a new bigger bag to hold all my books. Have you finished your gym class?

Dalya helped her friend to close her bag:

- Yes, I've just finished my course. And I, too, must return borrowed books. How were your classes today?

On the way to the Library, Amira told her:

- The History Teacher gave us a 20 pages' assignment, due tomorrow. The Geography Professor was in an angry mood today. The Latin Professor tripped on a step; he broke his glasses. The Mathematics Professor sprayed the entire class with chalk powder; I must wash my hair tonight. There were two explosions in Chemistry class. And my week isn't over yet, it's only Tuesday!

Dalya laughed:

- It looks like a busy day! I want to know all the details. I miss the lessons in class, with you.

Immediately, Amira exclaimed in astonishment:

- The Teachers' reprimands, the 20 pages' homework, and the sudden explosions ... you miss that? I will trade my schedule for yours, willingly! 2 classes only, you're lucky this semester!

When they arrived at the entrance of the Library, Amira had described all the incidents that took place in her classes.

- Anyway, you never get bored in this school! Dalya laughed.

Amira opened her bag to pull out her borrowed books, and she sighed:

- It's a school of the crazy!

At the entrance to the College Library, there was the office of Miss Guendolyn Knigaski, the Library assistant. She was a very soft, kind, helpful woman, and easily recognized thanks to her ruby red hair. Her office was always meticulously and impeccably well-ordered.

- Hello Mesdemoiselles. I am glad to see you today!

Dalya and Amira smiled at her, placing their books in a large cart.

- We have some books to return.
- Lots of books to return! My bag broke!

Sitting at her desk, Miss Guendolyn smiled happily:

- It's a pleasure to see you using so many books. You are among the students who borrow the most books.

Approaching her office desk, Dalya asked in a polite voice:

- I was wondering, Miss Guendolyn … if you have received the new collection of Mr. Theodor Seuss Geisel's books?

Immediately, Miss Guendolyn indicated a place in her office:

- I have just received these books this morning! It is the 2nd box on the left. Open it. Apparently, he is a very gifted Author. The waiting list for his books is several months long. I insisted a lot to be served among the first.

A happy smile appeared on Dalya's face when she opened the indicated box:

- His books are astonishing, very funny, and very motivating. I love his stories! it is a real pleasure to read them.

Amira came close to her friend Dalya, and she read a title:

- Mr. Theodor Seuss Geisel … this is the first time that I hear this Author's name. Looks like an interesting book.

Dalya confirmed:

- I'm sure you'll like these books, Amira. I discovered one of his books by chance in the Library of the grand Mansion. But there was only one.

Amira flipped through a book briefly, thinking aloud:

- You said these books are funny and motivating? With my crazy schedule, my weird classes, and tons of homework, I really do need funny and motivating books... Miss Guendolyn, when can we borrow them?

With an amused smile, Miss Guendolyn replied to these two impatient students:

- They are not yet registered in my directory. However ... I can make an exception. You can borrow 2 books each. Help yourself, Mesdem...

Suddenly, a young boy came into the office, and he asked:

- Hello. I am looking for a woman. Miss Guendolyn Knigaski. I was directed to an office down the hall.

Miss Guendolyn stood up from her chair:

- It's me. How can I help you?

The young boy took out of his bag a magnificent bouquet of pink peonies.

- This bouquet is for you, Miss. And this card is sent to you with this bouquet.

At that moment, Miss Guendolyn froze in her place. Dalya and Amira exchanged curious looks, not daring to speak or move. In front of the woman's surprise and immobility, the delivery man placed the bouquet and the card on the office table. And he asked politely:

- May I have your signature on this document, Miss? Confirmation that you have received the bouquet.

Miss Guendolyn pulled herself together with difficulty, she signed the confirmation paper.

- Thank you, Miss. Have a good day!

Immediately, the young boy left quickly toward the exit, he seemed to have other deliveries.

Silence invaded Miss Guendolyn's office. She remained motionless, observing the magnificent bouquet of pink peony flowers. It was the first time in her life that the young woman received flowers and a card. Dalya and Amira didn't dare to move or say a word; they stared in silence at the young woman, the bouquet of flowers and the card.

At one point, Miss Guendolyn took the card with a trembling hand, she read the contents. Instantly, her cheeks reddened and a beaming smile lit up her face.

Dalya Bouvard repressed her curiosity. But Amira Mounier...

- Who is it from?

Immediately, Dalya whispered to her friend:

- It does not concern us. It's private.

Except that Amira pretended not to hear her friend, she insisted:

- It's a beautiful bouquet of flowers, Miss Guendolyn. The pink peonies are gorgeous. It must be someone who thinks highly of you to send you this bouquet. Who is it from?

Miss Guendolyn turned her face away, her cheeks turning scarlet. She whispered in a confused tone:

- Yes... it's a... pretty bouquet... very pretty peonies... splendid...

Dalya held back her friend Amira by her arm, so as not to move toward the office desk.

- Stop intimidating her. It does not concern us.

Except that Amira pulled away quickly, and she asked with an innocent smile:

- These are pink flowers, Miss Guendolyn. Pink is a beautiful spring color. Pink is a great attention color. Pink flowers are a nice gesture. It surely comes from an admirer! It is clear that he is a Gentleman, with excellent taste. Who is it from, Miss Guendolyn?

Miss Guendolyn quickly put the card away in a drawer, and she moved the bouquet with a confused move:

- He's... no one... just a... an acquaintance... that's all.

Dalya and Amira exchanged an amused look. It was quite clear that it was not just an acquaintance. Dalya tried to reason her friend, she whispered to her:

- It does not concern us. Leave her alone. Come on, we have homework to do!

Amira replied to her friend Dalya, in a pleading tone:

- I need to know! Curiosity will give me a migraine!

Turning toward the young woman, Amira flashed her innocent smile:

- So, Miss Guendolyn... is he handsome? Is he tall? Is he nice? Since when do you know each other? Did he invite you to dinner? Is this the first bouquet he offers you? Is he gallant with you? Is he attracti...

Suddenly, Miss Guendolyn came close to the two students, and she gently pushed them toward the exit of her office, answering in an intimidated voice:

- You have a lot of homework, Mesdemoiselles. The Library is over there. I recommend the armchairs in the left section; they are very comfortable. Good luck with your studies, Mesdemoiselles.

Amira protested, braking with her foot to slow her exit from the office:

-   I just want to know who he is! Just a first name! When is your next date? I can help you choose your outfit! I can help you with hair! Is he a handsome man? Is he tall? Just a first name! Please!

Dalya was also pushed out of the office. And she, too, protested, braking with her foot:

-   But I didn't say anything! Why are you kicking me out? And my book then? You told me I could borrow 2 books today! I said nothing!

Miss Guendolyn repressed an embarrassed laugh, and tried to sound serious:

-   Come on, Mesdemoiselles. Outside, please. I have a lot of work. Come back tomorrow. Homework awaits you. Good luck with your studies, Mesdemoiselles!

In a second, Dalya and Amira found themselves outside Miss Guendolyn's office. Exchanging a confused look, Dalya and Amira had a giggle for a long minute.

When Dalya walked inside the Library, toward the armchairs of the left section, she sighed amused:

-   I couldn't even take the book I was expecting!

Amira laughed as she followed her:

-   You are quite right, Dalya. We are never bored in this school!

Chapter 17

Closer

Saturday, March 18th, 1893. The afternoon, in the grand Mansion.

In her bedroom, Dalya was searching for something under her bed, repeating in a stressed voice:

- I am late! I am late!

Dalya ran to the dressing room and she actively searched the closets:

- But where are they? I'm sure I put them somewhere here! I am late! I am late!

At one point, a silhouette entered the room and exclaimed joyfully:

- I am bringing you your washed and ironed pajamas, Mademoiselle. They are soft as a cloud!

Dalya quickly put on her coat:

- Thank you, Océanie. Have you seen my navy-blue shoes?

The help Cook Océanie put the clothes on the bed, and she walked toward the dressing room:

- I think your navy-blue shoes are in the left closet.

While wearing her shawl around her neck, Dalya informed her:

- No, they are not there. I've been looking for them since a while. And I'm late.

Océanie took some shoes out of a closet and she presented them to the little girl:

- You can wear the black shoes.

For a long second, Dalya stared at herself in the mirror, and she thought aloud:

- My dress is light pink, my coat is navy blue, the shawl and bonnet are light pink … I think I need the shoes in navy blue.

Océanie approached the little girl:

- Black and navy blue are close colors. Black shoes will go very well with your outfit.

Except that Dalya politely insisted:

- I prefer to wear the navy-blue shoes. The difference between black and navy-blue will appear, and it will ruin my outfit.

Immediately, Dalya ran to search in the bathroom, murmuring:

- And I'm late! I'm late! But where did those shoes go?!

Océanie remained motionless and confused in her mind:

- *Black and navy-blue are two almost identical colors. I myself often confuse them. It's very strange that Mademoiselle is so meticulous so suddenly. She has always worn outfits regardless of colors. Where does this sudden interest in perfectly coordinating its colors, come from?*

Suddenly, Dalya came out of the bathroom, and she exclaimed:

- Found them! Finally!

Putting on her navy-blue shoes, Dalya smiled happily:

- My outfit is complete now!

Océanie stifled an amused laugh:

- Thanks to the found navy-blue shoes. You are very elegant and refined, Mademoiselle.

Without wasting another minute, Dalya took her bag and she quickly left:

- I won't be late, Océanie. I'll be home before dinner. See you soon!

Océanie picked up the pajamas to put them away in the dressing room, and she smiled:

- Understood, Mademoiselle.

A few hours later, in the house of the French family, the Poirier.

Dalya closed her eyes, she focused hard, and she recited slowly:

- Dualism is … the coexistence of two different elements, the soul and the body. The man is made up of the body relating to sensible matter, and the soul relating to the spiritual nature. An extended substance and a thinking substance. The body belonging to the sensible world, and the soul belonging to the intelligible world.

Opening her eyes, Dalya waited for Richard Poirier's verdict. Sitting on the chair in front of her, the young man followed in a book he held in his hands:

- Good. And the definition of monism?

Dalya breathed for a second, and then she answered:

- Monism is … it is a system of thought for which the universe is composed of only one substance, either matter or spirit. It is the opposite of dualism. Monism removes the distance between the real world and consciousness.

Without raising his eyes from the book, Richard said:

- Good. And who is Descartes?

It was an easy question, Dalya answered without hesitation:

- Mr. René Descartes is a French mathematician, physicist, and philosopher. He defines the soul by the thinking substance and the body by the extended substance, differentiating them absolutely and suppressing all intermediary. According to him, the body has its own characteristics: continuity, divisibility, infinity, exteriority, mobility. The spirit also has its characteristics: unity, interiority, individuality, will, freedom.

Richard continued:

- It's correct. And who is Berkeley?

Dalya thought for a second:

- Mr. George Berkeley is an Irish Anglican bishop and philosopher. He is opposed to the theory of René Descartes. Berkeley affirms that all the beings that we call material are reduced to perception, to the ideas that we have of them. Berkeley denies the existence of material substance defined by Descartes as extended substance. For Berkeley, there are not two substances, one material and the other thinking, but only one: the mind. Matter is an abstract idea without any reality; it designates only the being perceived by the mind. Berkeley affirms that the only substance is the mind.

At this moment, Richard Poirier raised his head, he observed Dalya, and he smiled:

- That's right. All your answers are correct!

Immediately, Dalya relaxed in her chair, breathless from the effort she was putting in to answer these questions. Richard closed the book and he put it down on the desk table:

- I assume that you have understood this chapter of Philosophy very well. I admit that matter and spirit are the most difficult subjects of the Philosophy course. The next chapters will be easy from now on.

Dalya exclaimed in an amused tone:

- I hope the next chapters will be easy! I feel that I have no more neurons in my brain.

The two young people exchanged a little laugh. Richard drank his tea, and he thought aloud:

- Anyway, I'm sure you'll pass the Philosophy class. You are studious and persevering, despite the difficulty of this subject. The Late Mr. Governor Iskander Balthazar was right in ensuring your educati...

Suddenly, Richard went silent. He realized his clumsiness:

- I am sorry. That's not what I meant. I …

Dalya smiled:

- You don't have to apologize. And you are quite right; the Late Mr. Iskander Balthazar saved my life by looking after my education and registering me in College. I admit that it was a big change for me. One day, I am selling vegetables at the market. And the next day, I am studying in a prestigious College.

Richard regretted his impulsive sentence; he never wanted to remind Dalya of her difficult past. Trying to make up for his clumsiness, Richard said:

- And it was a change for the better.

Dalya explained:

- Certainly, yes. But it was not an easy change. I had a hard time fitting in at school. The classes, the students, the Professors, the Director … it was not easy to adapt to them.

For the first time, Dalya dared to confide in the young man. And for the first time, Richard dared to ask personal questions to the little girl.

- Have you always wanted to study at school?

Dalya exclaimed:

- Oh yes! When I worked in the market, I often observed the students in uniforms going to their schools. I tried to imagine what they were learning in class and how their days were going.

Strangely, that day, Dalya opened up sincerely, and Richard listened attentively.

- My parents did not have the conviction, nor the resources to register me in a school. I was more profitable working at the market.

Richard observed Dalya for a moment:

- However, working in the market has gifted you with important qualities; the discipline to wake up very early, the perseverance and strength to work 7 days a week, the sense of communication with customers, the speed of calculating prices.

Dalya smiled:

- That's quite correct, yes. The work at the market trained me well. And I was also happy to help my family, as best as I could.

Richard was curious:

- You helped your family, even though the work at the market was difficult?

Without hesitating for a second, Dalya replied with a confident voice:

- My family is my priority. Just like Madame your mother is your priority. We make efforts and sacrifices for the people important to us.

Richard smiled:

- We have one thing in common then, you and me. Our families are our priority.

Dalya drank her tea, while asking in a curious voice:

- Mrs. Glorina once told me that you took on responsibility for your family, way too soon.

Richard relaxed in the chair:

- When my father passed away, I had no choice but to continue the family business. It is true that my schedule is very busy; between my career in the Government, managing my family's business, and watching over my mother and sister. However ... like you said so well, the family is our priority.

With an amused voice, Richard continued:

- I admit that, sometimes, I am so overloaded with work that I sleep on my office table.

Dalya exclaimed:

- Me too! During the exam period, I often sleep at the Library of the grand Mansion.

Richard smiled proudly:

- This is our 2nd point in common then. We're more alike than I thought.

The young man and the little girl exchanged a happy smile. The two young people discovered things in common, they opened up and confided in each other, and they grew closer and closer. At a moment, Dalya picked up her bag, and she stood up:

- I held you longer today. We did almost 2 hours.

Richard stood up to greet her:

- Quite the contrary. I was delighted with our conversation, Mademoiselle.

Dalya slipped away before her cheeks would turn scarlet red:

- See you soon.

Richard insisted:

- See you very soon.

Chapter 18

A construction at the grand Mansion

Sunday March 26th, 1893.

March was everyone's favorite month, including Lawyer Sloan Wilfrid. The gentle sun and fresh air filled you with positive energy. The green color covered every corner of the city; the trees proudly displayed their foliage, the flowers multiplied day by day. Spring was a beautiful season.

This Sunday morning, the Lawyer Sloan Wilfrid decided to visit the grand Mansion. The Lawyer made a point of visiting the little girl regularly, in order to inquire about her news.

When he arrived at the grand Mansion, Sloan Wilfrid got out of his car, and he immediately noticed a strange large construction in a corner of the garden. The head of the great Mansion greeted him at the entrance:

- Good morning, Mr. Wilfrid.
- Good morning, Mr. Bûchebois. I came a little early this morning. I will have a coffee, please, while waiting for Mademoiselle Dalya to wake up. I just came to check on her, and see how she is doing.

The head of the grand Mansion smiled:

- Mademoiselle Dalya has been awake since 6 AM this morning.

Sloan Wilfrid wondered:

- She is early this morning, on a Sunday. Why?

At this moment, the head of the grand Mansion indicated the large construction:

- The Gardener is building a greenhouse in the garden, to grow vegetables and fruits. They've all been working on it since very early this morning.

Curiosity invaded Sloan Wilfrid; he walked toward the construction:

- A vegetable and fruit greenhouse? At the grand Mansion? ...whose idea is it?

The head of the grand Mansion didn't need to answer this question. The answer was quite obvious. Sloan Wilfrid understood:

- Mademoiselle Dalya Bouvard!

A few steps later, Sloan Wilfrid arrived at the construction site. He was curious and surprised by the planning around this new site.

Several people were there. The Gardener Mr. Weil Rosenwald, the assistant Igor, Dalya Bouvard, and her friends Alfie Jaq and Maurice Gus. They were all holding aluminum poles, trying to build the structure of the greenhouse. The Gardener directed the building work and the people:

- Igor ... a little further to the right. Mademoiselle Dalya, come a little further. A little more. A little more. Perfect. Fix the poles securely to the ground. Alfie...come forward...come forward...stop. Maurice, raise your pole a little. Yes. That's good. Fix the poles to the ground. Perfect. How many poles do we have left to install?

In front of the construction site, a small office table was installed on the grass. Amira Mounier, Dalya's best friend, was sitting at the table. Dozens of books and architectural plans were spread out on the table. Amira Mounier answered the Gardener's question, following a large paper in front of her:

- You still have ... 2 poles to install on the right. 6 poles to be installed on the left. 4 poles in the center. And the greenhouse will be complete.

The Gardener ordered:

- Igor, Mademoiselle... you will go to the left now. Hold your poles. Wait for my signal. Alfie, Maurice ... we need to reinforce the center of the greenhouse. Install 2 poles in the center. Igor, Mademoiselle...move now...move. Yes, that's good.

Lawyer Sloan Wilfrid observed the building with admiring eyes. He came close to Amira Mounier's desk.

- Good morning, Miss Amira. It's a beautiful greenhouse that is being built at the grand Mansion!

Amira smiled and proudly explained to him:

- It's true. We looked for plans of this construction in architectural books. The structure of the greenhouse is metal, in aluminum poles, installed on the right, on the left, and in the center, in order to ensure the stability of the greenhouse. Aluminum requires less maintenance than wood, and lasts longer.

Sloan Wilfrid asked in a curious tone:

- The greenhouse will be covered in glass, I imagine.

Amira Mounier corrected him:

- No, Monsieur. It is true that glass is better for light transmission, but glass is heavy and fragile. We need a light coating, which will resist the wind. We decided to use plastic films.

Pointing to the other side of the garden, Amira continued her explanations:

- The maid Cristelle takes care of cleaning the plastic films. They will be well fixed on the poles with ropes. And since the greenhouse needs ventilation, to maintain an optimal temperature for the plants, the plastic films will be easier to open and close. It will be easier to evacuate excess heat and humidity.

The maid Cristelle took care of the covering of the greenhouse. About twenty large squares of transparent plastic were spread over the huge garden. Cristelle cleaned them with two sponges at the same time.

While observing the planning in the garden of the grand Mansion, Sloan Wilfrid thought aloud:

- It's fascinating…simply fascinating!

Lawyer Sloan Wilfrid noticed a few more people present. Dalya's twin little sisters were picking flowers from the garden. Ari and Adi were easily recognizable by their little pink hats, gray coats, and black gardening boots.

And naturally, following Dalya Bouvard like a shadow, the Snow Panther was lying on the grass, watching with interest the activity in the garden of the grand Mansion.

A few steps further, the help Cook Océanie was busy setting a table in the garden, near the greenhouse. We could clearly see cold drinks, sandwiches, and pastries. At a moment, the Cook came out of the outer door of the kitchen; he walked toward the table, carrying a large container of fruit cut into squares, sprinkled with honey.

At one point, Alfie screamed enough to be heard on the other side of the garden:

- Miss Océanie… more chocolate pastries, please!

And Maurice also screamed, but in a furious tone:

- Look in front of you! You idiot! You were about to crush me with the pole!

Océanie laughed out loud:

- Understood, Mr. Alfie. A second plate of chocolate pastries, just for you!

Everyone was taken by an amused giggle. On this beautiful Sunday, the grand Mansion was full of activity. Everyone was busy with their work. The head of the grand Mansion asked in a courteous tone:

- Would you like me to call Mademoiselle Dalya for you, Mr. Wilfrid?

Sloan Wilfrid replied:

- It would be useless to bother them, Mr. Bûchebois. Let them finish building.

Before leaving the garden of the grand Mansion, Sloan Wilfrid stopped for a long minute, and he observed Dalya Bouvard. The little girl wore blue overalls, gardening boots, a white shirt, a black cap was holding back her hair. Her hands were covered in mud, her outfit was stained with dirt, her hair was dirty, and she was laughing heartily as she helped build a vegetable and fruit greenhouse.

At this moment, the Lawyer Sloan Wilfrid asked the head of the grand Mansion, Mr. Bûchebois:

-   She still doesn't realize she's the Heiress to the greatest fortune in this Country, doesn't she?

Having failed to change the spontaneous habits of the little girl, Mr. Bûchebois sighed:

-   No, Monsieur. She still doesn't realize it.

Lawyer Sloan Wilfrid turned around and he left the grand Mansion, with an amused laugh.

Chapter 19

Give up willingly

Wednesday, March 29th, 1893.

On this end of that March Day, the air was calm and peaceful in the city of Georgetown. Except in the house of the Edelmen family.

- We can't watch her succeed one Challenge after another, cross our arms and do nothing! We only have 8 months left before this damn 4th Challenge!

This evening, in the luxurious living room of this residence, many people were gathered there. The nephew Mr. Ferdinand Edelmen seemed very upset, nervous, and impatient. Mr. Ferdinand sat down on an armchair and he continued:

- We need a radical solution, once and for all!

His sister, Mrs. Honoré Edelmen put down her tea, she answered in a calm and confident tone:

- And since I am in charge of it personally this time, we will not fail.

The Lawyer Mr. Ernest Laszlo did not share Mrs. Honoré's confidence and calm:

- This little beggar seems to have a chance that protects her. It's almost impossible for me to remove her from this inheritance in a legal way. I have tried everything!

Another voice in the luxurious living room that evening, answered calmly:

- If you can't get her out of the inheritance ... then she needs to give it up.

At that moment, the Lawyer Mr. Ernest, the nephew Mr. Edelmen, and his sister Mrs. Honoré, they all turned around toward a man. Of a slim and posed silhouette, perfectly neat blond hair, a dark black suit with a very elegant white shirt and an impeccably arranged tie. From his appearance, the man appeared to be a Government employee. He watched the landscape outside through the windows of the living room, looking peaceful and confident. Mrs. Honoré had called on him to help them in this matter.

The Lawyer Mr. Ernest Laszlo asked the question that everyone was thinking:

- That she gives up this inheritance? How?

Without turning around, the Government employee replied in the same still calm voice:

- Information about her family reveals that her father Antman Bouvard has an addiction to card games. He is not very skillful, he often loses. Therefore, he is forced to borrow big sums of money... which he will certainly not be able to pay back.

The Lawyer Mr. Ernest Laszlo thought for a moment about the new idea that presented itself to him:

- If he can't pay his debts ... then we can corner him ... and therefore, she will have no other choice but to give up this inheritance.

The Government employee confirmed, without turning toward the present people:

- Exact. She will give up this inheritance, on her own free will.

The nephew Mr. Ferdinand Edelmen did not understand the plan of the two men, he asked his friend the Lawyer:

- Ernest ... how will she give up this inheritance? Willingly?

Before the Lawyer could answer, the Government employee affirmed:

- This little girl cannot access this fortune. It is not just about money. Public opinion is more and more interested in this matter, and the Government Ministers are worried about the turn of events. One more Challenge won, and this success will create a mess in our Society. That is the reason why it is imperative that she gives up ... willingly!

At that precise moment, the Lawyer Mr. Ernest Laszlo understood what he had to do. He stood up from his chair and he picked up his coat. Before leaving the luxurious living room, Mr. Ernest Laszlo announced in an arrogant and determined voice:

- I will start the procedures tonight!

And even if the plan did not seem very clear for the nephew and the niece, Mr. Ferdinand Edelmen and Mrs. Honoré Edelmen relaxed on their armchair, and they exchanged a reassured smile. While the Government employee serenely contemplated the landscape outside the luxurious living room.

Chapter 20

Detained

Saturday April 1st, 1893.

The classes' day at the Royal Georgetown College ended. And as usual, Dalya headed toward the grand Mansion. As soon as she passed the front door of the big residence, Dalya noticed the head of the grand Mansion and the Gardener. The two men were at the front door, in front of the parked car, and they seemed to be waiting for someone. Dalya greeted them with a smile:

- Good evening, Mr. Bûchebois … Good evening, Mr. Gardener.

The serious faces of the two men revealed to Dalya that something serious had happened. The head of the grand Mansion cleared his throat, and he announced with a worried tone:

- Mademoiselle … I'm sorry to bring you bad news. You must go immediately to the police station.

Dalya was surprised by this request:

- Police station? Why? What happened?

The two men exchanged a worried look. They hesitated to break the news to Dalya. The Gardener came close to her and he replied:

- Your father, Mademoiselle … he was detained by the police.

The announcement slapped Dalya in the face; her throat choked and her brain stopped:

- My… my father… police… detained… but why?

Mr. Bûchebois walked toward the parked car:

- We don't know why, Mademoiselle. The Gardener will take you to the police station right away, to find out more.

Immediately, Dalya gave her school bag to Mr. Bûchebois, and she got inside the car, with the Gardener at the wheel.

The road from the grand Mansion to downtown city seemed like an eternity for Dalya. When the Gardener stopped the car in front of the police station, Dalya immediately got out and she walked toward the entrance.

The building was huge, gray brick, thousands of windows showing the thousands of offices that were there, a black fence surrounding the entire place. At the entrance to the police station, a reception desk was set up. An elderly policeman in a spotless uniform was arranging papers in folders. Dalya approached him:

- Good evening, Sir... My Da...

The policeman interrupted her in a firm voice:

- No visits are allowed for today!

Dalya insisted:

- I just want to know why my da...

The policeman stood up from his chair to place some files in a huge cupboard behind him:

- Come back with your parents, child!

Dalya wanted to know her father's fate, and it was urgent. Except that before she spoke another word, the loud voice of the Gardener behind her spoke:

- This girl's father was detained today, Sir. We want to know why.

The policeman turned toward the Gardener and the little girl; he watched them for a long second. And realizing that the little girl was not going to leave the reception without hearing from her father, the policeman sighed:

- Full name?

Dalya jumped:

- Antman Bouvard, Sir.

The policeman searched through a pile of papers in front of him, and after a few long seconds he replied:

- Antman Bouvard. Detained for reason of bad checks. His trial will take place in 5 days.

Dalya was stunned by this news:

- But... bad checks? ... How? When?

The policeman put the paper back in the file:

- I can't tell you more than that, kid.

The Gardener approached the policeman:

- Can we see him? Just for a few minutes?
- Sorry, all the visits are over for today. And you need a visit permit from a Lawyer.

This news was terrible and shocking. Dalya never thought she would see her father detained. Forced to recover from her shock, Dalya asked the policeman again:

- What can we do to help my father?

The policeman picked up his files and turned around to store them in the cupboard:

- Get him a Lawyer!

The Gardener and Dalya didn't need words to understand each other. Immediately, the Gardener and Dalya left the police station at a rapid pace, and they got back into the car.

The Law firm was busy and noisy. The employees were all busy processing their files. Dalya entered the office, and she immediately went to Mr. Sloan Wilfrid's desk. The office door being closed, an employee informed her:

- Mr. Sloan Wilfrid went out just a moment ago. He seemed to have an urgent business to attend to.

Dalya stood still thinking for a second. She had no choice but to head to a 2nd office to ask for help. With a forced move, Dalya knocked on the office door of the Lawyer Mr. Ernest Laszlo. A cold voice replied:

- Come in.

Dalya walked inside the office. And as always, an icy cold invaded this place, even though the fireplace was well lit. The Lawyer was sitting behind his desk. And a beautiful woman was sitting in a chair across from him. Dalya recognized the Governor's niece, Mrs. Honoré Edelmen.

And one would have thought that the Lawyer and the niece were certainly and patiently awaiting the arrival of Dalya Bouvard.

- Good evening, Mr. Ernest. I'm sorry to bother you, I ne...

Ernest Laszlo interrupted her, with a not the least reassuring smile:

- You never bother me. Come close ... come close ... what can I do for you?

The politeness of the Lawyer toward Dalya was a very unusual thing. The niece's calm and scrutinizing gaze was intimidating. Dalya took a few steps toward the desk. In a trembling voice, Dalya announced:

- My father was detained ... today.

The Lawyer displayed an icy smile and replied in a calm voice:

- Yes, it is very unfortunate. I was made aware of his arrest a few hours ago. And I'm sincerely sorry for you and your family.

The Lawyer's smile did not affirm any desolation for this incident. And although she was shaking, Dalya continued:

- The policeman at the police station told me that it was because of bad checks, and that my father needed a Lawyer. Mr. Ernest, can you...

The Lawyer interrupted her in a strangely joyful tone:

- There's no need to beg me to help your father. One, I handle only the Governor Iskander Balthazar's Will, not your family. And two, bad checks are a serious offence; there is a risk of a year in detention. Nothing can be done to help him. The Law is the Law!

With these words, Dalya almost collapsed on the floor; her face became pale, and her body trembled. Dalya never thought of facing such a situation. Remaining still and standing, Dalya did not know what to do to help her father. She clearly felt the scrutinizing looks of the niece Mrs. Honoré, and the arrogance of the Lawyer Ernest Laszlo.

After a long second of a heavy silence, and for the first time since Dalya's arrival in this office, the niece Mrs. Honoré Edelmen spoke. Her voice was so piercing and cold:

- Unless ... unless ...

Dalya jumped:

- Unless what? What can I do to help my father?

The Lawyer and the niece exchanged a determined look. At that precise moment, the Lawyer Ernest Laszlo presented a paper to Dalya, and he displayed a frightening smile:

- It is all in your hands ... you can get your dad out, tonight!

Few minutes later, Dalya left the office of the Lawyer Ernest Laszlo, in a state of shock and confusion, even more than before she entered. Dalya instantly headed toward the car parked across from the Law firm. When a hand stopped her:

- Dalya ... I called you several times, didn't you hear me?

Lawyer Sloan Wilfrid looked worried. Dalya had not seen him and even less heard him, having a busy mind:

- Sorry ... Sir ... I ... am ... I ...

The young Lawyer did not need more explanations to understand the state of the little girl. Sloan Wilfrid ordered Dalya to follow him. After leaving the office, Wilfrid walked toward a passage between two small Alleys, which was almost invisible. Dalya followed him. The passage between the two Alleys was quiet and empty. Sloan Wilfrid turned toward Dalya:

- I heard about your father an hour ago. I'm just coming back from the police station. He was arrested for bad checks.

Dalya asked in a terrified voice:

- What will happen to my father?

Sloan Wilfrid sat down on an empty crate, he looked worried:

- If it was a small amount of money, we would have paid for it and he would have been released this very evening. But the amount of bad checks is very big. Legal proceedings have already been initiated. His trial will take place next week, and the judge will decide on his detention sentence. First thing Monday morning, I'll check his Court records. I will try my best to reduce his time in detention!

Having exhausted all her strength that day, Dalya's legs no longer held her; she sat down against her will on an empty crate, opposite to the Lawyer. Sloan Wilfrid asked her in a curious tone:

- Why were you at the Law firm?

Dalia replied:

- After being at the police station, I came here to tell you about it. You were away. So, I asked for help from … Mr. Ernest Laszlo.

For a moment, Dalya hesitated to speak. And when the young Lawyer sensed her hesitation, he insisted on knowing. Sloan Wilfrid knelt before Dalya:

- What's going on? What did Ernest Laszlo tell you? Dalya, I need to know everything!

The words hesitated to come out of the little girl's lips. With a pale face, a choked throat, a trembling heart, Dalya answered in a crushed voice:

- He … he … Ernest Laszlo said that it was all in my hands, and that I could get my father out of detention tonight ... he handed me a paper ... and he advised me to ... he advised me to … to …

Sloan Wilfrid stood up and he finished Dalya Bouvard's sentence:

- He advised you to give up this fortune, in exchange for freeing your father from detention!

At that moment, tears streamed down Dalya's cheeks. With trembling hands, she buried her face in her hands, and she cried. Sloan Wilfrid couldn't hold back his anger. Immediately, the young Lawyer took an empty crate and he crushed it with all his might, against a wall:

- YOU BASTARD!! YOU GARBAGE!!

The Gardener was waiting for Dalya at the entrance to the passage between the two Alleys. He whirled around at the sound of the crushed wooden crate. The Gardener watched Dalya from a distance, with a sad and worried look. And without intervening, the Gardener turned around to watch that no intruder disturbed the conversation between Dalya Bouvard and the Lawyer Sloan Wilfrid.

After several long seconds of a heavy silence, Sloan Wilfrid regained his calm with difficulty:

- Please excuse my manners, Mademoiselle.

Dalya fully understood the young Lawyer's anger. She herself was still in shock from the situation. Sloan Wilfrid sat down on a crate across from her, and he sighed:

- These are the trickeries of Ernest Laszlo. He is ready to do anything to make you give up this fortune!

At that precise moment, Dalya thought aloud:

- If I sign this paper and give up this inheritance, my father will be free tonight. And Mr. Ernest Laszlo said that my father will keep his delivery job at the Toscana restaurant. He said that I could even continue my studies at the Coll...

Immediately, Sloan Wilfrid got up quickly, and he knelt in front of her:

- Dalya!! Dalya!! Look at me!! You can't give up this inheritance!! It's not just about money and fortune; it's so much more than that!! This Will does not influence your life alone, but the life of thousands of people!!

Dalya felt her throat tighten:

- But Mr. Wilfrid ... my father is detained because of me!

Sloan Wilfrid screamed:

- False!! Your father is detained because of his mistakes, and not because of you!! Ernest Laszlo wants you to believe it's your fault. This is how he hopes to force you to give up this fortune!!

Sloan Wilfrid's argument was true, somehow. The young Lawyer continued in a determined tone:

- Dalya ... Dalya ... listen to me!! ... In any way possible, your father can't get out of detention in one day. The procedure has already started; we must wait until the judge pronounces next week. I will personally follow this case. I will use all my contacts and means to get your father out of detention as soon as possible!! You have always trusted me, and I never break my word! ... Dalya, I ask you to trust me, once again!!

Sloan Wilfrid came closer to Dalya, and he insisted:

- But I beg you, Dalya... Whatever happens, whatever occurs, whether I am present or absent, I beg you, don't sign Ernest Laszlo's paper!! Please don't give up on this inheritance!! Thousands of lives are affected!! Promise me! It's the life of thousands of people!! Promise me you won't give up and you won't sign the paper!!

Dalya thought for a few long minutes. The decision to be made was incredibly difficult. At one point, between the two Lawyers, Ernest Laszlo and Sloan Wilfrid, Dalya Bouvard decided to trust only one man:

- You have my word, Mr. Sloan Wilfrid. I will not sign the paper.

Chapter 21

A long night

The same day. Saturday April 1st, 1893.

The return to the grand Mansion was in painful silence. At one moment, in the car, the Gardener affirmed with a confident tone:

- Mr. Sloan Wilfrid is a brave and honest man. You can trust him, Mademoiselle Dalya. He will never disappoint you. If he promises to help your father, he will do it at any cost. He is a man of his word !

Dalya Bouvard was worried and dejected for her father's detention. But the Gardener's words and Sloan Wilfrid's promise reassured her somehow a little.

Approaching the entrance to the grand Mansion, the car stopped and it was surrounded by all the employees. Cristelle could not restrain her concern:

- So ? What's going on?

The Cook asked:

- Why was Mr. Antman detained?

The head of the grand Mansion opened the car door for Dalya:

- We were worried about your lateness… is everything alright, Mademoiselle?

Océanie made her way between Cristelle and Mr. Bûchebois:

- What happened? When will he come out?

Igor drove the car inside the garage, after the Gardener got out. Dalya gathered her strength and she explained her father's situation to the employees of the grand Mansion. Without wanting to worry them more, Dalya did not divulge the offer of the Lawyer Ernest Laszlo, in order to abandon the inheritance.

A tense and sad silence followed Dalya's explanations. The head of the grand Mansion was the first to react:

- We are sincerely sorry for this news, Mademoiselle.

Dalya thanked him with a forced smile. Cristelle and Océanie hugged Dalya simultaneously:

- Really sorry, Mademoiselle.
- We are all here, if you need anything!
- Yes, whatever it is, we are at your service!

The Gardener informed the employees:

- Lawyer Sloan Wilfrid has promised that he will take on this case. He is a man of his word. He always watched over Mademoiselle and her family. He will succeed in getting Mr. Antman Bouvard out of this situation, I'm sure of that!

The Cook exclaimed spontaneously:

- I will serve the best cakes to Mr. Sloan Wilfrid!

Although the situation was grave and serious, Dalya was somehow reassured by the presence and the support of the employees. And when everyone went back to the grand Mansion, to resume their work, Cristelle asked:

- Would you like to have your dinner now, Mademoiselle?

Although she was tired from this long difficult day, there was one thing left for Dalya to do:

- I must visit mother and my two little sisters, at the annex house.

Cristelle smiled at Dalya's kindness:

- Understood, Mademoiselle. You will find your dinner tray in your bedroom, at your return.

Dalya thanked her, before heading toward the annex house.

Before arriving at the front door of the annex house, Dalya heard crashing noises and deafening screams. Dalya ran and she quickly climbed the front steps. The noises and screams came from the kitchen. And when Dalya entered there, the scene she discovered was terrible...

Dalya's mother, Augustine Bouvard, was in a hysterical state. She crushed to the floor, everything her hands touched. She was breaking dishes, cutlery, pots... the kitchen floor was full of broken debris. All the kitchen cupboards were open. All items were broken and strewn across the floor. Chairs were broken, fruits and vegetables were smashed on the walls, milk was scattered on the floor, kitchen utensils and dishes were shattered. And while destroying everything her hand touched, Augustine Bouvard screamed with all the might of her lungs:

- WE WILL ALL STARVE!! HE IS DETAINED NOW!! WE WILL ALL STARVE!! HE LEFT US WITHOUT MONEY!! WE WILL ALL STARVE!!

Dalya stood motionless and shocked for a long moment, trying to figure out what was going on. It was known that Mrs. Augustine Bouvard did not handle well the problems and incidents of life. Dalya's mother had always been pessimistic, violent, angry, unpredictable, and unable to handle the slightest incident of life.

- HE WILL NEVER GET OUT OF DETENTION NOW!! WE WILL ALL STARVE!! HE IS AN INCAPABLE WHO LEFT US WITHOUT MONEY!! WE WILL ALL STARVE!! HE WILL NEVER GET OUT OF DETENTION!!

A shadow of hidden silhouettes in a corner of the kitchen, caught Dalya's eye. The little twin sisters watched their mother breaking and screaming like a madwoman. Wearing their usual onesies and nightcaps, Ari and Adi looked terrified and frightened by their mother's attitude; the twins didn't dare to come out of their hiding place.

The kitchen floor was filled with broken items, and the twins were at the other end of the kitchen. Mrs. Augustine was throwing glasses against the kitchen wall hysterically:

- HE'S A MORON!! AN INCAPABLE!! AN IDIOT!! HE WILL NEVER GET OUT OF DETENTION!! HE WILL ROT DETAINED !! INCAPABLE !! MORON !!

It only took a second for Dalya to decide what to do in this situation. With quick steps, taking advantage of the turned back of her mother who was pulling a saucepan out of a cupboard, Dalya crossed the kitchen like an arrow to arrive at the place of her little sisters. And immediately, Dalya took her twin sisters back in her arms, she hugged them tightly. Mrs. Augustine threw the pan on the floor, with all her might, until the metal object broke in two:

- HE LET US TO DIE OF HUNGER!! HE WILL ROT IN DETENTION AND WE WILL DIE OF HUNGER!! INCAPABLE!! HE LEFT US WITHOUT MONEY!!

Dalya waited until her mother turned toward the cupboards. And in a second, Dalya walked back across the debris-filled floor in fast steps, while hugging tightly her little sisters. When Dalya came out of the annex house with her little sisters, the sound of an object broke against the wall, and her mother's hysterical screams continued:

- WE WILL ALL STARVE!! HE LEFT US WITHOUT MONEY!! MORON!! IDIOT!! INCAPABLE!!

Several steps further from the annex house, Dalya arrived at the garden of the grand Mansion. The debris sounds and her mother's screams were no longer heard. Out of breath from her rapid walk, Dalya put her little sisters back on the ground to catch her breath. The little twins were confused and terrified by what was happening. They asked their big sister, in a trembling voice:

- Why is mom screaming?
- Why is mom breaking?

Dalya knelt down in front of her little twin sisters, and she adjusted their nightcaps. Clearing her voice and trying to sound calm, Dalya explained to her little sisters:

- Mom is… she's a little sick. She needs to rest a bit. So, I'm going to take you to sleep with me, at the grand Mansion, for tonight. Alright?

The little twins exchanged a surprised look at this news. And immediately, a big smile appeared on the faces of the little twins:

- Sleep with Dindin ? Tonight ?
- And Dindin tell us a story?

Dalya fastened the buttons of her twin sisters' onesies, and she forced herself to smile at them:

- Certainly, yes! ...I'll tell you a good funny story. But you must be nice tonight, with me at the grand Mansion, alright?

The little twins quickly forgot the scene of their mother's rage, they jumped joyfully:

- Yes!! We nice Dindin!!
- We sleep with Dindin!!

Before Dalya stood up, Ari and Adi asked their big sister one last question:

- And papa Ant... he come and kiss us before sleep?
- Papa Ant... come and see us before sleep?

At this question, Dalya's heart stopped, and her brain froze. Dalya had to use incredible strength to pull herself together and smile:

- Dad is... he's on a trip for a while. Dad will come back, that's for sure! And ... and he will bring you from his trip, some lovely toys for you both. And until he gets back, you must be nice and do whatever I ask of you, alright?
- Oki Dindin!! Oki Dindin!!

Ari and Adi took their big sister's hands, and the three girls headed toward the grand Mansion. And as expected, Dalya found a dinner tray in her bedroom. After helping her younger twin sisters eat dinner and wash up, Dalya settled them into her big bed.

It only took a few minutes for the twins to fall into a deep serene sleep. Sitting near them, Dalya observed her little sisters peaceful in their sleep.

Earlier, in the kitchen of the annex house, the only idea that occurred to Dalya was to get her little sisters out of the house quickly, and away from their mother's mad rage. Having endured the difficult and ruthless character of Augustine Bouvard, Dalya did not want to see her little sisters suffer this same mad anger.

That night seemed very long and difficult. A detained father, a mother in a mad rage. The only thing that reassured Dalya a little, was that her little sisters were with her, safe and sound, at the grand Mansion. At least for tonight.

After several hours, Dalya could not sleep. Every time she closed her eyes, thousands of questions flooded her mind:

- *When will my father be released? What will happen now, for me and my family? Wouldn't it be easier to abandon this inheritance? Lawyer Ernest Laszlo told me that my father will be freed in one day. But ... I promised Mr. Wilfrid, that I would not sign anything, and that I would let him take care of it. How long will my father be detained? Is he alright?*

Dalya felt a migraine invade her brain, and a wave of anxiety carried her away. A whirlwind of questions, doubts and worries took hold of her. Finally, Dalya sat back on her bed, and she watched her little twin sisters sleeping peacefully.

For a moment, Dalya's gaze crossed a small object placed on her desk. The Excelbox. The strange box shone in all its glory. A small rectangular opening was always open on one side. An oval shaped cage, made of transparent glass, was silently charging under the moonlight. The cage was welded by 4 yellow gold cylinders, forged in the shape of a vine plant. A golden clock appeared inside the glass cage. Its small needle was still fixed on December 12th, 1893. Its large needle wavered between the night of April 1st and 2nd, 1893.

Without hesitation, Dalya stood up and she walked to her desk. Dalya needed answers to her worries. She sat down in front of the strange box. She wrote on a small piece of paper, and she inserted it into the rectangular opening.

What is the 1st clue?

When the piece of paper was swallowed inside, the strange box awoke. The oval glass cage lit up with a sparkling light. And without hesitation, the Excelbox answered the little girl's question:

Breathe. Exhale. Wait.
To survive the outside, look inside.

Dalya picked up the piece of paper emitted by the Excelbox, and she whispered the first two words of the clue:

- Breathe ... exhale ... breathe ... exhale.

Voluntarily, Dalya complied. She relaxed in her chair, she closed her eyes, she took a deep breath, and then she exhaled slowly. Dalya made this movement several times. And strangely, it was as if Dalya breathed in calm, and she breathed out anxiety. Filling her lungs with fresh air, Dalya exhaled the doubts and worry that invaded her.

On the 5th time, strangely, Dalya felt better. She continued to read the clue:

- Wait ... wait ...

This single word was able to calm the little girl's anxiety. Since the first time this strange box was handed to her, Dalya learned to trust the Excelbox. Why and how, Dalya didn't know anything about this strange box. But over the many clues, the Excelbox always proved that its answers were true and correct.

And that night, even if Dalya didn't understand the clue at first, the Excelbox answered the little Dalya Bouvard's anxiety and concern, with only 3 words; breathe, exhale, wait.

Chapter 22

A thoughtful help

The next morning. Sunday, April 2nd, 1893.

Although the day before was a difficult day full of painful events, the beginning of this Sunday morning seemed calmer. Dalya woke up at the first light of day. Her little twin sisters were still asleep, next to her. And before getting out of bed, Dalya heard a knock on her bedroom door.

- Come in.

It was the head of the grand Mansion. Because of the events of the previous day, Mr. Bûchebois insisted on bringing himself the breakfast tray to Dalya's bedroom.

- Bonjour, Mr. Bûchebois.
- Bonjour Mademois...

While coming inside the bedroom, Mr. Bûchebois realized the presence of the two little twin girls. Ari and Adi immediately woke up to the sound of voices. Their little curly hair in the air, their eyes half open, their mouths yawning with sleep, the little twins slowly sat up on the bed, and they came closer to their big sister. Mr. Bûchebois was still holding the breakfast tray in his hands, and he seemed confused:

- They... your little sisters... they spent the night here, in your bedroom? At the grand Mansion?

After a few seconds of hesitation, Dalya answered in a dejected voice:

- I...yes, Monsieur ...they spent the night with me...here...in my bedroom.

The head of the grand Mansion had to recover from his astonishment. He took a few steps forward and he put the tray down on a table. Then, Mr. Bûchebois addressed Dalya in a formal tone:

- You should have warned me, Mademoiselle!

Dalya got up from the bed:

- I'm sorry, Monsieur. Yes, I had to warn you of their presence ... it's just that ... when I was at the annex house ... mother was not ... she was not ... she ...

The head of the grand Mansion interrupted Dalya, in a serious voice:

- Follow me, all three of you. Immediately, please.

The little twins got out of bed instantly. Dalya took them by the hand, and they followed Mr. Bûchebois who was leaving the bedroom. Dalya trembled:

- I'm sorry, Monsieur. You are the head of the grand Mansion, and I should have asked your permission to bring my sisters here. It was just for one night...mother wasn't feeling well last night...I'm sorry Monsieur...sorry Monsieur ...

The little twins followed their big sister with a quick step, in the corridor of the grand Mansion. Ari and Adi did not understand what was really going on, but they were imitating their big sister, and they repeated:

- Sorry Monsieur!!
- Sorry Monsieur!!

The head of the grand Mansion took a few steps down the corridor. Dalya understood that he was going down the stairs toward the hall and the exit of the grand Mansion. The formal and serious state of Mr. Bûchebois indicated that he was angry by Dalya's decision, and that he was about to take the little twins out of the grand Mansion. After all, the orders of the Lawyer Mr. Ernest Laszlo were very clear; Dalya alone would live in the grand Mansion, and no one else!

Except that... Mr. Bûchebois didn't come down the stairs. He suddenly stopped in front of a door to the right of the hallway. Dalya and her little sisters stopped, and they went silent instantly. Mr. Bûchebois observed the 3 sisters for a few long seconds. When he opened the door, Mr. Bûchebois ordered:

- Go inside, please.

The room that Dalya and her little sisters discovered was far beyond their imagination. It looked like a bedroom. Almost all furniture were in soft pink color. There were two beds with luxurious blankets, large windows with white cloud curtains, small tables and chairs, a large Library containing books and pencils in a thousand colors, a hundred toys and stuffed animals placed everywhere, a huge wardrobe filled with clothes of all sizes and seasons, a corner with strange and funny swings, a large bathroom with a tub in the shape of a yellow duck...

Dalya and her little twin sisters were amazed by the splendor of this room. Ari and Adi released their big sister's hand, and they stepped inside the room, being fascinated by what their eyes discovered:

- Oh!! It's zoli!! Look Dindin!! Oh!! Many toys and swings!!
- Oh!! Look look!! Princess beds!! Oh, that's zoli!! Look funny bathtub!!

Dalya also stepped inside the room, surprised by this splendor. And yet, she turned toward the head of the grand Mansion, to better understand what the man was offering them:

- Monsieur Bûchebois ... is it... it's a room with two beds... is it...

The head of the grand Mansion explained to Dalya:

- The Governor's wife, Mrs. Irea Senderlson often received modest and orphaned children. She ordered us to always keep rooms tidy for children and visitors.

At this precise moment, Mr. Bûchebois knelt in front of the little twins:

- Miss Ari... Miss Adi... this bedroom is yours. From now on, there is no need to sleep in your big sister's room.

Ari and Adi exchanged a confused look:

- We sleep here? These beds? Next to Dindin room ?
- Toys to us? Swings to us? Beds to us?

Mr. Bûchebois smiled:

- This entire room is yours, Mesdemoiselles.

Instantly and abruptly, Ari and Adi jumped at the old man's neck; they squeezed him with their little hands and they kissed him on the cheeks, exclaiming joyfully:

- Thank you!! Thank you much!! Thank you!! Thank you!! Thank you much!!

The head of the grand Mansion did not expect this spontaneous gesture from the little twins. And it's clear that he wasn't used to kisses and hugs. Mr. Bûchebois turned red with emotion. When the little twins let go of him, they ran to discover their new room and its treasures. Dalya was moved by the gesture of the head of the grand Mansion, she replied with tears in her eyes:

- Thank you, Monsieur Bûchebois ... thank you so very much!

Mr. Bûchebois stood up and he addressed Dalya in a thoughtful tone:

- Mademoiselle ... you must let us know of all your needs and desires! The grand Mansion and all its employees are at your service. It is our job.

Dalya hesitated for a few seconds, before asking:

- Mother ... mother wasn't well last night. And... and I can't bring my sisters back to the annex house, at least not this week... and I have my classes and exa...

Mr. Bûchebois interrupted Dalya:

- Mademoiselle ... focus only on your studies. You absolutely must pass your exams this semester. The employees of the grand Mansion will take care of your little sisters. Mesdemoiselles can stay at the grand Mansion for as long as you wish. It would be a great pleasure to serve you, Mademoiselle.

Dalya was very touched by the offer of the head of the grand Mansion. And always spontaneous by nature, Dalya hugged Mr. Bûchebois with a grateful and moved gesture. Immediately, the little twins stopped running in their new room, and they imitated their big sister, each hugging Mr. Bûchebois' legs. The old man smiled at the natural gesture and the happiness of the three little sisters.

Sunday afternoon.

After lunch, the little twins took a nap for a few hours. The employees of the grand Mansion busied themselves with their work. Dalya took advantage of the calm of this afternoon, and she stayed in the Library of the grand Mansion.

Despite having an interesting book in her hands, Dalya couldn't clear her brain out of questions, of worry and of anxiety. Her father's detention was a painful shock for her entire family.

Suddenly, a voice interrupted Dalya in the Library:

- Mademoiselle ... someone wants to see you.

The head of the grand Mansion stepped back and he introduced a man. Immediately, Dalya stood up:

- Uncle Giorgi! Good afternoon. Come in, please.

The old man had replaced his tools apron with a simple green coat. His peppery hair was still frizzy and messy. He walked toward his little niece, and he hugged her, with a very strong gesture. Dalya understood that Uncle Giorgi knew about his brother's detention.

- I came as soon as I heard the news. How are you? How are your sisters?

Dalya invited him to sit on the armchairs, and she replied with a sad smile:

- We are well. Thank you for coming to inquire about our news. My little twin sisters are taking a nap at this moment. They will stay with me for a few days, here at the grand Mansion. The employees are nice, and they take care of us.

Even though Uncle Giorgi seemed upset by this event, he smiled:

- It's good...it's good...I'm reassured that you and your little sisters are in good hands. The employees of this grand Mansion seem to be honest and generous people.

A long minute of silence settled between Dalya and her Uncle. The old man didn't know what to say to comfort his niece, and Dalya didn't know what to say about her father's detention. At one point, Uncle Giorgi affirmed with a confident voice:

- Biggo... I'm just a poor inventor and handyman. I don't know what to do to help my brother. I don't know how I can help you and your little sisters. However, if you need anything, I am always always available!

Dalya expected no less from her uncle Giorgi. He was always thoughtful and considerate of her and her little sisters.

- Thank you, Uncle Giorgi.

Before getting up to leave her, the old man asked in a polite voice:

- Will Antman have a Lawyer for his defense?

Dalia replied:

- Yes, Mr. Sloan Wilfrid will take care of helping my father. He will take care of this matter himself. And tomorrow I'm going to visit my dad in... in...

Little Dalya Bouvard's throat choked, she didn't dare utter the name of the place where her father was being held. Without needing more words, Uncle Giorgi understood exactly what he had to do:

- You won't be alone tomorrow. I will come with you.

Chapter 23

The visit

Monday, April 3rd, 1893.

It was a sunny day, with a clear blue sky and a cool breeze. A beautiful spring day. And yet, Dalya Bouvard was sad and anxious. Lawyer Sloan Wilfrid informed the Royal Georgetown College that Dalya Bouvard will be absent that day. Dalya will visit her father, in detention.

Usually, having a big appetite in the morning, Dalya couldn't eat a single bite that day. When serving her hot milk, the head of the grand Mansion realized the anxiety of the little girl. And usually reserved and formal, Mr. Bûchebois served Dalya slices of bread, displaying a thoughtful smile:

- Everything will be fine, Mademoiselle.

Dalya forced herself to smile back at him. In all her life, Dalya never thought that one day she would visit her father in detention. This ordeal was difficult and painful.

Before leaving the grand Mansion, Dalya met the maid Cristelle in the hall:

- Here is the basket you requested, Mademoiselle. There is food and clothes for your father. I also included newspapers that Igor had brought me.
- Thank you, Cristelle.

The maid Cristelle clearly felt the girl's sadness, despite Dalya trying to hide it. Finding no words to relieve her, Cristelle just hugged Dalya tightly.

At the exit of the grand Mansion, Dalya found the car parked in the front. The Gardener and Uncle Giorgi were waiting for her. Both men greeted the little girl with silent smiles. Immediately, the Gardener got behind the wheel. Uncle Giorgi and Dalya got inside the back of the car.

Several minutes later, the Gardener stopped in front of the police station:

- I will wait for you here. Take your time.

When Dalya and her uncle Giorgi entered the reception of the Police Station, they met the Lawyer Mr. Sloan Wilfrid, who was talking to a policeman. And as soon as he noticed Dalya, Sloan Wilfrid cut his conversation short and he walked toward them. The young Lawyer tried to appear natural and even smiling:

- Good morning, Mademoiselle. Good morning, Monsieur Giorgi. You are on time!

Dalya cleared her throat:

- Good morning, Monsieur Wilfrid.

Sloan Wilfrid needed no more words to recognize the pain in Dalya's voice. He smiled tenderly at her:

- I got you permission to meet your father. This policeman will escort you to the visiting room. You have 1 hour with him.

Dalya forced a smile:

- Thank you, Monsieur Wilfrid.

The Lawyer approached Dalya and he whispered to her:

- I have contacts here. Your father is well treated, rest assured!

Before Dalya could answer, a policeman approached them, and he addressed Dalya in a respectful tone:

- Please follow me, Mademoiselle. The visiting room is on this side.

Sloan Wilfrid gave Dalya an encouraging smile. He was well aware of the difficulty of this situation, which is why he insisted on being present at this visit.

The policeman took several steps ahead of Dalya and he opened a door. Dalya took a few steps forward. Then, suddenly, she stopped just before the opened door. The policeman turned around:

- Come in, Mademoiselle.

At that moment, in front of the opened door, Dalya could not feel her legs, her heart was beating at full speed, her throat was tight, and her cheeks turned red.

The policeman repeated for the second time:

- Come in, Mademoiselle.

Dalya stood motionless like a statue in front of the door. She gripped the basket tightly in her hands. It looked like her brain stopped working, and her body went paralyzed.

The policeman repeated for the third time:

- The visiting room is on this side… come in.

Sloan Wilfrid and Uncle Giorgi exchanged a worried look. They observed Dalya's stillness in front of the opened door. Dalya felt her body become paralyzed, her face turned pale, her legs refused to move, and her brain froze.

After long seconds of a difficult silence, Lawyer Sloan Wilfrid approached the little girl:

- Is everything alright, Mademoiselle ?

At that moment, tears streamed down Dalya's cheeks, and she turned toward Sloan Wilfrid, whispering in a crushed voice:

- I ... I .... I ...

Needing no more words or explanations, Sloan Wilfrid and Uncle Giorgi understood why Dalya didn't dare to enter the visiting room. Uncle Giorgi came close to his little niece, he took the basket from her hands, and he smiled kindly at her:

- Biggo ... it would be better if I went in your place. Not only for this time, but also for all future visits. On the agreed dates, bring me the basket of provisions to my workshop, and I will pass it on to your father.

Lawyer Sloan Wilfrid confirmed this idea:

- It will be better that way, Monsieur Giorgi. I'm going to prepare the visiting permit in your name, this afternoon.

Dalya had no words in mind to say, her tears flowed silently and painfully. With a caring gesture, Lawyer Sloan Wilfrid hugged the little girl, and he whispered in a sorry tone:

- Everything will be fine, Dalya ... everything will be fine.

As brave and courageous as Dalya Bouvard was, she never dared to visit her father in detention. No child should do that.

It is true that this story is inspired by real events. And as brave as the Author was in daring to tell the real scenes, the detention of Antman Bouvard was incredibly difficult and painful for the Author to live, and also to write.

Chapter 24

Mentioned for the last time

Tuesday April 4th, 1893. The morning, in the Gymnasium of the Royal Georgetown College.

- Mademoiselle ... Mademoiselle ... Dalya ...

The young Professor Tudi called Dalya several times. The little girl was sitting on a bench in the Gymnasium, observing her gloves, her mind busy with questions and worries. Her body was present in the Gymnasium, but Dalya's mind was elsewhere.

- Sorry Professor, I didn't hear you.

Dalya Bouvard looked clearly troubled and distressed, although she forced herself to act normal and hide her sadness. With a kind smile, the young Professor came close to her:

- Are you ready for today's session, Mademoiselle? ... Follow me.

The young Professor took 2 small mats, and she left the Gymnasium. Dalya followed her, curious about this next training. A few corridors and a few stairs later, the young Professor and Dalya found themselves in the garden of the Royal College.

On this spring morning, the weather was cool, the greenery embellished the garden, several flowers were not even awake yet, the water flowed gently from a small fountain. The school garden was a real paradise.

The young Professor Tudi placed the 2 carpets on the grass, and she explained to Dalya:

- Today's training will take place here in the College's garden.

Since the beginning of her education in this school, 4 years ago, Dalya has never taken a class outdoor. She exclaimed:

- We ... we will train here? In the garden?

The young Professor Tudi smiled:

- Yes, in the garden. Take off your shoes and socks. Sit on the mat in this position. Take off your gloves, they won't be needed today.

Dalya complied. She took off her shoes and socks, and she sat down on the carpet next to the young Professor.

- Straighten your back. Bend your legs. A little more ... a little more ... perfect. Raise your chin. Put your hands on your knees like that. That's good, Mademoiselle.

The young Professor Tudi and Dalya Bouvard sat in the middle of the garden, surrounded by green trees, multicolored flowers, and a water fountain.

- Today's practice is to calm the mind.

One would have thought that the young Professor Tudi clearly sensed Dalya's worry and anxiety. And strangely, the young Professor Tudi understood exactly what the little girl needed, that day.

- The training is simple. Close your eyes. Breathe in and out slowly. Fill your lungs and empty them. Focus on the sounds of the garden.

For several hours, Dalya sat on the carpet in the middle of the school's beautiful garden. Her repetitive breathing movements emptied her lungs and eased her tight throat. Closing her eyes, Dalya felt the questions and worries gradually evaporate from her mind, giving way to the sounds of water flowing from the fountain, the sounds of birds barely waking up, the cool breezes of the wind caressing her face, the smell of fresh grass and sweet flowers. Nature's serenity managed to calm Dalya's mind.

The young Professor Tudi had chosen the perfect workout to calm the little girl's anxiety. The Gymnastics class that day was incredibly relaxing and soothing.

The afternoon.

After finishing her Gymnastics class, Dalya picked up her bag and she headed for the College exit. On a bench near the exit door, Dalya found two familiar silhouettes; her friend Amira Mounier, and the Library assistant, Miss Guendolyn. It was quite clear that the two were waiting for Dalya.

When she found out that her best friend's father was being detained, Amira was devastated by the news. Usually cheerful and encouraging, Amira lost her words for the first time in a long time. As soon as she appeared, Amira hugged Dalya so tightly, and she whispered in a trembling voice:

- I'm sincerely... sorry about your father.

During this difficult time, Dalya was grateful for all the kind words and gestures she received. She forced herself to smile and look strong :

- Thank you, Amira.

The Library assistant, Miss Guendolyn, approached Dalya, and she also hugged her:

- I'm sure everything will be alright soon, Mademoiselle.
- We hope so, Miss Guendolyn. Thank you very much.

When Dalya turned around to leave the College, Miss Guendolyn held Amira back by the arm, and she whispered quickly to her:

- Watch over her!
- Count on me, Miss Guendolyn!

The road to Dumbarton Oaks Park was quiet and peaceful. And as agreed, Amira insisted on accompanying her friend Dalya to the grand Mansion:

- My father will reprimand me if I go home without accompanying you, to your house. We were both worried about you and your family.

Dalya was relieved to have company. And in order to clear her friend's mood, Amira told Dalya everything that was happening in the other classes, and the latest news about school.

When they arrived at the entrance of the grand Mansion, Dalya and Amira were greeted by the little twins. Ari and Adi had come home early from kindergarten, and they were picking flowers from the garden.

- Hello Dindin!!
- Hello Mia!!

Amira knelt and she hugged the little twins:

- Hello pretty Demoiselles! Such beautiful bouquets of flowers you have picked, both of you! Who is it for?

The little twins replied simultaneously and happily:

- For Mom!! Pretty flowers!!
- Yes!! Flowers for mom!!

Dalya smiled as she addressed her little sisters:

- Mom will be very happy to receive your bouquets of flowers. We go to visit her and give her the flowers, now?

Since Saturday, when Dalya brought her twin sisters out of the annex house, under the mad rage and the screams of Mrs. Augustine who was breaking the entire kitchen, Dalya didn't dare to come back to the annex house. She preferred to give her mother a few days off to calm down.

And that day, walking toward the annex house, Dalya and Amira marched behind the little twins, who were impatient to offer the bouquets of flowers to their mother.

Meanwhile, at the grand Mansion, a black car stopped in front of the front door. Immediately, the head of the grand Mansion greeted the visitor with a courteous smile:

- Good afternoon, Monsieur Wilfrid.

The Lawyer got out of the car:

- Good afternoon, Monsieur Bûchebois. I came to check on Mademoiselle Dalya. Did she come home from school?
- Yes, Monsieur. A few minutes ago. I saw her heading toward the annex house with the little Demoiselles and her friend Amira.

While standing at the front door of the grand Mansion, Sloan Wilfrid asked:

- Good... good... I take it you know about her father?
- Yes, Monsieur. Mademoiselle informed us about his situation.

At that moment, Sloan Wilfrid addressed the Manager in a serious and grave tone:

- Honestly, I don't know how her father's case will end. The trial will take place in a few days, and his case is complicated. Mr. Bûchebois, you absolutely must watch over Dalya Bouvard! The next few days may be difficult for her. You must warn me at the slightest concern !

The head of the grand Mansion didn't hesitate for a second:

- Rest assured, Monsieur Wilfrid. All the employees watch over Mademoiselle Dalya, and also the little twins who live here at the grand Mansion. I myself make sure that all their needs are met.

A detail caught the attention of the Lawyer. Sloan Wilfrid asked in a curious tone:

- What? The little twins live at the grand Mansion? They no longer live in the annex house? Why is that?

Mr. Bûchebois answered sincerely:

- I don't know why, Monsieur Wilfrid. Mademoiselle brought her little sisters to the grand Mansion, the very day her father was detained. I didn't dare to ask Mademoiselle for more explanations. I moved the little twins to another bedroom, and we all adjusted our work schedule to better serve the 3 little girls.

The Lawyer Sloan Wilfrid thought aloud:

- It's strange... if Dalya moved her little sisters from the annex house; it must be for a serious reaso...

When suddenly, the Snow Panther came out of the front door of the grand Mansion, and she pushed away the head of the grand Mansion Mr. Bûchebois who was on its way. The animal ran with all the might of its paws, like an arrow, and she headed to the annex house.

At this precise moment, the voice of Amira Mounier was heard screaming with all the strength of her lungs:

- HELP!!! HELP!!! HELP!!! SHE WILL KILL HER!!! HELP !!!

The Gardener was in another side of the garden. And when he noticed the Snow Panther running toward the annex house, the Gardener dropped a vase which broke on the ground, and he followed the Panther, running with all his might. Amira Mounier continued to scream:

- HELP!!! HELP!!! HELP!!! SHE WILL KILL HER!!! HELP !!!

The Lawyer Sloan Wilfrid recovered rapidly from his shock, and he ran at top speed toward the annex house. The Manager Mr. Bûchebois stood up quickly from his fall, and he ran after the Lawyer. The Cook and Igor came out of the back door of the kitchen, they had heard the screams for help too, they ran straight toward the annex house.

- HELP !!! HELP !!! HELP !!!

Hearing screams for help, the maid Cristelle dropped her bucket of water in the hall of the grand Mansion. And when she saw all the men running toward the annex house, Cristelle rolled up her apron, and she ran too.

The help Cook Océanie was cleaning the windows of the living room, when suddenly she saw through the windows several silhouettes running toward the annex house. Océanie understood that something serious was happening. Océanie released her sponge, she went out through the back door of the living room, she held her big belly with both hands, and she ran as fast as she could.

When everyone arrived at the annex house, they found themselves in front of a horrible scene...

In the hall of the annex house, Amira Mounier had fallen to the floor, out of breath and fainted, for having screamed too much for help with all her might. The little twins were standing terrified and paralyzed in a corner; they were sobbing hard, hugging each other. And... Mrs. Augustine Bouvard was strangling her daughter Dalya!

Mrs. Augustine was squeezing Dalya's neck very tightly with both hands. The mother repeatedly banged her daughter Dalya's head against a wooden wall, so hard that a crack formed on the wall. Dalya had pale cheeks and blue lips; she seemed to have stopped breathing and lost consciousness. Mrs. Augustine was screaming as she strangled her own daughter:

- IT IS BECAUSE OF YOU THAT HE IS DETAINED!!! IT IS BECAUSE OF YOU THAT WE ARE GOING TO STARVE!!! EVERYTHING IS YOUR FAULT!!! IT IS BECAUSE OF YOU THAT HE IS DETAINED!!! YOU IDIOT!!! YOU VERMIN!!! HE WILL ROT DETAINED!!! EVERYTHING IS YOUR FAULT!!! EVERYTHING IS YOUR FAULT !!!

And that was not all. Having arrived first at the annex house, and fortunately, the Gardener had jumped with all the weight of his body on the Snow Panther. He held the animal by the neck leash. The Gardener quickly understood that the Panther will try to save the little Dalya

Bouvard from the hands of her mother. With all his strength, the Gardener tried to prevent the Snow Panther from jumping on the mother Mrs. Augustine Bouvard and killing her.

The Snow Panther roared and wrestled furiously to get out of the hands of the Gardener, in order to save Dalya Bouvard. And The Gardener struggled hard to hold the Snow Panther and avoid a slaughter:

- CALM DOWN SÉRAPHINE!!! CALM DOWN!!! I BEG YOU!!!

The new arriving people had to recover quickly from their shock to contain the situation in front of them.

The head of the grand Mansion Mr. Bûchebois, the Cook and the assistant Igor, they ran toward Mrs. Augustine and they tried to move her away from Dalya. Enraged and hysterical, Mrs. Augustine struggled like a madwoman, squeezing her hands tighter on Dalya's neck.

At one moment the Cook lifted Mrs. Augustine by the waist and he pulled her back. Igor and Mr. Bûchebois struggled to loosen Mrs. Augustine's fingers which were strangling Dalya's neck.

Amira recovered her breath; she got up quickly. Lawyer Sloan Wilfrid and Amira picked up the unconscious Dalya, and they carried her to a nearby divan.

As soon as they freed Dalya from the hands that were strangling her, Mr. Bûchebois, the Cook and Igor, they locked Mrs. Augustine with difficulty in a room. Mrs. Augustine was screaming at the top of her lungs and banging on the door like an enraged dog:

- IT IS BECAUSE OF YOU THAT HE IS DETAINED!!! WE ARE ALL GOING TO STARVE!!! EVERYTHING IS YOUR FAULT!!! HE WILL ROT DETAINED!!! EVERYTHING IS YOUR FAULT!!! YOU VERMIN!!!

At this moment, noticing that Mrs. Augustine was locked in a room, and therefore far from the claws of the Panther, the Gardener released the animal. Instantly, the Snow Panther ran straight to Dalya, lying and passed out on the divan. With a thoughtful gesture of her paw, Séraphine caressed Dalya's lifeless hand, letting out a worried and anxious meow.

In the midst of the chaos, the help Cook Océanie rushed to the little twins who were shaking and crying in a corner. With a single move, Océanie lifted the little twins Ari and Adi, she hugged them very tightly, and she left at a rapid pace, heading toward the grand Mansion.

The maid Cristelle stumbled over a broken chair, running toward the kitchen. She filled a container with cold water with a trembling hand, she took a towel from the counter, and she joined Dalya in the living room. With trembling hands, Cristelle wet the towel and she placed it on Dalya Bouvard's inflamed, red neck.

All the employees of the grand Mansion, the Lawyer Sloan Wilfrid, Amira Mounier, and the Snow Panther... they were all holding their breath, standing around Dalya Bouvard. And those were long, tense, serious seconds. Lying on the divan, her cheeks gradually turned pink, her lips recovered progressively their natural color, and her eyes slowly opened.

Dalya regained consciousness. She was alive. Everyone breathed in relief.

After a minute of a heavy silence, Lawyer Sloan Wilfrid took a deep breath, he stood up, and he ordered in a grave tone:

-   Mr. Gardener, Miss Amira … help Mademoiselle to get back to her bedroom, in the grand Mansion.

Immediately, the Gardener lifted entirely the little girl's weakened body and he headed toward the exit. Amira Mounier followed him, trembling and still in shock at this scene. The Snow Panther didn't take her eyes off Dalya, and she didn't leave her side for a second. Séraphine followed the little girl lifted by the Gardener. Lawyer Sloan Wilfrid continued his orders:

-   Cristelle… make sure the little twins are safe and sound. I saw Océanie take them to the grand Mansion.

Cristelle left the annex house in a hurry. Turning toward a young man, Lawyer Sloan Wilfrid ordered:

-   Igor … bring a Doctor to the annex house. We will wait for you here.

The Manager, Mr. Bûchebois, and the Cook exchanged a confused look. The assistant Igor dared to correct the Lawyer:

-   You mean … bring a Doctor to the grand Mansion, Monsieur Wilfrid.

At that precise moment, Lawyer Sloan Wilfrid answered in a decided and definite tone:

-   No, Igor. The Doctor is not for Mademoiselle Dalya. This little girl is brave; she will pull through. The Doctor is for Augustine Bouvard. It's time for this woman to get treatment, in a psychiatric hospital!

This is how, Dear readers, it will be the last time you will hear of Augustine Bouvard. In this story and in reality, Augustine Bouvard is a monster; she doesn't deserve to be a mother. And she doesn't deserve another drop of ink on these pages.

Chapter 25

A counter-attack

The next morning. Wednesday, April 5th, 1893.

Revenge was never the character of Lawyer Sloan Wilfrid ... Until this day.

After witnessing the pain of Dalya Bouvard visiting her father in detention, and the violent scene of the mother strangling her daughter, Sloan Wilfrid had only one thing in mind; prepare the counter-attack against the Lawyer Ernest Laszlo, and make him pay well much for his plot!

Using little shenanigans to achieve your ends, is one thing. But imprisoning a man to force his daughter to give up a fortune that is her right, break up an entire family and make 3 innocent sisters suffer ... that is quite another thing!

Sloan Wilfrid was furious, angry, and most of all determined to protect Dalya Bouvard and Iskander Balthazar's Will ... at all costs!

In his office at the Law firm, Sloan Wilfrid was sitting in his chair, looking calm but boiling inside. Motionless, he was observing a paper for several long minutes. Sloan Wilfrid understood well that he could not defend the case of Antman Bouvard. The Lawyer Ernest Laszlo will never allow it. That's why Sloan Wilfrid wrote a list of names of competent Lawyers to handle Dalya's father's case. The list included many Lawyers. Except that, in this difficult situation, only one name stood out from the list. As crazy as his idea was, Sloan Wilfrid had no choice but to try.

After long minutes of silence and intense thinking, Sloan Wilfrid stood up, he took his coat, and he left his office. Passing by Lyor in his office, he ordered him in a determined tone:

- Take your coat, Lyor. Follow me. We have a matter to settle!

Lyor didn't need to be asked twice. He put down the papers in his hand, and he got up to take his coat. And before leaving the office, an object caught Sloan Wilfrid's attention. Lyor's brown leather file bag was placed on a pile of books. With a quick move, Sloan Wilfrid picked up the large file bag. Putting on his hat, Lyor asked him in a curious tone:

- Why do you need my bag? It's empty.

Sloan Wilfrid looked a little worried:

- Just in case ... just in case.

Curiosity overwhelmed him; Lyor Laszlo followed Sloan Wilfrid out of the office:

- How? Why just in case? What matter do we have to settle?

Lawyer Sloan Wilfrid called for a cab with a wave, and he affirmed in a determined tone:

- Antman Bouvard.

Lyor wasn't surprised that Sloan Wilfrid took on this case. From their first meeting, it was very clear that Sloan Wilfrid was defending Dalya Bouvard and this Will, against everyone. Yet, Wilfrid didn't inform the young Lyor about the offer his father Ernest Laszlo had made to Dalya. The relationship between Lyor and his father was already difficult and strained enough because of the management of the BalthEnterprise Holding. And knowing Lyor very well, Sloan Wilfrid was sure he would disapprove of his father's methods. So then, Wilfrid decided not to keep Lyor informed of his father's blackmail.

Getting inside the taxi, Lyor asked hesitantly:

- Are you sure you want to handle the Antman Bouvard case?

On the way, Sloan Wilfrid explained to him:

- I cannot represent Antman in Court. Your father will never accept it. Therefore, we'll go see someone else who can defend him and take care of this case.
- And ... who do you have in mind? Asked Lyor curiously.

After a few minutes of travel, Lyor had the answer to his question. The car stopped in front of an old gray brick building in a quiet, forgotten street of Georgetown city.

Followed by Lyor, Sloan Wilfrid entered the building, and he went up to the 3rd floor. The stairs were in a dusty gray marble. The windows were opened, sheltering the pigeons, the wallpaper was pale, the chandelier had only one small bulb lit among twenty, plunging the stairs into an almost invisible darkness. The building appeared to be uninhabitable.

On the 3rd floor, the two Lawyers stopped in front of an old, faded wooden door. Sloan Wilfrid looked worried, something that rarely happened to him. Except that the situation was grave, and Sloan Wilfrid was more determined than ever to overcome the Challenge!

With a serious tone, Sloan Wilfrid ordered Lyor:

- Hold this bag ... you'll need it to protect yourself!

Although confused, Lyor took the file bag from his mentor.

Sloan Wilfrid gathered all his energy, he took a long breath, he displayed on a calm and courteous smile, then he knocked on the door. A few seconds later, the door opened. The two Lawyers were greeted by an old man. Over sixty, the old man was very very short, very fat with a large belly, a bald head in the center with pepper curly hair on both sides, a beard of several days, and big glasses. The old man was wearing dark green pajamas, and a large fluffy dark gray bathrobe.

As soon as the old man noticed Sloan Wilfrid at his door, he screamed in a furious tone:

- OUT OF THE QUESTION!! NO!!

And immediately, the old man slammed the door in the face of the two Lawyers. With a quick move, Sloan Wilfrid stopped the door closing on him, by placing his foot over the small opening:

- And I didn't expect any other answer from you, Master Barold!

Pushing the door to close it, with his two arms and his shoulder, the old man screamed annoyed:

- Then why are you here?! Cook me dinner tonight? Clean up my house? Give me a bath? Go away!! Leave me alone!!

Sloan Wilfrid meanwhile tried to open the door with both hands, while keeping his foot stuck in the entrance. Stifling an amused laugh, Sloan Wilfrid replied:

- Sorry, Monsieur ... I can't cook, let alone clean ... but I would like 5 minutes of your time ... please!! ... Only 5 minutes!!

Lyor Laszlo watched the two men, with confusion and curiosity. One struggled to close the door, and the other to keep it open. The old man understood that Sloan Wilfrid would not let go of the door. At one point, the old man stopped pushing the door to close it, he observed the two Lawyers for a moment with an angry and furious look:

- I have 1 minute, no more! Hurry up!

The old man let go of the door he was trying to close, and went back inside his apartment. Sloan Wilfrid straightened his tie, smiling victoriously at finally getting a minute from the old man.

A few steps inside, Lyor and Wilfrid discovered the apartment. Everything seemed to be old and almost antique. The furniture and armchairs were filled with piles of books and files, piled on top of each other. It seemed that the old man is an avid reader and an avid of mess. And although the curtains were wide open, the light of day entered timidly in this place, rocking the living room in a soft and calm light. The smell of papers mixed with the smell of dust. The apartment looked like it hadn't been tidied or cleaned since ... centuries.

The old man walked over to a lamp, and he lit it. The dim light wasn't enough to brighten up the living room, but enough to lift it out of the darkness somewhat.

Sloan Wilfrid addressed the old man courteously:

- I hope you remember me, Monsieur. We met a long time ago. I am Lawyer Sloan Wi...

The old man interrupted him in an annoyed and impatient tone:

- Yes, yes Sloan Wilfrid, I know who you are!! ...and who is this?

At that moment, Sloan Wilfrid cleared his throat, he gathered his energy, and he answered hesitantly:

- This is ... I present to you ... Ly... Lyor Laszlo.

Suddenly, anger invaded the old man. In a second, his cheeks turned red, his curly hair rose in the air, his eyes opened wide, and he screamed out with all his might:

- AND HE DARES TO COME HERE??!!

Immediately, Sloan Wilfrid moved away from Lyor, stepping back a few steps. Lyor didn't understand the old man's anger, and he had a feeling that the situation was going to get worse.

With a sudden and unpredictable move, the old man grabbed a book and he threw it vigorously toward the young Lyor Laszlo. It was only then that Lyor understood the usefulness of the file bag that Sloan Wilfrid handed him. Lyor protected himself with the file bag, while the old man threw a second book toward him, screaming furiously:

- AND HE GOT THE NERVE!!! TO STAND HERE IN FRONT OF ME LIKE THIS!!! NONCHALANTLY!!!

Lyor Laszlo took a few steps back, holding the file bag firmly in front of him, to protect himself from the books thrown at him. Lyor whispered in a worried and confused tone:

- Wilfrid!! What's going on? What is happening to him?

Sloan Wilfrid took a few more steps back and he answered in a low voice:

- It's Master Barold ... the famous Lawyer ... who lost his license...

The old man threw a shoe at Lyor, which the young man blocked with the file bag. At this moment, Lyor exclaimed:

- Master Barold? ... Master Victor Barold? ... the famous Lawyer who lost his license to practice Law because of ... because of my father?

Sloan Wilfrid smiled nervously at Lyor:

- Himself, flesh and bone!

In an astray moment, Lyor unintentionally lowered his file bag, and he received a slipper on his cheek. The old man exclaimed happily after his hit:

- IT'S YOUR DAY TODAY!! I WILL TEACH YOU A GOOD LESSON!! THE NERVE TO COME AND SEE ME!! IT'S YOUR LUCKY DA...

The old man was about to pick up a large book and throw it away. When Sloan Wilfrid decided to act:

- Listen to me!! Listen to me, please!! It's his son but he has nothing to do with what happened!!

The young Lyor understood the old man's anger, he took a few steps back and he firmly held the file bag in front of him. The old man exclaimed:

- I DON'T CARE IF IT'S HIS SON OR HIS AUNT!! HE IS A LASZLO, AND SO HE DESERVES A GOOD LESSON!!

The old man threw a big book with a clumsy move, that instead of hitting Lyor, the book deflected and it broke a mirror. Sloan Wilfrid bravely advanced toward the old man, and he insisted:

- Listen to me!! Master Barold!! Please!! … Lyor Laszlo was only 5 years old when the incident happened!! He is not responsible for what his father did!!

At this moment, silence and calm settled in the living room. The old man stopped in his move, he observed the young Lyor Laszlo with an angry look, and he observed Sloan Wilfrid with an even more furious look. Then, the old man decided to put down the 500 pages book he was about to throw toward Lyor. Sloan Wilfrid's point was correct.

Forced to repress his anger, Master Barold sat on an armchair, muttering incomprehensible and angry words. And before they too sat down, Lyor Laszlo held Sloan Wilfrid by the arm, and he whispered to him:

- Wilfrid?! He was a great Lawyer once, yes … but he hasn't practiced Law for 20 years!! Are you crazy?! It's madness to ask this man to take care of this case! We don't even know if he's sane!

At that moment, Sloan Wilfrid turned toward his young student:

- Crazy worries require even crazier reinforcements!

The voice of the old man interrupted the two Lawyers in their whispers:

- And these 5 minutes that you want … is it for today or the week of the 4 Thursdays?!

Immediately, the two Lawyers sat down. Lyor settled into the chair next to Wilfrid, and he still held his file bag, just in case the old Lawyer changed his mind. And even before Sloan Wilfrid began his argument to convince the old man, Master Barold affirmed in a rigid and angry tone:

- I will not handle Antman Bouvard's case! I retired 20 years ago. You are wasting your time with me! There was no need to disturb me from my nap!

At that moment, Lyor asked Sloan Wilfrid in a surprised tone:

- How did he know what you were going to ask him?

Getting ahead of Sloan Wilfrid, Master Barold replied with an annoyed air:

- I don't go out much, but I read the newspapers. This case is public. And I know Ernest Laszlo's Firm is handling the Governor's Will ... it's not that hard to guess, kid!

Sloan Wilfrid whispered to Lyor:

- Genius one day ... Genius forever! Master Victor Barold has not lost his talent!

Straightening up on his chair, Sloan Wilfrid cleared his throat:

- Master Barold...I wouldn't have bothered you if it wasn't a grave and serious situation. You were and remain the best Lawyer in the defense pleading. We need a helping hand from you!

The old man affirmed:

- He will be condemned for bad checks. Anyway, his fate is already decided, even before the trial. I can't help you at all !

Sloan Wilfrid approached the old man:

- Master Barold ... this is a matter of great importance! The fate of thousands of people rests on this condemnation. It's not just about Antman Bouvard!

In a second, the old man understood the underside of this case:

- So then, Iskander Balthazar's Will is at stake...

Sloan Wilfrid confirmed the idea:

- Exact!

At this moment, Lyor lost the thread of the conversation between the two men. Lyor asked in a confused tone:

- How? ... one second, one second... Wilfrid, what are you talking about? ... What does the Will have to do with it? Why is the Will linked to the Antman Bouvard case?

Apparently, Sloan Wilfrid and Master Victor Barold understood each other without needing more words. Relaxing on his chair, the old man reflected aloud:

- He's going to use the father against the Will. Ernest Laszlo did not change his methods. He uses everything to achieve his ends.

Sloan Wilfrid offered the old man a few seconds of thinking, before trying to convince him one last time:

- Master Barold ... your help will be precious to us!

Despite all the arguments of Sloan Wilfrid, the old Lawyer did not change his decision:

- You have wasted your time here. I can't do anything for you.

Not wishing to insist more than that, Sloan Wilfrid greeted the old man and he withdrew, followed by the young Lyor. Sloan Wilfrid had some doubts that Master Barold would refuse to help him. He had done his best to convince him. Too bad, Sloan Wilfrid will find another Lawyer.

Coming down the old stairs, the young Lyor was curious:

- I don't understand why you chose to consult Master Barold on this matter. He is very old; he hardly moves around his apartment. This case requires a dynamic and hard-working Lawyer. Yes, Master Barold was an expert in pleading, but 20 years ago! He seems not to have had contact with a human for years! I wonder who will want to work with him?! It was a waste of time to come here.

At that precise moment, and as unlikely as it was, a tiny idea slowly seeped into Sloan Wilfrid's mind. It was an absurd, insane ... and above all diabolical idea!

Sloan Wilfrid stopped on a step of the old stairs, and he thought aloud:

- Dynamic...hardworking...to kill two birds with one stone...it would be crazy...but if it succeeds, he'll lose his mind...and I'm not the only one who wants to teach him a good lesson...that's the only argument to bring him out of retirement!

Lyor turned around and he asked in a worried tone:

- Wilfrid, what are you talking about?! I don't understand what you are saying.

Lawyer Sloan Wilfrid had one last argument to convince Master Barold to help him. With a quick step, Sloan Wilfrid turned around and he walked up the stairs toward the old man's apartment:

- I'll be back in a minute, Lyor! Wait for me in the taxi!

If there's one thing you need to be sure of, Dear readers ... it's that something was brewing in the city of Georgetown. A counter-attack!

Chapter 26

The little twins in the grand Mansion

Friday, April 7th, 1893.

It only took a few hours for the employees of the grand Mansion to adjust their schedules, and accommodate themselves with great pleasure to the service of the new residents; the little Bouvard twins.

That day, early in the morning, the employees of the grand Mansion were all gathered in the kitchen, around their usual breakfast.

Helping himself to the bread, the Gardener informed the head of the grand Mansion:

- Last night, I added 2 small seat belts in the car. The little twin girls will be well settled now.

The head of the grand Mansion smiled, putting down his cup of coffee:

- Well thought, Rosenwald. The little twins are very small in size. Seat belts in their sizes, is a great idea!

The Gardener had offered to drive the little twins to their kindergarten school every morning and bring them back to the grand Mansion every afternoon. The Gardener insisted on dropping off Dalya too, at the College every morning, by car. Which saved Dalya from being late for her classes.

Adding sugar to his coffee, the head of the grand Mansion asked:

- Igor… did you move the small chairs to the little twins' room?

Igor's mouth was so full that not a word could come out despite his effort to speak. Seated next to Igor, the maid Cristelle answered for him:

- Yes, Mr. Bûchebois. Igor brought the small chairs; I installed them in their bedroom. We have also placed small desks and small chairs in the Library. The little twins love to do their homework near their big sister.

Cristelle and Igor took care of arranging the bedroom and the furniture for the little twins. Adding butter to his bread, the Gardener thought aloud:

- We must install the fireplace covers in the Library, the living rooms, and their bedroom, in order to prevent the little twins from being injured by fire and wood chips.

The help Cook Océanie sat back down in her place, after taking a large spoon from the drawer. Océanie took care of the baths and meals of the little twins. She replied to the Gardener, with a little amused laugh:

- Oh, the little twins won't appreciate the fireplace covers, I can confirm that! Last night, after giving them their baths, I found them stewing marshmallow in their bedroom fireplace. They had fun turning the skewers in the fire!

The head of the grand Mansion was surprised:

- Stewing Marshmallow? All by themselves? Who gave them the marshmallows and the skewers?

At this moment, all eyes looked at the Cook. Mr. Ferrero Lutché nearly choked on a bite of muffin. He smiled nervously:

- Signorina Ari e Adi siamo simpatico and adorabile. They asked me for marshmallows and skewers to cook them. I couldn't refuse them!

An amused laugh invaded the kitchen of the grand Mansion. The Manager regained his formal voice after a few moments:

- Océanie, I would still like you to make sure that the little twins stay away from the fireplace, and out of danger.
- Understood, Monsieur.

The Cook was quite right; the little twins were adorable and kind, it was hard to refuse them anything. And the Cook was very happy to prepare the little girls' favorite dishes, he even allowed them to play with dough and decorate a few dishes in his kitchen.

All the employees were well organized to serve the new guests of the grand Mansion. And the strangest thing is that even the Snow Panther joined the employees to watch over the little girls. Panther Séraphine watched the little twins every minute after they returned from kindergarten.

And it must be said that Ari and Adi were very nice, obeying to all the employees of the grand Mansion, to the great happiness and relief of their big sister Dalya. Ari and Adi got used very well to their new life in this house. They even learned the names of all the employees; the head of the grand Mansion was Mr. Bois, the Cook was Mr. Feo, Cristelle was istelle, Océanie was Nini, Igor was Or, the Gardener was Mr. Ald.

In no time, Ari and Adi had won the hearts of all the employees of the grand Mansion. And Dalya was sincerely grateful to the employees, for watching over her and her little sisters.

Chapter 27

The canteen

Monday April 10th, 1893. At the Royal Georgetown College.

This April day was very busy for everyone. The sky was busy between gray clouds and bright sunshine. The birds were busy roaming the skies. The people on the street were busy with their errands and work. And the Royal Georgetown College was busy preparing for exams in the next few weeks.

At the end of their morning class, Dalya and her friend Amira headed to the canteen.

- We still have to do the summaries of the last Philosophy lesson. Dalya sighed with a stressed air.
- It will be easy, don't worry! Amira reassured her.
- To learn by heart 6 long lessons in a few days?! I need more than a summary!

Amira paused for a moment in the hallway:

- Why 6 lessons?! In Philosophy, we have 3 lessons this semest...

Dalya corrected her friend:

- 6 lessons, Amira. The Professor told us that we will be questioned about the lessons of the previous semester as well.

In a second, Amira Mounier turned very pale:

- And ... when did the Professor tell us that?!

Dalya smiled in an amused air:

- Last week, in his class.

Amira couldn't believe her ears:

- And where was I ?!

Taking her friend by the arm and leading her to the canteen, Dalya continued:

- Your body was in the classroom, but your brain was somewhere else. Come on, we'll have lunch quickly, and we'll work on the summaries this afternoon.

Amira allowed herself to be led to the canteen, murmuring in a shocked tone:

- 6 lessons to learn in a few days! We are in trouble! I thought I was early for the exam studies!

The canteen was already full at this hour. Dalya and Amira helped themselves to their meals, following the queue in front of the counter.

- Amira … are you sure you can eat the 4 verrines of crème caramel?

Amira added a 5th verrine to her tray, and she answered in a serious tone:

- We have 6 lessons to summarize! I need strength !

Dalya and Amira exchanged a little laugh. Taking a seat at a table in the canteen, Amira continued in a determined tone:

- So … in my opinion, we must start with the first chapter of Philosophy. It only contains vocabulary definitions.

While eating her salad, Dalya carefully followed her friend Amira's directions:

- Exact! Great plan! Let's start with the first chapter then.

Amira skipped the salad and the main dish, to eat the verrine of crème caramel first:

- And after, for the 2nd chapter… it will take us 1 day to summarize it and 2 days to lea…

When suddenly, a loud noise was heard in a corner of the canteen. Dalya and Amira noticed many students exclaiming and laughing loudly, while reading newspapers. Amira turned around and she continued to think about her study program:

- So … 1 day of summaries, and 2 days to learn by heart!

Dalya asked her:

- Do you think we can do summaries of all the lessons this weekend? In just 3 days? If your father wouldn't mind that you spend the weekend at the grand Mansion, we will finish faster if we work on weekends, until late at night.

Using her 3rd verrine of crème caramel, Amira replied:

- Yes … I admit that it is a good idea! Work and finalize all the summaries first, and then learn by heart. My father will certainly not refuse if I spend the weekend with y…

A 2nd noise was heard in another corner of the canteen. Several students burst out laughing and surprised while leafing through newspapers. Dalya wondered aloud, curiously:

- What are they reading?

Amira replied in a careless tone as she finished her dessert:

- Probably nothing that is useful for our next exams. If I finish the studies for the Philosophy course with you quickly, that will give me plenty of time to work on my other courses.

Dalya turned toward her friend:

- Certainly, yes! And if you need help in your other courses, I will be more than happy to help you. I have free time.

Amira finally helped herself to her salad:

- Thanks a lot! I have already prepared the summaries for Mathematics, Latin, and History. I still must do the summaries of Geography. And the chapters this semester are very long.

Dalya jumped up from her chair:

- I can write you summaries of Geography, while you study History and Lat...

For the 3rd time, a big noise of laughs and exclamation exploded in the canteen. And this time, not only was the noise close to Dalya and Amira's table, but the students were familiar. Eriem, Gael and their entire court laughed loudly, heartily, and were unable to contain themselves. They each held a newspaper in their hands.

- What's going on? Why are they all laughing while reading the newspaper? Dalya whispered.
- I don't know what got into them, all of them. replied Amira

At one moment, a student came close to the table of Dalya and Amira. Lakita Fleuritel was a short size, slender appearance, with a large nose and a slim mouth. The student wore a small cap on her head. Due to an incident, Lakita Fleuritel had lost all her hair ... But apparently, she hadn't lost her ignoble character.

Under the curious eyes of Dalya and Amira, Lakita Fleuritel offered them each a newspaper. And with an arrogant smile, Lakita announced to them:

- I imagine that you are already aware of the latest news.

Dalya and Amira took the newspapers, and they exchanged a confused look. Lakita's strange attitude didn't foresee anything good. As soon as Dalya opened the newspaper, she was stunned by what she read in the headline:

The Heiress to the Country's greatest fortune...

And her father detained for bad checks!

At that moment, the entire canteen burst into a nasty, insolent laughter. Dalya finally understood that since earlier, the laughs were on her and her father. Dalya's heart stopped beating, her throat tightened, her cheeks blushed, her eyes watched all the students pointing at her, her ears were stunned by the laughs and mockeries of the other students. Dalya Bouvard had trouble breathing.

Before Dalya could even continue reading the article, Amira Mounier snatched the newspaper from Dalya's hands with a swift move. And fortunately, Amira was present with her friend at that moment. Dalya was unable to move and think for herself. With a sudden move, Amira stood up; she took her backpack and also Dalya's. Amira's cheeks were flushed with anger, and despite her tight throat, Amira screamed at Lakita Fleuritel:

-   You will pay for it, Lakita! ... Very very hard! ... You are a real pest! ... You will pay for it!

Lakita Fleuritel ignored Amira's threats and she returned joyful and triumphant to her friends' table. Eriem Eyelord was giggling, Gael was reading the newspaper article aloud, and their entire court was laughing loudly.

Instantly, Amira took her friend Dalya by her arm, and she dragged her out of the canteen, under the laughs and mockeries of all the College students.

Immediately in the corridor, Amira led Dalya to a quiet and empty place, the large stairs at the end of the corridor. As soon as she arrived, her legs didn't hold her anymore, Dalya sat down on the big stairs, and instantly tears flowed from her eyes. She cried silently, not even daring to make a sound. Her heart was burning. Never did Dalya thought she would undergo such evilness. Making fun of her, Dalya could accept that. But making fun of her father who was detained ... that was pure free evilness!

With a sudden move, Amira put down the two bags on the floor, she took the newspaper in her hands, and she tore it into small pieces with an angry reaction. Amira couldn't hold back her anger:

-   That vermin Lakita! She misses no opportunity to report the news of others! She dared to give out the newspaper to the entire school! But what a pest! She will pay for that! Very very hard, believe me! I would have liked to give a slap to this pes...

A familiar voice interrupted Amira in her anger and Dalya in her tears:

-   What's going on ?

At that precise moment, Professor Canfield appeared in front of Dalya and Amira. He was holding books in his hands, indicating that he was heading to the Library to bring them back. Immediately, Amira fell silent, and Dalya didn't dare to answer or speak a word.

Except that Professor Canfield was a wise and clever man, he didn't need any explanation to understand what was going on. Professor Canfield noticed Dalya Bouvard's tears, her friend Amira Mounier's anger... and he saw this morning's newspaper, torn on the floor.

Approaching Dalya, Professor Canfield said with a thoughtful tone:

-   I am very sorry about what happened to your father, Mademoiselle.

Dalya Bouvard remained still, silent, her head down, tears streaming down her cheeks in silence. She didn't dare to raise her gaze and she had no words to say. Professor Canfield had never seen Dalya in such a state; she was beaten down and crushed.

After a moment of a heavy silence, Professor Canfield turned to Amira Mounier, and he ordered her in a serious tone:

- I am aware of the difficulty of the current situation. Except that, Mademoiselle Dalya Bouvard must absolutely pass the Philosophy exam. If she has an eliminatory score, a zero or less than 5/20…

Amira immediately understood:

- … Her College admission will be cancelled.

Professor Canfield looked worried:

- Right, Miss Amira. So … can I count on you to help her with her exam studies?
- Yes, Professor!! Rest assured!! Amira affirmed, in a confident and determined tone.

Professor Canfield continued:

- Good, very good. If you need additional lessons or the assistance of a Teacher, let me know immediately. Notify me about any concern! This exam is very important, Miss Amira! Am I clear enough?
- Very clear, Professor! And she will pass the Philosophy exam, I guarantee it!

Observing the silence and stillness of Dalya Bouvard, Professor Canfield continued his instructions to Amira Mounier:

- Now, you are both excused from class, this afternoon. I will notify your Teachers of your absence. Given the state of Mademoiselle Dalya, it is useless for her to continue her lessons for today.

Amira picked up the two school bags with a motivated move:

- Thank you, Professor. I'm going to accompany her right away to the grand Mansion. Dalya will pass her exams; you have my word!

Immediately, Amira Mounier held Dalya by the arm, and she led her through the corridor. And despite the heavy silence and crushed tears of Dalya, Amira was determined to help her friend:

- Everything will eventually work out Dalya, don't worry! I'll go with you to the grand Mansion. You'll have a good dinner, and you'll sleep early tonight. Tomorrow, we will start the exam studies. I bet you'll get the best grade of the class this semester! And don't worry about Eriem, Gael and their court, they laugh at everyone. They are all fools! This pest of Lakita Fleuritel will pay very hard for it! I'll let you know!

Through the large windows of the Royal Georgetown College, Professor Canfield observed the two young students leaving the school and crossing the street. He couldn't help Dalya Bouvard with her personal worries. However, Professor Canfield was as determined as Amira to help Dalya succeed her schooling.

Suddenly, a silhouette approached Professor Canfield, and observed as well the two girls walking along the street. Professor Canfield sighed worriedly.

- Do you think she's strong enough ... to face what awaits ahead of her?

The Music Teacher of the College, Miss Haîyang replied in a calm and confident tone:

- She is way much stronger than what she thinks!

Professor Canfield turned toward the young woman:

- I hope so, Miss Haîyang ... I hope so ...

Chapter 28

Lessons well understood

Tuesday, April 11th, 1893. In the afternoon, at the Royal Georgetown College.

When Amira Mounier finished her History course, she hurried out of the classroom and she headed to a specific place; the College Library. Amira was not looking for her friend Dalya, but for another person.

In the back of the left section of the Library, 3 students were quietly sitting, reading, and doing their homework. Assami Eyelord and her 2 friends Hélène Lagénéreuse and Esteban Warner. It was the favorite and usual corner of these 3 students.

Assami Eyelord was Eriem's younger sister and her complete opposite. Calm, kind, polite, the young Assami did not share the character, and even less the wickedness of her older sister and her court. And above all, the young Assami was brave; she always and clearly expressed her disagreement with injustice and free evilness.

While the 3 students were busy reading, Amira Mounier observed them from afar. This afternoon, in the Library, Amira was about to do something unusual, for the first time in her life. It is true that Amira was shaking all over her body, but she was determined to act.

At one point, taking a long breath, Amira decided to approach the 3 students, for the first time since ever.

Feeling a presence in front of them, the 3 students raised their heads toward a silhouette. Assami, Hélène and Esteban looked at Amira, curious about her presence, in front of their work table. In a determined and serious voice, Amira Mounier spoke:

- Yesterday, in the canteen … she didn't deserve to be humiliated in front of everyone.

Assami Eyelord closed her book. Esteban took off his big glasses. Hélène put down her pen. They all watched Amira Mounier, with all their attention. No more words were needed for the 3 students to understand who Amira was talking about. The entire school knew about the incident that took place in the canteen.

Amira continued in a sad voice:

- After the mocking in the canteen, I walked her home. Arriving at the grand Mansion, she hugged her little twin sisters, and she cried all the tears in her body.

Hélène and Esteban exchanged a serious look. Assami Eyelord continued to listen to Amira. Unable to hold back her anger, Amira affirmed:

- There was no need for Lakita to distribute the newspapers to all the students in the canteen. There was no need for Lakita to reveal a student's personal worries to the entire school. There was no need for Lakita to humiliate and mock a detained father.

The silence in the Library became heavy and serious. The 3 students remained motionless and attentive to the words of Amira Mounier. And one must admit that her words were true and sincere.

Since the day of Antman Bouvard's detention, Amira tried by all means, to help and support her only and best friend Dalya. Except that day, Amira was sadly aware that she wasn't brave and strong enough to face Lakita Fleuritel, Eriem Eyelord, and her court. Amira felt powerless to defend her friend Dalya.

With a choked and crushed voice, with tears of anger and powerlessness, with tightened and furious hands, standing in front of the 3 students, Amira Mounier repeated:

- She didn't deserve the mocking in the canteen ... she didn't deserve that!

After a long minute of silence, and for the first time since Amira's presence in front of them, Assami Eyelord spoke. And she said a small sentence only:

- We'll take care of it.

Amira Mounier didn't need to say another word, or ask for help. Instantly, the 3 students understood what they had to do.

Before leaving the Library, Amira Mounier dried her helpless tears, and she smiled at the 3 students. A grateful smile.

Left alone, Hélène Lagénéreuse picked up her pen, Esteban Warner took back his glasses, and Assami Eyelord took back her book. Silence resumed in this left section of the College Library. A light and a decided silence. At one moment, the 3 friends exchanged a determined and accomplice smile.

Because, you see, Dear readers, sometimes some people ... like Lakita Fleuritel ... need a helping hand to help them understand some lessons. Once and for all!

The next day Wednesday, April 12th, 1893. In the canteen of the Royal Georgetown College.

At lunchtime, the school canteen was noisy and full. All the students ate their meals and finished their homework at the same time. In a remote table, 3 friends were seated, in a usual calm. Esteban Warner was reading a book, Hélène Lagénéreuse was tasting her dessert, and Assami Eyelord was writing a few notes in her notebook. And strangely, it looked like the 3 friends were patiently waiting for someone to come at their table...

- Good morning! Have you heard the latest news about the Latin Professor?

As usual, Lakita Fleuritel made the rounds of the tables in the canteen, in order to report and reveal the latest news and rumors. As soon as she showed up at their lunch table, Assami, Hélène and Esteban stopped in their moves, and they exchanged an accomplice and determined look.

Assami and Esteban closed their books, and they watched Lakita intently. Hélène Lagénéreuse asked with a soft and interested voice:

- What's going on with the Latin Teacher? Sit with us. Tell us.

Lakita Fleuritel was happy to be invited to sit down, and to join the 3 students. As soon as she sat down, Lakita informed them:

- A person confirmed to me that the Latin Teacher will be replaced at the end of this semester!

With a natural hand move, Hélène Lagénéreuse took a fruit out of her school bag, she cut it into few pieces, and she exclaimed in a serious voice:

- The Latin Teacher? Are you sure, Lakita? He has been a Teacher in this school for several years!

Lakita Fleuritel replied in an arrogant voice:

- My source of information is always sure and certain!

While offering Lakita a piece of a green fruit with tiny black seeds, Hélène asked her:

- And who will be the new Latin Teacher then? Do you have an idea? Do you know who?

Lakita tasted the piece of fruit offered, and she let out an amused laugh:

- Of course, I know who the new Professor will be! I always know the latest news!

During this time, Assami and Esteban remained motionless, silent, focused on the conversation between their friend Hélène and Lakita Fleuritel.

Taking a second piece of fruit offered by Hélène, Lakita relaxed in her chair, and she informed them:

- The new Professor is a woman. She was a Latin Teacher in a College in New York. She recently moved to this city, because of her husband's work. He became an official in the Town Hall of Georgetown.

Hélène wondered:

- A Professor from New York! So, she must be very experienced in Latin. I heard that the best language schools are in New York.

Lakita took a 3rd piece of fruit from Hélène's hand, and she laughed arrogantly:

- And that's not all. The new Professor is a woman on a wheelchair! Apparently, they get anyone into this school! First, this little vegetable and fruit seller, Dalya Bouvard. Now, this Professor in a wheelchair. Next year, I bet we'll study with the butcher's son and the housekeeper's daughter! It's scandalous!

Assami and Esteban exchanged a calm and patient look. Hélène placed a 4th piece of fruit in front of Lakita, while answering in a soft voice:

- It is the School Council that decides on admissions and recruitments. If the Council thinks these people are competent and gifted, they deserve to be in this school.

Finishing the 4th piece of fruit, in one bite, Lakita Fleuritel laughed aloud:

- You are so naive Hélène! The Council never admits someone for free. The Latin Teacher was recruited because of her husband, who is an official in the Town Hall. The School Council wants permission to expand the school, so they're going to use this new contact. As for this seller of … vegetables and fruits … Dalya … she was admitted … admitted to this school … only because … because … the Wi… the Wi…

Suddenly, Lakita Fleuritel stopped talking. She felt a strange and unpleasant sensation in her mouth.

Dear readers… apparently there are some fruits that can cause irritation of the tongue, burning on the lips, and even canker sores in the mouth. The person affected will have difficulty eating, drinking, and especially speaking, for at least 2 weeks. No medical treatment is effective for this allergy… except silence.

The green fruit with tiny black seeds, was Esteban Warner's idea. Making Lakita Fleuritel eat the fruit, without her realizing it, was Hélène Lagénéreuse's idea. As for Assami Eyelord … she was in charge of the menaces.

Lakita Fleuritel felt her mouth burn, her lips tighten, and her tongue dilate:

- What... I can't... my ton... what is... I... my mou...

At that moment, Assami Eyelord came close to Lakita, and she whispered in her ear:

- Lesson number 1 … you are going to lose that bad habit of mocking others and revealing their personal worries to everyone. Lesson number 2 … you will leave Dalya Bouvard alone. I will not repeat it a 2nd time.

With a calm movement, Assami Eyelord, Hélène Lagénéreuse, and Esteban Warner gathered their books and their bags, and they left their lunch table. While Lakita Fleuritel remained frozen and paralyzed in her chair; her mouth was swollen, her cheeks red, her eyes terrified. Lakita Fleuritel lost her evil tongue, and she trembled.

Dear readers … lessons well understood.

Chapter 29

The inside

Thursday, April 13th, 1893. In the Law firm.

Lawyer Sloan Wilfrid's request was very simple:

- Lyor ... all I ask of you is to assist Master Victor Barold to prepare the defense speech for the Antman Bouvard case. Master Barold is a very gifted Lawyer, the best in defense pleading. Nevertheless, I am afraid that Master Barold is old, and he seems well overwhelmed by paperwork and administrative procedures. This is a very important matter, and I need to know that all the details will be in order. I ask you to only assist him in this case.

And the decision of young Lyor Laszlo was very clear:

- I will not be Master Barold's Secretary! It is out of the question that I help anyone to prepare the defense of Antman Bouvard. Master Barold will find another assistant than me. I want to know nothing about this trial! I want nothing to do with that girl and her father! She has ruined my life enough as it is! This year, I will myself submit to Court, the withdrawal of my name from this Will!

Sloan Wilfrid understood that Lyor will not help Master Barold to prepare Dalya's father's defense pleading. Lyor's decision was made. Sloan Wilfrid left the young Lyor's office, and he closed the door.

2 days later. Saturday April 15th, 1893.

Spring had packed up and left the city of Georgetown, giving way to the splendor of summer to settle in. The sun was more and more present; the blue sky was deserted of clouds. A little cool wind blew from time to time between the Alleys.

Upon entering the Law firm, Sloan Wilfrid had an idea in mind, and he was determined to carry it out that day. Opening the door of an office, Sloan Wilfrid coughed painfully:

- Good... Goo... Good morning Lyor...

At this hour, the young Lyor Laszlo was already advanced in writing his report. He only had a few sentences left to correct. And noticing the state of his mentor, Lyor greeted him:

- Hello Wilfrid. You seem very ill, you look terrible!

Sloan Wilfrid collapsed on the chair across from Lyor's desk, coughing louder and louder.

- Yes...I... didn't...sleep a minute last night...I think I caught a cold...

Lyor asked in a worried tone:

- You should have stayed home, to rest. At least today !

Straightening up on his chair, Sloan Wilfrid coughed with all the might of his lungs:

- I...no...today I have a... very important...matter to settle...

Immediately, the young Lyor closed his report:

- I can replace you! You don't look like you're in good shape to do anything today. What case is it ?

Sloan Wilfrid cleared his throat:

- It's a little errand to do... today... it's Antman Bouvard's visit day in detention... Dalya's Uncle, Giorgi Bouvard is held busy in a job... he asked me if I ca... He asked me if I can... ... bring Dalya's basket to her father... she dropped it off to me yesterday, here at the office... I can't miss this appointment... it's the least I can do for her and her father...

In an instant, Lyor Laszlo stood up from his chair and he took his jacket:

- Antman Bouvard's basket will be delivered to him today! I'll do it for you then!

Sloan Wilfrid coughed a little, while handing the basket to the young man:

- Thank you … Lyor … thank you very much …

When Lyor Laszlo picked up the basket and walked out of the Law firm, Sloan Wilfrid watched the young Lyor's silhouette through the big windows of his office.

A few hours later.

Lawyer Sloan Wilfrid was busy reading his newspaper, when he noticed a familiar shadow pass through the open door of his office. He was expecting Lyor Laszlo's return from his visit. Immediately, Sloan Wilfrid put down his newspaper, and he headed to the counter to make coffee.

A few seconds later, Sloan Wilfrid entered Lyor's office, and he placed the cup of coffee in front of the young man, who sat in his usual chair. The young Lyor looked terribly shocked, he was confused and seriously troubled, his face was pale, his eyes were lost, his throat was tight. Lyor Laszlo seemed to be struck down by something serious.

And Sloan Wilfrid understood the reason of young Lyor's condition. Settling in a chair in front of him, Lawyer Sloan Wilfrid explained in a serious tone:

- Today was your first visit inside a detention place, Lyor. There are more than 50 people sleeping on the floor, in a room of 6 square meters. Each prisoner has 3 squares of 25 cm on the floor, to sleep there. The few wealthy prisoners buy 1 or 2 more squares to lengthen their legs. I let you imagine the bending position that prisoners use to sleep on the floor, all condensed in this cell.

Lyor was paralyzed in his chair. Sloan Wilfrid continued:

- It is a cell with a capacity of only 20 people, and yet it's filled with more than 50 people. Each inmate has 3 floor squares to sleep on. The detainees avoid drinking water, so as not to have to trample 50 people and go to the bathroom. Men condensed together...in stinking dirt...and a bending position.

Sloan Wilfrid cleared his throat:

- For his first night in detention, I called on all my contacts to ensure that Antman Bouvard slept in the infirmary. It's a less full room, even if it's with seriously ill inmates...several skin diseases...grave infections...a foul smell.

Lyor whispered in a shocked voice:

- Wilfrid...this...this place...is...

Sloan Wilfrid finished the young man's sentence:

- This place is hell. And if I tell you about the living, the food and work conditions in these places of detention, believe me Lyor, you won't sleep for months.

For long seconds, a heavy and serious silence settled in Lyor's office. Sloan Wilfrid continued:

- For several months now, I have been following very closely an important Law bill that improves the living and detention conditions in our Country. This project was signed and voted 2 days ago, during the monthly assembly of the Government. In a few weeks, all the detainees will each live in separate cells, instead of being condensed into a single large room.

Despite this news, Lyor Laszlo remained disturbed and paralyzed by what he discovered during his visit. Sloan Wilfrid wanted to relieve him somewhat by diverting the conversation:

- Did you drop off the basket? How is Atman Bouvard?

Recovering from his shock with difficulty, Lyor forced himself to speak:

- Yes... I... I dropped off the basket ... Antman is... he's fine... I think... by the way, he was repeating some very strange words. I didn't understand what he meant exactly.

Sloan Wilfrid asked in a curious tone:

- What was he saying?

In a confused voice, Lyor informed him:

- Antman Bouvard was repeating a sentence; the only remedy is patience... the only remedy is patience. But the remedy for what? And why patience?

At that precise moment, Sloan Wilfrid smiled. He didn't need any further explanation to understand Antman Bouvard's sentence. And in front of Lyor's confusion, Wilfrid explained:

- It means that Antman Bouvard is alright. He is a brave man. He understood his mistakes, and he accepts the price to pay. Antman knows there's nothing he can do to change his current situation, other than to be patient with his detention... getting upset, depressed, or stressed won't do him any good. The only remedy for his fate is patience... the only remedy is patience.

After a short moment of silence and thinking, Lyor straightened up on his chair and he announced:

- Antman Bouvard must get out of this detention! We absolutely must get him out of this hell!

Sloan Wilfrid repressed hardly his proud smile at the determination of the young Lyor. The plan that Sloan Wilfrid had devised, several days ago, was working more easily than he had expected. Suddenly, Lyor jumped to his feet, and he decided aloud:

- I'm going to Master Barold. I'm going to help him prepare the defense pleading of Antman Bouvard!

With an innocent little voice and a proud smile, Sloan Wilfrid asked Lyor:

- Are you going ... now?

At the door of his office, a small detail detained Lyor and prevented him from leaving the Law firm. Lyor Laszlo turned around and he asked in a curious tone:

- Wilfrid... you're not coughing anymore?

It happens that sometimes ... trickeries can serve a good cause.

Chapter 30

The insolence and the bandage

Saturday, April 15th, 1893. The morning. The insolence.

The head of the grand Mansion asked the same question for the 5th time:

- The Gardener can drive you wherever you want, Mademoiselle. Are you sure you want to walk till downtown?

In the hall of the grand Mansion, Dalya Bouvard gave the same answer:

- Yes, Monsieur Bûchebois. We will go to the Saturday Market, my little sisters and I. It will be a nice good walk. I'll buy them ice cream.

Immediately, the little twin sisters jumped joyfully:

- We go to market with Dindin!!
- We have ice cream!! We have ice cream!!

The head of the grand Mansion smiled:

- Understood, Mademoiselle. We will wait for you, for lunch.

Dalya adjusted her little twin sisters' hats, replying:

- Thank you, Monsieur Bûchebois. We won't be late.

The weather announced a beautiful sunny and cool day. After the difficult events of the past few days, Dalya needed very much, a good walk to clear her mind. And that morning, she decided to bring her little twin sisters for a walk to the Saturday market.

Dumbarton Oaks Park was quiet and peaceful. The gardens were decorated with greenery and beautiful colorful flowers. At one point, Dalya and her little sisters stopped in front of the lake on their way. The little twins had fun feeding the birds with bread crumbs.

A few minutes later, Dalya and her little twin sisters arrived downtown. The streets were busy, the Saturday market was lively, kiosks were filled with a multitude of foods and products. Sellers and customers were in full swing. It was a beautiful April day in the Georgetown market.

From a distance, Dalya noticed several familiar faces among the sellers and customers she had worked with before.

As soon as Dalya and her little twin sisters took a step toward the market, suddenly three men blocked their way. Tall figures, wearing black jackets and caps, the three men had piercing black eyes and mocking smiles.

- Hello little Bouvard girls!
- It's been a long time since we've seen you here!
- What a pleasure to meet you today!

Dalya knew these three men very well. They threatened her one day, because of her father Antman's debts. Dalya even remembered the name of the one with the coal-black beard; Agadir.

Dalya held firmly the hands of her little twin sisters, and she walked to the left side of the street, pretending not to see or hear the three men. Except that the three individuals were determined to have fun that day. Blocking her way on the left side of the street, the three men asked:

- How's your dad doing in detention? Not so hard?
- It's far from the luxury of the grand Mansion, isn't it?
- Has he become accustomed to the conditions of detention?

Dalya felt her throat tighten, her hands tremble, her face became pale. She didn't dare to respond to the mockery of the three men. Dalya just lowered her head, and she held the hands of her little twin sisters. She decided to turn around and walk toward the right side of the market. The three men were quick; they blocked her way, this time too.

- Your father deserved to be detained! He was always arrogant!
- Get used to this situation, kid! Your father will not be freed so soon!
- Your father will rot in detention, that's for sure!

It seems that no matter how hard she tried, the three men blocked the way for Dalya and her little sisters. They could not enter the market. And the mockery of the three men became more and more cruel.

- How does it feel to have your father in detention?
- He was looking for trouble, Antman!
- How many years will your father be detained?

All Dalya wanted that day was to get some fresh air, take her mind off things, meet her friends, visit the market, and take her little sisters out for a walk.

Quickly, Dalya turned around, still holding firmly her little twin sisters' hands, and she walked away from the market. Little Ari and Adi asked in a pleading voice:

- But we did not take ice cream!
- We here for ice cream!

The mockery of the three men got louder and crueler:

- Say hello to your father when you visit him in detention!
- Let us know when your father is released ... in 10 years!
- We wish him a very good weekend in his detention!

In a strangled voice, Dalya replied to her little twin sisters:

- I... the... the Cook is going to prepare you a delicious ice cream... at the grand Mansion.

As sad as it was, little Dalya Bouvard was chased out of the market, by the insolence of the three men.

The same day. The afternoon. The bandage.

The air at the grand Mansion was quiet and heavy, and it wasn't because of the April heat. In the living room of the grand Mansion, the little twins Ari and Adi were lying on the floor on the big cushions, they were coloring drawings. Dalya was sitting close to them, on an armchair, with a book in her hands, and her mind elsewhere.

Since the scene this morning in downtown market, Dalya looked dejected and sad. Never Dalya had imagined that there were such mean people to make fun of a father in detention, and humiliate his little girls. Dalya did not expect such cruel and hurtful words. Neither Dalya nor her little sisters deserved this insolence.

Dalya was so lost in her thoughts that she didn't see the head of the grand Mansion enter the living room. Mr. Bûchebois approached Dalya, and he announced in a surprised voice:

- Mademoiselle ... there is... there is someone who wishes to see you... you and your little sisters.

Gathering her strength and her mind, Dalya asked in a curious tone:

- Why me and my sisters? Who is it ?

When the head of the grand Mansion let the visitor inside, Dalya jumped:

- Mrs. Marianne Poirier!

It was the French neighbor, herself! The great woman walked slowly and gracefully into the living room. Mrs. Marianne Poirier wore a magnificent long emerald green coat, and a luxurious brown hat. She was leaning on a cane. Despite her advanced age and her illness, the great woman was intimidatingly beautiful.

The head of the grand Mansion hastened to help the great woman to settle on an armchair.

Dalya was surprised by this unexpected visit. From what she knew, Mrs. Marianne Poirier hardly ever left her house. Dalya smiled as she sat down next to the great woman:

- It's a nice surprise to see you here, Madame! Welcome to the grand Mansion!

Immediately, Mr. Bûchebois bowed before the great woman and he asked in a formal tone:

- Madame would like some tea?

After a nod and a smile from the great woman, Mr. Bûchebois left the living room to join the kitchens, and also to inform the other employees of this prestigious visit. It was the first time since ever that the grand Mansion received Mrs. Marianne Poirier, the French neighbor.

And although curious and surprised, Dalya didn't dare to ask the great woman for the reason of her visit. However, Mrs. Marianne Poirier radiated a contagious calm. Even the little twin sisters stopped drawing, and they stared eyes wide open at the new visitor.

Dalya asked her little twin sisters to come closer:

- Come say Good afternoon to Madame. Come closer.

Ari and Adi did so, in an unusual silence and calm. When the little twins were in front of the great woman, Ari and Adi were amazed by her beauty and intimidated by her allure. Magnificent silver white hair, brilliant emerald green eyes, a porcelain skin, it is true that Mrs. Marianne Poirier had lost none of her beauty and her grace. Instantly, the little twin sisters bowed in reverence before the great woman, and they exclaimed in a serious voice:

- Good afternoon, Majesty!

Mrs. Marianne Poirier displayed an amused smile. Dalya corrected her little sisters:

- Her name is Mrs. Marianne Poirier. It is our French neighbor. You will call her Madame...not Majesty...Madame!

The little twin sisters defended their decision:

- Why is that? Majesty is prettier!!
- Yes, it's true!! She is majesty!

Dalya begged her little twin sisters:

- But why do you always have to twist people's names? It's Madame! Not Majesty!

Ari and Adi exchanged a confused look. Then, they asked their big sister in an innocent tone:

- Princess then?

Mrs. Marianne Poirier held Dalya's hand, before she corrects her sisters. And one must admit that it was very difficult to correct the little twins once they had chosen a name for someone.

At one point, Mrs. Marianne Poirier took a small notebook and a pencil out of her little bag, she wrote a note, then she handed the paper to Dalya, who read:

I am glad to know that you and your little sisters are doing well.

And I'm sure everything will work out for the best for your family.

On reading this message, Dalya was touched by the kindness and benevolence of the great woman. Dalya finally understood the reason for this visit; Mrs. Marianne Poirier knew about Dalya's father's detention, and she came herself to the grand Mansion to make sure that Dalya and her sisters were alright.

With her throat tight, Dalya answered in an emotional voice:

- It's… it's nice of you to come see us, Madame. Thank you for asking about us… Thank you very much.

The great woman smiled, and tenderly squeezed little Dalya Bouvard's hand. Mrs. Marianne Poirier made no comment about Dalya's father, and she asked no questions about his detention. The only things the great woman did, was being present and checking on 3 little girls. Despite her illness, the great woman left her house and she came to the grand Mansion, for 3 little girls. Touched by this attention, Dalya Bouvard had tears in her eyes.

Slowly, Mrs. Marianne Poirier took a small box from her bag and she opened it in front of the little twin sisters. Ari and Adi were amazed when they discovered what was inside. Little Macaroons in several colors and tastes. Ari and Adi jumped joyfully:

- Thank you, Majesty!! Thank you thank you!!
- Oh macaroons!! Thank you, Majesty!!

With great pleasure, the woman bowed to receive the kisses of the little twins.

The afternoon ended more happily than expected. The head of the grand Mansion served tea to the prestigious guest. The other employees of the grand Mansion were curious about this visit, they discreetly observed the great woman, through the opening of the living room door. The little twin sisters proudly showed their drawings to Mrs. Marianne Poirier.

And the heart of Dalya Bouvard was warmed up by this unexpected visit. The presence of the great woman changed the air and the mood in the living room of the grand Mansion.

In the most difficult moments of our life, we always remember two types of people; the people who hurt us, and the people who supported us.

The real Mrs. Marianne Poirier was a true bandage for 3 little girls. The author of this story will never forget the thoughtful visit and the kind gesture of the real Mrs. Marianne Poirier.

It is with immense sadness that the real Mrs. Marianne Poirier left us, a few days after the end of this 4th book. Nevertheless, in homage to this great woman, the character of Mrs. Marianne Poirier will continue with us, until the end of this story.

Chapter 31

Worried

The beginning of April was turbulent and chaotic. The detention of Antman Bouvard, the blackmail of the Lawyer Ernest Laszlo, the mockery in the school canteen, the insolence at the Saturday market… difficult events happened one after another, in the life of the little Dalya Bouvard, without respite. The end of April seemed to be calmer and less hectic. There was no further mockery or humiliation or blackmail.

That day, after lunch, the help Cook Océanie took the little twins back to their room for a nap. The other employees went back to their usual jobs. Dalya decided to read a book in the Library of the grand Mansion.

The Snow Panther followed the little girl like a shadow. Entering the Library, Séraphine stretched out on a divan, and she observed Dalya with all her attention. After a few seconds of research, Dalya pulled a book from a shelf, and she settled into a chair.

After the difficult weeks she had, Dalya needed to change her ideas and clear her mind. She chose a book on the History of Mathematics, her favorite course. Except that, after each page turned, Dalya's mind drifted away from the book:

- *The Egyptians used Mathematics for salary calculation, harvest management, area, and volume calculations, and in their irrigation and construction work. They used a… a… how long will my father be detained? It's been almost a month. Mr. Sloan Wilfrid promised me to do everything possible to release my father as soon as possible. But Lawyer Ernest Laszlo wants revenge on me and he will keep my father detained for as long as he can.*

Straightening up in her chair, Dalya turned over a page:

- *The … the Egyptians used an additional number writing system. They knew the four operations, and they were able to solve first-degree equations and also the… and also the… what if Mr. Sloan Wilfrid fails to release my father? What will become of me and my sisters? How are we going to live?*

Dalya took a deep breath, and she turned the pages with trembling hands:

- *In Greece, Mathematics becomes a branch of Philosophy. Of the philosophical argument comes the mathematical argument. It was not enough to apply; it was necessary to prove and convince. Hence the birth of the … of the demonstration. I must sign Lawyer Ernest Laszlo's paper, I must give up this fortune, I must help my father out. Since I was nominated in this Will, I find myself facing difficult Challenges. I cannot continue in these trials. I must give up this fortune. I must give up this fortune. I must give up!*

Suddenly, Dalya felt her lungs choke and her throat tight. Dalya closed her book. There was no need to continue reading. Despite the calm of this afternoon, Dalya's mind was invaded by doubts, unanswered questions, and worry. The Snow Panther raised her head to better observe the little girl. Séraphine felt and fully understood Dalya's worry.

Although it was too early for her lesson appointment this afternoon, Dalya decided to go out for a walk and breathe some fresh air. Above all, she wanted to escape the anxiety that was invading her.

Adjusting her coat, Dalya met Mr. Bûchebois in the hall. The head of the grand Mansion asked in a polite tone:

- Would you like something, Mademoiselle?

Dalya wore her bag over her shoulder, and she replied:

- No, thank you Mr. Bûchebois. I'm going out for a little walk, before visiting the French neighbors, the Poirier.
- That's a great idea, Mademoiselle. A bit of fresh air and a good walk will do you good.

Pulling an item from a closet in the hall, Mr. Bûchebois continued:

- On the other hand, I advise you to take a shawl with you, I feel some wind this afternoon.

Dalya was touched by the kindness of all the employees of the grand Mansion, toward her and her little sisters. Dalya took the shawl from Mr. Bûchebois, and she smiled at him:

- Thank you, Monsieur.

This afternoon, Dumbarton Oaks Park was quiet. The sun shone timidly; white clouds floated slowly in the sky. Mr. Bûchebois was quite right; a few breezes of cold wind blew from time to time. Dalya walked while admiring the stunning gardens and beautiful houses on the road. The gardens were adorned with splendid trees and plants; white roses, orange tulips, blue irises, yellow lilies, pink orchids, apple and apricot trees stood proudly, spreading their foliage.

Dalya stopped in front of the little lake on the road, where a dozen white swans were resting there. She took out of her bag, bread crumbs, and she offered them to the birds. With a graceful and happy movement, the swans approached the little girl.

That day, Dumbarton Oaks park was a beautiful, peaceful, and welcoming garden. Strangely, nature absorbed the little girl's worry and anxiety.

A few minutes later. In the house of the French neighbors.

In his office, Richard Poirier observed the landscape through the large windows. For almost an hour, the young man was watching the slightest movement outside. He was eagerly awaiting someone's arrival. Suddenly, he noticed from afar a little silhouette walking slowly and heading toward his own house. At this moment, Richard Poirier murmured:

- She came.

Immediately, Richard went back to his desk, he put some books aside, he closed a folder, he took out a notebook, and he resumed reading his newspaper. Richard Poirier was anxious and impatient for this meeting; he had been waiting for it for several days.

After a few minutes, the door to his office opened, and a person appeared.

- Good afternoon, Mademoiselle. Come in, please.
- Good afternoon.

Dalya tried her best to look natural. Except that the dark eyes circles, her pale face, her strangled voice, and her tired appearance, it clearly showed that Dalya had been tormented for several days. When he put down his newspaper, Richard Poirier offered her:

- Do sit down, please. You come at the right time. I was going to have my tea. Would you like some milk with it?

Dalya politely replied:

- Yes, thank you.

By serving tea in 2 cups, Richard Poirier was trying to start a subject with Dalya. Except he didn't know what to say and where to begin. It was a sensitive and personal subject; he didn't want to offend Dalya. When Richard placed a cup of tea in front of her, Dalya got ahead of him to it:

- Madame visited me and my sisters, last week. We were happy to welcome her in the grand Mansion.

Quickly, Richard Poirier finally found the words to say:

- Mother wanted to check on you, herself.

Dalya tasted her tea:

- It's nice to think of us. My little sisters were happy to meet Madame. They loved the macaroons she brought them.

Richard smiled:

- And it was mutual, Mother was delighted to meet your little sisters. She informed me that they are lovely Demoiselles. They even nicknamed her Majesty.

Dalya and Richard exchanged a smile. The two young people were uncomfortable, but not like the previous times. Dalya didn't dare to talk about her father's detention, she was sad and tormented. And Richard didn't dare to bring up the subject with her, so as not to offend her.

Opening her bag, Dalya took out a book, muttering in an amused voice:

-   Luckily the Philosophy class keeps me busy. The new theme is so difficult; it forces me to use every neuron in my brain. And I thought the Latin course was diff...

And as usual, the words escaped from Richard Poirier, without him being able to control them:

-   You are not alone.

At this precise moment, Dalya looked up at the young man, she was surprised by what she heard. Richard Poirier seemed sure of his words, he repeated:

-   You are not alone, Mademoiselle Dalya Bouvard.

For a long second, Dalya watched the young man. She was surprised by his words. It is true that Dalya was touched by the support of many people; the Lawyer Sloan Wilfrid, the employees of the grand Mansion, her friends Amira, Alfie, and Maurice. Except that Richard Poirier's words touched her differently, and gave her inner strength.

At that precise moment, having the support of Richard Poirier, Dalya Bouvard felt strong and brave to face the next Challenges.

Chapter 32

The exam studies

Sunday, May 7th, 1893. In the grand Mansion.

May seemed calmer than the previous month. Strangely, the Gymnastics class with Professor Tudi consisted only of relaxation and breathing exercises. Dalya Bouvard always felt better after this class. And the end-of-year exams being close, the Philosophy class occupied Dalya's mind more frequently.

This morning, Dalya Bouvard woke up very early. She hoped to take advantage of the calm of this Sunday day to study Philosophy. This course required focus and total calm.

After dressing up quickly, Dalya took her books and went down to the dining room. The head of the grand Mansion was unerringly punctual. He was carefully arranging the breakfast table.

- Bonjour, Monsieur Bûchebois.
- Bonjour, Mademoiselle. Did you sleep well?

Settling down on a chair, Dalya smiled:

- Yes, very good, thank you.

Mr. Bûchebois poured some orange juice into a glass and he offered it to her:

- You are very early today. Do you have anything planned, Mademoiselle?

The chocolate croissants were freshly baked. Dalya put one on her plate:

- Yes, I woke up early this morning to study for my Philosophy exam in the Library. I absolutely must pass this course.

Mr. Bûchebois brought the jam closer to Dalya:

- Understood, Mademoiselle. I will serve you coffee in the Library. We will take care of your little twin sisters, in order to offer you calm for your studies.

Eating quickly, Dalya replied:

- Thank you Monsieur Buch…

Suddenly, a silhouette entered the dining room. Dalya's best friend, Amira Mounier affirmed with a confident tone:

- And the studies for the Philosophy exam won't happen without me!

Dalya smiled:

-   Good morning, Amira!

Immediately, Amira Mounier sat down next to Dalya, and she whispered with an amused air:

-   Honestly, I need you to pass my Philosophy exam. You understand better than me, the subjects of this course. I don't get it at all!

Dalya laughed:

-   With great pleasure! I will tell you everything I know about this course. After breakfast, we will settle in the Library to work better, it's calm and quiet.

The head of the grand Mansion placed a plate in front of Amira, and he asked her:

-   Would you like coffee or hot chocolate, Miss Amira?

Without hesitation, Amira replied:

-   Lots of coffee, please. This Philosophy class needs my neurons to be awakened!

In this difficult period, Amira Mounier made sure to be present for her only and best friend, Dalya Bouvard. By all means, Amira tried to support her friend, to make her laugh, and to help her with the studies.

When the head of the grand Mansion poured coffee for Amira, two silhouettes entered the dining room, screaming happily:

-   Delivery of the week newspapers!
-   Delivery of the best pears of the market!

Since her father's detention, Dalya Bouvard received punctual visits from her two friends, Alfie Jaq, and Maurice Gus, at the grand Mansion. The two boys delivered to her every weekend, the newspapers of the week, and some fruit from the market. Being poor and powerless, newspapers and some fruits were all Alfie and Maurice could do to support their friend in this difficult time. And for this gesture, however small, Dalya Bouvard was grateful to them.

-   Welcome Alfie! Welcome Maurice! Come in, sit down, serve yourself!

Dalya greeted her friends with a big happy smile. Alfie placed the pears in front of Dalya, repeating proudly:

-   The best pears of the market! They will be delicious in a pie!

Instantly, Amira Mounier exclaimed:

-   And especially if the pears are caramelized with brown sugar, with a crème anglaise!

Dalya laughed at her friends' appetite:

-   Thank you very much for the pears. They look delicious!

Sitting down in front of Dalya, Maurice presented the papers to her, with a serious voice:

- Read the front page of the Wednesday newspaper. The session in Congress was quite eventful. It ended in a big fight! A big brawl!

Dalya dropped her chocolate croissant, and immediately leafed through the newspapers:

- A fight in Congress? Are you serious? So, they still didn't agree on the Immigrant Law?

While Maurice and Dalya were discussing the latest news in the newspapers, Alfie and Amira were discussing the different pear recipes. The head of the grand Mansion placed plates and cutlery in front of the two boys, and he served them fresh orange juice.

Maurice Gus spread butter on his toast, affirming in a confident tone:

- Anyway, this new Immigrant Law is not that simp…

A little amused laugh appeared in the dining room:

- Everyone is early, this Sunday!

Dalya and her friends turned toward Lawyer Sloan Wilfrid. And immediately, Dalya stood up from her chair to greet him:

- Good morning, Monsieur Wilfrid!

The Lawyer handed his hat and his coat to the head of the grand Mansion, and he walked toward Dalya:

- Good morning, Mademoiselle. I had a few appointments today. The grand Mansion was on my way, I thought to visit you before starting my day. How are you? How are your lessons going? How are your little twin sisters?

Lawyer Sloan Wilfrid visited Dalya, even more frequently than before. He asked about her at the grand Mansion and at the College. He insisted on knowing if Dalya and her little sisters were alright. He ordered the employees of the grand Mansion to take good care of the 3 little girls. Since a long time, Dalya was touched by the kindness of Lawyer Sloan Wilfrid.

When the Lawyer and Dalya sat down again, the head of the grand Mansion asked:

- Would you like a coffee, Mr. Wilfrid?
- With great pleasure! This will be my second coffee of the day. Are there butter croissants?

The head of the grand Mansion prepared a cup of coffee and a plate of croissants, while Dalya was informing the Lawyer of her upcoming exams.

Suddenly, two tiny chubby silhouettes entered the dining room. The little twins were followed by the help Cook Océanie. Ari and Adi woke up just a few minutes ago. Their curly brown hair was in the air, and they were still wearing their pink onesies. The little twins walked all around the breakfast table, greeting the present people.

- Hello Dindin! Hello Frite!
- Hello Afie! Hello Mauice!
- Hello Mia! Hello Mr. Bois!

It was well known that the little twin sisters called everyone by the nicknames they invented. Too bad if you like it or not, the little twins were incorrigible.

Within minutes, the dining room in the grand Mansion had become crowded and noisy. Lawyer Sloan Wilfrid and Maurice Gus were discussing the week's newspapers. Alfie Jaq and Amira Mounier served themselves pastry. The little twins insisted on pouring the orange juice themselves. Because of their small hands and the big jar, the little twins spilled orange juice on the floor. Immediately, the help Cook Océanie looked in a drawer for a towel to clean up the juice on the floor. The maid Cristelle entered the dining room, carrying a plate of croissants in her hands. Cristelle didn't see the juice on the floor, she slipped. Just behind her, assistant Igor managed to save the plate of croissants from Cristelle's hands. Discreetly, the Cook, Mr. Ferrero Lutché, appeared at the dining room's door. The Italian Cook was counting the number of people who will be present for lunch, in order to adjust his menu. The head of the grand Mansion walked around the table to fill the coffee cups.

At one moment, in the dining room of the grand Mansion, Dalya Bouvard observed the din, the laughs, the serious discussions, the cups of coffee filled, the juice poured on the floor, the slide, the plate of croissants saved from the fall... at this moment, the little Dalya Bouvard smiled.

It is true that Dalya woke up early this morning, in order to take advantage of the calm and to study for her exam. Except that in the middle of this chaos, she was sure she won't study anything that day. However, Dalya Bouvard was grateful for all these visits. And above all, she was happy in the middle of this chaos, on this beautiful Sunday day.

Chapter 33

Summaries of Philosophy

Saturday, May 13th, 1893. In the garden of the grand Mansion.

- Meli Melon !! Meli Melon !! Meli Melon !!

On this May morning, in the fruit and vegetable greenhouse, the little twins were singing and dancing. They picked up the melons from the ground and put them in a big basket. Despite the hundreds of toys in their room, Ari and Adi preferred to play outside in the garden, and especially in the fruit and vegetable greenhouse.

Every weekend, the little twins wore overalls and gardening boots. And just like their big sister Dalya, Ari and Adi loved doing crafts and gardening.

Sitting on the ground, the Gardener would cut up the melons, and immediately the little twins brought them back into the big basket, singing and dancing:

- Meli Melon !! Meli Melon !! Meli Melon !!

When Dalya entered the greenhouse, she reprimanded her little sisters:

- Your noise can be heard all the way to the grand Mansion! I couldn't read a single page! Wouldn't you rather play in your bedroom or in the living room, instead of disturbing Mr. Gardener?

Without even looking up, Mr. Rosenwald continued to slice a melon:

- The Demoiselles don't bother me. They have fun picking melons.

Only a few years ago, the Gardener was an antisocial man, cold, and preferring solitude more than anything. And today, he defended the presence of two little girls, having fun and working beside him, in the garden of the grand Mansion.

Immediately, the little twins exclaimed:

- We nice!! We help pick up Meli Melon!!
- We don't bother at all!! We nice!!

Dalya sighed; her little sisters were stubborn and incorrigible. Approaching a big basket, Dalya smiled:

- We have a good harvest of Melon!

The Gardener stood up and he put a melon in the big basket:

- Some melons ripened too quickly due to the heat of the previous days. That's why I decided to pick them up today.

Taking a knife out of his pocket, the Gardener cut a melon into several pieces, and he offered it to them:

- Most melons are sweet and delicious.

Dalya and the little twins helped themselves. Instantly, the 3 sisters exclaimed:

- It's very sweet! It's very good! Delicious!

Suddenly, the help Cook Océanie entered the greenhouse, and she let out an amused laugh:

- So, you're tasting melons without inviting me?

The Gardener cut up a melon and he offered it to Océanie:

- The Cook will be busy for the next few days.

Tasting the melons, Océanie thought aloud:

- We are going to prepare ... a salad of cucumber cheese and melon, a filet mignon with caramelized melon, a tomato and melon soup, a green salad of melon and chicken skewers, a charlotte with white chocolate and melon, a juic...

The little twins jumped up and interrupted Océanie:

- Ice cream Melon! We want ice cream Melon!
- Yes! with marshmallow and Socolate chips!
- And also melon jam, with bread! Very very good!
- And we want pie with yellow cream and melon!

The Gardener and Océanie exchanged an amused smile. All the employees of the grand Mansion understood that the little twins were intelligent, clever, and above all with a big appetite, they loved sweets. Océanie answered the request of the little twins:

- Understood, Mesdemoiselles. Ice cream, jam, and pie. I will let the Cook know right away. But ... these desserts will be served only after you finish your plates.

The little twins were obedient to the employees of the grand Mansion. Ari and Adi affirmed:

- Yes! Promise! We finish plate!
- And then desserts! Promise promise!

The Gardener thought aloud:

- First, I must separate the ripe melons. These are the most urgent to cook. Hard melons will wait a few days.

The big basket contained more than 70 melons. Dalya dared to ask:

- Mr. Gardener, can I take 3 or 4 melons? It's for the French neighbors. I would like to bring them this afternoon.

Océanie advised her:

- It is better to offer ripe melons to the old French neighbor. It will be easier for her to eat.

Dalya found a bag in the tool corner, to pick up the fruit. And while Dalya Bouvard carefully chose the melons to take away, Océanie watched her silently, and smiling.

The same morning. In an office at the Government Headquarters.

Mrs. Louise has been Richard Poirier's Secretary for almost 6 years. Having worked with politicians for over 30 years, Mrs. Louise was very familiar with her secretarial duties. She was meticulous, very organized, and fast in her work. In her late fifties, Mrs. Louise was a small, slender, dynamic woman, with gray hair always in a neat chignon, a long, neat gray dress, and round glasses following her everywhere.

The Secretary was organizing papers in a folder, when a young man entered the office:

- Good morning, Mrs. Louise.

Immediately, Mrs. Louise raised her head and she smiled:

- Good morning, Mr. Richard.

The young man walked straight to his office. Mrs. Louise waited a few seconds for him to take off his coat and settle down, before joining him in his office.

- Next week will be busy, Mrs. Louise.

The Secretary placed the newspapers on Richard Poirier's work table, saying:

- Certainly, Monsieur. The Law voting is always a busy time. Here are today's newspapers. I have highlighted important articles for you to read.

As he settled down in front of his desk, Richard immediately picked up the newspapers:

- Thank you, Mrs. Louise. I need a …

The Secretary knew Richard Poirier's needs, even before he pronounced them:

- Your coffee cream without sugar, is on your right. I retyped your notes on the Finance Law and the Immigration Law. The folders are on your left.

Richard Poirier highlighted a news article, asking:

- Very well, thank you. What about my appointments today?

Reviewing a small notebook in her hands, Mrs. Louise announced:

- Lunch with Mr. Karl Richter at 1 PM. Tea with Mr. Bastien Luc at 6 PM. Meeting at the General Secretary's office at 9 PM.

The young man closed a newspaper, and he took up another:

- Before the 9 PM. meeting, I need to review my n...

Mrs. Louise smiled:

- Your notes on the Party Elections are retyped and ready. They are ordered in this yellow folder. If there are any changes, I can rewrite them before tonight's meeting.

Mrs. Louise simplified the work of Richard Poirier; she helped him to be productive and fast. The Secretary continued to read in her little notebook:

- For the meeting after tomorrow, Monday, I need your report, Mr. Richard. I must retype it today, so that you can correct it. Did you finish it?

Immediately, the young man took out a few papers from a folder:

- Yes, and here it is. 12 papers to rewrite. Please include side notes. It must be in attachment, and in 3 copies.

Mrs. Louise took them, and she thought aloud:

- 12 papers, side notes to be included. Understood. It will be ready in three hours, Monsieur.

Before Mrs. Louise would turn around and leave the office, Richard Poirier called her back:

- And... I will also need these 4 papers, retyped and rearranged, please.

When the Secretary took the papers in her hands, she read the contents. Mrs. Louise could not contain her confusion:

- These notes are about ... matter and spirit? George Berkeley... Descartes...

Richard Poirier repressed a little amused laugh, and he explained to his Secretary:

- These are summaries of a Philosophy course. A student needs it; her exams are close. Would it be possible to have these papers retyped, for this afternoon? Before 4 PM?

It was the first time since ever that Mrs. Louise helped Richard Poirier in a work unrelated to politics. Without daring to ask questions, the Secretary looked at the papers in her hands, and she affirmed:

- Alright, Mr. Richard. Before 4 PM, these summaries will be ready. I will retype these 4 papers first. And then, I will start the Monday reports.
- Thank you, Mrs. Louise.

Richard Poirier picked up the files on his desk and he began his work. Before Mrs. Louise would close the office door, she turned around and she observed the young man, in a curious stare, while thinking:

- *Summaries of Philosophy? To help a student? That's unusual of Richard Poirier... strange ... very strange ...*

Chapter 34

The last day at school

Friday, June 2nd, 1893.

On this late afternoon in June, Dalya Bouvard and Amira Mounier left the Royal Georgetown College with a relieved heart. It was the day of the exam results, and the last day at school.

The return to the grand Mansion was in a less stressed spirit than at the beginning of the day. Having passed her Philosophy course, despite the difficult events that her family was going through, Dalya's heart was a little lighter. At one point, on the way to Dumbarton Oaks Park, Dalya stopped for a moment, and she hugged her friend Amira:

- Thank you for helping me with the exam studies. Without you, I would have not passed my course this semester!

Amira Mounier smiled:

- You are welcome, it's the least I can do for you. You would have done the same for me. And ... to be honest, I helped you mostly for the apple pie the Cook is making!

Dalya laughed heartily:

- And you totally deserve it! I will ask the Cook, Mr. Ferrero Lutché, to prepare this pie, just for you!

Amira exclaimed:

- And don't forget to insist that he caramelizes the apples!

When suddenly Amira said in a serious voice:

- On the other hand, Dalya ... don't count on me for our holiday homework! My brain is paralyzed until August!

Dalya laughed:

- When the Philosophy Professor dictated the summer homework to us, at a certain point, I had no more space in my notebook to write. I had to use a blank paper to keep writing.

Suddenly, Amira became furious:

- The Professor of Philosophy is crazy! He probably thought we had 15 months' vacation instead of just 3 months! He gave us 5 pages of words to define, it's completely insane!

Arriving at the grand Mansion, Dalya and Amira noticed a black car parked at the entrance. And at the same time, the silhouette of Lawyer Sloan Wilfrid appeared coming out of the hall of the grand Mansion. When he saw them, Sloan Wilfrid greeted them with a cheerful smile:

- Good evening, Mesdemoiselles. It's your last day at school, I presume?

Amira was the first to answer:

- Yes, but this is not the start of vacation. We have mountains of homework!

Sloan Wilfrid let out an amused chuckle:

- I wonder if there is a student who loves homework.

Immediately, Dalya and Amira exchanged a confident look:

- Not us, anyway!

Amira preceded her friend, toward the Library of the grand Mansion, in order to take back her books. Lawyer Sloan Wilfrid asked Dalya in a curious tone:

- I take it you got your exam grades, Mademoiselle?
- Yes, Monsieur. I managed to get an 11/20 in Philosophy. It was a very difficult and complicated course. But my friend Amira and I managed to get the average score, it was hard to believe it. Professor Canfield gave us our grades, himself. And he was impressed that we got the average score.

Placing his hand on Dalya's shoulder, Lawyer Sloan Wilfrid smiled at her:

- This is great news, Dalya! Bravo! Despite all the problems and worries, you passed your exam! Bravo !
- Thank you, Monsieur.

After a moment of hesitation, Lawyer Sloan Wilfrid cleared his throat and he addressed Dalya in a serious tone:

- I came today to inform you of your father's situation. There is what we call judicial holidays, during the summer months, where all trials are suspended until September. I am sorry to inform you that there is nothing we can do for your father for the next 3 months. The administrative procedures are tight. We are forced to wait for the judicial reopening.

Dalya was surprised and sad by this news, she had hoped that her father would be released this summer. Lawyer Sloan Wilfrid continued in a decided voice:

- On the other hand, I asked to bring forward the date of the trial. It will be held in the first week of September. And since I can't represent your father, I hired another Lawyer. Your father will be defended by the best Lawyer in this town!

In a brave and sincere tone, Dalya smiled at him:

- Thank you for everything you are doing for me and my family, Monsieur Wilfrid.

At that moment, Sloan Wilfrid approached Dalya, and he said in a determined tone:

- Your father's case is my priority. I gave you my word, and I will not fail!

Chapter 35

Much more

Summer seemed to be calm and serene in the city of Georgetown. The grand Mansion was also preparing for a change of season. The Gardener put away the firewood in the garage. Assistant Igor removed all the heavy winter carpets. Cristelle changed all the wool sheets and the velvet curtains, replacing them with lighter fabrics. The Cook took out his notebook of summer recipes, based on the fruits and vegetables of the season. The head of the grand Mansion decided to change the cutlery and the serving plates, he took care himself of shining the new tableware of the season. The summer at the grand Mansion followed the same habits as the previous summers.

This afternoon, Dalya had finished putting away her summer clothes in her closet. Despite the employees' offer of help, Dalya insisted on putting away and folding her own clothes.

Having an appointment in a few minutes, Dalya wore a yellow dress, and a light beige cardigan with golden buttons. Before leaving her room, Dalya hesitated for a second between beige shoes and black shoes.

- Yellow dress ... beige cardigan ... therefore, beige shoes! Decided!

As she walked down the corridor, Dalya heard laughs and screams emanating from her twin little sisters' bedroom. And opening the door, Dalya discovered why her little sisters were laughing heartily.

Since their first night at the grand Mansion, all the employees carefully watched over the little twin sisters, and they held no idea to entertain them and fill their days.

That day, in the little twins' room, Dalya discovered the employee Océanie sitting on the floor, surrounded by a pile of little party dresses, of all colors and shapes. The little twins wore party dresses, in blue and purple, with large tutu, and shiny silver shoes. Several necklaces of fake pearls decorated their small necks. Their light brown hair was arranged in a crown of braids. Ari and Adi modeled in front of the big mirror in the bedroom, laughing and turning around like spinning tops. Their dresses grew larger with each turn.

When Océanie noticed Dalya's presence, the employee exclaimed happily:

- Welcome to our costume party afternoon, Mademoiselle!

Dalya was touched by the kindness of all the employees toward her little twin sisters. Dalya walked into the room, and she smiled:

- It looks like a party in here.

Océanie explained to her:

- We had planned to put away the summer clothes this afternoon, in the dressing room. But when the little Demoiselles saw the party dresses, they wanted to try them on. And there's no rush, we'll put the clothes away another day.

Immediately Ari and Adi ran to their big sister:

- Look Dindin!! Our lovely dresses!! Our shiny shoes!! Look look!!
- We zolies!! We princesses!! Look at the hair braids!! It's crown of braids!!

Dalya knelt in front of her little sisters:

- Yes, it's true, you are very beautiful! I love your dresses. And your hairstyle is really pretty!

The little twins were happy to dress up and parade in party dresses. And one must admit that Océanie also had fun dressing up the little girls. At one point, Océanie proposed:

- Mesdemoiselles Ari and Adi … how about changing your dresses, now? Do you want to try white party dresses with silver paddles? You can wear the white feather furs, and the flower crowns on your head. And I think I have seen the white pearls somewhere here...

Ari and Adi immediately complied:

- Yes!! White party dress!! And white pearls too!!
- And white shoes with it? Where are feather fur?

Dalya observed her little twin sisters and the employee Océanie, actively looking for a new disguise and its accessories. With a hesitant move, Dalya approached the employee, and she asked her:

- Océanie... I was wondering if... if you would like to fix my hair, like what you did with my little sisters. In crown of braids. It's pretty. And I've never tried it.

Suddenly, Océanie exclaimed:

- Of course, Mademoiselle! With great pleasure!

Océanie was surprised by this unusual request. Dalya has always kept her hair in a simple bun. It was the first time that Dalya wanted to change her hairstyle. And despite Océanie's surprise, she was delighted to do Dalya Bouvard's hair.

- Sit on this chair, Mademoiselle. The crown of braids is easy; it will take 5 minutes to do. Mesdemoiselles Ari and Adi...will you bring me the hairbrushes, and the hair ties, please?

The little twins were happy to have their big sister join their fancy dress party. They jumped happily, bringing the brushes and hair ties back to Océanie. The young employee brushed Dalya's hair; she affirmed in a sincere voice:

- The crown of braids will suit very well your hair and your outfit, Mademoiselle. It changes a lot from the usual bun you do. I admit I always hoped that you would change your hairstyle, one day. You have very pretty hair.

Sitting on a small chair, Dalya smiled:

- Thank you, Océanie.

The employee Océanie was delighted that Dalya changed her hairstyle, for the first time since ever. And even if curiosity invaded Océanie on this sudden change, Océanie did not dare to ask Dalya more questions, contenting herself with arranging the new hairstyle.

A few minutes later. In the house of the French neighbors.

The housekeeper Mrs. Glorina opened the outer kitchen door, and she exclaimed happily:

- Good afternoon, Mademoiselle Dalya! What a pleasure to see you today!

Dalya entered timidly:

- Good afternoon, Mrs. Glorina. I brought you and Madame some Madeleines, freshly made this morning.

Closing the door, Mrs. Glorina let out a little amused laugh:

- Your Madeleines arrive at the right time! I was so busy with the summer cleaning; I didn't have enough time to bake a cake today. I was going to offer Mrs. Marianne Poirier only tea.

Dalya put her basket on the kitchen table:

- Would you like me to help you with the housework, Mrs. Glorina?

With a caring voice, Mrs. Glorina smiled:

- That's very nice of you, Mademoiselle. But I'm done for today. I still have the curtains and sheets to wash. I'll take care of that, next week.

Pulling out another cup from the cupboard, Mrs. Glorina continued:

- Would you like to have tea with Mrs. Marianne? She asked after you, last night. Go ahead, get ahead of me to Mrs. Marianne's bedroom. I'll follow you upstairs as soon as the tea is ready.

Dalya readjusted her cardigan and she left the kitchen. Barely she went up 2 steps of the staircase leading upwards, Dalya heard a familiar voice behind her:

- Your new hairstyle is very pretty.

Immediately, Dalya turned around, and she discovered the young Richard Poirier in the living room. He was choosing a book from the Library, and he repeated his remark:

-   Your new hairstyle is very pretty. You should wear a crown of braids more often.

And as usual, Dalya felt her cheeks blush without being able to stop it. She was happy that the young man noticed her hairstyle, and she was delighted by this compliment.

-   Thank you. I brought some Madeleines this afternoon. While Mrs. Glorina is preparing tea, I thought I would say hello to Madame.

Richard Poirier took a second book off the shelf. And with an innocent voice, Richard Poirier asked:

-   And a hello to me too?

Dalya Bouvard was surprised and intimidated by the words of young Richard Poirier. She remained motionless and frozen in her place, near the stairs. Richard Poirier displayed an attractive smile; he was happy to see the little girl this afternoon. And apparently, Richard Poirier was increasingly enjoying in making Dalya Bouvard blush.

Avoiding the young man's gaze, Dalya whispered:

-   Yes...I...I thought I'd say hello to you, too. And... and I came to let you know that I passed my Philosophy exam. I had a hard time believing my grade. My mentor, Professor Canfield was impressed with my success in this course.

Richard Poirier smiled:

-   Congratulations, Mademoiselle. You have well worked and studied this course. You succeeded because of your perseverance.

Dalya came closer to Richard Poirier:

-   I succeeded because of your explanations and the summaries you wrote for me. Your summaries helped me tremendously to study well for the exam. I clearly understood the questions and was able to answer them easily. Thank you for all the hours you devoted to me on Saturday afternoons, despite your busy schedule. And thank you for being patient with me.

This time, it was Richard Poirier who was intimidated. Although trembling, Dalya Bouvard's voice was sincere. The young man froze in his move, in front of the Library in the living room. Despite his tight throat and a fever running through his body, Richard Poirier affirmed with a confident voice:

-   It was a real pleasure to help you, Mademoiselle Dalya Bouvard. And I confirm to you that you will always have a place in my schedule, no matter how busy.

Dalya smiled at him:

-   Thank you very much.

The Philosophy courses between Richard Poirier and Dalya Bouvard revealed many things between the two young people. During the many Saturday afternoons, Richard and Dalya studied, they laughed, they confided in each other, they discovered common points, they encouraged and gave each other strength. They were much more than Philosophy courses. Much more.

Chapter 36

The baby is coming

Thursday June 22nd, 1893. In the grand Mansion.

It was the slowest day of June. A blue sky and a bright sunshine covered Georgetown city. The heat was sweltering, the air dense to breathe, and the activity was slower and less dynamic than other days of the year.

At the grand Mansion, Dalya and her friend Amira were lying on the armchairs of the Library, reading books in a sleepy silence. At the end of the afternoon, boredom settled in the grand Mansion.

At one point, Amira closed her book and she affirmed with a confident tone:

- Dalya, I never thought I would say that ... but I miss school!

Immediately, Dalya laughed at her friend's remark:

- Me too, I admit !

Lying on her back, Amira stared at the ceiling of the Library, thinking aloud:

- I will die of boredom during these 2 months. We need to be busy doing something ... any activity! Except our holiday homework, of course! My brain is still damaged from the last exams of the semester.

Closing her book, Dalya sighed:

- I wonder what other students do as an activity during their vacati...

When suddenly, rapid footsteps entered the Library of the grand Mansion:

- DINDIN!! DINDIN!! DINDIN!!

The little twins ran toward their big sister, screaming with all their might. Amira said in an amused laugh:

- Anyway, your little twin sisters don't seem to be bored!

Dalya straightened up on her chair and she addressed her little sisters in a serious tone:

- Ari, Adi... if you screwed up again, there is no way I am covering this ti...

The little twins interrupted their big sister, and they jumped up, screaming:

- DINDIN! BABY IS COMING NOW! BABY IS COMING NOW!

Dalya needed several seconds to understand what was happening. Amira straightened up on her chair, too:

-   Baby coming? Océanie's baby?

The little twins screamed happily:

-   YES!! BABY IS COMING NOW!! COME COME!! BABY IS COMING NOW!! COME COME!!

During a second of silence, Dalya and Amira exchanged a confused look, before finally understanding and screaming too:

-   OCEANIE IS DELIVERING HER BABY NOW!

Dalya, Amira, and the little twins, they all ran toward Océanie's bedroom. All the employees of the grand Mansion were already in the employee's room. Lying on her bed, Océanie seemed to be in pain and sweating. The maid Cristelle was holding her hand, and she announced in a worried voice:

-   The contractions have already started!!

The Gardener affirmed:

-   I will bring the Doctor immediate...

Cristelle interrupted him:

-   The Doctor is too far away! The baby will arrive before the Doctor! We need a midwife, and now! Océanie's contractions are too close!

The head of the grand Mansion had difficulty composing coherent sentences:

-   The woman...the old woman who takes care of the neighbors' house...the French family...she...that old woman...

Dalya jumped:

-   Mrs. Glorina?

The head of the grand Mansion exclaimed:

-   Yes! Glorina! She was a midwife before!

It only took one look between Dalya and the Gardener to understand each other. Immediately, Dalya and the Gardener left Océanie's room at a rapid pace:

-   We'll get Mrs. Glorina, right away!

The maid Cristelle ordered the rest of the employees:

- Mr. Cook, prepare the boiling water!! Mr. Bûchebois, we will need disinfectant!! Igor, go get me the white sheets!!

Immediately, the 3 men quickly left. Cristelle turned to the little girls:

- Miss Amira, bring me some bath towels, as many as you can find!!
- Yes, immediately!!

The little twin sisters asked in a serious voice:

- And us bring toys for baby?

Amid the chaos and pain, Océanie let out an amused laugh:

- This baby will have to come out of my womb first!!

Cristelle stifled her laugh, and she ordered the little twins:

- Ok! Ari, Adi... bring only one toy each from your rooms! Go for it !

The little twins ran and screamed:

- BABY IS COMING!! BABY IS COMING!!

A few minutes later, Amira Mounier brought back about fifteen bath towels of all sizes. Ari and Adi brought back two pink and green stuffed animals. Igor had brought back a dozen white sheets. The Cook and the head of the grand Mansion returned...empty-handed.

- THE BOILING WATER!!! AND DISINFECTANT!!! Cristelle screamed with all the might of her lungs. HAVE YOUR BRAINS STOPPED WORKING?!

Sure enough, the Cook and the head of the grand Mansion seemed to be lost and confused. Mr. Ferrero Lutché and Mr. Bûchebois left the room murmuring:

- I... yes... boiling water...
- Yes... exact... right away... disinfectant...

Océanie suffered and screamed out of pain. Cristelle held her by the hand:

- Breathe Océanie... slowly... gently... breathe....

Igor asked:

- Does she need pillows? Covers?

Cristelle confirmed:

- Yes!! Bring us the long pillows in the guest room!! And the cotton blanket!!

When Igor left the room, Amira suggested:

- Something else?

Cristelle shook Océanie's hand:

- Breathe... breathe... perfume, Miss Amira... breathe Océanie... breathe... you'll find some in the bat...
- In the bathroom near the living room!! Amira screamed while leaving the room.

Ari and Adi approached the bed and they jumped:

- And us? And us? Bring something? And us? And us?

Cristelle ordered the little twins:

- The baby needs clothes... in your room, in the clothes closet... remember those pajamas that were too small for you? Those in blue with little yellow stars... bring them!!

Ari and Adi screamed while running outside the room:

- Blue pajamas!! Yellow stars!! Right away!! Quick quick quick!!

And to think it was a boring day at the grand Mansion...

Barely a few seconds later, Igor placed pillows behind Océanie's back, and a blanket on her stomach. Amira emptied a few drops of perfume on a small white towel and she gave it to Océanie to breathe a little and regain strength. Ari and Adi entered the room proudly holding the requested pajamas in their hands. Cristelle smiled at them:

- Well done, Ari! Well done, Adi! ... you brought exactly the pajamas I told you about... Miss Amira, open the window a little, plea... FERRERO!! BUCHEBOIS!! BUT WHAT'S HAPPENING TO BOTH OF YOU TODAY??!!

The Cook and the head of the grand Mansion had been going around in circles since earlier, without bringing the requested things. As soon as they found themselves in the kitchen, the Cook and the Manager had a memory lapse and they forgot what they had to bring.

And this time, the assistant Igor and Amira Mounier did not need Cristelle's instructions. Immediately, Igor asked Amira:

- Follow me into the kitchen! I'm going to put some water on to boil and...
- ... and I will bring back the disinfectants! Amira continued.
- Exact! They are in the pantry, in the lower shelf. A jar in blue and another in green!

While Igor and Amira disappeared into the kitchen, the little twins approached Cristelle:

- Baby need a nightcap?
- Baby need socks too?

Between pain and giggles, Océanie replied:

- These little girls are incredibly smart!!

Cristelle spoke to the Cook and the head of the grand Mansion, in a furious tone:

-    These 5-year-old girls are more efficient than you two!

At this moment, a new silhouette entered Océanie's room:

-    Good afternoon, everyone! I hope I am on time!

Instantly, the presence of the neighbor's employee, Mrs. Glorina, reassured everyone present. The old woman was smiling joyfully and calmly. As soon as she came, Mrs. Glorina immediately took off her coat, and she rolled up her sleeves, announcing in a soft and joyful voice:

-    Well, well … we have a baby to deliver today! I will need boiled wat...

The voices of Igor and Amira interrupted the old woman:

-    Here comes the boiling water!
-    And here are the disinfectants!

Cristelle explained to the old woman, without letting go of Océanie's hand:

-    We brought bath towels, sheets, pillows, blankets, baby clothes…

Mrs. Glorina exclaimed happily:

-    Well then, you are very well prepared, bravo! … now, I would like everyone to leave this room, please. I need only one person here. Come on, come on… everything will be fine!

Cristelle volunteered to stay in the room with Océanie. All the employees of the grand Mansion, Dalya Bouvard, Amira Mounier, and the little twins, they all left the room, and they waited in the corridor.

The minutes that followed were difficult. Everyone stood still, stressed, and anxious. Cristelle's encouragement became more and more anxious. Only Mrs. Glorina's voice sounded calm and serene.

With each contraction, the screams of Océanie became more and more painful. Intense screams. Louder screams. Slower screams. When suddenly … a terrible silence settled in, all of a sudden. No sound emanated from Océanie's room. Everyone outside in the corridor exchanged worried looks. And suddenly … a beautiful new scream was heard in the grand Mansion for the first time since ever … a baby has arrived!

Chapter 37

Wonderfully surrounded

Thursday, June 29th, 1893.

In the house of the French Poirier family, the employee Mrs. Glorina had finished putting away the last dishes of lunch. She put the folded towels in the closet, thinking aloud:

- The soup for dinner is ready, in the pot. I will have to cut the bread into slices and butter it. The laundry is out to dry. So, everything is in order!

After finishing her work, Mrs. Glorina took off her kitchen apron, and she put on her light coat. While adjusting her little hat, the silhouette of Richard Poirier interrupted her in the kitchen:

- Mother is taking a nap. She asked me to tell you that she doesn't want her tea now, but later in the evening.

Turning toward him, Mrs. Glorina smiled:

- Understood, Mr. Richard. I will serve tea to Mrs. Marianne when I get back then.

Before closing the kitchen door, Richard asked:

- Do you need the Chauffeur to drive you downtown for your shopping?

Picking up her handbag, Mrs. Glorina replied:

- Thank you, Mr. Richard, but I'm not going downtown today. I'm going to the grand Mansion.

Richard Poirier's curiosity kindled. He asked in an interested tone:

- The grand Mansion?

Mrs. Glorina informed him, letting out a happy little laugh:

- Yes! … a week ago, when you were absent, Mademoiselle Dalya and Mr. Gardener of the grand Mansion came to ask me to help a young girl give birth to a baby. And I must admit that they did well to warn me just in time! The baby came out quickly, just a few minutes after my arrival!

Richard was surprised by the news he was hearing:

- A baby? Delivered in the grand Mansion?

Mrs. Glorina exclaimed proudly:

- A beautiful, healthy baby boy! And I am going today to the grand Mansion, in order to check on the baby and on the mother. Unless you need me here?
- No, go ahead … I have work to do, I'll be in my office. And mother is taking a nap.

As he closed the kitchen door, Richard Poirier murmured in confusion:

- A baby in the grand Mansion …

Several minutes later, Mrs. Glorina arrived at the front door of the grand Mansion. She noticed the Gardener, who was moving a large wooden plank inside the house. Mrs. Glorina greeted him with a smile:

- Hello Monsieur Rosenwald.

The Gardener stopped in his way, and he looked at Mrs. Glorina with a surprised stare. The old woman continued:

- I came to get news about the baby and the young mother. I hope they are well. Are they inside ?

It seems that the Gardener had trouble formulating understandable sentences:

- Hello…you…the baby…yes…Océanie…

Mrs. Glorina didn't understand the Gardener's strange paralysis. She noticed the planks of wood he was carrying, and she asked curiously:

- Are you doing any renovations at the grand Mansion before the fall?

The Gardener's brain seemed to be stuck, not knowing what to say and what to do. Mrs. Glorina felt embarrassed by the tall man's bizarre behavior.

At this moment, a small silhouette came out of the door of the grand Mansion. Dalya held a large crate in her hand:

- Hello Mrs. Glorina … Welcome! Please come in! … Mr. Gardener, I found the pins you need.

The Gardener asked in a curious tone:

- Pins? What for?

This question seemed strange to Dalya. She replied in a confused voice:

- For the baby's bed that you are making, Mr. Gardener ... you asked me to get you pins, a minute ago.

Apparently, the Gardener's brain has stopped working normally. Mrs. Glorina let out an amused chuckle. Immediately, the Gardener pulled himself together, and he continued his way to the inside of the grand Mansion:

- Yes, yes. The pins, for the baby's bed. Yes, I need it. Thank you, Mademoiselle.

Dalya thought in a low voice:

- But what's wrong with him?!

When the Gardener preceded them carrying wooden planks inside the house, the neighbors' employee Mrs. Glorina asked Dalya:

- I wanted to get some news about the baby and the young mother Océanie. How are they? Are they well rested? Is everything going well?

Dalya took Mrs. Glorina to Océanie's room. And without holding back her happy smile, Dalya affirmed:

- This baby has revived the grand Mansion!

It's true that the second Océanie's baby was born, he captured everyone's hearts. Océanie named him Philippe Shell. He was a healthy baby, full cheeks, chubby, and soft, a smile imprinted on his face, he had inherited the magnificent big honey eyes of Océanie and her light brown hair.

All the employees of the grand Mansion were at the service of baby Philippe. The Gardener and Igor were busy building a small wooden bed, so that the baby would be comfortable there. The head of the grand Mansion brought the best sheets, pillows, and towels for the baby. The Cook decided to get prepared in advance for cooking to newborns; every afternoon he experimented with different recipes and purée dishes. Cristelle took turns looking after the baby, alternating with Océanie. Dalya and her friend Amira were busy reading all the books about babies that were in the Library of the grand Mansion, and they informed the employees of all the useful information and advices for the baby.

The little twins were very generous and caring toward the baby; they brought him their stuffed animals and clothes, and they insisted on helping to take care of the baby.

- Baby need socks? Us bring toys for baby?
- Baby want piece of cake? Baby drink hot Socolate?

The young mother Océanie had resumed her usual work at the grand Mansion. She was moved and touched by the kindness and benevolence of everyone, toward her and her child.

Arriving at Océanie's room, Mrs. Glorina rejoiced at what Dalya had told her. At this moment, Mrs. Glorina smiled:

- Well... this baby is wonderfully surrounded, Mademoiselle!

Chapter 38

Defending the baby

Friday, June 30th, 1893.

Dalya and Amira were on their way back to the grand Mansion, after a visit downtown. The employees of the grand Mansion were all busy with their work, and being on vacation, Dalya and Amira offered to go shopping at the market.

- It was a good outing. Amira thought aloud.
- Yes, and the weather is nice, today. Dalya replied.

The two girls continued on their way. At one point, Amira exclaimed:

- Haven't you noticed that everyone at the grand Mansion has been in a good mood since the arrival of baby Philippe?

Dalya exclaimed:

- Of course! Even my little twin sisters do less fooleries! They spend their days entertaining the baby and bringing him toys!

Amira affirmed:

- Your little sisters Ari and Adi are adorable! I would have loved to have brothers or sisters!

Hardly stifling her laugh, Dalya corrected her:

- You would have loved to have brothers and sisters, really?! You forget the fooleries that comes with them! Last night, the little twins had fun turning off all the lamps that Mr. Bûchebois lit! And the other day, they decided to wear winter coats in the hea…

Suddenly Amira stopped, and she interrupted Dalya:

- It's the police.

Dalya also stopped, and she asked in a confused air:

- What? What are you talking about?

Amira pointed to a car parked at the entrance to the grand Mansion:

- It's a police car.

When Dalya saw it, her heart froze and a worried feeling invaded her. Amira affirmed in a serious voice:

- Dalya, something is happening at the grand Mansion!

Running with all the strength of their feet, Dalya and Amira arrived breathless at the entrance of the grand Mansion. And they discovered a terrible scene in the hall of the grand Mansion...

Five police officers were present. The Lawyer Mr. Ernest Laszlo stood in the same row of the policemen, he looked angry. Young Lawyer Sloan Wilfrid looked worried and tense. And on the other side of the hall, all the employees were present. And it looked like the employees were blocking the way to the policemen. The Gardener, the Cook, the head of the grand Mansion, Igor, and Cristelle... they all seemed anxious and stressed.

Dalya was confused about what was happening. But, she would soon understand the situation.

The Lawyer Mr. Ernest Laszlo ordered the policemen in a furious tone:

- Bring me that baby, now!! He will not spend a minute more in this house!! He is an illegal child; he belongs to the orphanage!!

At that moment, a shiver ran through Dalya Bouvard's body. What everyone had feared for months, has finally happened. The Lawyer Mr. Ernest Laszlo knew about Océanie's baby, and he was determined to get him out of the grand Mansion.

In a corner of the hall, Océanie was standing, trembling, clutching baby Philippe with all her might. The fear was clearly displayed in the eyes of the young mother. Cristelle was standing near Océanie, and for the first time in a long time, Cristelle seemed worried and she looked pale.

After the order of the Lawyer Mr. Ernest Laszlo, the policemen advanced a step toward the employees. Except that not only the Gardener, the Cook, the head of the grand Mansion and Igor, they blocked their passage to Océanie and her baby... But, a fearsome silhouette roared with a frightening sound and it released its sharp claws. The Snow Panther forced the policemen to step back.

Young Lawyer Sloan Wilfrid rushed to his employer:

- Mr. Ernest, maybe we can discu...

The Lawyer Ernest Laszlo ignored Sloan Wilfrid and he ordered the employees of the grand Mansion:

- This baby won't stay here! He will come out willingly or by force! Let the police take him!

At this moment, a small voice spoke. Dalya Bouvard gathered her courage, she placed herself near the Gardener, and she asked in a curious tone:

- The baby doesn't bother us, Mr. Ernest Laszlo. Why can't he stay here at the grand Mansion?

Furious at this question, Ernest Laszlo screamed:

- Because I will not allow it! He is an illegal child; his place is in the orphanage and not here!

The small voice of Océanie was heard in a pleading and trembling tone:

- Please... Sir... please...

Cristelle hugged Océanie and the baby in her arms, also suppliant:

- Please Mr. Ernest ... he's only a baby...

Amira Mounier who had joined the rank of the employees, she affirmed in a trembling voice:

- The baby is nice... we don't even hear him... he's...

Except that the Lawyer was determined to be obeyed:

- GET THAT BABY OUT RIGHT NOW!!

The policemen advanced toward the employees. The Cook, Igor, and the head of the grand Mansion, they did not move from their position, they remained motionless in front of the young mother and her baby. The Gardener raised his baton and he screamed with all his might:

- STEP BACK!! STEP BACK IMMEDIATELY!!

Never had the Gardener looked so angry, until this day. Monsieur Weil Rosenwald held his baton firmly, he seemed to be ready to fight. And endowed with a formidable maternal instinct, the Snow Panther hardly held back from jumping on the policemen. The animal looked furious and determined to defend the baby. Séraphine roared with all her might, pointing her claws and canines at the policemen.

Suddenly, the Lawyer Ernest Laszlo let out an arrogant little laugh:

- Well... well... a Gardener who disobeys the Master of the place? This behavior is quite new.

The Gardener restrained his anger with great difficulty, he tightened the baton in his hands. After a minute of tense silence, the Lawyer Ernest Laszlo addressed the Gardener:

- You are fired!!

At this precise moment, as improbable as it was, and for the first time since the beginning of this confrontation, the head of the grand Mansion, Mr. Bûchebois spoke in a calm and courteous tone:

- Sorry to have to correct you, Mr. Ernest Laszlo. But you can't fire the Gardener.

The Lawyer was thunderstruck by this answer and by this audacity:

- Sor... Sorry?!

The head of the grand Mansion, Mr. Bûchebois continued in the same calm tone:

- With all due respect, Mr. Ernest Laszlo… you are not the Owner of the grand Mansion, you have no right to fire or recruit anyone in this Mansion.

The words of the head of the grand Mansion echoed in the hall, like lightning from the sky. Dalya and Amira exchanged a surprised look. Océanie and Cristelle became paralyzed in their corner. The Cook and Igor shared a surprised smile. The policemen did not know what to do and whom to obey. Even the young Lawyer Sloan Wilfrid couldn't help but display a surprised smile.

The Lawyer Ernest Laszlo lost his temper:

- BÛCHEBOIS!! HOW DARE YOU?! I AM THE OWNER OF THE GR...

At this moment the Gardener also lost his temper and he addressed the Lawyer Ernest Laszlo in a threatening tone:

- YOU ARE NOT OUR EMPLOYER! DALYA BOUVARD IS THE GOVERNOR'S HEIRESS! SHE IS THE SOLE DECISION-MAKER IN THIS HOUSE!

Immediately, the Cook and Igor exclaimed enthusiastically:

- Yes! You are not our employer!
- Exact! She is the sole decision-maker here!

Cristelle dared to say in a trembling but confident voice:

- Only she can fire us!

Amira exclaimed:

- It's her name, which is written in the Will!

And apparently the Snow Panther understood the words of this discussion, she too joined in the conversation, roaring in a loud and defiant tone, to the point that the hall windows shook. The Panther Séraphine stood in front of Océanie and her baby, scrutinizing the slightest moves of the policemen, with a piercing and terrifying blue stare.

Having held his tongue enough until now, Lawyer Sloan Wilfrid decided to act to temper this incident. In front of the tension between the employees of the grand Mansion and Mr. Ernest Laszlo, Sloan Wilfrid approached the Lawyer and he whispered in a respectful tone:

- Mr. Ernest, it would be preferable, in my opinion, to retire now. From a legal point of view, we have no authority in this house. The Will makes it clear that Dalya Bouvard is the sole decision maker of what happens here inside the grand Mansion. It would be wiser to forget about this baby and to retire.

Except that Ernest Laszlo was not a man to give up and to retire easily. The Lawyer didn't like being challenged, let alone disobeyed. Mr. Ernest Laszlo turned to his employee Sloan Wilfrid, and he asked him in a cold accusatory tone:

-   Wilfrid … why do I have the gradual impression that you are defending Dalya Bouvard?

Sloan Wilfrid replied without a second of hesitation, barely suppressing an amused laugh:

-   Honestly, Monsieur … that Dalya Bouvard authorizes a baby or a goat to live here in this grand Mansion, that's the least of my worries. I'm rather concerned about the Snow Panther. The police can very well mobilize all the employees … who will stop the Snow Panther from slaughtering us?

One must admit that Sloan Wilfrid was right on this point. The policemen seemed to be terrified already just by the presence and the roars of the animal. And although docile and nice, none of the employees of the grand Mansion could hold back Séraphine… not even Dalya Bouvard!

And as strange as it was, the Snow Panther understood the idea of the young Lawyer Sloan Wilfrid. Séraphine took several steps toward the policemen, she opened her jaw wide, her canines terrified everyone, her tense fur made her look frightening, her claws lit up in the light of the lamps… the Snow Panther had a maternal instinct to protect the baby, and she was impatient to slaughter anyone who dared come near!

For a few long seconds, a heavy silence invaded the hall of the grand Mansion. No one dared to move or say another word. At a moment, the head of the grand Mansion Mr. Bûchebois broke this silence, addressing the intruders in a calm, courteous and above all defiant tone:

-   Gentlemen policemen … Mr. Ernest Laszlo … you are requested to leave the grand Mansion, immediately!

Chapter 39

Intensive courses

Saturday July 1st, 1893. In the grand Mansion.

Cristelle was leaving the Library when she met Dalya:

- There you are, Mademoiselle. I was looking for you. I am bringing your tea and some cake.

Dalya froze on the hall stairs; she answered with a hesitant voice:

- I ... I am sorry, I forgot to tell you not to bother making me tea. I was thinking of going out this afternoon.

Instantly, Cristelle looked at the tray she was holding in her hands, and she thought aloud:

- No worries, Mademoiselle. In this case, I will add another cup and a 2nd piece of cake to this tray. The little Demoiselles will soon be awake from their nap. And it's time for their afternoon meal.

Dalya came down the last step of the staircase:

- Thank you very much, Cristelle. I won't be late; I will be back in few hours.
- Understood, Mademoiselle.

Putting a book inside her bag, Dalya asked:

- How is Océanie? How is the baby? I hope they have recovered from the terrible scene of yesterday. I was really worried about Océanie and her baby.

Cristelle let out an amused laugh:

- Oh, I was much more worried about the Lawyer Ernest Laszlo who was kicked out of the grand Mansion, yesterday! I'm curious to know if he slept well last night! Océanie and the baby are perfectly fine, Mademoiselle. And all employees are relieved and reassured that you are the sole decision-maker in the grand Mansion. This Lawyer Ernest Laszlo must learn to better read the Wills, before acting as Master of the universe!

For a long minute, Dalya and Cristelle shared a giggle. Before Dalya would leave the grand Mansion, Cristelle called her back:

- One second, Mademoiselle.

Dalya turned around. Cristelle placed the tray on a small table in the hall, and she approached Dalya:

\-   The back knot of your dress is not well done.

Dalya smiled:

\-   Thank you, Cristelle. I admit that it is difficult to make a perfect knot backwards.

While readjusting the knot of the dress, Cristelle noticed that Dalya was wearing a pretty summer dress, pastel green, a light open cardigan in light pink. Cristelle was delighted to see Dalya wearing dresses, especially on weekends. And a while ago, Dalya had learned to arrange her hair in a crown of braids, all by herself.

When Cristelle finished readjusting the knot of the dress, and a few locks of hair, she exclaimed:

\-   It's done! You are very pretty in a dress, Mademoiselle!

Dalya thanked Cristelle with a smile, before leaving the grand Mansion.

A few minutes of walk later.

The home of the French family, the Poirier, was quiet and calm. Way too quiet. Richard Poirier had been locked in his office since this morning. Although it was vacation time for most people in the city of Georgetown, it was a busy time for Richard Poirier. A big event was happening in September, and he only had 2 months to prepare for it.

The worktable was filled with files, reports, papers, and books. Richard Poirier was sitting in front of his desk, writing notes, and busy with his work.

Suddenly, a silhouette knocked on the door. Without even looking up from the file, Richard replied:

\-   Thank you for the coffee, Mrs. Glorina. It comes at the right time.

A little amused voice replied:

\-   Sorry, but I brought you only a honey fruit bowl. Mrs. Glorina asked me to bring it to you.

Suddenly, Richard Poirier looked up at the door to discover a familiar silhouette.

\-   Good afternoon, Mademoiselle Dalya. Come in, please.

The little girl placed the bowl of fruit on a small table nearby. It took considerable effort for Richard Poirier to repress his joy and reduce his happy smile. However, the words betrayed him and they escaped from him without him being able to control them:

\-   We missed you.

Dalya got used to the young man's awkward and intimidating words. And Richard got used to the little girl's blushing cheeks. Despite the many meetings, the tension and the embarrassment between the two young people, were still very much present.

It is true that the month of June was hectic at the grand Mansion. Yet, Dalya also missed the French family. Looking at the many files and papers scattered around the office, Dalya easily guessed what was going on:

- You are preparing for the Political reopening in September. It will be with the new Government. And you must be ready for the vote on the new budget and the new Laws.

Richard Poirier relaxed on his chair, and he watched for a long minute the little girl standing in front of his desk. She fascinated him and surprised him at each meeting.

- It is quite correct. Mademoiselle is up to date with her Political information. I have 2 months to prepare for the Political reopening in September.

Dalya was delighted to have guessed correctly:

- Good luck, then!

Richard replied, even more delighted:

- Thank you, Mademoiselle. It gives me strength.

And it was so very true. The presence and words of Dalya Bouvard filled the young Richard Poirier with strength.

Looking at the stacks of files and papers all over the office, Dalya seemed to have a question on her lips, but she was hesitant to ask:

- I... I was wondering if... I see you're busy for the next few months... and I understand...

The young man easily understood Dalya's hesitation, he encouraged her to speak:

- Do you need my help, Mademoiselle?

Dalya asked shyly:

- I was wondering, when you have a free minute, if you would like to help me, this summer, in the Philosophy lessons, for the next semest...

Richard Poirier interrupted her immediately and he straightened up on his chair:

- Sure! It will be with great pleasure, Mademoiselle!

In an embarrassed voice, Dalya insisted:

- Only in your free time, and when you are rested. I would like to use the summer holidays to study, and to advance in my course.

The two young people had not seen each other for a month. After the end-of-year exams, Richard Poirier thought that Dalya no longer needed support courses in Philosophy. Their meetings on Saturday afternoons, their hours of study, their laughs, and their sincere conversations; these moments were very much missed by Richard Poirier. And more specifically, one person was very much missed by Richard Poirier.

Opening a small notebook, Richard Poirier leafed through few pages:

- I propose to you every Saturday ... does 4 PM suit you, Mademoiselle?

That day, despite being overbusy with work until September, Richard Poirier insisted on setting a time in his schedule for Dalya Bouvard. After a long month of June without meeting, Richard decided not to let Dalya be absent for so long.

Chapter 40

Fatigue mistake

Tuesday, July 4th, 1893. In the Law firm.

The summer month promised to be calm and peaceful. The streets were full of passers-by and visitors, enjoying the beautiful rays of sunshine and the summer heat. After a freezing and harsh winter, the entire city of Georgetown was grateful for the warmth of the summer month.

At the Lawyer's office, Sloan Wilfrid was peacefully reading a report given to him by Lyor the day before. The young apprentice Lyor Laszlo had become more experienced in preparing the pleadings that Sloan Wilfrid didn't hesitate to entrust him with several cases.

Sipping his iced tea, Sloan Wilfrid corrected the report in his hands. When suddenly, the Lawyer was surprised by a sentence in the report. Sloan Wilfrid sat up from his chair and he readjusted his glasses to read it again. After a few seconds of confusion, Sloan Wilfrid decided to get up and search for Lyor Laszlo in his office to get more explanations.

Lyor's office was in the usual chaos; books and files covered all the empty spaces, the large armchair clearly confirmed several nights spent at the office, a dozen empty coffee cups were piled on the work table. The only object that seemed to have escaped the chaos of this office was the Crocus flowerpot placed on the edge of the window. Gorgeous purple-blue petals with orange interiors and fresh green leaves. The delicious smell filled the office. Apart from the flowers near the window which seemed to be peaceful, all objects in Lyor's office were in a big mess.

When Sloan Wilfrid entered the office, he found Lyor busy writing a report. Sloan Wilfrid walked over to the work table, and he announced in a worried tone:

- You look tired, Lyor.

The young apprentice looked up at his mentor, and he asked in a curious tone:

- What makes you say that?

With dark eyes circles, a gray face, messy hair, a crumpled shirt, Lyor Laszlo seemed to have slept several nights at the office. But that wasn't what caught Sloan Wilfrid's attention. While sitting down in an armchair, Sloan Wilfrid handed Lyor some papers:

- In the report you gave me yesterday, you mixed up the defense of the Adjutor case with the numbers of the Gantt case. You rarely make such mistakes. I take it you're exhausted. A fatigue mistake.

At this announcement, Lyor Laszlo took the document from Sloan Wilfrid and he examined it:

\- I ... did I really mixed up the two cases? ... I ... I'm sorry; I'm going to redo right away the rep...

Sloan Wilfrid took the report from Lyor and he ordered him:

\- You will first go home, take a good cold shower and sleep for a few hours!

Lyor Laszlo protested:

\- I can't! I still have three files to prepare for next wee...

Sloan Wilfrid interrupted him:

\- For next week, yes, I know. I'll take care of it, myself!

Lyor Laszlo thought aloud:

\- And I haven't started the defense pleading of Antman Bouvard yet ...

Lying back on his chair, Sloan Wilfrid explained:

\- Currently, there is nothing we can do for Antman Bouvard, it is the judicial holidays. All Courts are on pause, until September. So, during these summer months, you have only two things to do; prepare for Antman Bouvard's defense and study for your Bar exam. Where are you in your exam studies?

At this question, Lyor Laszlo froze:

\- I... my Bar exam... yes... my studies... by the way, I...

Sloan Wilfrid sighed:

\- You didn't have time to start your exam studies, did you?

Because of the files and cases at his father's office, Lyor Laszlo didn't touch a single study paper of his Bar exam. In front of the confused silence of Lyor Laszlo, Sloan Wilfrid stood up from his chair, he closed the file in front of Lyor and he ordered him:

\- Today, a shower and a good night sleep. Tomorrow, you will start the studies for your Bar exam and the defense pleading of Antman Bouvard... 2 assignements only, nothing more!

In front of Sloan Wilfrid's determination, and realizing his state of fatigue, Lyor Laszlo had no more strength or energy to discuss the directives of his mentor. The young Lyor stood up and he took his coat, repeating to himself:

\- Yes, today, a shower and a good night sleep. Tomorrow, I will begin the studies for my Bar exam and the defense pleading of Antman Bouvard. I will come here to the office early in the morning to star...

Sloan Wilfrid handed Lyor his hat:

- No, out of the question! If you come here to the office, you'll be distracted by the Law firm cases.

Lyor Laszlo asked in a curious tone:

- Where do you want me to work?

Opening the door to the office, Sloan Wilfrid answered:

- The grand Mansion's Library seems to me to be the best place to work, even better than the National Library of Georgetown city. I will inform the head of the grand Mansion Mr. Bûchebois that you will be spending a few days there at the Library, so that he can prepare a room for you next door. You will have all day to work in it quietly, and rest in the evening. And I am sure that Mademoiselle Dalya Bouvard will see no inconvenience in your presence.

Exhausted and weary, Lyor Laszlo didn't argue with his mentor Sloan Wilfrid's orders, for once. Lyor Laszlo left his father's firm, murmuring:

- Shower, sleep, studies of the Bar exam … defense pleading of Antman Bouvard … Library of the grand Mansion.

Chapter 41

A peaceful night … more or less

Friday, July 7th, 1893. In the dining room at the grand Mansion.

Dalya woke up early that morning. Her friend Amira Mounier joined her to work together on their holiday homework. While the head of the grand Mansion Mr. Bûchebois was serving the orange juice to the little girls, he informed them:

- Mr. Lyor Laszlo will remain at the Library of the grand Mansion, for his own studies, for a few days. I thought you would be more comfortable somewhere else. We have arranged a work table and armchairs for you in the living room.

Dalya replied with a smile:

- Thank you, Mr. Bûchebois.

Spreading butter on her bread, Amira asked the same question for the 100th time:

- Dalya, are you sure you want to work with me, my holiday homework in other courses?

Using the jam, Dalya gave the same answer for the 101th time too:

- Yes, very sure! I had only one course the past semester, Philosophy. And I don't want to be behind in the other courses. So, I will work the holiday homework with you, to be up to date in all the other courses!

The head of the grand Mansion placed a basket of chocolate croissants on the table, and he murmured:

- Well thought, Mademoiselle.

Between sips of milk, Amira thought aloud:

- Good point! I think we must start with the most difficult courses. We are attacking History and Geography courses this week. And after that, we will still have Mathematics, Physics, and Chemistry… What do you think?

Dalya helped herself to a chocolate croissant:

- It's a good plan! But, as long as we don't stay too long in History and Geography, it gives me headaches. And for Latin, what do you suggest?

Before Amira could answer, the little twin sisters entered the dining room, and they exclaimed in a happy tone:

- Hello Dindin !!

- Hello Mia!!
- Hello Monsieur Bois !!

Dalya was surprised by the morning presence of her little twin sisters:

- Why did you wake up so early?

The little twin sisters were already wearing their blue overalls and white sweaters, their light brown hair was in buns, and they were barefoot. Ari and Adi sat down on their special chairs, and they answered proudly:

- We have lot of homework today!!
- We also study!! We are very busy!!

Dalya and Amira exchanged an amused look. Dalya asked in a curious tone:

- What homework? You are in kindergarten; the only homework you have is coloring.

Amira jumped up from her chair and she asked the little twins, in a pleading tone:

- Ari, Adi... do you want to swap homework? Please please !

Ari and Adi helped themselves to the chocolate croissants, and they answered in a serious voice:

- Everyone is studying today! We also study today!
- We are very busy! We have important homework!

The head of the grand Mansion filled the milk glasses of the little twin sisters and he smiled:

- And you are very right to do your homework, Mesdemoiselles Ari and Adi. I will ask Igor to set up small desks and chairs for you in the living room, right away!

Dalya and Amira laughed. When suddenly, the dining room door swung open.

- That was a very bad joke, Dalya!!

Lyor Laszlo came into the dining room, and he was very upset. Instantly, all the laughs and moves stopped. Dalya answered all confused:

- What joke? What are you talking abo...

As he advanced toward Dalya, Lyor raised the tone of his voice:

- I'm not here at the grand Mansion for a vacation!! I have important matters to settle!! You kept me up all night!! Because of you, I had to get up every 2 hours to turn them off!!

The head of the grand Mansion tried to intervene and calm down the young Lyor Laszlo:

- Would you like a coffee, Monsi...

Except that Lyor was furious, he continued to pour out his rage on Dalya:

- It wasn't funny at all!! Hiding alarm clocks in the corners of my room and make them ring every 2 hours of night... it wasn't funny at all!!

At this moment, Amira Mounier turned toward her friend, and she exclaimed in a surprised tone:

- Dalya Bouvard ... since when do you make jokes without my help?!

Confused by this accusation, Dalya replied sincerely to Lyor:

- I didn't do anything!! I didn't go into your room!! By the way, yesterday I was busy putting things away in my own room!!

The head of the grand Mansion confirmed Dalya's words:

- Mademoiselle didn't leave her room, yesterday afternoon. She was even served dinner in her bedroom, so she could finish her tidying up.

Except that Lyor didn't want to know anything, he was convinced that the joke was Dalya's idea:

- Try to provoke me with your jokes again, and you will regret it!! I don't have time to waste with you !!

Slamming the dining room door, Lyor Laszlo stormed out. The head of the grand Mansion broke the silence, announcing in an amused voice:

- I think it is better to serve breakfast to Monsieur Lyor Laszlo in the Library. He doesn't seem to be in a good mood this morning.

While Mr. Bûchebois was preparing a plate and a cup of coffee on a tray, Amira turned toward Dalya, and she asked her in a surprised voice:

- You hid alarm clocks in Lyor Laszlo's room! And they rang every 2 hours of night! Without telling me and including me in your plan?! I could have helped you! Why didn't you tell me?!

Dalya leaned back on her chair:

- I swear it wasn't me! I don't know why Lyor wants to make me responsible for all the problems of the world! I didn't leave my room yesterday; I tidied up my dressing room, my desk, my school ba...

When suddenly, Dalya straightened up on her chair, and she asked in a worried tone:

- Ari ... Adi ... the alarm clocks you took from me yesterday, did you...

At this moment, Dalya, Amira, and the head of the grand Mansion, they all observed the little twins with a curious air. Ari and Adi jumped up from their chairs, and they defended themselves with an enthusiastic voice:

- We are zentilles!! We did nothing!!
- We help Riri wake up early to study!!
- So, we put clocks in Riri's room!! That's all!!
- Yes, that's all!! We zentilles!! We did nothing!!

Suddenly, Amira Mounier burst out laughing uncontrollably:

- It's brilliant!! It's totally brilliant!!

The head of the grand Mansion barely stifled his amused laugh. Dalya addressed her twin sisters in an angry tone:

- Help him wake up early?! Are you being serious?! He didn't sleep all night because of the alarms going on every 2 hours!! And it's me he's yelling at!! Ari! Adi! Stay away from Lyor Laszlo and don't get any close to him!! He's a furious nut, and I don't need any more worries!! Don't piss him off!! Stay away from him !!

Ari and Adi answered in a sincere voice:

- Oki Dindin!! We stay away from Riri!! Oki!! Promise!!
- Yes, Dindin!! We not piss off Riri!! We zentilles !!

The little twins always obeyed their big sister's orders ... almost always.

Chapter 42

A calm Library ... more or less

Monday, July 10th, 1893. In the salon of the grand Mansion.

In this afternoon, the grand Mansion was calm. All the employees were busy with their work. Lyor Laszlo locked himself in the Library to study. And in the living room, Dalya and Amira were working on their vacation homework. Everything was quiet...

Suddenly, an explosion was heard. Dalya continued writing, thinking aloud:

- It must be Mr. Gardener fixing something.

Her friend Amira didn't answer, busy looking for a word in a book. Barely a few seconds later, a 2nd explosion was heard. Amira Mounier opened a book and she copied out a definition, muttering:

- Renovations in the summer, it's well thought. This is the best season for housework.

Dalya and Amira continued their homework. When a 3rd explosion sounded bigger and louder. Curious this time, Dalya stopped writing, and she turned toward the living room door:

- It's strange; the sound comes from inside the grand Mansion.

In an indifferent tone, her friend Amira replied, while continuing to write in her notebook:

- It must be renovations inside the house.

Dalya turned around and she continued her work. Except that after a 4th explosion shook the windows, the doubt about these strange noises invaded the two girls. Amira stopped writing, and she asked in a curious tone, this time:

- Dalya ... did you know about these renovations?

And before Dalya could answer her friend, a 5th explosion shook the windows and the vases of the living room, and it had the effect of an earthquake. Immediately, a scream of pain was heard at the grand Mansion. And immediately afterwards, the living room door swung open. The little twins Ari and Adi were breathless, they ran to their big sister Dalya, whispering:

- We did nothing Dindin!! We swear we did nothing!!
- Hide us!! Hide us quick quick quick!!

Amira and Dalya exchanged a confused and surprised look. Dalya worried:

- The explosions were you two? But what have you done ag...

An enraged scream was heard throughout the grand Mansion. With an amused giggle, Amira ordered the little twins:

- Get under the table … quick quick quick!!

Ari and Adi didn't need to be repeated twice. They immediately hid under the office table, and Amira lengthened the tablecloth to better hide the little twin sisters.

The living room door suddenly opened. And Lyor Laszlo seemed enraged:

- AREN'T YOU GOING TO STOP YOUR FOOLERIES??!! I HAVE AN EXAM AND AN IMPORTANT FILE TO PREPARE!!! HAVE YOU NOTHING BETTER TO DO!!!

Dalya calmly replied to Lyor:

- We too have important homework to do! We haven't moved from this living room, me and Amira, since this morning!

Amira also replied to Lyor:

- And we are not deaf, speak less loudly!

The young Lyor Laszlo advanced toward Dalya, and he screamed furiously:

- Are you having fun provoking me?! I have no time to waste on your fooleries!! Do you think hiding firecrackers between books is fun?! I get a firecracker in my face every time I take a book out!! This is a very bad joke !

Dalya and Amira exchanged an amused look. Picking up her homework notebook, Dalya calmly replied to Lyor:

- It's a genius idea. But sorry, me and Amira have nothing to do with this foolery!

In front of the calm and indifference of Dalya and Amira, Lyor Laszlo seemed confused:

- If it's not you two… then who?

In a second, Lyor Laszlo finally understood who was having fun provoking him:

- It's them, aren't they? Where are those little twins?

Suddenly, two small voices under the work table answered simultaneously and honestly:

- They not here!! They not here!!
- They far away!! They not here!!

Dalya and Amira couldn't hold back their giggles any longer. Lyor Laszlo muttered a few threats for a second, and then he left the living room, slamming the door behind him.

Raising the tablecloth to allow the little twins to come out of their hiding place, Amira choke with laughter:

- Firecrackers between books! Ari, Adi … you are geniuses!!

Dalya continued her friend's sentence:

- Geniuses in fooleries, yes. One more foolery and Lyor will lose his brain.

Ari and Adi sincerely defended themselves:

- But we did nothing!! We are zentilles!!
- We nice!! We did nothing!!

And before continuing her homework, Dalya asked her little twin sisters in a curious tone:

- Ari… Adi… How many firecrackers did you hide in the Library?

If there's one thing you need to be sure of, Dear readers, it's that the little twin sisters never lied. Ari and Adi replied sincerely and proudly to their big sister:

- 237!!

At that moment, an explosion and a scream of anger was heard in the grand Mansion. Amira laughed in tears:

- This is the 6th explosion. Lyor is almost there … he still has 231 firecrackers to discover!!

Dalya also laughed heartily:

- It will be a long summer vacation for Lyor Laszlo!

A 7th explosion was heard. And immediately, Dalya, Amira and the little twin sisters laughed with one voice:

- 230!!

Chapter 43

Gardening

Saturday August 19th, 1893. The afternoon. In the garden of the grand Mansion.

The summer heat was getting heavier. The sky was clear blue, the sun was shining brighter and longer, a few windy breezes passing by from time to time. It was a beautiful summer day.

After lunch, the little twins took their usual nap. Dalya took advantage of the calm to help the Gardener in the immense garden of the grand Mansion.

- These sunflowers are gorgeous!

Dalya was amazed by the bright colors of the flowers which the Gardener was about to plant. Emptying a small carriage filled with flowerpots, the Gardener said:

- Yes, you are quite right; Mademoiselle. Sunflowers have a beautiful fresh yellow color. It wakes up the garden and illuminates it.

Helping to empty the carriage, Dalya marveled:

- This is the first time you've brought these flowers here to the grand Mansion, Mr. Gardener. They are very pretty, and their pink color is very beautiful!

The Gardener sat down on the ground, and he began to make holes in the earth:

- They are called oleanders; they are summer flowers only. Easy to plant and resistant to summer heat.

At that moment, Dalya had an idea. She emptied the carriage of the last pot of flowers, and she asked in a polite tone:

- Mr. Gardener … can I have 4 or 5 flower pots? I would like to offer them to the French neighbors.

The Gardener replied, indicating with a shovel:

- Take as many as you want, Mademoiselle. The carriage is empty, use it. I advise you to also bring them the Lupins. The purple flowers…the ones next to the water pipe…yes, those are the Lupins.

Rolling up her sleeves, Dalya followed the Gardener's directions, and she began to fill the small carriage. When a voice joined them:

- These are splendid flowers, Mr. Gardener! The garden will look like an Eden!

The help Cook Océanie was also amazed by the bright colors of the new flowers. She approached the Gardener and she asked him:

- The Cook needs chives and cilantro. Can I have some?

The Gardener turned toward a corner of the garden:

- Sorry Océanie, there are only a few left. I plan to plant them tomorrow, including mint and basil.

Océanie thought aloud:

- No worries, I'll tell Mr. Ferrero to use the parsley, in the meantime.

At one point, Océanie observed Dalya picking out flowerpots and putting them in a small carriage. A small detail caught Océanie's attention, she asked in a curious voice:

- You're not wearing summer dresses today, Mademoiselle?

For several months, Dalya assiduously wore refined dresses during the weekends. Except that day, Dalya wore her usual blue overalls, a white shirt, and gardening shoes. With an amused chuckle, Dalya explained to her:

- Dresses are not very practical for gardening work. This afternoon, I'm going to bring some flowerpots to the French neighbors. They have a small garden. These flowers will embellish the place.

Before going back inside the grand Mansion, Océanie smiled as she watched the little Dalya Bouvard fill in the carriage with flowerpots.

The afternoon. In the house of the French family, the Poirier.

Mrs. Marianne Poirier loved the summer days. The wind was non-existent, and the heat didn't affect her as much as the winter cold. In the afternoons, the great woman often liked to read books, sitting on a large armchair, facing the huge windows of her bedroom. The sun offered a magnificent spectacle every day.

At one moment, a silhouette interrupted the calm of the room:

- I bring your tea, Mrs. Marianne.

The house employee, Mrs. Glorina took care to all the needs and desires of the great woman. And having served her for several years, Mrs. Glorina knew all her habits and tastes. Placing a tray on a table in front of the great woman, Mrs. Glorina explained to her:

- As you wished, I have prepared some black tea for you, with a cinnamon stick. And I served you a lemon meringue pie.

Mrs. Marianne answered with a smile, and she put down her book on the table. As she poured the tea into a cup, Mrs. Glorina repressed an amused laugh.

- It was almost a salty pie. While preparing the meringue cream, I confused the salt with the sugar. Fortunately, I was able to remove the salt in time, before mixing everything.

Mrs. Marianne laughed silently and she picked up her cup of tea. Before leaving the room, Mrs. Glorina turned to the great woman:

- I'll be outside for a while to hang up the laundry while the sun is still bright and warm. If you need anything, Madame, ring me. And... speaking of sunshine, would you like me to open the window a bit? There is no wind today. And the warm rays of the sun will do you good.

Before eating her spoonful of pie, Mrs. Marianne replied with a nod. Mrs. Glorina opened one of the bedroom windows. And instantly, a ray of sunshine entered and crept up to the great woman's legs. Mrs. Marianne felt gentle warmth on her legs.

Mrs. Glorina left the room, and she returned to her household chores. Mrs. Marianne continued her reading, while tasting her tea.

At one point, a giggle was heard outside the house. Mrs. Marianne took a spoonful of pie again, and she continued to read.

A few minutes later, two voices were heard outside the house. Mrs. Marianne finished her cup of tea, and she turned the page of her book.

Barely a second later, two voices laughed their hearts out. This time, Mrs. Marianne was disturbed by the sounds of laughs and talk, emanating from outside the house.

The noise seemed to be close to the French family's house. Curiosity invaded her, Mrs. Marianne put down her book, she stood up slowly from her chair, and she approached the open window. From the top of her bedroom, Mrs. Marianne put on her glasses to better see who was the origin of the laughs and the conversations.

At that precise moment, Mrs. Marianne Poirier saw her son Richard Poirier and Dalya Bouvard in the garden. The two young people were sitting on the lawn, busy talking. For months, Richard and Dalya had been meeting inside the house; in the office or in the living room. It was the first time that the two young people met in the garden. Mrs. Marianne opened the window a little more, in order to listen to their conversation and understand what was going on.

Dalya took a pot from the carriage:

- And this flower here is called the Lupin. It is appreciated by bees. Its purple color is beautiful. It grows quickly. And it smells great, especially at night.

Richard said in a serious tone:

- The only word that I retained from all your explanations is the word bees!

Dalya couldn't hold back her amused laugh. She explained to him:

- Some flowers attract more bees than others. But don't worry, bees are not dangerous, they are only interested in flowers.

Richard Poirier murmured in a worried and amused tone:

- They're still bees! With painful stings!

Pulling a large fork out of the carriage, Dalya politely asked:

- Have you really never done any gardening? In your entire life? Not even once?

Richard smiled:

- No, I've never tried gardening, until today. I admit that I am an interior man; I spend all my days in offices.

Dalya looked up at the bright sun:

- It's a beautiful sunny day. Better to spend it outside, in the open air.

Handing the flower pot and a large fork to Richard, Dalya exclaimed happily:

- And it's a beautiful day to plant these flowers!

Hesitantly, Richard took the items from Dalya. The young man was gifted in strategies, in politics, in detailed reports and analysis, in dealing with Government people. Except that when it came to gardening, Richard didn't know where to start.

That day, Dalya had suggested that she go out into the garden for some fresh air. She had brought flowerpots with her from the grand Mansion. Richard agreed to take a break from his work, and he followed her outside.

Continuing to empty the carriage of flowerpots, Dalya explained to Richard:

- You must make a small hole in the ground with the fork. And plant the flower. Afterwards, we will water the plants and the entire garden.

Richard followed Dalya's directions, muttering:

- A hole in the ground, with the fork.

Dalya was delighted to have convinced Richard to get out of his office and spend some time in the garden, for once. Putting the flowerpots on the ground, Dalya continued her explanations:

\- Mr. Gardener advised me to bring you this flower too. The Sunflower is such a happy flower with this beautiful yellow color. Mr. Gardener thinks the sunflower wakes up the garden. I think he is quite right!

Richard was busy making a hole in the ground. He felt a pleasant sensation while working with his hands in the garden. He listened attentively to Dalya.

\- And ... these flowers are called oleanders. Isn't it a splendid color? It looks like roses. Mr. Gardener confirmed to me that this flower resists the heat of summer.

With a proud move, Richard straightened up and he announced:

\- I planted a flower!

The young man had put the earth back around the flower. And the flower was standing, gracefully. Dalya smiled:

\- It's perfect! Your first flower planted in the garden! Well done!

Richard thought aloud:

\- After all, gardening is not so difficult. I should try it more often.

Dalya confirmed:

\- And it's relaxing too. Gardening empties and refreshes the mind.

By offering a second flower pot to Richard, Dalya asked him:

\- I will let you plant the flowers, while I clean up the dead plants. When you're done, put the empty pots in the carriage. The Gardener reuses the empty pots for other plants.

Richard took the flower from Dalya's hands, and he asked in a curious voice:

\- What empty pot?

Turning toward him, Dalya explained:

\- The empty pot that you removed before planting the flower.

Richard's confused face was enough to answer Dalya. She approached the flower that Richard had planted; she stirred the earth with her fingers, to discover that the pot was planted with the flower. At that moment, Richard Poirier and Dalya Bouvard exchanged a look, and immediately an uncontrollable burst of laugh invaded them both. The two young people laughed heartily.

\- I am really not good at gardening.
\- No, not at all.

Dalya took a flowerpot, and she started her explanations for the 2nd time. Richard focused seriously on the techniques of gardening.

While Richard and Dalya were busy in the garden, a silhouette watched them from her bedroom window. Mrs. Marianne Poirier was surprised that her son Richard tried gardening for the first time in his life. And when hearing the laughs of the two young people, Mrs. Marianne understood that her son was having a good time, on this summer afternoon.

Since their first meeting, Mrs. Marianne Poirier felt that the little Dalya Bouvard was very special. It is true that the little girl had spontaneous manners, unusual clothes, and strange ideas. However, Mrs. Marianne was very fond of Dalya Bouvard. And above all, the great woman appreciated the influence of this strange little girl, on her son Richard.

Before closing the window and returning to her reading, the great woman stared for a long minute at the two young people laughing and working in the garden. And at that precise moment, Mrs. Marianne Poirier smiled.

Chapter 44

The last days of vacation

Tuesday August 29th, 1893.

Leaving a shop in downtown, Amira Mounier put her new notebooks in her bag:

- And there you go! We bought all the school supplies we need.

Dalya checked the list one last time:

- Notebooks, white papers, black pencils, erasers, pencil case, cardstock, plastic folders ... yes, I think we bought everything.

The two little girls were preparing for the back to school, for next week. They bought their school supplies well in advance. Closing her bag full of new materials, Amira thought aloud:

- All I have left to arrange, is the school uniform. I must hang up my jackets and pants, iron my shirts, and have my shoes shined. I must buy new socks, and hair bands.

At that moment, Dalya exclaimed:

- I completely forgot my school uniform! Thank you for reminding me. I too need to clean and iron it.

On this beautiful day at the end of August, the entire city of Georgetown was preparing for the back to school. Dalya and Amira parted each their way, at the school supply store. They each went home to get their uniforms ready for next week.

On the way back to the grand Mansion, Dalya organized her next days in her head:

- I must put away my summer clothes first; I won't have time to do it after the start of the school year. Then, I must wash my shirts and jackets. Afterwards, I must sew on the buttons of my jackets. I will ask Cristelle for a needle and thread. And I'll shine my shoes in the garage, so as not to dirty the floor. Amira is right; I also need new black socks and hair bands.

Several minutes of walking later, Dalya arrived at the grand Mansion. She had a lot of work to do, to prepare for the back to school. Dalya decided to go straight up to her bedroom to organize her closet.

Except that as soon as she entered the grand Mansion, Dalya heard a deafening din. Standing frozen and motionless in the hall of the grand Mansion, Dalya watched a strange scene happening before her eyes.

Within a minute, the assistant Igor ran up the stairs quickly. The furious screams of young Lyor Laszlo were heard upstairs. The head of the grand Mansion came out of the kitchen and he ran toward the Library. The maid Cristelle went back down the stairs and she ran toward the living room. The grand Mansion was overwhelmed by the sounds of songs, the banging on the pots, and the furious screams of Lyor.

Only the Snow Panther acted normally; Séraphine was lying on the edge of a window in the hall, watching all these people running in all directions. And it almost looked like the Snow Panther was watching the scene with an amused look.

Dalya Bouvard didn't understand why the employees were running everywhere, and what was the origin of all these noises. Suddenly, the help Cook Océanie entered the hall. She carried her baby Philippe in her arms. And strangely, in the midst of all this chaos, pots noises, rapid steps, furious screams, baby Philippe was laughing heartily.

Océanie easily guessed Dalya's confusion. And even before Dalya would ask what was going on, Océanie approached her, and she informed her in an amused voice:

- Earlier, little Demoiselles Ari and Adi were having fun and singing as usual. Apparently, Mr. Lyor Laszlo does not like songs, and even less children. He asked the little Demoiselles to stop singing like pots. Well…the little Demoiselles took that comment to heart. They took the pots from the kitchen, and they are running around all over the grand Mansion, singing very loudly, and banging on the pots.

Dalya was amazed by what she heard, and what she saw.

- My little sisters... the pots… I... I've only been away for a few hours, and I'm coming back to find this... they're running around... with pots...

Océanie continued with the same amused tone:

- The employees and Lyor Laszlo have been trying to catch them for a while now. Except that the little Demoiselles are fast and small, they easily sneak around everywhere.

At one point, the Cook Mr. Ferrero Lutché appeared in the hall. He seemed worried:

- When do I get my pots back? ... le mie padelle … I need them for tonight dinner sauce!

Without being able to restrain her amused laugh, Océanie replied to the Cook:

- I don't think your pots will be caught up so soon, Mr. Cook. The little Demoiselles are too fast.

At that moment, in the hall of the grand Mansion, in the midst of chaos and din, the Cook, the help Cook Océanie, her baby Philippe, and Dalya Bouvard… they were all overcome by an uncontrollable laugh.

While the entire town of Georgetown was preparing for the back to school, the grand Mansion was busy catching little twin girls, singing and banging on pots. This is what the last days of vacation look like in the grand Mansion.

Chapter 45

Ready

Wednesday, August 30ᵗʰ, 1893. In Master Barold's apartment.

The date of Antman Bouvard's trial was approaching. And since several days, Lawyer Sloan Wilfrid had trouble focusing on the other files of the firm. This matter occupied his mind completely. That day, Sloan Wilfrid decided to visit the Lawyer handling the case, Master Victor Barold.

- Good morning, Master Barold … good morning, Lyor. It's a beautiful sunny day outside!

With his usual smile, Lawyer Sloan Wilfrid greeted the two men seated on the armchairs in the living room. The old Lawyer's apartment had not changed its decor; books and files covered all the furniture, and the large curtains kept the sun out of the living room. The old Lawyer's mood didn't change either, he was still wearing his cozy pajamas and bathrobe, his hair curled in the air, and an annoyed grin was imprinted on his face. Master Barold whispered:

- I don't like sunny days! I don't like the sun! I don't like summer! I don't like the heat!

Sloan Wilfrid sat down on the chair next to Lyor, and he asked in a curious tone:

- I thought I'd visit you today to find out how the defense pleading is progressing. Where are you in this case?

The young Lyor Laszlo seemed to have accumulated weeks of sleepless nights; dark eyes circles, a wrinkled shirt, and an unshaven beard. He was lying on the couch looking exhausted and tired. Lyor replied in a dejected tone:

- It's not progressing at all. The case is very clear and previously judged; an offense of bad checks.

Sloan Wilfrid thought for a moment:

- Yes, I am well aware that the defense pleading will not be easy to write. But … can we use Antman Bouvard's difficult financial situation?

Master Barold remained indifferent and motionless in his armchair; he was reading a file, without paying attention to the conversation between the two young men. Only Lyor Laszlo replied:

- It would be useless to use this point, Wilfrid. The judge knows that Antman Bouvard and his family live in the annex house of the grand Mansion; he has a job at the Toscana restaurant, providing him with a secure and decent salary. And his daughter is a candidate to inherit a fortune. The alibi of the difficult financial situation does not work in this case.

Sloan Wilfrid leaned back on his chair, and he whispered:

- Surely there must be a solution ... surely there must be a solution ...

Laying his head on the edge of the armchair, Lyor Laszlo closed his eyes for a long minute, and he replied in a tired voice:

- This case seems to have already been decided. We looked for a solution in all legal texts. We've been looking for weeks. We searched for days and nights. The case is already judged.

A heavy silence settled in the living room. Lawyer Sloan Wilfrid knew that getting Antman Bouvard out of this situation would not be so easy. However, he clung to a small glimmer of hope that the great Master Victor Barold and the young Lyor Laszlo, would certainly find a solution to this case. Except that after several weeks of searching without results, this hope was beginning to fade away.

At one moment, the authoritative voice of Master Barold broke the silence in the living room:

- Lyor, go get us some croissants!

The young Lyor woke up from his brief nap; he seemed surprised by this request:

- I brought the croissants, barely an hour ago. The plate is still fu...

Master Barold displayed a sarcastic smile:

- These are chocolate croissants. I want jam croissants.

The young Lyor straightened up on his chair and he answered all confused:

- There are no jam croissants. The pastry shop only sells chocolate croi...

Master Barold ordered:

- The pastry shop two streets away, opposite to the public garden. They sell my jam croissants. Go get them for me! Hurry up!

The young Lyor Laszlo complied reluctantly; he stood up and he took his jacket before going out. Sloan Wilfrid needed no further assistance to understand that the old Lawyer wanted to speak to him in private, sending Lyor back for the croissants.

As soon as the apartment door closed, Master Barold handed a folder to Sloan Wilfrid. The young Lawyer took it, and he flipped through it quickly:

- This is the police report on the detention of Antman Bouvard.

Sloan Wilfrid observed the old Lawyer for a moment, trying to figure out what Master Barold wanted to say to him. And for the first time since their meeting, Master Barold displayed a worried air, he announced in a serious voice:

- Ernest Laszlo did not act alone in this affair.

Surprised by the words of the old Lawyer, Sloan Wilfrid was curious:

- How do you know that?

Pointing at the file he gave him, Master Barold explained:

- The police report is too rapid. Response times are abnormal.

At that moment, Sloan Wilfrid leafed through the folder in his hands for the 2nd time, and he was shocked by what he learned:

- Right ... that's right. The bank notified the police 15 minutes after the bad checks were deposited. The legal investigation was done in 30 minutes. The police order for Antman's arrest was done within 30 minutes. And the Lawsuit was written 10 minutes after the detention.

Master Barold said:

- The procedure for bad checks takes at least 3 days, between the bank and the police. In this case, the procedure was completed in an hour and a half. It is too rapid.

At that moment, Sloan Wilfrid came close to Master Barold's chair. Stunned by this discovery, Sloan Wilfrid thought aloud, leafing through the file for the 4th time:

- Yes, it's way too rapid! The procedure must go through several offices, and it requires legal paperwork. From 3 days to an hour and a half, it is strange. But... Master Barold, why do you think Ernest Laszlo did not act alone?

Master Barold laid back on his chair:

- Ernest Laszlo is haughty and arrogant. He uses threats and blackmail to achieve his ends. Nevertheless, he is a fearful and cowardly man, he rarely dares to bypass or defy the Law. Except for this case, he acted with full confidence, he forced the procedure so that the case could be dealt within an hour and a half, instead of 3 days ... and that can be explained by a single thing, Ernest Laszlo has the support of a high placed person!

Having worked with Lawyer Ernest Laszlo for several years, Sloan Wilfrid agreed with the old Lawyer on this point. In a worried and curious tone, Sloan Wilfrid asked:

- Who do you think helped him?

Master Barold remained silent, thinking for several long seconds. And Sloan Wilfrid used every neuron in his brain to find an answer to his question.

- Wilfrid... do you think that Ernest Laszlo and the Edelmen family are the only ones who want this little girl to fail in these Challenges of the Will?

The question was weird, but the answer was simple. Sloan Wilfrid replied with certainty:

- Well yes, of course! They are the only ones affected by this fortune!

Master Barold jumped up from his chair and he exclaimed:

- Wrong answer, Wilfrid! Very wrong answer! Think a little more. Who would it hurt if this girl succeeds to obtain this fortune?

Sloan Wilfrid's brain was working at full capacity, he thought aloud:

- Ernest Laszlo ... the Edelmen family ... their friends, their acquaintances ...

Master Barold ordered him:

- Think higher!

Sloan Wilfrid observed the old Lawyer:

- The Nobility ... the Bourgeois class ...

Master Barold repeated:

- Think higher!

In a second, a crazy idea crossed Sloan Wilfrid's mind, so crazy that he hesitated to speak his words. Surprised and confused, Sloan Wilfrid whispered:

- The ... the Government?

This time, Master Barold smiled. The old Lawyer leaned back on his chair:

- Dear Wilfrid ... you were wrong from the start on this matter of the Will! You thought that Ernest Laszlo and the Edelmen family were the only ones affected by this Will. Well, I correct you; it's about much more than money!

At this moment, Sloan Wilfrid was struggling to understand:

- How? Why would the Government interfere with this Will?

Master Barold continued:

- Imagine that a poor little girl, without lineage, without education, who passes the Challenges of the Will, and who succeeds to obtain this fortune. A poor little girl, a seller of vegetables and fruit at the market, who succeeds to obtain her place among the Nobility, willingly and above all by force. If she succeeds ... she will be a symbol of hope and courage for the people.

Stunned by this idea, Sloan Wilfrid fell back in his chair, looking surprised:

- This matter of the Will is taking on much larger dimensions than I thought! I understand better now the fury they all have against Dalya Bouvard. They are afraid that she will succeed!

A few moments of silence passed away. Sloan Wilfrid barely recovered from his shock; he asked in a determined voice:

- Master Barold ... What should I do?

The old Lawyer thought aloud:

- To fight better, you must use the same weapons as the enemy. If Ernest Laszlo has allies in high places, you must have them too!

Immediately, Sloan Wilfrid answered without hesitation:

- Congressman Yolan McKlain! He helped me twice to stop Ernest Laszlo's scheming against the Will. I will ask for his full support. He won't refuse it to me.

Master Barold approved this choice:

- And I wouldn't have chosen a better man than him. He is a man of integrity, honest, and above all a strong character when necessary. I would also like to propose a 2nd man to you ... Mr. Bahadir, he is the Private Secretary of Senator McGrover. He's a great friend. I'll send him a note. He will be very useful to you.

It seems that on this day, the two Lawyers decided about their side and their weapons.

Master Barold affirmed:

- If they want to fight...

And Sloan Wilfrid continued:

- ... We will be ready!

Chapter 46

Green stars

Friday, September 1ˢᵗ, 1893. In the morning, at the Royal Georgetown College.

Two days before Antman Bouvard's trial, many people were stressed and anxious by this event. At the end of her lessons at noon, Amira Mounier walked quickly toward the office of a Professor. When she knocked on the door, a man's voice was heard:

- Come in, Miss Amira.
- Good morning, Professor Canfield.

Professor Canfield was sitting behind his desk; dressed in his usual checkered suit, he was writing notes in a large register. When the student appeared before him, Professor Canfield stopped writing; he looked up at her and he smiled:

- What can I do for you, Miss Amira?

Amira asked in a courteous tone:

- I wanted your permission, Professor, to be absent on Monday, so that I could support my friend Dalya Bouvard.

Professor Canfield leaned back on his chair, and the tone of his voice became more serious:

- The trial of Mr. Antman Bouvard is the day after tomorrow?
- Yes, Professor. Morning at 9 AM.

Without hesitation, Professor Canfield replied:

- Certainly, Miss Amira! I will inform your Professors of your absence. It's the least we can do for Mademoiselle Dalya Bouvard.
- Thank you, Professor.

Before Amira would leave the office, Professor Canfield held her back for a moment:

- If I may ask you a favor, Miss Amira. Monday, I will be held up with a school board meeting. However, I would like to know what will happen in this trial.
- Understood, Professor Canfield. As soon as the trial ends, I will report the judgment to you, immediately.

The day before the trial. Sunday, September 3rd, 1893. Morning.

Very early this Sunday morning, Amira Mounier had finished preparing caramelized peach and crème anglaise tarts. When her father came down to the kitchen, he exclaimed:

- Good morning, Champion! The smell of the tarts is delicious!

Pouring coffee in a cup, Amira informed her father:

- Good morning, papa. So, your breakfast is on the tray. I made you sandwiches and a salad for lunch. I'll leave you a peach tart, if you want to have it with tea this afternoon.

Mr. Jacob Mounier smiled:

- Thank you, Champion! Are you going now?

Arranging the peach tarts in a basket, Amira replied:

- Yes, I'm going out right now, papa. Her father's trial is tomorrow. I absolutely must be near her today, to support her. I made these peach tarts just for her, they are her favorites. Professor Canfield has given me permission to be absent tomorrow, Monday, to attend the trial with her.

Helping his daughter to close the basket, Mr. Jacob Mounier thought in a worried voice:

- She's a brave demoiselle. I sincerely hope that everything will go well tomorrow.

Amira Mounier also prayed:

- I hope so too, papa. I hope so too.

Several minutes of walking later, Amira Mounier arrived at the front door of the grand Mansion. She paused for a moment in the large garden. Dalya Bouvard was her only and best friend. Dalya helped her overcome her stuttering, she always defended and supported her. So that day, Amira was determined to help her friend and support her. On the eve of the trial, Amira was certain that Dalya would be distressed and anxious. And knowing her since a long time now, Amira was convinced that Dalya will have panic attacks and difficulty breathing.

Regrouping her forces, and displaying a determined smile, Amira Mounier entered the grand Mansion. Suddenly, in the hall, Amira Mounier found herself in front of a chaotic scene.

In the hall of the grand Mansion, Lyor Laszlo was red with anger, he screamed out with all the might of his lungs:

- I LEFT MY FILES FOR A DAY!! ONE DAY ONLY!! AND YOU FOUND NOTHING BETTER TO DO THAN COLOR MY PAPERS!!

And across the hall, the little twin sisters Ari and Adi were fiercely defending themselves:

- NO THAT'S NOT TRUE!! NOT ONE DAY!! ONE AFTERNOON ONLY!! NOT ONE DAY!!

Between Lyor Laszlo and the little twin sisters, there were the maid Cristelle, and Dalya Bouvard. It seems that the young Lawyer Lyor Laszlo and the little twins were quarreling, Cristelle and Dalya being in the middle, they were trying to calm them down and keep them away from each other.

Amira approached Dalya and she whispered to her in a worried tone:

- What's going on?

Repressing a laugh, Dalya tried to push her little sisters away and lead them back into the living room:

- My little twin sisters colored the papers of Lyor … the usual fooleries!

And with an amused smile, Cristelle tried to move young Lyor away, pushing him toward the Library:

- The young Demoiselles just wanted to have a little fun!

Lyor Laszlo was mad with rage:

- NO BUT THEY NEVER STOP THESE TWO PESTS!! THEY COLORED EVERYTHING!! ALL MY PAPERS ARE COLORED!!

And Ari and Adi were seriously pissed off:

- WE NOT PESTS!! WE ZENTILLES!! AND WE NOT COLORED ALL THE PAPERS!! WE ONLY COLOR MOST PAPERS!! THERE'S STILL 2 PAPERS NOT COLORED!!

The arguments of the little twins provoked even more the anger of the young Lawyer, and the laughs of Cristelle and Dalya.

- MY FILES ARE FULL OF PINK FLOWERS, BLUE HEARTS, AND YELLOW STARS!!

The little twins replied with one voice:

- NO THAT'S NOT TRUE!! WE DREW STARS IN GREEN, NOT IN YELLOW!!

In front of this scene, Amira Mounier remained motionless and frozen in the hall of the grand Mansion. She didn't know what to do to help. A laugh escaped from Cristelle who pushed an enraged Lyor Laszlo toward the Library. And Dalya barely repressed her laugh, pushing the little twins toward the living room.

Amira Mounier observed this quarrel with surprise. And at one point, Amira smiled. A small detail caught her attention; her friend Dalya was struggling to breathe. But it wasn't because of anxiety and distress. Dalya Bouvard was struggling to breathe because of holding back her giggles, in front of the quarrel between Lyor Laszlo and her little twin sisters.

A few hours later.

The young Lyor Laszlo finally arrived at Master Victor Barold's apartment. As soon as Lyor appeared in the salon, Master Barold closed his book, and he asked in a curious tone:

-   And my croissants?

On the living room table, already inundated with books, Lyor placed a box of pastries and a file full of papers. Immediately, Lyor collapsed on the armchair with a dejected air, and he announced in a grave voice:

-   We have a problem, Master Barold.

While taking a croissant, the old Lawyer answered in a monotonous tone:

-   One problem more or less, it doesn't matter, tomorrow's trial is lost in advance!

In a frustrated voice, Lyor explained:

-   I'm going to have to rewrite your entire defense pleading for tomorrow.

Master Barold observed Lyor with a curious look, while tasting his croissant. Lyor straightened up from his chair, he opened the file, and he spread the papers on the table:

-   I left this file for one day, in the grand Mansion. And the little pests had fun coloring it!

Master Barold stretch out his neck to look at the colored papers, while finishing his last bite of croissant. Spreading the papers on the table, Lyor muttered furiously:

-   A work of several weeks!! Days and nights of research!! And the only papers they found to color are those in this folder!! They filled all the papers with flowers, hearts, and stars!! These little twins do fooleries all the time!!

Master Barold stretched out his hand to get a 2nd croissant, while thinking in an annoyed voice:

-   It will be difficult to focus tomorrow, during the trial, reading a file full of scribbles!! Try to convince the judge, with arguments colored in pink flowers, blue hearts, and green stars... green stars... green sta...

Suddenly, Master Barold froze in his movement. Young Lyor Laszlo did not realize it, he continued to spread all the papers on the living room table, muttering furiously:

-   I must rewrite the entire file!! I will spend another sleepless night because of these pests!! They are wasting my time!!

Before taking a 2nd croissant, Master Barold lengthened his neck to better read a small detail on a paper left by Lyor on the living room table. A long minute of thinking later, Master Barold smiled. It was a very rare and strange thing from an old Lawyer with a difficult character and always upset. Master Barold murmured in an amused voice:

- Green stars ... green stars ... green stars ...

At one point, Master Barold pulled himself together. He took his 2nd croissant, and he announced to Lyor in a calm and confident tone:

- It won't be necessary to rewrite the file, Lyor. We'll manage tomorrow. You have worked enough so far, it is better that you rest tonight, a long day awaits us tomorrow!

Lyor Laszlo stopped rearranging the papers, he looked at the old Lawyer with a surprised stare:

- Are you sure, Master Barold? I can rewrite the most important papers. I can spend a sleepless night, and prepare them for you, tomorrow first hour!

The old man relaxed in his chair and he tasted his croissant with a slow move:

- Unnecessary ... unnecessary. These drawings do not disturb, quite the contrary. I admit that these colors embellish the defense file. And by the way... these are pretty green stars, don't you think?!

For a long minute, Lyor Laszlo watched the old Lawyer, with a confused air. Just a second ago, the old Lawyer complained about the difficulty of being in front of the judge, holding a document full of scribbles. Lyor Laszlo did not understand this sudden change of mind.

And the strangest thing was Master Victor Barold's smile. During all these months of work and research, Lyor never saw the old Lawyer smiling.

That evening, Master Victor Barold smiled, while savoring his croissant with a slow move. And Dear readers, I confirm to you, it was not at all an innocent smile!

Chapter 47

The 2nd clue

The day before the trial. Sunday, September 3rd, 1893. The night.

Finally, the grand Mansion fell into silence. The employees finished their work for the day, the little twins fell asleep in their beds, and Dalya Bouvard returned to her room.

Tomorrow's trial will change the life of the Bouvard family forever. Remaining alone in her room, anxiety and worry overwhelmed increasingly Dalya Bouvard. It was quite useless to lie down in bed, Dalya was certain that sleep would not visit her that night. She sat down on an armchair in front of the fireplace, and she took a book in her hands. Except that difficult questions caught up with the little Dalya Bouvard.

- *What will happen tomorrow at the trial? What will become of my father? What will the judge's decision be tomorrow? What will become of me and my little sisters? How are we going to get out of this situation? What will the judgment be tomorrow? ... what will the judgment be tomorrow? ... what will be the judgment be tom ...*

Dalya slammed her book shut; her throat was choking and her hands were shaking. Anxiety invaded her, Dalya couldn't sit still for a second. She stood up and she walked toward the windows of her bedroom, to get some fresh air.

Suddenly, Dalya stopped. A strange little box caught her eye. It has been several months since the Excelbox's help was not asked. Placed on the desk, the Excelbox was recharging on the moonlight. The cage was welded by 4 yellow gold cylinders, forged in the shape of a vine plant. Inside the cage, the clock peacefully counted the time passing; the small needle was fixed on the date of the 4th Challenge, December 12th, 1893. The big needle was heading toward the next day September 04th, 1893. A power and serenity emanated from the Excelbox.

Strangely, Dalya felt attracted to this strange box.

- *The Excelbox has always provided me with answers to difficult questions. Could this strange box have the answer for tomorrow's judgment? Does the Excelbox know what the judge will decide tomorrow? Does the Excelbox know my father's fate tomorrow?*

Dalya Bouvard came forward and she sat down in front of the desk. Mechanically, without even thinking, she wrote on a small piece of paper, and she placed it on the rectangular opening.

What is the 2nd clue?

Immediately, the small piece of paper disappeared inside the box. A blinding spark emanated from the Excelbox and lit up the entire room with a powerful and intimidating light. And a small piece of paper appeared at the rectangular opening. For the 2nd time in several months, Dalya Bouvard asked. And the Excelbox answered.

Breathe. Exhale. Confront.
To survive the outside, look inside.

When Dalya picked up the piece of paper, she was surprised by what she read.

- This 2nd clue is almost identical to the 1st clue. The words, breathe, and exhale, were also in the 1st clue.

And just like in the 1st clue, Dalya spontaneously obeyed the directives of the Excelbox. She closed her eyes, she took a deep breath, and she exhaled all her anxiety and fear. Strangely, after only a few times, this simple move helped her feel good and it calmed her anxiety. Dalya continued to read this 2nd clue.

- The same phrase repeats itself ... to survive the outside, look inside. But, survive what? What does outside mean? Looking where? Inside of what?

Even if Dalya didn't understand this 2nd clue, she was confident that she would find the right explanation at the right time. This has always been the Excelbox method; enigmatic clues, explained at the right time.

Before Dalya would put down the piece of paper of the 2nd clue, she noticed that only one word changed.

- At the 1st clue, there was the verb wait. In this 2nd clue, the verb is to confront. This is the only change from the 1st clue. Breathe, exhale, confront ... confront ... confront ...

Thanks to a single word ... confront ... the Excelbox succeeded in rekindling a small flame inside the little Dalya Bouvard. By murmuring this word several times, Dalya clearly felt the encouragements of this strange box.

It happens that sometimes, when we are invaded by fear, distress, worry ... when we find ourselves in a difficult and painful situation ... the only thing we can do, at this precise moment, is ... to confront!

Chapter 48

The trial

Monday, September 4th, 1893.

This September day was crucial; the fate of Antman Bouvard and his family will be decided. Some people were eager for the judgment, other people were confident about their plan, and most people were anxious. It promised to be a long day.

The Court was a huge, intimidating building, icy gray marble, hundred-step stairs, and windows indicating thousands of offices.

The young Lyor Laszlo was leaning on a beam at the entrance of the Court. He awaited the arrival of his mentor Sloan Wilfrid and Lawyer Master Victor Barold. Lyor Laszlo consulted the defense pleading file for the last and the 100th time.

- Good morning, Lyor.

Sloan Wilfrid joined Lyor on the immense stairs of the Court. And for the first time in a long time, Sloan Wilfrid looked worried and tense. He had promised Dalya to do everything possible to help her father. Except that the judgment was very clear even before the start of the hearing. Antman Bouvard risked a few more months of detention.

The young Lyor Laszlo handed him a file:

- Good morning, Wilfrid. Here is the defense pleading file. I checked it several times last night.

At first glance at what was handed to him, Sloan Wilfrid looked surprised:

- What is ... why are there pink flowers and green stars on all the papers? The entire defense pleading file is colored.

Lyor took a long breath to repress his anger:

- The little twin girls have added their personal touch! ... anyway, I believe that Master Barold can manage to lighten the judgment for a few months with these arguments. It's really all we can do for Antman Bouvard.

Sloan Wilfrid reread a few paragraphs, thinking aloud:

- Good ... good ... the defense is well written, nice job Lyor. This case is not easy to deal with; it seems to have already been decided. Antman Bouvard risks at least 7 more months of detention. But if we manage to lighten his sentence, we will have gained 1 or 2 months. Master Barold will join us in a few minutes. I met him in the café at the corner of the street, he is having breakfast there.

Lyor exclaimed:

- He could eat on this important day?! I barely had my coffee this morning!

Sloan Wilfrid forced himself to smile:

- Master Barold is not someone who stresses easily. That's why I chose him to lead this case. And besides, I thank you for having assisted him in the preparation of the defense pleading, you were a remarkable help to him, Lyor!

The two Lawyers waited on the stairs of the Court, exchanging a few ideas on the defense file. When a few minutes later, Master Barold joined them.

- Good morning, Gentlemen!

For the first time in 20 years, Master Victor Barold wore a suit and tie, instead of his usual pajamas and cozy bathrobe. The old Lawyer looked elegant in a perfectly polished azur blue suit, impeccable white shirt, and matching blue tie. He arranged his curly hair as best he could, but it rebelled all the same. And despite his big belly, his very small size and his bald head, Master Victor Barold had made a great effort to be particularly elegant, that day.

Except that the strangest thing was not the old Lawyer's elegance, but his mood. Master Victor Barold seemed in a happy mood, which was very strange for his usual upset character, and very strange on this day when everyone was stressed and anxious.

Sloan Wilfrid and Lyor Laszlo exchanged a surprised look. Sloan Wilfrid forced himself to sound less worried:

- Good morning, Master Barold, we were waiting for you.

Immediately, the young Lyor hastened to hand over a file to the old Lawyer:

- Here are all of your defense pleading documents, Master Barold. I have included all the notes that you indicated to me. Everything is organized and ready for today !

Clutching the file in his hand, Master Victor Barold turned toward the huge building of the Court, and he announced in a determined voice:

- Gentlemen, it's time to end this case!

Sloan Wilfrid and Lyor Laszlo exchanged a confused look, and they followed the old Lawyer inside.

In the Courtroom.

The place was quiet and serene, yet no one felt comfortable there. All the people who entered there felt distress and uneasiness. It was a large room, illuminated by a multitude of small windows. Fifteen rows of black wooden benches were arranged in parallel all along the room.

And at the end of the rows, two long tables were separated, clearly indicating the place of the defense Lawyers and the place of the accusation Lawyers. And at the front of the room, a large table raised by a few steps, faced all the people present; it was the place of the judge.

When Dalya entered the Courtroom, she immediately sat down in the 1st row of the benches, just behind the defense Lawyers' table. One, her legs no longer held her because of the distress. And two, Dalya wanted to see and hear everything that will happen in this trial. It seemed like a long day.

Amira Mounier was absent from school that day to support her friend Dalya. Amira followed Dalya like a shadow, and she sat down near her. Giorgi Bouvard was brave to visit his brother Antman in detention, and deliver the baskets of clothes and food to him. And on this important day, Uncle Giorgi Bouvard was also present to support his little niece. Sitting down next to her, Uncle Giorgi whispered to her in a caring voice:

- Everything will be fine, Biggo! You'll see, everything will be fine!

The Courtroom was filling up quickly. The Lawyer Ernest Laszlo entered with an arrogant and confident step. He headed straight for the long accusation table, and he put down his briefcase and files there. Observing the room with a scrutinizing air, the Lawyer Ernest Laszlo stared at the little Dalya Bouvard for long seconds, with a devilish smile.

A familiar face entered the Courtroom, and he sat on the first row of benches, just behind the Lawyer Ernest Laszlo. Dalya was surprised to see the Governor's nephew; Mr. Ferdinand Edelmen. The old man had a calm face and a haughty smile. The Lawyer Ernest Laszlo turned to his friend Mr. Ferdinand Edelmen, they chatted and laughed quietly. Dalya Bouvard remained silent and anxious, watching the two men share a laugh.

Amira Mounier barely repressed her anger:

- Why is the Governor's nephew attending your father's trial?! It's none of his business! Doesn't he have anything else to do but follow other people's worries?! No, but what a family of vultures!

Suddenly, the Lawyer Ernest Laszlo and the Governor's nephew Ferdinand Edelmen, stopped in their discussion, and they looked confused, when they saw a man enter the Courtroom. Dalya turned toward the entrance, and she noticed a man over sixty, very short in stature, with a big belly, a bald head, and curly hair, wearing an azur blue tie suit. The old man walked straight to the long defense table, he put his file there, and he sat down on the chair.

Sitting just behind the long defense table, Amira, Dalya, and Uncle Giorgi whispered:

- Is this the Lawyer in charge of defending your father?
- Yes, I think so... he sat in front of us... I think that's him.
- He seems to be well experienced.

Immediately, the young Lyor Laszlo and the Lawyer Sloan Wilfrid entered the Courtroom, and they settled in the 3rd row of benches. Lyor and Wilfrid wanted to keep their help and support in this matter secret, so they sat away from Dalya and Master Victor Barold, so as not to arouse the suspicions of the Lawyer Ernest Laszlo.

Sloan Wilfrid forced himself to look calm, he smiled discreetly at Dalya.

Looking confused and surprised, the Lawyer Ernest Laszlo asked his right arm to come closer:

-   Wilfrid ... what is Victor Barold doing here? He lost his Lawyer's license 20 years ago! Why is he sitting at the defense table?

Sloan Wilfrid replied in an innocent tone:

-   I don't have the faintest idea, Mr. Ernest Laszlo. No idea!

And as I told you before, Dear readers, everyone who enters the Courtroom feels a distress and uneasiness. The Lawyer Ernest Laszlo was confused by the presence of Master Victor Barold. The Governor's nephew Mr. Ferdinand Edelmen was eager to get this matter over with. Dalya Bouvard was anxious by her father's trial. Amira Mounier was worried about her only and best friend. Uncle Giorgi Bouvard was stressing over the fate of his niece and brother. Lyor Laszlo and Sloan Wilfrid were nervous to know the judgment of this case. And Master Victor Barold ... he was readjusting the little flower pinned to his jacket. So, everyone was anxious. Almost everyone.

The start of the trial.

When the judge entered the Courtroom, all the discussions died down, and everyone present stood up. The judge sat down in his big armchair, and he ordered the people to sit down again. He wore a long black outfit, and large glasses, snow-white hair clearly indicated his advanced age and years of experience in the job.

Immediately, the judge knocked his desk with a small wooden gavel, announcing in a loud voice:

-   Ladies and gentlemen, I announce the start of the trial for case No. 19/05/21. The detainee is Antman Bouvard.

Immediately, Amira Mounier felt her friend's anxiety; she held her hand:

-   Everything will be fine, Dalya ... everything will be fine.

Leafing through a file, the judge continued to announce:

-   In this case, the accusation Lawyer is Master Ernest Laszlo. Would you come before me, please.

The Lawyer Ernest Laszlo stood up and he walked toward the judge, replying in an arrogant voice:

- Present, your honor.

And as expected since the beginning of her father's detention, when Dalya refused to sign the abandonment of the inheritance, the Lawyer Ernest Laszlo had promised her to appear to Court and incarcerate Antman Bouvard, at the maximum of his legal sentence. Ernest Laszlo was known to be the best Lawyer in town. At that moment, Dalya's entire body trembled, and her throat tightened.

The judge continued reading:

- And the detainee's defense Lawyer is ... is ...

At this moment, the judge seemed confused by the name he had to announce. After a few seconds of astonishment, the judge cleared his throat and he announced:

- And the detainee's defense Lawyer is ... Lyor Laszlo.

It was as if lightning paralyzed everyone in the Courtroom. All surprised eyes turned toward the young Lyor Laszlo, seated far away, in the 3rd row of the visitors' benches. And spontaneously, Lyor Laszlo uttered two words:

- Oh shit!

Silence and utter confusion settled in the Courtroom. The judge continued:

- Lyor Laszlo, would you please come before me.

Dalya Bouvard was paralyzed in her place; she did not understand what was announced by the judge. Amira Mounier became mute, she had no more words to say to reassure her friend. Uncle Giorgi seemed surprised by this announcement. The Lawyer Ernest Laszlo lost his arrogant smile and haughty confidence when he heard his son's name. The Governor's nephew Ferdinand Edelmen sat up from his seat, and he looked surprised at the announcement. Sloan Wilfrid and Master Barold exchanged an accomplice look.

As for Lyor Laszlo, he was thunderstruck when he heard his name; his brain stopped working, his throat tightened, his face went pale, his heart raced, and his body trembled.

The judge repeated with an impatient air:

- Lyor Laszlo, in front of me! Come on young man, I don't have only this case to deal with, today!

Unable to think for himself and make the slightest move, Lyor Laszlo was pushed by Sloan Wilfrid to get up and to appear before the judge. At one moment, the father and the son stood side by side, in front of the judge. The father represented the accusation, and the son represented the defense.

Immediately, Dalya turned her head back, toward the Lawyer Sloan Wilfrid, and she whispered in a trembling voice:

- Lyor? Will it be Lyor who will defend my father? Are you sure?

Sloan Wilfrid whispered with a confident tone:

- Lyor Laszlo is our best chance!

Standing in front of the judge, Lyor Laszlo did not dare to raise his eyes toward his father Ernest Laszlo. This is the 2nd time that the name of young Lyor Laszlo is mentioned in a situation that did not concern him. And above all, this is the 2nd time that Lyor did not know how his name was written in this case. Except that the answers to these questions won't take long to come.

- Master Victor Barold ... come before me, please.

At the judge's command, Master Barold stood up and he walked over to the large table. The judge seemed surprised:

- Master Victor Barold, I did not expect to see you here today. It's been almost 20 years since you left this profession. To what do we owe the honor of this visit?

The old Lawyer replied with an innocent smile:

- It seemed like a nice day for some fresh air, Your Honor. I came out to stretch my legs ... after 20 years of rest.

The judge froze in his chair, and Lyor Laszlo looked more confused than ever. The Lawyer Ernest Laszlo affirmed in an impatient and angry tone:

- Victor Barold lost his Lawyer's license 20 years ago! He has nothing to do here!

And the answer didn't take long to come; Master Barold immediately retorted:

- I am here as Legal Counsel only. I assist Lyor Laszlo in his defense.

This news shocked not only the judge and the Lawyer Ernest Laszlo, but especially the young Lyor Laszlo, who turned to observe Master Barold. For several months, Lyor was Master Barold's assistant. And today, Master Barold claims to be Lyor's assistant?! But what is really happening?

The judge resumed reading the file, thinking aloud:

- Master Victor Barold ... Legal Counsel ... Alright ... Noted.

The three Lawyers stood before the judge in a tense silence. Without looking up from the documents, the judge asked in a curious tone:

-   Ernest Laszlo represents his own Law firm. Lyor Laszlo, which firm do you represent?

Immediately, Master Barold replied :

-   Your Honor, Lyor Laszlo will present the defense as independent Lawyer.

The judge straightened his glasses and continued reading:

-   Alright … Alright.

Confused by what was unfolding in front of him, Lyor Laszlo said in a trembling voice:

-   But I ... I'm not a Lawyer yet, Your Honor. I don't have my Lawyer's license, yet!

In front of this objection, Master Barold replied by pointing to a few papers, placed on the judge's table:

-   Your Honor, enclosed in the file, you will find the Certificate of 3 years of Law courses at the University of Georgetown, the Certificate of training at the Law firm, as well as the Registration receipt for the Bar exam of Mr. Lyor Laszlo.

At that moment, the young Lyor Laszlo and his father turned toward the old Lawyer. It seems that Master Barold has prepared his move very well. The judge found the papers indicated by Master Barold, and he affirmed in a decided tone:

-   Good ... very good ... all documents are in order. I accept that Lyor Laszlo represents the defense of the detainee Antman Bouvard.

This confirmation made Lyor Laszlo tremble, and it enraged his father Ernest Laszlo, and it made Master Victor Barold smile. The judge observed the three Lawyers for a few long seconds, thinking aloud:

-   The father and the son ... against each other. This is the first time in my career that I will decide in such a situation. And on top of that, a Lawyer reappears after 20 years of absence.

At one point, the judge pulled himself together and he ordered the Lawyers still standing in front of him, in an authoritative tone:

-   Gentlemen ... I want a calm and simple trial. The defense and accusation Lawyers will have 10 minutes each to present their pleading. I will make a judgment today. This case has gone on long enough. We start in 5 minutes, get ready !

In the private defense room.

The defense room was small; a desk and a few armchairs were installed there. Lyor Laszlo entered first, his legs no longer held him, he immediately sat down on the first chair he found in front of him. Master Victor Barold followed him into the private room, smiling calmly. Sloan Wilfrid joined them a second later, and he closed the door of the private defense room.

Sitting in a state of shock, the young Lyor Laszlo clutched his brain with both hands, trying to figure out what had just happened. Sloan Wilfrid and Master Barold remained calm and silent, standing in front of Lyor.

After a minute of a tense silence, Lyor Laszlo couldn't take it anymore; he needed answers, he needed to understand. The young Lyor Laszlo looked up at Sloan Wilfrid, and he asked in a trembling voice:

- What is happening? Why does my name always appear in the most insane places? First the Governor's Will, and now the defense of Antman Bouvard!! How was my name written for the defense of this case?

At this moment, Master Victor Barold replied with an amused smile:

- You're asking the wrong person, kid.

Sloan Wilfrid remained silent. And the young Lyor Laszlo was even more confused:

- How? ... Why am I involved in this case? What's going on?

Master Barold and Sloan Wilfrid exchanged an accomplice look. They've been hiding their plan for months. It was time for Lyor Laszlo to find out the truth.

With a calm move, Master Barold took a long black Lawyer's robe from his bag and he affirmed in a determined voice:

- I've been waiting 20 years for this revenge! 20 years patiently waiting for revenge on your father Ernest Laszlo! And when you came to my apartment a few months ago, I knew it was an opportunity not to be missed!

Lyor Laszlo observed the old Lawyer with a curious look:

- But... I don't understand... what opportunity are you talking about? When Wilfrid asked you to defend Antman Bouvard, you refused! You threw us out! ... What made you change your mind?

A smile appeared on Master Barold's face:

- You, Lyor! ... Thanks to you, I changed my mind. I easily understood Ernest Laszlo's blackmail in this case. He had the father of this little girl imprisoned, in order to force her to give up this inheritance. The idea of defeating Ernest Laszlo's plan was interesting. But, defeating Ernest Laszlo's plan with his own son ... beating Ernest Laszlo with his own son ... oh, that was a very, very interesting idea!

Master Barold advanced toward Lyor, and he confirmed his plan:

-   You're the only reason why I agreed to help you with this case. During all these months, I prepared you for this trial!

Lyor Laszlo was stunned by the revelations he just heard. During all these months, Lyor Laszlo thought to only help and assist Master Barold. Except at that moment, Lyor understood that Master Barold and Sloan Wilfrid were preparing him to face his father in this trial.

Immediately, the young Lyor turned toward his mentor:

-   You sold me, Wilfrid?! … To beat my father, you sold me?!

Walking a few steps toward Lyor, Lawyer Sloan Wilfrid explained in a calm tone:

-   I must help Antman Bouvard get out of this situation, at all costs. And the only ones who can do it, are Master Barold… and you, Lyor!

Lyor Laszlo's body trembled with shock and fear:

-   But ... but I'm not yet a Lawyer! … I can't defend him! … I can't defend him!

Spontaneously, Master Barold put the long black Lawyer's robe on young Lyor Laszlo's shoulders, and he said:

-   It's already decided, kid! You will appear before the judge, in 5 minutes!

Sloan Wilfrid buttoned up Lyor's black Lawyer's robe:

-   Listen to me carefully ... you have mastered this case perfectly well, Lyor! You know the defense pleading by heart! You've been working on it for months! Do everything you can to reduce Antman Bouvard's sentence! Give it all your best!

Quickly, Lyor Laszlo unbuttoned his black Lawyer's robe:

-   Wilfrid … please don't do this to me! It's my first case, and I must confront my father, he's going to crush me! … This case has already been judged, I will fail, my career will be over before it even begins! … Please don't do this to me, Wilfrid!

Master Barold readjusted the dress on Lyor's shoulders, letting out an amused laugh:

-   I admit that in both cases, I am a winner. If you fail in this defense, your father will be humiliated by his son's failure. And if by any miracle you succeed in beating him, your father will be humiliated by the success of his son … funny situation!

Sloan Wilfrid repressed a giggle, and he buttoned up Lyor's black Lawyer's robe.

-   Take a deep breath, and defend Antman Bouvard in front of the judge!

Lyor unbuttoned his black Lawyer's robe, murmuring in a trembling, pleading voice:

-   Wilfrid…I can't…he's going to crush me…I can't…I'm begging you…I can't…

For a long minute, Sloan Wilfrid and Lyor Laszlo fought to close and open the buttons of the black Lawyer's robe. Lyor Laszlo didn't want any of this responsibility, and Sloan Wilfrid was determined to make his plan work. At one point, Master Victor Barold held the hands of the young Lyor, and he gave him a file, ordering in a serious tone:

- Come on, kid! Pull yourself together!

Tired of the shock of events, and tired of struggling to unbutton his Lawyer's robe, Lyor Laszlo gave up his fight. With a quick movement, Sloan Wilfrid buttoned up the Lawyer's robe. And Master Barold gave his instructions to Lyor Laszlo:

- Take a deep breath. Stand straight. Speak your defense pleading slowly. Take it one point at a time. Do not rush. Watch the judge a few times. Review your notes between two sentences.

This time, Lyor Laszlo begged the old Lawyer:

- Master Barold ... I can't ... I beg you ... Master, I can't ...

Except that it was too late, Master Barold's decision had been made several months ago. Master Barold adjusted Lyor's tie, while insisting on his last instruction:

- And above all, above all... don't forget the green stars! Wonderful green stars! It's your most formidable weapon!

At that moment, Lyor Laszlo asked in a confused tone:

- What green stars?! But what are you talking about?! The fate of a man will be decided today, my career is at stake today, and you speak to me of green stars!! You're kidding, I hope?!

Master Barold answered in a serious voice:

- No, I'm not kidding, Lyor! And I insist, don't forget the green stars! They are wonderful!

At this moment, a man knocked on the door:

- The trial resumes. The defense Lawyer is requested to come to the Courtroom.

Immediately, anxiety invaded the body of Lyor Laszlo and he screamed:

- WILFRID!! REMIND ME TO KILL YOU AT THE END OF THIS TRIAL!!

Pushing Lyor Laszlo out of the private defense room, Sloan Wilfrid let out an anxious and amused chuckle, at the same time:

- You can count on me!

In the Courtroom.

Sitting next to Dalya, Amira Mounier perfectly felt her friend's worry. And even if with a trembling voice and a tight throat, Amira tried to reassure her:

- Everything will be fine, Dalya. Mr. Sloan Wilfrid promised to arrange this situation. Everything will be fine.

Uncle Giorgi thought aloud:

- The Lawyers seem competent. They seem to have worked on this case for several months.

Dalya whispered in a worried tone:

- I should have given up this inheritance... I should have signed Lawyer Ernest Laszlo's paper... I should have given up this inheritance... I should have obeyed what he asked me to d...

Immediately, Amira interrupted her:

- Abandoning this inheritance would be a mistake! Governor Iskander Balthazar himself put your name on this Will! He didn't choose you at random, Dalya! ... and even if you give up this inheritance, what guarantees do you have that Lawyer Ernest Laszlo will keep his word and he will help your father in his detention?

Amira Mounier's arguments were very true and fair. Dalya had no trust in Lawyer Ernest Laszlo.

When a door opened, three men entered the Courtroom. Lyor Laszlo wore a long black robe, he held a file in his hand, he advanced with a forced step toward the long table of the defense, and he settled there for the first time in his career. Master Barold and Sloan Wilfrid sat in the visitor's benches, just behind Dalya, Amira, and Uncle Giorgi.

Immediately, a second door opened, letting in the Lawyer Ernest Laszlo. And just like his son Lyor, Ernest Laszlo wore a long black robe. When he arrived at the long accusation table, Ernest Laszlo dropped his files with a snap that clearly indicated his anger. Ernest Laszlo observed his son Lyor with a furious and confused look; he still did not understand why his son was running against him in this case.

Seated a few benches back, Master Barold muttered in an interested tone:

- Today, we will find out if the young Lyor Laszlo is gifted at being a Lawyer!

Sloan Wilfrid crossed his arms, and he thought aloud and worried:

- I hope so ... I hope so. Good luck Lyor!

When the judge came in and he sat down in his big chair, everyone present fell silent. The judge spoke in a clear, authoritative voice:

- The trial for the Antman Bouvard case begins. Ernest Laszlo, representing the accusation, will start first. Then, it will be the turn of Lyor Laszlo, representing the defense. 10 minutes each for the pleading. Ernest Laszlo, it's your turn.

The Lawyer Ernest Laszlo had been preparing for this day for months. He had forced Dalya Bouvard to abandon this inheritance. And since she refused to sign the abandonment paper for this inheritance, Ernest Laszlo had sworn to keep her father Antman Bouvard in detention for as long as possible. Lawyer Ernest Laszlo was determined to make Dalya Bouvard pay for her disobedience.

With a confident move, the Lawyer Ernest Laszlo stood up, he took his file in his hand, he advanced toward the judge's table, and he delivered his accusation pleading:

- Your Honor ... Ladies and gentlemen. I present to you today the charges against Antman Bouvard.

First, Antman Bouvard is guilty of having issued four bad checks. The offenses were committed on March 9th, March 17th, and March 24th, to the detriment of physical persons, his card game friends. Antman Bouvard, currently working as a courier in a restaurant, said he had a bank account with a checkbook. The checks were not honored because there was not enough money in the defendant's account.

Second, the element of bad faith is present in this case. The accused knew well that there was no money in his bank account when he issued the checks to his friends.

Third, the accused's addiction to the game of cards makes him a risky element for all physical persons. It is true that the game of cards is not illegal, and prohibited by Law. Addiction to playing cards, however, is detrimental to the order of our Society.

Fourth, the accused uses manipulation and lies to extort money from his friends. Antman Bouvard uses the position of his daughter, Dalya Bouvard, named Heiress in the Will of the Late Governor. However, this little girl did not yet pass all the Challenges of the Will, and therefore she has not yet inherited this money. The accused misleads his friends by promising them sums of money that he does not yet have.

Your Honor ... Ladies and gentlemen. This case is quite clear. There are 4 charges; writing bad checks, bad faith, cards' game addiction, and manipulation.
I, Ernest Laszlo, Lawyer representing the accusation in this trial, request the maximum sentence against the accused Antman Bouvard. That is 11 months of detention. The role of all of us, is to protect our Society and ensure order.
Thank you, your honor.

When the Lawyer Ernest Laszlo finished, he turned and sat down at his accusation table. Ernest Laszlo displayed an arrogant and proud smile. The nephew Mr. Ferdinand Edelmen did not repress his joy, after having heard the accusation pleading of his friend. The two men exchanged a confident and happy look.

Seated a few steps away, Dalya Bouvard felt her heart ache, her hands trembling and her face become pale. Dalya was certain that the Lawyer Ernest Laszlo would drag down her father Antman in this case; he had sworn it to her.

A bench behind Dalya, Lawyer Sloan Wilfrid crossed his arms. He looked worried and anxious. Sloan Wilfrid thought aloud:

- Ernest Laszlo outdid himself in his accusation pleading today! He mentioned all the points of the defense. There is no argument left for Lyor Laszlo to defend. The judge already looks convinced. Lyor Laszlo is grilled. Antman Bouvard is condemned. But what are we going to do now? How are we going to get out of this situation? How are we going to get out of this situation?

Sitting next to Sloan Wilfrid, Master Barold whispered in a strange calm tone:

- The green stars ... Lyor Laszlo has only the green stars left to use...

Sloan Wilfrid turned toward the old Lawyer, and he looked at him with a confused look, not understanding why the old Lawyer insists on the green stars. From the beginning of this case, Sloan Wilfrid was sure that Master Barold was the best Lawyer in town. And despite the old Lawyer's eccentric ways and crazy ideas, Sloan Wilfrid had complete faith in him. Except that, after hearing Ernest Laszlo's perfect accusation pleading, Sloan Wilfrid got worried.

The judge announced:

- Lyor Laszlo, it's your turn now.

After his father's perfect accusation pleading, Lyor Laszlo seemed struck by lightning. Since the beginning of his legal internship in his father's firm, the young Lyor was aware of his father's exceptional skills in pleading. And even though they were increasingly in conflict in recent years, Lyor Laszlo admired his father's intelligence in handling legal matters.

Except that day, the young Lyor Laszlo did not want to oppose his father in front of the judge. Lyor Laszlo never imagined one day being in this situation; he remained paralyzed in his chair. The judge grew impatient:

- Must I come down to bring you myself, Lyor Laszlo? Move forward, please!

A grave silence reigned in the Courtroom. Having no other choice, the young Lyor Laszlo got up, and he advanced toward the judge's table, with a hesitant step. With a trembling voice and pale lips, Lyor Laszlo delivered the first defense pleading of his career:

- Your Honor. Gentlemen and lad... sorry... Ladies and Gentlemen... I... I... represent the defense of the accused Antman Bouvard. The points ... all the points raised by the accusation are ... are exaggerated and ... and ... I will present to you the points of defense of ... of ... Antman Bouvard ... which are the following ... the ... the ... it is true that the checks were ... bad checks ... except ... except that ... the ...

Lyor Laszlo's throat choked increasingly, and his sentences became more incomprehensible. In the benches, people's reactions differed. The Lawyer Ernest Laszlo and the nephew Ferdinand Edelmen exchanged an amused and arrogant smile. Dalya Bouvard was stressed; she still did not understand why it was Lyor Laszlo who was defending her father. Uncle Giorgi and Amira Mounier became mute. Sloan Wilfrid looked increasingly worried; he thought that Lyor Laszlo would present a good defending pleading, and that he would succeed in reducing the prison sentence by at least a few months. While Lyor couldn't even pronounce a single correct sentence.

The judge leaned back on his chair; he seemed bored by the pleading of this confused young apprentice Lawyer. At one moment the judge announced:

- You have five minutes left, Lyor Laszlo.

It is true that Lyor Laszlo was a hard-working young man; he was always well organized, assiduous, and good at preparing legal cases. But that day, Lyor Laszlo seemed lost and confused in his defense pleading. The young apprentice Lawyer leafed through his file, muttering in a stressed voice:

- I... yes, Your Honor... 5 minutes... in Antman's... defense... checks... checks that... I... argument of... I...

There were only 5 minutes left to convince the judge, and Lyor Laszlo's brain completely froze. Sweat appeared on his forehead, his face turned pale, his hands trembled, Lyor Laszlo thought:

- *I can't...I can't...Master Barold was supposed to do the defense pleading today, not me...Sloan Wilfrid and Master Barold forced me and sacrificed me...my father has already used all the arguments I had...there's nothing left for me to say...and Master Barold wants revenge on my father and to destroy my career...all that old Lawyer is talking about is the green sta...*

At this precise moment, Lyor Laszlo became paralyzed standing; he noticed a tiny little detail in the folder he was holding in his hands. And at that precise moment, a few benches away, Master Victor Barold smiled and he affirmed:

- Lyor Laszlo has found the green stars, and he's going to use them!

Sloan Wilfrid turned toward the old Lawyer, looking confused:

- What? What green stars?

Without wasting another second, Lyor Laszlo turned to the judge, and he announced in a much more certain and confident voice than before:

- There's an error in the accusation file, Your Honor.

At this announcement, everyone present in the Courtroom was surprised and curious. The judge straightened up on his chair:

- Which is?

Lyor Laszlo answered easily:

- Your Honor, the checks were issued on March 9th, 1892 ... March 17th, 1892 ... and March 24th, 1892. The dates of the checks are one year and one day past the deadline. However, according to the Law, when the checks exceed one year and one day, without being presented to the bank for cashing, the checks become invalid, and the person will not be prosecuted or accused.
Your Honor, today is September 4th, 1893. These checks have been expired for 5 months. Antman Bouvard should not even have been detained!

Lyor Laszlo's words shocked everyone in the Courtroom. Immediately, the judge leafed through a few papers in the file of this case, he stopped in front of a page, and he readjusted his glasses to better read a date.

Dalya Bouvard and her friend Amira Mounier exchanged a surprised look. Uncle Giorgi crossed his arms and he seemed surprised by this discovery. Nephew Ferdinand Edelmen sat up from his chair. The Lawyer Ernest Laszlo immediately opened a file, with a brusque move, to verify the statements of his son Lyor. Immediately, Sloan Wilfrid turned toward the old Lawyer:

- Master Barold... is that true? Are the checks expired?

The old Lawyer relaxed in his chair, and he just smiled. The young Lyor Laszlo regained his voice and his self-confidence:

- Your Honor, Mr. Antman Bouvard should not have been detained, not even for an hour. I request the opening of an investigation against the bank and also against the investigation office. Is it a simple verification error, or a deliberate error to hold Antman Bouvard for other purposes?

The Courtroom was overwhelmed by a sudden, paralyzing shock. The Lawyer Ernest Laszlo was nailed to his chair, the nephew Ferdinand Edelmen turned very pale, Dalya Bouvard seemed confused by what she heard, Sloan Wilfrid used all his neurons to understand what had escaped from him in this file.

The judge took off his glasses and he asked:

- Do you have anything else to add to your pleading, Lyor Laszlo?
- No, your honor. This is the only argument in my defense pleading.

When Lyor Laszlo returned to his defense table, the judge decided:

\- The judgment will be pronounced in two minutes. Session adjourned!

The judgment.

When the judge left the Courtroom, a heavy silence weighed on everyone. The accusation pleading of the Lawyer Ernest Laszlo was perfect, he presented several arguments, and his speech was impeccable. Lyor Laszlo meanwhile, he presented only one argument, and his defense pleading was less than good. None of the people present could guess the final judgment of this case. But everyone seemed stressed and worried.

The nephew Ferdinand Edelmen tightened his cane with all his might. The Lawyer Ernest Laszlo looked tense. Dalya Bouvard's heart was beating at full speed. Lyor Laszlo's throat choked. Amira Mounier and Uncle Giorgi were paralyzed on their benches.

In this intense moment, and while waiting for the return of the judge to the Courtroom, Master Victor Barold approached the Lawyer Sloan Wilfrid and he whispered in a serious tone:

\- I bet 20 dollars that Ernest Laszlo will tear his hair out after the judgment.

After a long second of thinking, Sloan Wilfrid whispered in a serious voice too:

\- I bet 20 dollars and a lunch that it will be the nephew Ferdinand Edelmen who pulls his hair out first.

Master Victor Barold confirmed without hesitation:

\- Bet accepted!

After what seemed like an eternity of waiting, the judge walked into the Courtroom, he settled into his chair, and he said:

\- Session resumed to announce the judgment in the Antman Bouvard case.

Adjusting his glasses, the judge addressed the audience:

\- Although it seems like a simple file, this case is strange. First, by the two defense and prosecution Lawyers, who are a father and a son, one against the other. Then, by the identity of the detainee, who is the father of an Heiress to a colossal fortune. And the arguments of the accusation and the defense are both valid.

After a long second of silence, the judge announced in a confident voice:

\- That said, by the right given to me by the State of Washington DC, I declare Mr. Antman Bouvard...

Everyone held their breath. No one breathed. All the hearts stopped.

- ...cleared of all accusations and charges against him!

Instantly, spontaneous screams of joy and utter astonishment filled the Courtroom. The judge banged on the gavel, and he decided:

- Antman Bouvard will be released. Case closed !

Dalya Bouvard could not believe her ears; she remained motionless, under the shock of events, repeating in a trembling voice:

- My father will be released ... my father will be released ... my father will be released ...

Her friend Amira Mounier did not hold back her happy laugh; she hugged her friend very tightly:

- Your father is cleared, Dalya! Your father will be released! Your father will be released!

Amira and Dalya laughed heartily; Amira was happy and relieved; Dalya was still in shock at the news. At one moment, Amira Mounier jumped:

- I must leave you and notify Professor Canfield, immediately! He asked me to keep him informed of the judgment, right away! He will be really very happy with this excellent news! He's waiting for me at the College!

Dalya replied in a trembling voice:

- Thank you for coming with me today, Amira. And thank you for being there during these difficult times, for me and my little sisters. I will always be grateful to yo...

Amira Mounier interrupted her:

- It's the least I can do for you, Dalya! You are my only and best friend, and I already owe you a lot!

A second later, Uncle Giorgi hugged his niece, repeating in a relieved voice:

- He will be released! Antman will be released! He will be released!

Dalya turned to the old man, and she answered him in an emotional voice:

- Uncle Giorgi...thank you for being brave to visit my father in detention, when I couldn't. Thank you for bringing him the baskets, all these months. And thank you for being there, for me and my little sisters.

Immediately, Uncle Giorgi smiled:

- That's what family is for, Biggo! I couldn't help the Lawyers, but bringing the baskets back to your father Antman, was all I could do to help. And I'm relieved and happy that this case is over. I will report the good news to the Merchants and friends of Antman. All the market sellers are eagerly waiting for the verdict of this trial.

Sitting at the defense table, the young Lyor Laszlo seemed to be struck by lightning:

- I... I succeeded... my first case... I... I succeeded...

His father the Lawyer Ernest Laszlo who was at the accusation table, he held his head in his hands. To see him, one would have thought that Ernest Laszlo was holding back his brain, which was about to explode, because of his failure in this case. As for the nephew Ferdinand Edelmen, he had trouble breathing, and he unfastened his tie with a sudden move.

And just then, a few steps away, Lawyer Sloan Wilfrid pulled 20 dollars bill out of his pocket, and he announced in an amused voice:

- You have won your bet, Master Barold... Ernest Laszlo is pulling his hair out... I have never been so happy to lose a bet!

Master Victor Barold took the 20 dollars bill, and he asked in a serious tone:

- What about lunch then?

Sloan Wilfrid announced:

- I invite you to the best restaurant in town, Master Barold!

The old Lawyer said :

- See you then at the Toscana restaurant! And I'm warning you, I'll probably order the entire menu!

Sloan Wilfrid let out a joyful laugh:

- There will be two of us then, Master Barold! This success deserves to be celebrated!

While Master Barold was putting the money won from the bet back into his jacket pocket, he asked in a serious tone:

- It was a real pleasure to work with you, Mr. Sloan Wilfrid. And... if you have any other business that might break a nerve of Ernest Laszlo, I'd be more than happy to help!

Watching the Lawyer Ernest Laszlo and the nephew Ferdinand Edelmen in a state of failure and confusion, Lawyer Sloan Wilfrid replied with a determined smile:

- Oh Master Barold... I feel that you will have a lot of work to do, from now on!

Before leaving, Lawyer Sloan Wilfrid had one last question:

- Regarding today's case, Master Barold ... I was only hoping that the detention sentence would be reduced by a few months. Making Antman Bouvard innocent is a real stroke of genius! ... The expired checks, I admit that I didn't think of checking the dates. Why didn't you speak to me or Lyor about it?

Master Barold answered with a confident tone:

- I didn't tell you about it, because it was up to Lyor Laszlo to find the trick in this affair, and to prove whether he was gifted. Today, your student has confirmed that he is destined to be an excellent Lawyer. At our lunch, I'll explain in more details how I noticed the expired checks. Anyway, you can be very proud of your student Lyor Laszlo! You trained him well!

Sloan Wilfrid watched Lyor Laszlo for a long second, and with a proud smile.

Still seated at his large table, the judge ordered the old Lawyer to approach. Repressing his amused laugh with great difficulty, the judge asked:

- Master Barold ... it's been 20 long years of absence, and you came to this trial today, to stretch your legs and get some fresh air ... just that? Really?

Master Barold approached the judge, displaying an innocent smile:

- Your Honor, the month of September was recommended to me by my Doctor. Apparently, the air is excellent for a good walk.

The judge affirmed with a serious tone:

- There are 11 other months in the year, Master Barold. I think you should go out and stretch your legs a lot more often. The young apprentice Lawyers can very well benefit from your experience.

Master Barold bowed his head in respect:

- I will consult my Doctor about this, Your Honor.

Leaving the judge, Master Barold turned and he walked over to the defense Lawyer's table. The young Lyor Laszlo seemed to be still in shock from his success. Master Barold smiled:

- Lyor Laszlo ... you did a great job today!

Immediately, Lyor Laszlo stood up and he asked in a curious voice:

- Master Barold ... the expired dates of the checks were colored with green stars! Is that what you've been talking about since this morning? Green stars?

Master Barold let out an amused laugh:

- From the first minute I read the case file, it seemed to be doomed already. All we could do for Antman Bouvard was to reduce the prison sentence by a maximum of one month. However ... the night you showed up with the colored papers, I noticed the expired dates of the checks, thanks to the colored green stars. And I admit ... I was myself surprised by this discovery! The dates of the checks were written in very small numbers; it was done on purpose to make the dates as unreadable as possible. Except that, being colored by green stars...

Lyor Laszlo understood and he finished the sentence:

- Being colored by green stars, the expired dates were more visible! And so, we could use this argument, we could release Antman Bouvard!

Master Barold corrected him :

- You used this argument, you released Antman Bouvard! ... I could have shown you these expired dates the day before this trial, but it was up to you to find this flaw in the file, it was up to you to make your neurons work, it was up to you to present the defense pleading!

Approaching a few steps, Master Barold explained in a serious voice:

- Your defense pleading was well organized and argued, Lyor. And although your father used all of your arguments in the accusation pleading, you still managed to come up with one last argument. Of course, there are points to correct in your defense pleading; your speech needs to be worked on, you need to master your composure, and you still have a lot to learn in Law. Nevertheless ... I confirm to you that you are gifted for this profession. You are hardworking and honest. I have no doubt that you will become a brilliant Lawyer! Keep on going !

Lyor Laszlo was touched by this opinion. And despite the old Lawyer's eccentric ways and ideas, Lyor Laszlo was well aware that Master Victor Barold was a heavyweight in the Legal profession, and one of the best Lawyers in the entire city, if not the Country.

Hearing these words of encouragements and validation, Lyor Laszlo was touched:

- Thank you, Master Barold. I am very grateful to you for your teachings. I would have not succeeded without your help !

Master Barold patted the young apprentice on the shoulders:

- It's your work today, Lyor! You can be very proud of it! And ... speaking of pride, by the way, I absolutely must greet your father, Ernest Laszlo. I missed him so much!

At this moment, Lyor seemed confused:

- You ... I thought you hated my father?!

Master Barold readjusted his tie and he smiled:

- But it's always true, my dear Lyor! ... And on this glorious day, I absolutely must give him back the slap he gave me 20 years ago!

As he advanced toward a man, Master Barold screamed in a joyful tone:

- Ernest Lazlo! My dear friend! How are you? You look like you received a slap! So how does it feel to be beaten by your own apprentice son, huh? It's his first case and he beat you with a single argument! Failure is not too hard? Do you need a glass of water?

Meanwhile, a few steps away, Sloan Wilfrid approached a small silhouette sitting on a bench, and he knelt in front of her. Dalya Bouvard asked in a trembling voice:

- Is it over, Monsieur?

Sloan Wilfrid answered in a touched voice:

- Yes. It's over. Your father will be released in an hour, Mademoiselle. Thank you for trusting me, and for not having abandoned the inheritance, by signing the paper of Lawyer Ernest Laszlo, despite all his pressure!

Instantly, and without notice, tears flowed abundantly down Dalya Bouvard's cheeks. And as strange as it sounds, watching Dalya Bouvard cry, Sloan Wilfrid smiled. The little girl found no words to say, and no moves to make. However, her tears of joy and relief were enough to thank Sloan Wilfrid.

For a long minute, the little girl was crying. And kneeling before her, the Lawyer smiled, repeating in a relieved voice:

- It's over ... it's over.

For the little Dalya Bouvard, her father's detention was a painful and difficult experience to live through. And for the Author of this story, these were painful and difficult memories to write. Nevertheless, in the difficult moments of our life, sometimes we have only one choice ahead of us ... to confront.

And just like the Excelbox has so aptly affirmed it before ... breathe, exhale, and confront!

Chapter 49

Sorry

The same day, a few hours later.

For the first time in several months, the road of Dumbarton Oaks Park seemed serene for Dalya Bouvard. The trees looked cheerful and green, the flowers smiled shyly to the rays of sun, the birds sang happy sounds. For the first time in a long time, Dalya Bouvard's heart was light.

Immediately after the end of the trial at Court, Dalya Bouvard returned to the grand Mansion, to announce the news to her little sisters and to the employees. Meanwhile, Lawyers Sloan Wilfrid and Lyor Laszlo were handling the final paperwork for Antman Bouvard's release.

The little twin sisters jumped happily upon receiving the news about their father:

- Ant returns from trip!! Ant returns from trip!! Ant returns from trip !!

The maid Cristelle and Océanie hugged Dalya:

- This is great news, Mademoiselle!! Finally!! After so many months of waiting and stress, your father is cleared!! Congratulations, Mademoiselle !! Congratulations !!
- We are relieved by this news. This experience was painful !

Dalya thanked them with a touched smile. The Gardener approached Dalya:

- Your father is a brave and hard-working man, Mademoiselle. We were sure that he would be released sooner or later.

The head of the grand Mansion continued:

- Yes, he didn't deserve to be detained. We are all happy with this good news, Mademoiselle!

Igor also seemed happy:

- It was a stressful and tense day. No one could touch breakfast this morning! We were all waiting for the judgement.

The Cook announced in a cheerful voice:

- And for this great news, I'll cook a feast for today's lunch!

Dalya Bouvard and the employees of the grand Mansion laughed heartily, relieved and reassured by the good news. Dalya sincerely thanked all the employees of the grand Mansion for their support and help during this painful ordeal.

A few minutes later.

The little twins had their noses glued to the windows of the living room of the grand Mansion; they were waiting the arrival of their father. Dalya Bouvard was finishing some homework, and watching the slightest movement at the front door of the grand Mansion.

When suddenly, the little twins jumped up and they exclaimed with one voice:

- Ant returned!! Ant returned!! Ant returned!!

Ari and Adi left the living room, and they ran toward the front door of the grand Mansion. Immediately, Dalya closed her homework notebook, and she followed her little sisters at a rapid pace. A black car parked right in front of the front door. The first out of the car was Lawyer Sloan Wilfrid. He greeted Dalya and the little twins with a happy smile:

- Good evening, Mesdemoiselles! I'm so glad to see you. I brought a nice surprise with me!

The second man to get out of the car was Antman Bouvard. The little twins ran toward him, and they jumped on his neck, laughing:

- Ant returned !! Ant returned !!

Antman Bouvard hugged his little girls in a strong move, and he smiled:

- Ari, Adi! I missed you so much! And you have grown so much! I am happy to see you again, my little twins!

Ari and Adi proudly announced to their father:

- We were nice!! We were good!
- We been to school and do our homework every day!

Kneeling in front of the little twins, Antman Bouvard laughed:

- That's very good Ari! That's very good Adi!

Dalya smiled while observing the reunion of her father and her little twin sisters. The Lawyer Sloan Wilfrid turned around and he got back into the car:

- Now, I must leave you. Lawyer Master Victor Barold is waiting for me for lunch and to celebrate the success of this trial. And Antman ... stay out of trouble!

Antman Bouvard stood up and he answered in a touched voice:

- Yes, Monsieur. And thank you again for your help. I am grateful to you!

Before starting the car and leaving the grand Mansion, Sloan Wilfrid turned around and he announced in an amused voice:

- Dalya ... for the next few days, avoid crossing paths with Lawyer Ernest Laszlo. He is enraged because of his failure. He will be in angry mood for a long time. You are warned.

Dalya smiled discreetly :

- Understood, Mr. Wilfrid. Thank you very much.
When Lawyer Sloan Wilfrid's car left the grand Mansion, Dalya addressed her little sisters:
- Our father needs to rest; his trip has been exhausting. Let's go inside, you still have some homework to finish.

Ari and Adi hugged their father, and they ran inside the grand Mansion, screaming happily:

- See you later, Ant!
- Good bye, Ant!

When the little twins disappeared inside the grand Mansion, Antman Bouvard spoke to his daughter Dalya, in a calm and hesitant voice:

- I received your letters ... with the basket you sent me, every week.

Throughout his period of detention, Dalya sent her father a basket every week, through her uncle Giorgi Bouvard. The basket contained clothes, food, newspapers. And in each package, Dalya included a letter to inform her father of the news of the little twins. Antman Bouvard continued:

- The little twins seem to settle well in this house. I think it would be better if the little twins stayed with you in the grand Mansion. If the employees don't mind it...
Instantly, Dalya replied to her father:
- The head of the grand Mansion, Monsieur Bûchebois told me that my little sisters can stay here for as long as they want to. The employees are delighted by the presence of the twins; they all adjusted their schedules to watch over Ari and Adi. And the little twins were very good and obedient to all the employees.

Antman Bouvard said :

- I will go see the employees of the grand Mansion this afternoon, to thank them.
- All the employees took good care of me and my little sisters. And today, they were all happy that you were released.

During a long minute of silence, Dalya felt that her father hesitated to say something. It was as if he was looking for his words, but couldn't find them. And after an awkward silence, Dalya announced to her father:

- Cristelle, the maid, cleaned the annex house for you, earlier. And the Cook, Mr. Ferrero Lutché, will prepare a good lunch for everyone. You are welcome to join us at the grand Mansion. If you are tired, the assistant Igor will take care of bringing you lunch to the annex house. I'm letting you rest. I'm going home to finish homework with my little sisters ... see you later, father.

232

Antman Bouvard remained silent, hesitating. Not wanting to embarrass him more than that, Dalya smiled at her father, and she turned to go back to the grand Mansion. When suddenly, unusual words were heard.

- I am sorry.

When she turned around, Dalya couldn't believe her ears. And yet, she had heard very well. Antman Bouvard addressed his daughter Dalya, and he pronounced these words for the first time since ever:

- I am sorry for everything you've been through.

These words paralyzed Dalya Bouvard; she remained shocked watching her father. Dalya never thought she would hear these words from her father. And yet, Antman Bouvard repeated them sincerely, in an honest voice:

- I am sorry.

Antman Bouvard smiled at his daughter; a sincere and regretful smile. Although he said no more words, it is certain that Antman Bouvard regretted having mistreated his daughter Dalya. He regretted forcing her to do things she didn't want. He regretted taking her money from her bags sales at the market. He regretted having let her mother beat her without intervening. He regretted having workloaded his daughter without worrying about her studies or her fatigue. He regretted having made life difficult for his daughter. He regretted that his daughter received menaces because of him. He regretted having taken risks with his game of cards and the bad checks. He regretted having put his family in a difficult situation because of his detention. At this precise moment, Antman Bouvard regretted many wrong decisions he made.

A moment of uncomfortable silence settled between the father and the daughter. Antman Bouvard seemed sad and full of regrets. Dalya Bouvard remained silent and shocked. She did not expect these confessions from her father. She found no words to say.

What can you respond to years of abuse, pressure, and mistreatment? What can you say to a father who takes money from his daughter's work? What can you say to a father who lets his daughter be beaten by a monster? What can you say to a father who makes his daughter work day and night, tirelessly? What can you say to a father when you receive menaces because of him? What can you say to a father who takes risks to the detriment of his family?

With a heavy heart, Dalya Bouvard smiled at her father. It was the only answer she could find to give. And Antman Bouvard smiled at his daughter, before leaving for the annex house.

In this story and in reality, Antman Bouvard apologized sincerely, and many times. Except that he never changed.

And it is how, Dear readers, the character of Antman Bouvard will stop here, in this scene. He will not continue the story with us. And it is very regrettable.

Chapter 50

On the road

Tuesday, September 5th, 1893.

The day after her father's release, Dalya Bouvard received congratulations from everyone she met on her way. The market Merchants, her father's friends, the Dean of Merchants Mr. Kenan Einsenberg, the flower vendor Lalla Fatim Fadl.

At the school gate, Dalya found her friends Alfie Jaq and Maurice Gus, waiting for her. And as usual during these last difficult months, Alfie and Maurice brought her the Monday newspapers and some fruit. Except this time, Alfie and Maurice were happy and relieved by the good news of their friend Dalya.

And apparently, Amira Mounier spread this good news throughout the entire school. As soon as Dalya walked through the front door of the school, the school Concierge Dadès congratulated her, Professor Canfield greeted her warmly, the Director's Secretary Miss Uplerine Amana applauded her, the Library assistant Miss Guendolyn hugged her, the Music Teacher Miss Haîyang smiled tenderly at her, even the Mathematics Teacher congratulated her while laughing happily.

And strangely, while walking in a corridor of the school, Dalya Bouvard noticed 3 students who smiled sincerely at her; Assami Eyelord, and her friends Hélène and Esteban. Dalya didn't understand the strange sincere smile of these 3 students. Amira Mounier explained to her the reason why.

For the first time in several months, Dalya Bouvard had a very good day at the Royal Georgetown College. Dalya was moved and touched by the reaction of all the people she met on her way that day.

At the end of the school day, Dalya left downtown and she headed back to Dumbarton Oaks Park. The landscape gradually changed. Downtown buildings were turning into beautiful big houses. The gardens became more numerous and splendid. The leaves were colored brown, yellow and red. Cold wind breezes were more present than before.

On this autumn late afternoon, Dalya was walking slowly down the road, observing the landscape. And for the first time in several months, Dalya Bouvard felt her heart light and serene. Her father being released, he resumed his usual work as a courier at the Toscana restaurant, and he remained in the annex house of the grand Mansion. All the employees insisted on keeping the little twin sisters Ari and Adi, in the grand Mansion, in order to better take care of them. And Dalya will be eternally grateful to the employees for this attention, toward her and her little twin sisters.

Suddenly, on the way of Dumbarton Oaks Park, a car with a chauffeur pulled up in front of Dalya. A young man got out of the car and he greeted her:

- Good evening, Mademoiselle. It's a nice coincidence to meet you on the road today.

Dalya was surprised to meet Richard Poirier.

- Good evening. Yes, I'm coming from school. I finished my classes, for today.

Richard Poirier smiled:

- I too finished my work, for today. May I drive you to the grand Mansion?

It was the same way as the house of the French family. Happy with this meeting, Dalya accepted, and she got into the car. When the chauffeur started driving, Richard Poirier asked in a polite tone:

- I hope your back to school is going well?

Sitting next to Richard, Dalya replied:

- Very well, thank you for asking. I have the same schedule as the previous semester, only 2 lessons. The Philosophy course and the Gymnastics course.

Richard affirmed:

- You have studied very well the chapters of Philosophy, during the summer month. I'm sure you will pass this course again and easily.

Dalya smiled:

- Because of your help. Thank you. And how is your start of political year going on?

With an amused voice, Richard confided in Dalya:

- I wouldn't have refused another month of vacation! This start of political year promises to be busy and eventful. I have prepared my files and my reports during the 2 summer months, wanting to be in advance of events. The first week of September isn't even over yet, and all my reports are already outdated.

Dalya and Richard exchanged a little amused laugh. At one point, Dalya announced in an emotive voice:

- My... my father's trial took place, yesterday. He was cleared and released yesterday afternoon.

Immediately, Richard turned toward Dalya, and he exclaimed:

- This is excellent news, Mademoiselle! I am happy for you and your family!

Dalya informed him:

- It's a big relief, yes. I'm glad this affair is finally over. My father returned to his work this very morning. And he will remain in the annex house of the grand Mansion.

While observing Dalya, Richard smiled:

- Everything ends up being alright.

The chauffeur interrupted the discussion, announcing:

- We have arrived at your house, Monsieur.

When the car stopped, Richard took his files back in his hands and he ordered the chauffeur:

- Do take Mademoiselle to the grand Mansion, please.

Dalya tried to continue walking, except that Richard Poirier insisted:

- After a long day of school, it's the least we can do for you, Mademoiselle. And I will announce your good news to Mother, immediately. She will be relieved and happy to hear it. Will we be expecting you next Saturday?

With a shy smile, Dalya replied:

- With pleasure. I will bring apple and cinnamon muffins.

Closing the car door after him, Richard smiled:

- In that case, I can't wait for Saturday! Very good day, Mademoiselle.
- You too. And thank you again for driving me home.

Returning on Dumbarton Oaks Park road, the car headed to the grand Mansion. Dalya Bouvard was happy to have met the young man.

At a moment, before going inside his home, Richard Poirier turned back toward the road on Dumbarton Oaks Park. And for a long minute, Richard Poirier watched the car carrying the little girl, until it disappeared from the road.

Chapter 51

Back to school

Wednesday September 6th, 1893. At the Royal Georgetown College.

Before the 8 AM bell, Dalya Bouvard found her friend Amira at the school entrance.

- Good morning, Amira!

Amira Mounier smiled as she descends a step of the stairs:

- Good morning, Dalya. I was waiting for you before school starts. Here are the books I borrowed from the Library of the grand Mansion. You saved me in Latin class, thank you!

Dalya took the books from her friend's, and she put them in her school bag:

- You're welcome. There are many Latin books in the Library of the grand Mansion. Apparently, the Late Mr. Governor was a big Latin reader. If you need more books, you are welcome to use them.

Entering the school, Amira let out an amused laugh:

- Thank you very much... but I admit, I don't need more books, I need less classes. I don't know how I'm going to pass 10 classes this semester.

Dalya and Amira laughed, walking down a hallway. Dalya confessed in a sincere voice:

- I wish I had as many classes as you. I thought Professor Canfield would fill my schedule this semester. But he enrolled me in the same 2 previous courses, Philosophy and Gymnastics. I don't know why only 2 classes, and I didn't dare to ask him.

Stopping in front of her class, Amira Mounier exclaimed:

- Anyway, I know that I can count on you to pass the Philosophy course. You saved me last semester, thanks to your explanations. So, I only have 9 classes left to work on this semester!

Dalya Bouvard and Amira Mounier parted ways with a laugh. Amira entered her History class, and Dalya continued on her way to Gymnastics class.

And as usual, on entering the immense Gymnasium, Dalya found the young Professor Tudi waiting for her. It is true that Dalya had hoped to have more courses and classes this semester. However, Dalya was happy to resume her Gymnastics lessons, and she greatly appreciated the young Teacher Tudi, for her patience, her encouragements, and above all her contagious calm. Strangely, every time she entered the Gymnasium, Dalya felt a strange serenity. In addition to the Library, the Gymnasium has become Dalya Bouvard's favorite place.

With a soft voice and a happy smile, the young Professor Tudi greeted her:

- Good morning, Mademoiselle Dalya Bouvard. It is a pleasure to see you again, after the summer holiday.

Dalya smiled:

- Good morning, Professor. It's a pleasure to continue lessons with you. And I confirm, it was a long, busy, and stressful summer holiday!

The young Professor Tudi smiled, and she gave Dalya her usual uniform:

- Are you ready for the first class of this semester, Mademoiselle?

Without hesitation, Dalya Bouvard replied:

- Yes!

After Dalya changed into her uniform, she found the young Teacher in a corner of the Gymnasium. Adjusting her gloves, young Professor Tudi announced:

- We will start the sessions just like before.

Having followed this course for 6 months, Dalya knew the program of the sessions perfectly well. Dalya continued the sentence of the young Professor Tudi:

- Now, we will do an hour of breathing. Then, an hour of stretching and warming up. At 10 AM, the exercises of kicking in the air. And after the lunch break, we continue the face-to-face exercises.

The young Professor Tudi smiled proudly:

- Exact, Mademoiselle. The exercise for this month of September is very easy. It consists of 3 moves, linked to 3 words. Block... repel ... defend. After your warm-ups, you will train against this Punchingball.

Dalya repeated aloud:

- 3 moves, 3 words ... block, repel, defend.

The young Professor Tudi continued to explain to her:

- I will show you the movement related to each word. Shall we begin?

Chapter 52

An admiring stare

Saturday October 21st, 1893. In the grand Mansion.

In Dalya's bedroom, the little twins were sitting on their big sister's bed, and they begged her for the 27th time:

- Please Dindin!! We zentilles!!
- We go out with you!! Please Dindin!!

For an hour, Ari and Adi had been imploring their big sister to go out with her. While putting few books into her bag, Dalya repeated the same answer to them:

- I am not going for a walk, but to study. I need help with my Philosophy class. I can't take you with me.

The little twins insisted:

- We nice!! We not bother Dindin!! Promise!!
- Please!! We go out with you!! Please!!

Before Dalya could answer for the 28th time, a silhouette entered the bedroom.

- And here is your perfectly ironed dress, Mademoiselle. I arranged it for you.

The help Cook Océanie slowly placed a sapphire blue velvet dress on the bed. Dalya took out a gray coat and black shoes from the dressing room:

- Thank you, Océanie.

Still sitting on the big bed, the little twins resumed their pleas:

- Please Dindin!! Just one ride!! We zentilles and nice!!
- Yes, promise Dindin!! Just take us out for a ride!!

Océanie asked in a curious voice:

- Do the Demoiselles want anything?

Taking the dress to change, Dalya explained to her:

- My little sisters want to go out with me today, but I can't take them. I am already expected at the house of the French neighbors.

Immediately, Océanie approached the little twins, and she suggested to them:

- I have an idea … do the Demoiselles want to go downtown with me? I must buy some cleaning products. The Gardener can take us there by car. We can take a walk in the city garden.

Ari and Adi asked in a pleading voice:

- And we have sweets?
- And we go to swing?

Océanie repressed an amused laugh, and she informed the little twins in a caring voice:

- Yes, I will take you to the swing. About the sweets, we will buy some. But we will eat them only after dinner. Monsieur Bûchebois insists that you finish your meals, before having desserts and sweets.

Dalya returned from the dressing room, having worn her velvet dress:

- Thank you very much Océanie. I don't know what I would have done without your help, you and all the employees of the grand Mansion.

With a sincere smile, Océanie replied:

- It is with great pleasure that we serve you and the little demoiselles.

Speaking to the little twins, Océanie asked them:

- Mesdemoiselles, you must wear your coats, your hats, and your gloves. It's chilly this afterno…

Without waiting for the rest of Océanie's words, the little twins jumped out of bed, and they left the bedroom running and screaming happily:

- We get dressed right away!! Coat and hat!! Gloves immediately!!
- Right away!! Us go out!! For swing and sweets!! And garden!!

Océanie and Dalya exchanged a little amused laugh. Dalya put on her gray coat, and she picked up her bag. Océanie noticed a detail, she approached Dalya:

- One moment, Mademoiselle. I will fix your dress. The bow tie should be on the side, not in the center. Like this. Voilà!

Taking a few steps back, Océanie exclaimed:

- You are very pretty in this outfit, Mademoiselle. This velvet dress is gorgeous on you! The sapphire blue color accentuates your beautiful eyes. And your hair is gorgeous in a crown of braids!

Dalya blushed a little; she always appreciated compliments on her dressing efforts. While leaving the bedroom, Océanie suggested to her:

- The French neighbors' house is on our way to downtown, we can drop you off at the way, Mademoiselle.
- That would be nice, thank you.

The afternoon. In the house of the French neighbors, the Poirier.

The housekeeper, Mrs. Glorina, had many things to do. A few hours before, Richard Poirier announced to her that he would receive friends for dinner the next day. In the kitchen, placing 2 cups on a tray, Mrs. Glorina thought:

- *It will be a dinner just like the other times. I already have all the necessary vegetables; carrots, potatoes, zucchini. I will start with a vegetable soup for the entrée.*

The milk became boiling, Mrs. Glorina added chocolate powder to it, and she stirred slowly in the saucepan:

- *And he wants steamed meat. I could serve the meat with mashed potatoes. And I'll add a sauce on the side.*

Filling a plate with macarons, Mrs. Glorina continued to lay out her plan:

- *Slices of bread, with butter and fine herbs. Cramberry juice, and definitely coffee after dinner.*

When the tray was ready, Mrs. Glorina carried it and she left the kitchen. Dalya Bouvard and Richard Poirier were installed in the living room, next to the well-lit fireplace. Dalya was reading the Philosophy course aloud, and Richard was explaining the words and the principles to her.

When Mrs. Glorina placed the tray on a small table, she announced proudly:

- Monsieur, Mademoiselle ... here is your hot chocolate.

The two young people thanked Mrs. Glorina.

- The macaroons look delicious, thank you very much.
- The hot chocolate arrives at the right time. Thank you, Mrs. Glorina.

Mrs. Glorina smiled:

- I'll be in the kitchen, if you want anything else.

Mrs. Glorina left the living room, while Dalya and Richard continued their work. Dalya continued reading:

- I'll reread the paragraph from the beginning ... Philosophy is the study of the nature of things. That is to say the principles, the foundations. Philosophy seeks the why and the meaning of phenomenon. Science, on the other hand, is a study of things in nature, that is, of physical phenomenon, organic...

Before going back into the kitchen, Mrs. Glorina paused in the hallway for a moment. She remembered that Richard hadn't told her what dessert he wanted for dinner tomorrow. Mrs. Glorina returned to the living room to ask him the question.

Dalya was reading the manual aloud, in a focused voice:

- Science analyzes how things in nature work. Science brings out necessary relations between them and establishes constant and universal Laws of nature. By proceeding in this way, science aims to build rational and objective knowledge, that is to say coherent, logical, orderly and methodical knowledge, free from all irrationality, subjectivity, all relativity and plurality of opinions.

Mrs. Glorina approached the young Richard, and she was about to ask him a question about dinner. Except that at this precise moment, Mrs. Glorina restrained herself, a detail caught her attention and her curiosity.

While Dalya Bouvard was focused, reading aloud, Mrs. Glorina noticed that Richard Poirier was focused too... but not on the Philosophy course. The young man observed Dalya Bouvard with an admiring stare. And that stare, Mrs. Glorina understood it perfectly well.

It is true that, on this afternoon, the little Dalya Bouvard seemed particularly different from the other days. Her hair, arranged in a crown of braids, was splendid. Her velvet dress embellished her waist. The sapphire color of the dress accentuated her beautiful blue eyes. The fires in the fireplace made her cheeks blush a little. While she was reading the Philosophy course, Richard Poirier observed and admired Dalya Bouvard, without being able to help it.

Not wishing to interrupt this moment, Mrs. Glorina discreetly withdrew from the living room. She returned to the kitchen, with no answer to her question, but with a smile on her lips.

Chapter 53

Ernest Laszlo's Revenge

Thursday, October 26th, 1893. At the Law firm.

Autumn has well settled in the city of Georgetown. The leaves had changed colors, the clouds were gray and filled, the cold became more regular, and the townspeople were all busy with their works.

Before entering the Law firm, Dalya Bouvard made a nice encounter in the street.

- Mr. Jacob Mounier ... good morning!

Mr. Jacob Mounier, her friend Amira's father, was easily spotted. With a little belly, full cheeks, an almost always brown suit and tie, Dalya instantly recognized him among the crowd of people. The accountant Mr. Jacob Mounier greeted Dalya happily:

- Good morning, Mademoiselle! What a great coincidence to see you today!

Dalya indicated the building in front:

- I'm bringing muffins to Mr. Sloan Wilfrid. He watches over me and my family. So, the least I can do for him is bring him his favorite muffins.

Mr. Jacob Mounier smiled:

- And those are well-deserved muffins! Mr. Sloan Wilfrid is a good and honest man. Having worked with him for years, I can confirm that. I too have an appointment with him this morning. Let's go inside then!

Sitting behind his desk, Lawyer Sloan Wilfrid seemed busy reading a file. It was a busy time for the Law firm. When a man knocked on the office door, Sloan Wilfrid stood up:

- Mr. Jacob Mounier ... Mademoiselle Dalya... good morning! Come in, please. Sit down, please.

Dalya greeted first:

- Good morning, Mr. Wilfrid. I bring you some pastry prepared this very morning. Muffins with caramelized apples and cinnamon. I hope you will like them.

Lawyer Sloan Wilfrid jumped off his chair:

- Of course, I'll like them! I never refuse pastry! ... Thank you, Mademoiselle; it's very kind of you. I've just needed some, with my next cup of coffee.

It wasn't much, but Dalya was happy to please Lawyer Sloan Wilfrid. Turning toward the accountant, Sloan Wilfrid asked:

- Mr. Jacob Mounier, you absolutely must taste these muffins! Would you like a coffee with it?

It is true that the smell of the caramelized apple muffins was mouthwatering. Mr. Jacob Mounier held back an amused laugh:

- I started a diet this very morning!

Before ordering to his Secretary 2 coffees, the Lawyer Sloan Wilfrid affirmed with a sure tone:

- A little muffin will do you good, Monsieur Jacob! You won't regret it, it helps productivity and focus at work!

Dalya confirmed :

- The Cook does not use a lot of sugar in his pastries.

Observing the cakes in the box placed on the office table, the accountant Mr. Jacob Mounier murmured:

- It looks very delicious … maybe half a muffin then … my diet can be delayed by a day… half a muffin only.

Sloan Wilfrid and Dalya exchanged an amused smile. And while waiting for the coffees, Mr. Jacob Mounier took out a file from his big bag:

- By the way, Mr. Wilfrid … I came to see you today because I finished the expert report you asked for. About the textile Factory, Cotton Factory, which belongs to BalthEnterprise Holding.

Immediately, Sloan Wilfrid straightened up on his chair:

- Thank you for your help and your quickness, Mr. Jacob. Your accountant's opinion is essential to resolve this situati...

When suddenly, Lyor Laszlo walked into Sloan Wilfrid's office, and he slammed the door shut behind him. The young Lyor Laszlo has never looked so pale and shocked; he announced in a trembling voice:

- He wants to close the Factory!

Sloan Wilfrid needed more words to understand what was going on:

- Who are you talking about? Which Factory ?

Lyor Laszlo approached Sloan Wilfrid's desk table:

- My father wants to close the Cotton Factory ... entirely!

The news was shocking and brusque. Lawyer Sloan Wilfrid leaned back on his chair; he was stunned by this bad news. The accountant, Mr. Jacob Mounier seemed to know this Factory, he asked Lyor Laszlo:

- How do you know that?

Lyor replied in a trembling voice:

- At the office of my father's Secretary, I saw the letter of cessation of activity, in the name of the Cotton Factory. He is in the process of preparing the file for the dissolution of the Factory, to submit it to Court.

The accountant Mr. Jacob Mounier's cheerful face changed to a worried and shocked expression. Dalya Bouvard dared to ask:

- How many employees work in this Factory?

Lawyer Sloan Wilfrid replied with a tight throat:

- Thousands of employees. Thousands of families.

At that moment, Lyor Laszlo's legs no longer held him, he sat down on the nearest chair he could find, and he announced in a dejected voice:

- My father is going to force me to sign the dissolution of this Factory. He's going to force me to fire thousands of employees.

Immediately, Dalya Bouvard turned to Lawyer Sloan Wilfrid, and she asked a question, even though she already knew its answer:

- Is Mr. Ernest Laszlo taking revenge on me? Because I didn't abandon the inheritance, and because I didn't give in to his blackmail? Is he taking revenge because he lost the case at Court, and because my father was freed?

The three men exchanged a serious and worried look. Nobody dared to answer these questions. Since the release of Antman Bouvard, everyone was sure that the revenge of the Lawyer Ernest Laszlo would not be long to come. Except that they were far from thinking that this revenge would be the closing of an entire Factory, firing thousands of employees!

After a long minute of a grave silence, Lawyer Sloan Wilfrid was first to pull himself together:

- Mr. Jacob Mounier ... you have studied the statement of accounts of the Cotton Factory. What is your opinion on it?

The accountant Mr. Jacob Mounier cleared his throat, and he replied:

- The statement of accounts and the documents you provided me, show a negative deficit. The Factory has suffered losses accumulated for 5 years. Practices are no longer up to date with market demand. Even assets and machinery cost more to maintain because of their oldness. I am sorry to inform you that the Cotton Factory is in a very bad condition.

This news was disastrous. Sloan Wilfrid closed his eyes, refusing to believe this nightmare. Lyor Laszlo murmured in a shaking voice:

- Thousands of jobs ... thousands of families ...

Dalya's heart tightened and her throat choked. She never thought the Lawyer Ernest Laszlo capable of such cruelty. Instead of helping the employees, Mr. Ernest Laszlo simply preferred to close up. An air of shock and seriousness invaded Sloan Wilfrid's office. No one dared to move or speak; everyone was heartbroken by what was about to happen. The Cotton Factory will close!

At a moment, the accountant Mr. Jacob Mounier thought aloud:

- Unless ...

Lawyer Sloan Wilfrid jumped:

- Unless ... ?

Lyor Laszlo and Dalya Bouvard asked with one voice:

- Unless what ... ?

Leafing through his report, the accountant Mr. Jacob Mounier continued to think aloud:

- Unless ... unless the Factory receives an injection of funds.

Sloan Wilfrid grew impatient:

- What do you mean by that?

The accountant Mr. Jacob Mounier explained:

- If the Cotton Factory receives money to erase its debts, renew the machines and pay for a stock of raw materials... and if the products are exported to neighboring countries and to new markets... sales can generate a profit after a few months ... and so jobs will not be lost.

Sloan Wilfrid understood the accountant's idea:

- Inject funds into the Factory, to revive it again.

The accountant Mr. Jacob Mounier confirmed:

- Exact!

The young Lyor Laszlo asked:

- And how much money does the Cotton Factory need?

The accountant Mr. Jacob Mounier consulted his documents for a long minute. While Sloan Wilfrid, Lyor Laszlo and Dalya Bouvard watched him impatiently. When finally, the accountant Mr. Jacob Mounier replied:

- According to the statement of accounts and the debts, it needs approximately ... 1 million and 200 thousand dollars!

This number seemed so huge that Dalya and Lyor repressed a scream of surprise. Lawyer Sloan Wilfrid answered with a shocked look:

- It's ... it's a lot of money ... I don't have enough contacts in the business community to ask for this amount of money.

Lyor Laszlo thought aloud:

- No Banker or Businessman will accept to support the Factory, by investing this amount of money... it's a fortune!!

Dalya asked:

- Mr. Sloan Wilfrid ... can I use the money in the bank of Late Mr. Governor Iskander Balthazar, to invest it in this Factory?

Sloan Wilfrid replied, rubbing his forehead:

- Sorry, Mademoiselle ... but all of Late Mr. Governor's bank accounts are frozen until you pass the final Challenge.

The accountant Mr. Jacob Mounier closed his file:

- I am sincerely sorry for this bad news. But getting this amount of money, seems to me the only way to save the Cotton Factory.

After a long minute of silence and thinking, Lawyer Sloan Wilfrid decided:

- Lyor ... how long can you delay your signing of the Factory dissolution?
- You know my father; I can't stand up to him for long. I can delay my signing for 2 weeks ... that's the maximum.

Sloan Wilfrid thought aloud:

- We will have gained 2 weeks to look for a solution! 2 weeks is better than nothing.

Observing the accountant Mr. Jacob Mounier, Lyor Laszlo and Dalya Bouvard, the Lawyer Sloan Wilfrid announced in a worried voice:

- We have 2 weeks to find this money and save the Factory!

A few hours later, at the grand Mansion.

The way to Dumbarton Oaks Park seemed very long. Dalya Bouvard ran toward the grand Mansion, as quickly as she could. And on the way, only 2 things occupied the mind of the little girl:

- Thousands of jobs. And 1 million 200 thousand dollars.

Dalya felt guilty; after all, it was because of her that the Lawyer Ernest Laszlo took revenge and decided to close the Cotton Factory. If she had agreed to give up this fortune, her father would not have been detained, there would not have been a humiliating trial for Ernest Laszlo, and the Factory would not be in danger. The lives of thousands of families and jobs were at stake. Not only was the amount of money huge, but it had to be found in … 2 weeks!

At the end of this afternoon, Dalya needed help. And as in all previous impossible situations, help was almost always found in one place.

Arriving at the grand Mansion, Dalya did not slow down, she ran toward her bedroom, and she walked toward the small desk. When she stopped in front of the Excelbox, Dalya sat down on a chair in front of the strange box. Dalya was breathless, worried, anxious, and shaking.

Placed on the desk, the Excelbox was calm and serene. The transparent glass cage, in an oval shape, was welded by 4 forged yellow gold cylinders in the shape of a vine plant. The round clock inside the cage was clearly visible. The little needle was fixed on a precise date, December 12th, 1893. The big needle indicated the date of this very day, October 26th, 1893. The Excelbox was simply magnificent and intimidating.

And as bizarre as it may sound, Dalya got used to talking to the Excelbox as if it were a living person. And the strange box always listened attentively to the worries of the little girl. Sitting in front of her desk and in front of the strange box, Dalya Bouvard begged in a trembling voice:

- Excelbox … you have always helped me overcome the worst situations and the most difficult times. This time, it is a serious and grave event. A Factory will close; thousands of jobs and thousands of families are at risk. And all of this is because of me, because I refused to give up the inheritance. Today, Excelbox … I ask for your help. I need a clue that will help us save this Factory. I will do anything to save these families. I will do anything!

Writing the question on a piece of paper, Dalya trembled:

What is the 3rd clue?

After a moment of hesitation, Dalya inserted the question into the small rectangular opening of the Excelbox, imploring:

- I will do anything to save these families … I will do anything!

The Excelbox quickly swallowed the small piece of paper inside. The strange box woke up and lit up with a powerful light. And a second later, a small paper appeared on the rectangular edge of the strange box. Dalya remained motionless and paralyzed for a long second. Then, she decided to take it and read:

The immense armored door opens simply with a small key
By the 106, amazed you will be
To survive the outside, look inside

Over the years and the Challenges, Dalya Bouvard had increasingly more confidence in this strange box. The Excelbox always delivered the best solutions to the worst difficulties, and delivered the right words to the worst anxieties. It is also true that the Excelbox never delivered easy-to-understand clues from the first time. The strange box liked to make the brains work.

That day, despite Dalya Bouvard not understanding this clue, she held tight the little paper in her hands, she observed the Excelbox, and she smiled at it:

- Thank you Excelbox! Thank you! Thank you! Thank you!

And like all the previous times, the Excelbox slowly turned off, confident that the little girl will find the meaning of the clue.

From that moment on, Dalya's brain lit up, and her neurons started working. The Excelbox provided a solution, and Dalya was determined to find it!

Chapter 54

The 106

Friday, October 27th, 1893. At the Gymnasium of the Royal Georgetown College.

This afternoon, Dalya was training in the Gymnasium. The exercise was simple; Dalya had to perform 3 moves, under the guidance of the young Professor Tudi.

- Block ... repel ... defend ... good. Again ... block ... repel ... good...

The 3 moves were easy to perform; it consisted of raising your arm to block an intruder, repel the intruder's movement, and moving your arm forward to defend. The movements were simple, and Dalya has repeated them for 2 months. Yet, that day, Dalya was making many mistakes, as if she were learning these moves for the first time.

- Block ... raise your arms ... block ... push away ... no, Mademoiselle, you must repel the intruder's move, and then move the arm forward ... yes, just like that ... block ... push away ... no, you must move the arm forward and not the body ... only the arm ...

At one moment, after several minutes of practice, Dalya stopped to breathe. The young Professor Tudi handed her a bottle of water and a towel:

- A break will do you good.

Dalya sat down and she drank:

- I'm sorry, Professor. I make a lot of mistakes in training, today. My mind is elsewhere.

Dalya was concerned about 2 things; figure out the 3rd clue, and save the Cotton Factory. Her entire brain was desperately trying to find a solution to save the Factory, that she had no neurons left to focus on Gymnastics training.

And from the first minute the little girl entered the Gymnasium, the young Teacher Tudi understood that Dalya was not mentally fit for today's class. Nevertheless, the young Professor Tudi was patient with Dalya, she explained to her:

- The key to any exercise is focus. Generally, all the movements are easy and simple. Except that, it is the focus that makes the movements successful. You must know how to empty your mind, and pause external ideas. Do you remember the breathing exercise we used to do in the school garden?

Dalya remembered perfectly well these exercises; it was during the period when her father was detained. In the garden, the young Teacher Tudi asked Dalya to clear her mind and listen to the sounds of the garden. This exercise was so relaxing and beneficial for Dalya.

Dalya put the bottle of water down, and she immediately stood up:

- Yes, I remember this exercise very well.

Young Professor Tudi continued in an encouraging voice:

- So, do the breathing exercise again here. Close your eyes. Breathe, exhale. Slowly. Keep the noises in your brain away. Now, open your eyes. Look at the Punchingball. Nothing exists in this Gymnasium except this Punchingball. Take a good look at it ... ready? ... block ... repel ... defend ... perfect, again ... block ... repel ... defend ... great, again ... block ...

Dalya Bouvard regained her determination and her focus, under the guidance of the young Professor Tudi.

Saturday, October 28th, 1893. In the Library of the Royal Georgetown College.

Dalya Bouvard and her friend Amira Mounier had spent long hours in the College Library.

The accountant Mr. Jacob Mounier had informed his daughter Amira of the dissolution of the Cotton Factory, belonging to BalthEnterprise Holding. Instantly, Amira Mounier understood that the Lawyer Ernest Laszlo was taking revenge on her friend Dalya Bouvard.

And as soon as Dalya received the 3rd clue from the Excelbox, she informed her friend Amira, to help her find the solution proposed by this strange box. Determined to save this Factory, Dalya and Amira used all the neurons in their brains and all the books in the Library to decipher this clue.

In a quiet section of the College Library, Dalya and Amira sat on armchairs, surrounded by a hundred books. At one point, Dalya affirmed with a sure voice:

- I feel that the solution to save the Factory is in this 3rd clue! The Excelbox has always provided me with answers to my questions.

Amira turned to her friend Dalya:

- I too feel that this clue contains the solution to save the Factory. Except that, the clue is not clear at all.

Dalya re-read a paper for the 40th time:

- The number 106 certainly indicates something. We have written all the possible ideas on this paper; row 106 of the Library ... shelf 106 ... a date maybe? June 10 or October 6. Page 106, but from which book?

While her friend Dalya was looking for the meaning of the number 106, Amira focused on the first sentence of the clue:

- The immense armored door … opens simply with a small key. What I understand is that the Excelbox wants us to look for a small key to open a door. Why do we have to open a door? Which door is it? The door of an office or a bedroom at the grand Mansion? … A small key … a small key … what key?

Dalya Bouvard and Amira Mounier were ardently searching for the meaning of the 3rd clue, with great determination. The Factory must be saved!

Sunday, October 29th, 1893. At the grand Mansion.

The afternoon at the grand Mansion was rather quiet and peaceful. Dalya finished her Philosophy homework. Closing her notebooks, Dalya decided to join her little twin sisters in the fruit and vegetable greenhouse, in the garden.

Since the weather was mild and the sun more present on this winter day, the little twins Ari and Adi decided to help the Gardener with his work in the greenhouse. The maid Cristelle dressed the little twins in waterproof coats, hats, and boots. The Gardener even managed to make plastic gloves for the little twins. Ari and Adi loved helping and working in the greenhouse, in the garden. They moved the pots, watered the plants, picked the fruits and vegetables, cleaned up the dead leaves, and moved the small filled carts to the kitchen. The little twins liked to spend all their free time in the greenhouse, in the garden of the grand Mansion.

When Dalya entered the greenhouse, she was surprised that the Gardener was there alone.

- I thought my little sisters were with you, Monsieur?

When he saw Dalya, the Gardener repressed a little amused smile, while turning the earth with a shovel:

- The little Demoiselles are in the kitchen … with the other employees.

Immediately, Dalya affirmed with a certain voice:

- They did fooleries again, these two! I feel it!

The Gardener hid his amused smile with difficulty. And Dalya understood it easily. She left the greenhouse, heading to the kitchen of the grand Mansion, while murmuring:

- It's almost impossible to spend a day without fooleries! It would take an army to guard my little sisters! They never stop their fooleries!

Entering the kitchen of the grand Mansion, Dalya had difficulty understanding what was happening. The little twins were both lying on the big divan near the kitchen window, they were murmuring in an exhausted tone:

- Stomach hurts ... stomach hurts ... stomach hurts...
- We no more eat strawberries ... no more eat ever...

The maid Cristelle added pillows under the heads of the little twins:

- Don't move ... lie down, Mesdemoiselles.

The Cook was actively looking for a jar in the kitchen pantry. The help Cook Océanie came into the kitchen and she handed a small jar to Cristelle:

- Here is some perfume. Put some on little towels, so they can breathe some of it. It will do them good.

Dalya approached her little sisters, and she asked in a worried tone:

- What is happening to them?

Cristelle and Océanie exchanged a look and an amused smile. After a second of hesitation, Océanie informed Dalya:

- Your ... your little sisters are ... they're a little sick. Nothing serious, don't worry, Mademoiselle! They just have severe diarrhea ... because of ... because of ...

Cristelle continued in an amused tone:

- The little twins ate the strawberries from the greenhouse.

Except Dalya was confused:

- How many strawberries did they eat?

At this question, the head of the grand Mansion appeared behind Dalya. When handing Cristelle some clean towels, Mr. Bûchebois replied:

- The Demoiselles ate all the strawberries in the greenhouse!

The little twins seemed to be in pain, lying on the couch, their bellies swollen. The employees of the grand Mansion repressed their amused laugh with great difficulty. Dalya reprimanded her little sisters:

- You ate all the strawberries in the greenhouse?! There must have been at least 4 kilos of strawberries!! But what got into you?! 4 kilos of strawberries is a lot!! Look at your condition now!!

Océanie handed a small towel filled with perfume to the little twins. Ari and Adi whispered breathlessly:

-   Sorry Dindin ... we never eat strawberries again ...
-   Stomach hurts ... stomach hurts ... stomach hurts ...

Dalya asked in a worried tone:

-   Should I look for a Doctor?

Océanie tried to reassure her:

-   It's nothing serious, Mademoiselle. They just ate too much fruits, and without washing them well. They only have severe diarrhea. They've cleared almost everything already.

The Cook approached them:

-   I am preparing an herbal tea for the Demoiselles, for today and also for tomorrow. It will do them good and empty their stomachs completely. I already have all the ingredients. On the other hand, I don't have much star anise spice left for tomorrow. And Igor is busy putting away the wood before the predicted rain.

Immediately, Dalya turned to the Cook:

-   I can get you that spice, downtown, Mr. Ferrero. I'm going to change right away.

Turning toward her little twin sisters, Dalya threatened them in a serious tone:

-   And you two, you will not move from here! Don't make a single move until I return! Understood?!

Under the discreet and amused laugh of the employees of the grand Mansion, and the murmurs of pain of the little twins, Dalya left the kitchen to go downtown.

Several minutes of walking later.

Dalya arrived at a small kiosk in the market, in front of the Toscana restaurant. The herbalist provided Dalya with the spice the Cook needed. And before Dalya could leave the market to return to the grand Mansion, she met a familiar silhouette.

-   Good afternoon, Lalla Fatim Fadl. I haven't seen you for a long time. How are you doing?

Lalla Fatim Fadl was a flower seller in the market. A kind, sweet old woman with long white hair with shiny highlights, respected and adored by everyone. The old woman turned around and she smiled at Dalya:

-   Moonlight! It's a pleasure to see you today. It seems like a busy month for everyone. I've just received my seeds to plant. The next flowers will be magnificent!

Dalya did not hesitate to take 2 heavy bags from the hands of the old woman:

- I finished my shopping here at the market. I can help you carry those bags of seeds.

Lalla Fatim Fadl replied with a caring voice:

- You are always helpful and kind, moonlight. Thank you!

The last days of October were calm. The trees were getting ready to change foliage, the sky was often gray and clear, the squirrels were assiduously cleaning their habitats. The city of Georgetown was living a serene autumn.

After several minutes, Dalya and Lalla Fatim Fadl arrived in a popular Alley. The houses were almost all the same; built with 2 floors, small windows, and wooden doors. One detail caught Dalya's attention; clay pots filled with flowers and plants were placed on all the windows and in front of all the doors. It seemed to be a popular and modest Alley, welcoming families of workers and employees. And the hundreds of pots of flowers and plants embellished the Alley, with a pleasant sight and a delicious fragrance.

When Dalya Bouvard followed Lalla Fatim Fadl inside a modest house, Dalya saw the old woman's house for the first time. Although with a modest income from her sale of flowers, Lalla Fatim Fadl's home was meticulously tidy and clean. At the entrance, a small kitchen was on the right, a small table and two wooden chairs were placed in the middle of the house. The old woman was known for her medicinal recipes; an entire wall of the house was in shelves, and thousands of jars were placed there, all filled with different herbs and ingredients. On the left of the house, there was a bed with colorful cushions, and a large closet.

At the back side of the house, there was a beautiful little garden. Thousands of flowers and plants were carefully planted there. A delicious smell of freshness invaded the air. Scarlet color petals and fresh greenery adorned the garden. Observing this place, Dalya exclaimed in wonder:

- It's ... it's magnificent, Lalla Fatim. Your garden is a paradise.

The old woman explained to her:

- Everything blooms and beautifies when it is well cared for.

Dalya put the bags of seeds in a corner of the garden:

- And thanks to your care, your flowers and plants are the most beautiful of the entire city, Lalla Fatim.

Lalla Fatim Fadl smiled proudly, before putting a small saucepan back to heat. She turned to Dalya:

- I made a delicious lentil soup, today. You will definitely like it!
- I don't want to disturb you more than that, Lalla Fatim. You definitely need to rest after your day's work.

Except that Lalla Fatim insisted on her tasting her soup. And not wishing to appear rude, Dalya agreed to stay a few more minutes.

Watching Lalla Fatim Fadl stir the pan, Dalya couldn't help feeling a sense of pity for the old woman. Lalla Fatim Fadl lived alone in this house. Yet, the loneliness and poverty did not erase the smile on the old woman's face.

By placing a bowl of lentils and a spoon in front of her guest, Lalla Fatim Fadl smiled at her:

- And there you go, Moonlight … this is my best lentil recipe!

At the first taste, Dalya exclaimed:

- It's very very good Lalla Fatim, really delicious!! Thank you very much !!

Lalla Fatim laughed:

- I was sure you will like my soup!

And although Dalya loved lentils, her heart tightened increasingly with each spoon of soup. Dalya couldn't help feeling sorry for the old woman, living alone, and having only a simple lentil soup for dinner.

When suddenly, a 5-year-old boy knocked on the door, and he entered the house. He wore modest clothes, a small coat, and a large cap on his head. The little boy seemed to be used to coming to this house:

- Lalla Fatim … Lalla Fatim. Good evening. Mother sends you this.

The little boy put the dish, covered with a small napkin, on the dining table in front of Dalya. Lalla Fatim Fadl greeted him with a joyful smile:

- Thank you, my boy. Wait for me a second!

Lalla Fatim Fadl poured lentil soup into a bowl, she covered the bowl with a small plate, and she gave it to the little boy:

- Hold this, my boy. Give it to your mom. And walk slowly so as not to spill anything!
- Thank you, Lalla Fatim. Until tomorrow!

Dalya silently ate her lentil soup, and although several curious questions invaded her mind, she didn't dare to ask the old woman any questions, so as not to appear rude and too curious. Lalla Fatim went back to sit next to Dalya, and she took off the napkin that covered the dish that the little boy brought:

- These are two fried sole fish. My neighbor cooks the fish deliciously well!

Dalya tasted the fish that Lalla Fatim placed on a plate for her:

- And I agree, it's delicious!! I have never tasted fried fish, with breadcrumbs of garlic and fine herbs. At the grand Mansion, the Co...

Suddenly, someone interrupted Dalya, and entered Lalla Fatim Fadl's house. A little girl gently placed a small bowl on the dining table, in front of Dalya. The little girl must have been a bit younger than Dalya's little sisters. She wore a pretty cotton dress with long sleeves, and braids in her hair. The little girl jumped up happily:

- Granny! Granny! Bowl to you! Bowl to you!

Lalla Fatim hugged the little girl in her arms, and she kissed her tenderly on the cheeks:

- How beautiful is my little flower! Thank you for bringing me this bowl, you are very helpful. Wait a minute for me, please.

The old woman stood up and she filled a small bowl with lentils. Covering it carefully with a plate, Lalla Fatim handed it to the little girl, ordering her:

- Take that bowl back to your mom ... don't run ... and walk slowly.

The little girl turned around and she left the house, walking slowly, holding the bowl of lentils firmly in her hands. When Lalla Fatim sat down again, she took the cover off the bowl that the little girl had brought back. Lalla Fatim let out a little amused laugh:

- My neighbor guessed right today! There's nothing better than a good tomato and onion salad to accompany my lentil soup.

Dalya's curiosity grew. And yet, she repressed her questions, and she ate the salad that Lalla Fatim Fadl served her:

- Yes, I must admit that I too like lentils with tomato and onion salad. My little sisters love it too!

While eating her dinner, Lalla Fatim Fadl exclaimed:

- Your little twin sisters are adorable. I meet them sometimes on their way to school.

Dalya laughed:

- They are not always adorable! They do a lot of fooleries, almost every day. When it's quiet and calm at the grand Mansion, it worries me, because I know a disaster is brewing!

Lalla Fatim and Dalya laughed heartily. When someone knocked on the door, and walked in quickly. A young boy, tall and thin, placed an oven mold on the table, repeating:

- Aie aie !! It's hot !! It's hot !! aie aie !!

Lalla Fatim exclaimed:

- You always forget your gloves, boy! The dishes are too hot for your fingers!

The young boy laughed nervously:

- Yes, I seriously must be careful; otherwise, I'll lose my fingers!

Lalla Fatim stood up and she served him a bowl of lentils. Handing him the filled bowl, Lalla Fatim gave the boy a kitchen napkin, and she ordered him in a serious tone:

- Hold the dishes with this napkin; use both hands, so your fingers will suffer less!
- Thank you, Lalla Fatim, I'll return the napkin to you later, when I've finished distributing the dishes.
- Walk slowly, don't run !

When the young boy left the house, Dalya immediately guessed the contents of the oven mold:

- The young boy has brought you a dish of potato gratin. It seems to be cooked with béchamel sauce and cheese. The smell is delicious!

Lalla Fatim sat down again:

- Yes, and he always forgets to wear gloves. The poor little boy always ends up with burns on his fingers.

Dalya didn't understand what was really going on. Within an hour, Lalla Fatim Fadl's dinner table was filled with several different dishes, brought in by several young children.

If Dalya holds the questions in her mind one more minute, her brain will explode. While tasting the potato gratin, Dalya asked hesitantly:

- It's delicious; I really like the béchamel sauce. The young boy said he'll bring the napkin back to you when he's finished distributing the dishes. Does the young boy work as a delivery boy ?

Lalla Fatim helped herself to a portion of the gratin, and she laughed innocently at Dalya's question:

- Oh moonlight ... all the kids in this Alley are deliverers.

Confusion invaded Dalya. She put down her fork and she asked in a polite tone:

- Why are the children deliverers?

Except that before the old woman could answer, a little girl entered the house, and she placed a small bowl on the table. The little girl angrily announced to the old woman:

- I poured some zucchini soup, Lalla Fatim. Just a little bit. I'm sorry, but it's because of Pierre who was carrying a dish of hot gratin, he was running and he pushed me!! It's his fault!!

With a little amused laugh, Lalla Fatim reassured the little girl:

- It's alright, my pretty. But I told him to walk slowly.

While serving a bowl of lentils to the little girl, Lalla Fatim asked her in an attentive voice:

- Take this bowl back to your aunt, walk around the edges of the houses and go slowly!
- Yes, Lalla Fatim!! I'm going slowly!!

The little girl waited for a few seconds at the door of the old woman's house, checking right and left that no one was running. And then, she went out, heading for a house in front.

For a long second, Dalya stared at Lalla Fatim Fadl's dinner table. Only a few minutes ago, Dalya felt sorry for the old woman's loneliness and poverty, eating lentil soup alone. Now, the table was full of such delicious and varied meals and dishes: fried sole fish with garlic and fine herbs, a tomato and onion salad, a potato gratin with béchamel sauce and melted cheese, zucchini and parsley soup. And apart from the food that arrived every two minutes at the old woman's table, it seemed that Lalla Fatim was never left alone. The door to her house almost never closed.

Dalya thought aloud:

- It's ... it really is a feast!

Lalla Fatim laughed heartily, helping herself to the zucchini soup:

- Yes, it is a particularity of this Alley. Every evening, all the women in the neighborhood share what they have cooked. And it is the children who deliver the dishes to neighboring houses.

Dalya finally understood everything that had been going on since her coming into Lalla Fatim Fadl's house. The old woman continued to explain:

- And the sharing isn't only in cooked meals. This Alley is mainly inhabited by employees, workers, and craftsmen. In the house in front of me, the hairdresser takes care of the children's hair for free, once a month. In the 3rd house on my left, there is a kind volunteer Teacher who helps the neighborhood children with all their homework. And at the end of the street, an ex-army doctor offers medical care to everyone.

Listening carefully, Dalya was amazed by Lalla Fatim Fadl's explanations. And slowly eating her varied dinner, Lalla Fatim Fadl smiled:

- This is what mutual aid looks like in Alley 106. My table looks like an amazing feast every night. I admit that many times, I can't eat everything. The portions I receiv...

When suddenly Dalya interrupted the old woman:

- Sorry… what did you say?

Lalla Fatim Fadl repeated her sentence, getting some bread to finish her zucchini soup:

- This is what mutual aid in Alley 106 looks like...

At that moment, an idea formed in Dalya's mind. She leaned back in her chair, and she thought aloud:

- The Alley n°106 … n°106 …

Suddenly, Dalya jumped up from her chair:

- The number 106 was in the clue! So, it was the number of this Alley. But why did the Excelbox made me come to this Alley? It's probably for a good reason! The Excelbox never randomly or mistakenly gives clues!

Lalla Fatim Fadl stopped eating her soup, and she looked at Dalya in a confused air:

- Are you alright, my child?

Dalya ignored the old woman's question, and she continued to think aloud:

- So, I am in the Alley N°106 that the Excelbox indicated to me … but why? What am I supposed to find in this Alley? What is the Excelbox trying to tell me? … It's a modest Alley, with families who share their meals every evening. Their table is an amazing feast … an amazing feast … 106 … by the 106, amazed you will be … an amazing feast … by the 106, amazed y…

And as clear as the water can be, at this precise moment, in this modest house, in this modest Alley, Dalya abruptly stood up, and she screamed:

- I FOUND IT!

The next day, Monday, October 30th, 1893.

This day was very long for Dalya Bouvard. She was in a hurry to finish her courses at the College, and return to the grand Mansion. An idea has been running through her mind all day since her dinner with Lalla Fatim Fadl the day before.

When the 5 PM bell finally rang, Dalya and Amira ran toward the school exit. Out of breath, Amira Mounier affirmed:

- I'm going to find my father. He must surely be at work at this hour.

Dalya replied, while adjusting her bag:

- And I'm going to get the Lawyer Mr. Sloan Wilfrid. We all meet at the grand Mansion!

At the exit door of the Royal Georgetown College, Amira Mounier ran to the right, and Dalya Bouvard ran to the left. With a hasty step, Dalya arrived at Mr. Sloan Wilfrid's Law office. Being absent for a trial, the Lawyer was not in his office. Therefore, Dalya left a message for Mr. Sloan Wilfrid at his Secretary, before returning to the grand Mansion.

2 hours later. At the grand Mansion.

When Dalya saw through the window a car entering the grand Mansion, she rushed out of her room and down the stairs. In the hall of the grand Mansion, Lawyer Sloan Wilfrid entered first, and he greeted her joyfully:

- Good evening, Mademoiselle!

On the last step of the stairs, Dalya replied to him:

- Good evening, Mr. Wilfrid. Thank you for coming.

The young Lyor Laszlo was the 2nd to enter the hall, and he asked in a usual annoyed tone:

- What is going on again here?

Before Dalya could answer, Amira Mounier and her father entered the hall of the grand Mansion. Amira informed Dalya:

- Mr. Wilfrid saw us on the way. He brought us with him in the car.

Lawyer Sloan Wilfrid took off his coat, and he placed it on a chair in the hall:

- I received your message, Mademoiselle Dalya. It was urgent. Nothing serious, I hope?

The accountant Mr. Jacob Mounier took off his hat and he looked worried:

- My daughter Amira picked me up from work. Is everything alright, Mademoiselle ?

Lyor Laszlo repeated his question in an annoyed tone, taking off his coat too:

- What is going on again?

Dalya cleared her throat and she announced:

- Messieurs … I think I have an idea to find the money that will save the Cotton Factory.

The three men exchanged a confused look. And they answered instantly:

- I need a tea!
- I need to sit down!
- I need to understand!

Immediately, everyone settled in the living room of the grand Mansion. In a calm voice, Dalya Bouvard explained the 3rd clue she received from the Excelbox, she talked about her dinner with Lalla Fatim Fadl in her modest house, and she explained the idea of the Excelbox to find the money which will save the Factory.

After several minutes of a focused silence, Lawyer Sloan Wilfrid was the first to speak. He relaxed in his chair, thinking aloud:

- So, if I understood correctly, the idea is to organize a feast. Invite businessmen to convince them to invest their money in the Factory.

Amira Mounier confirmed her friend Dalya's idea:

- It is quite correct. And Thanksgiving is coming up. During this period, people are more empathetic and generous. Dalya had the idea of organizing a feast on Thanksgiving Day.

The accountant Mr. Jacob Mounier murmured in a serious voice:

- A fundraiser and a Thanksgiving feast ... to save the Cotton Factory.

Lyor Laszlo straightened up on his chair; he seemed interested in the new idea:

- Instead of visiting businessmen one by one and separately, you want to invite them all to one lunch? ... a Thanksgiving feast?

Dalya Bouvard affirmed the idea:

- Yes, one lunch, one Thanksgiving feast. It would be easier to convince them all. And the Thanksgiving period is always generous.

Lawyer Sloan Wilfrid was curious:

- And this idea ... this idea of a feast, was given by this strange box? The Excelbox?

Amira and Dalya exchanged an accomplice look and smile. Dalia replied:

- We searched for the meaning of the clue for days, without succeeding in figuring it out. And by pure chance, I found myself in the Alley N°106, and I attended a generous feast. That's how I understood the idea of the Excelbox... a feast to save the Cotton Factory.

The Excelbox has always impressed and intimidated everyone, without exception.

A long second of silence and thinking followed. When the head of the grand Mansion entered the living room, he presented the tea to the people present. Lawyer Sloan Wilfrid sat up from his chair and he asked him in a serious voice:

- Monsieur Bûchebois ... with the current staff and expenses, how many people can we accommodate for lunch at the grand Mansion?

The head of the grand Mansion replied immediately:

- We can very well serve 100 people, Mr. Wilfrid.

The accountant Mr. Jacob Mounier made calculations in his head, in a loud voice:

- 100 people ... 100 people can finance at least 10% of the amount the Factory needs. If you collect at least $120,000, you can already start restructuring the Factory.

Lyor Laszlo continued the sentence of the accountant Mr. Jacob Mounier:

-   … and by restructuring the Factory, we can delay its closing for a few more months, while we find other funds!

Lawyer Sloan Wilfrid repeated aloud:

-   A Thanksgiving feast…100 people…at least 10% of the amount needed…I think it's doable! We will be far from the needed amount of 1 million and 200 thousand dollars. But for the future of these thousands of families, we must at least try!

Dalya Bouvard, Amira Mounier, and her father the accountant Mr. Jacob, Lyor Laszlo, the head of the grand Mansion Mr. Bûchebois, and the Lawyer Sloan Wilfrid… all the people present in the living room, they exchanged a determined look, in front of the Challenge that awaited them.

Chapter 55

Not unpleasant

Saturday, November 4th, 1893. At the grand Mansion.

In the kitchen of the grand Mansion, the help Cook Océanie was seated in front of the table, she was busy peeling a basket full of pomegranates. The outside door opened, the maid Cristelle and Dalya came back from the garden, and they placed 2 baskets filled with pomegranates on the kitchen table. Cristelle sighed:

- Pomegranates are delicious, but still heavy to carry!

Dalya laughed :

- We should have used the carriage to carry them here to the kitchen. I too didn't think it was that heavy!

Observing the 3 pomegranate baskets on the kitchen table, Océanie exclaimed:

- The pomegranates' harvest has been good this season. Usually, the Gardener fills only one basket. This time we have 3 baskets to peel.

While Cristelle was using the water to reduce her thirst, Dalya offered to Océanie:

- I can stay and help you peel the pomegranates. It will go faster.

Océanie exclaimed :

- Certainly not, Mademoiselle! It's nice of you to offer us your help. But surely you have other more fun things to do this afternoon.

Cristelle picked up a knife, and she sat down next to Océanie to help her peel the fruits. Tasting a few pomegranate seeds, Cristelle said:

- The mini grains are sweet and delicious. The pulp is juicy. The pomegranates juice will be a delight! I wonder if the Cook has any savory pomegranate recipes.

Océanie replied immediately :

- Of course! There are many savory pomegranate recipes. A lentil salad with foie gras and pomegranate seeds. Avocado, goat cheese and pomegranate toast. Salmon with fine herbs and pomegranates. Pomegranate Shrimp Curry...

Dalya and Cristelle exchanged a surprised look:

- It looks very delicious! I can't wait to taste it!
- Just hearing these recipes makes me hungry!

Before leaving the kitchen, Dalya asked in a polite voice:

- Can I take 2 or 3 pomegranates? It is for the French neighbors. I was thinking of visiting them this afternoon.

Océanie exclaimed :

- Certainly, Mademoiselle. Take a small basket from the Pantry, and choose as many pomegranates as you want. Mrs. Glorina is a very nice woman, I adore her. Bring her 5 or 6 pomegranates.

Cristelle continued to peel the fruit:

- Mrs. Glorina is… the midwife who helped you give birth? Isn't she?

Océanie replied while taking another pomegranate to peel:

- Yes. She is the housekeeper of the French neighbors, the Poirier family.

While Dalya was looking for a basket, Cristelle and Océanie chatted around the kitchen table. Cristelle tasted a few seeds :

- Sometimes on the road, I meet the son of the old woman, in a car driven by his chauffeur. Richard is his name? … Yes, Richard Poirier. He seems very calm and polite. Apparently, he's gifted, and he has an important position in politics.

Dalya approached the kitchen table, and she selected the pomegranates. Océanie drank from her cup of tea, and she continued to peel:

- Yes, that's what I heard about Richard Poirier. This young man is so smart that they recruited him despite his young age. And… Richard Poirier is also a handsome man! I met him once, downtown. He was wearing a very elegant black-tie suit; it gave him an attractive allure.

Océanie took a pomegranate and she asked in a curious voice:

- Mademoiselle Dalya … you have surely met Richard Poirier, in his house. Is he really that attractive up close?

At that precise moment, Océanie looked up at Dalya. And she noticed a strange thing. Dalya Bouvard had blushing cheeks, and she looked intimidated. Whispering a few words, Dalya forced herself to sound natural:

- He…I…he's…Richard is nice…I…I'll take 5 pomegranates. I'm going to change to go out. I won't be late.

Quickly, Dalya took the full basket and she hurried out of the kitchen. The maid Cristelle suspected nothing; she continued to peel the fruit:

- I can't wait to taste the Lentils with Foie Gras and Pomegranate recipe. I'm curious about the taste !

As for the help Cook Océanie, she was curious about something completely different. Océanie was the only one who noticed that Dalya had blushed and she seemed intimidated when asked about Richard Poirier. And for a long minute, the help Cook Océanie turned around and she watched the little Dalya Bouvard leaving the kitchen.

A few hours later. In the house of the French neighbors.

On this November afternoon, in the living room, Richard Poirier was sitting next to the fireplace. On the armchair in front of him, Dalya Bouvard was focused on writing down all the young man's explanations. When Richard put down his cup of tea, he continued:

- The Law of the 3 states of Mr. Auguste Comte, a positivist Philosopher, considers that each branch of human knowledge passes through three successive theoretical states: theological, metaphysical, and positive.

Dalya muttered, writing quickly :

- Theological … Metaphysical …

Richard finished her sentence :

- And positive. About the Theological state, it is the stage where the human spirit tries to explain the phenomenon of nature, the existence of man, the genesis of the universe, through myths and direct intervention of divine and supernatural being.

Dalya quickly turned over a paper, and she whispered while noting:

- Through ... direct intervention ... of ... divine and supernatural being.

After giving her a second to write it all down, Richard continued:

- The 2nd state is metaphysical… It is the same search for the phenomenon of the Theological state, but instead of attributing them to divine and supernatural being, metaphysics thus replaces supernatural and divine powers, with constructions conceptual abstract of the spirit. The Metaphysical state prepares the ground for the sciences.

As she wrote the last sentence, Dalya reread her notes:

- So… One, the Theological state. Two, the Metaphysical state. And three, the Positive state.

At that moment, Dalya thought aloud:

- It seems to me that we have already studied the positive state.

Richard confirmed :

- Yes, that's right. Last week, we studied how scientific knowledge is constructed. There was a notion of the Philosopher Auguste Comte and his positive state. It was in the chapter on scientific progress ... page 150 ... I believe ... or 160 ...

At this precise moment, a strange incident happened. In the living room, near the fireplace, Richard and Dalya were sitting opposite to each other. And in the middle of them, there was a small table, where were placed some books and a tray of tea. Strangely, Richard and Dalya had the same idea and at the same second; to consult the book of Philosophy, in order to be sure of the exact page which indicated the notion of the positive state.

The book was placed on the table, in the middle of the two young people. Richard and Dalya rose from their chairs at the same time, and they stretched out their arms to pick up the same book. When suddenly...their hands touched, and a powerful sensation invaded the two young people.

Immediately, Richard and Dalya backed away, their hands shaking. They felt a strong, uncomfortable, electric sensation... but not unpleasant.

Their meetings were already intimidating enough; the contact of their hands only aggravated this embarrassment. Regardless of the many hours of lessons and the many meetings, time did not calm this strange feeling of embarrassment between the two young people. Each time, Richard still felt his throat tighten, and his words slip away. Dalya still blushed at the young man's words and stares.

And even though their meetings were embarrassing and intimidating...even though the touch of their hands was an uncomfortable but not an unpleasant feeling...Richard and Dalya never missed an opportunity to meet.

Chapter 56

The volunteers

Sunday, November 5th, 1893. At the grand Mansion.

Autumn has well settled in the city of Georgetown. The sky was embellished with gray clouds; the trees were tainted with many colors. Although the sun was present, the air was cold. The wind was blowing a little stronger than usual. And you think the wind only carried the leaves of trees? Oh no. Throughout Georgetown city, the Autumn wind was blowing something else ... by word of mouth, a little rumor was spreading quietly and certainly.

On this beautiful Sunday morning, Dalya got up early. She put on her blue overalls, a cotton sweater, and her gardening boots. Although it was Sunday, it was a busy day for Dalya and for many people too.

When Dalya arranged up her hair in a bun and hid it in a cap, she heard the footsteps and joyful screams of her little twin sisters entering her room:

- Coucou Dindin !
- Coucou Dindin !
- We help today !
- Istelle said we wear hats and boots !
- We help today !
- We ready to help !

Dalya knelt down in front of her little sisters, and she zipped up their pink waterproof coats:

- Alright, alright ... you can help. But I don't want any fooleries today! Is that clear? We are planning an important party. And if you mess up, it might delay us and ruin the party! No fooleries today!

The little twins were determined to obey, for once:

- Oki Dindin! We are nice today!
- Yes! No fooleries, promise Dindin!

Dalya led her little sisters downstairs to have breakfast. When entering the dining room, Dalya was pleasantly surprised to find several familiar silhouettes there. Seated around the table, the Lawyer Sloan Wilfrid was chatting with the accountant Mr. Jacob Mounier and with Lyor Laszlo, while enjoying coffee and toasts.

- If the bank allows us to pay the debts of the Factory, in installments payments...
- Yes, it would be a big time saver for the Factory. How soon can you convince them, Mr. Jacob?

- If they offer us 2 and a half years, or even 3 years, the Factory can survive, Mr. Wilfrid.
- 3 years of payment terms would be perfect! Replied Lyor, serving himself some jam on his toast.

The other people around the table were: her friend from College Amira Mounier, and her two friends from the market Maurice Gus and Alfie Jaq. The two boys did not hesitate for a second to respond to their friend Dalya's call for help in organizing this party.

Amira Mounier was eating breakfast, while listening carefully to Maurice Gus' explanations:

- So, if we manage to get this amount of money, in 7 or 6 years from now... me and Alfie, we can rent a place and open our own grocery store!

Amira Mounier was very impressed with Maurice and Alfie's business ideas:

- It's really awesome! I'm sure your business will do great! And do you need a permit to open the grocery store? Do you have an idea of the products you want to sell?

Maurice Gus was answering Amira's questions, while putting maple syrup on his pancakes. As for Alfie Jaq, he filled his plate and his mouth with whatever was on the breakfast table. Eating to his fill, Alfie Jaq didn't care about any conversation going on around the table, that day.

The head of the grand Mansion, Mr. Bûchebois went around the table, serving the present people coffee, hot chocolate, or orange juice. As soon as the little twins entered the dining room, they settled into their special seats. Immediately, the help Cook Océanie served the little twins two bowls of oats with a spoonful of honey:

- Who wants raspberries? And who wants strawberries?

Ari and Adi answered joyfully:

- Me want strawberries!
- And me want raspberries !

Dalya greeted everyone present, before settling herself on a chair. Lawyer Sloan Wilfrid announced aloud, while getting a 2nd toast:

- We are all gathered here today to discuss a plan to prepare this party. We need to determine the menu, the guest list, the place to prepare, and the jobs to distribute. Monsieur Bûchebois was kind enough to prepare this hearty breakfast for us. We have a long day ahead of us, and we need strength!

The head of the grand Mansion smiled proudly:

- It's the least we can do for you, Mesdemoiselles and Messieurs.

The maid Cristelle entered the dining room, carrying a large plate of omelette with cheese:

- Make way! Aie aie it's hot! Make way, please!

Alfie Jaq was the first to react. Immediately, he stood up and he pushed aside the basket of toasts. Cristelle placed the plate right in front of Alfie:

- Thank you, young man !

Amira Mounier and Maurice Gus barely repressed their laugh. It was no coincidence that Alfie made room for the omelette plate, right in front of him. Alfie sat back in his chair, his eyes wide open and amazed, watching and smelling the large omelette with cheese.

Dalya served herself omelette and bread. The head of the grand Mansion refilled her cup of coffee. And the conversations around the table resumed their course.

When suddenly, the door of the dining room swung open. The assistant Igor came in and he announced in a serious and alarmed tone:

- I think you should all come see what's going on outside. Right now !

Igor didn't need to be repeated, all the people present in the dining room left their plates and cutlery behind, and they followed Igor, with a quick and worried step. At the exit of the hall of the grand Mansion, everyone found the Gardener and the Cook. The two men were motionless, their worried stare watching the fence entrance door of the grand Mansion. And when the people present turned their eyes toward the point fixated by the two employees, surprise and confusion invaded them.

In just a few seconds, about 40 people walked through the entrance door of the grand Mansion, and they were heading toward the house. Men and women, of different looks and ages. Dalya and her friends exchanged worried looks. Lawyer Sloan Wilfrid thought aloud:

- Who are all these people? Why are they coming here?

When suddenly, Alfie Jaq and Maurice Gus recognized familiar faces from afar:

- The man who walks with the crutch… it's the Dean of Merchants, Mr. Kenan Einsenberg!
- The flower seller is there too… Lalla Fatim Fadl… yes, that's her!

Dalya thought aloud:

- They are the vendors of the market. But what do they want? Why are they here?

The answer to this question will soon come. When the 40 people arrived at the entrance of the grand Mansion, a man preceded them. And it was the Dean of Merchants Mr. Kenan Einsenberg. He was easily noticeable thanks to his copper beard, his usual green coat, and his crutch. The Dean of Merchants addressed a little person:

- Good morning, Demoiselle Dalya !

In a hesitant and confused voice, Dalya smiled:

- Good morning, Mr. Einsenberg.

The employees of the grand Mansion, Dalya's friends, the Lawyers, they were all impatient to know the reason of the presence of all these many men and women. The Dean of Merchants announced in a serious tone:

- A little rumor spread these last days, in Georgetown city. We heard that a little girl was planning a Thanksgiving party to raise money, in order to save the Cotton Factory.

Dalya answered in a timid voice:

- Yes, that's quite true.

Mr. Kenan Einsenberg smiled proudly:

- Well then Demoiselle ... this Factory you're trying to save, is the jobs of our brothers, our sons, and our friends. This Factory is the main source of income of our families. If you think the Cotton Factory can be saved, then we're here to give you a helping hand!

All the people behind Dalya Bouvard were surprised by this offer. The employees of the grand Mansion exchanged surprised stares. Amira Mounier, Maurice Gus, and Alfie Jaq let out a surprised laugh. The accountant Mr. Jacob Mounier and Lyor Laszlo smiled. Lawyer Sloan Wilfrid walked toward the Dean of Merchants, and he asked in a surprised voice:

- If I understand correctly ... you all want to help us organize this Thanksgiving party? Here at the grand Mansion?

The Dean of Merchants replied to the young Lawyer in a determined tone:

- That's right! If you accept our help, we will participate. And it's going to be the best party this town has ever had; you have my word!

Lawyer Sloan Wilfrid let out an amused laugh:

- Your help is more than welcome! We need it badly! Thank you!

Dalya Bouvard approached the Dean of Merchants, and she said to him in an emotional tone:

- Thank you, Mr. Einsenberg. Thank you so much for your help!!

At that moment, the Dean of Merchants bowed to Dalya, and he replied in a caring voice:

- Oh no... thank you, Demoiselle. You were not concerned by this Factory, and yet you wanted to save these jobs. It is a generous and noble act. The employees of this Factory and their families, they will not forget your gesture.

Immediately, the Dean of Merchants asked the Lawyer Sloan Wilfrid:

- So, Monsieur ... do you have a plan for this party?

Exchanging a confused look with the employees of the grand Mansion, Lawyer Sloan Wilfrid ran his hand through his hair, and he laughed nervously:

- To tell the truth, we have not yet discussed the organization of this party. And I admit, I'm only good at Law, I don't know anything about party planning. I don't know where to start.

The Dean of Merchants smiled:

- We've come at the right time, then!

The minutes that followed were impressive. The organization of the party began, under the directives of the Dean of Merchants Mr. Kenan Einsenberg:

- Who is in charge of the kitchen at the grand Mansion?

The Cook and Océanie advanced forward:

- I take care of the cooking, Ferrero Lutché … and Océanie Shell is my assistant.

The Dean of Merchants indicated for a few men and women to advance toward the Cook, and he proudly introduced them:

- Mr. Ferrero Lutché … you have at your disposal 10 of the best Cooks in the city of Georgetown. Each in a culinary specialty. And here are 5 assistants to take care of the cooking and the dishes!

The Cook and Océanie exchanged a delighted look. The Dean of Merchants presented 5 big men:

- And here are sellers of vegetables, fruits, meats, herbs, and dairy products. All market vendors offer their products for free, for this lunch. Order anything you want!

The Cook Mr. Ferrero Lutché quickly recovered from this good surprise, he asked the volunteer Cooks to follow him inside the kitchen of the grand Mansion, while informing them:

- We will start by establishing the menu. Then, we will decide how many plates to serve, how many products to order. And afterwards, we will distribute the dishes to be cooked, according to the specialty of each one.

The help Cook Océanie accompanied the women to the kitchen pantry, explaining to them:

- While the Cooks decide on the menu, we will take out the plates and cutlery to wash and dry them. Then, table linens and napkins. When the Cooks have ordered the ingredients for the menu, we will help them with the cooking.

When the Cook and Océanie disappeared inside the grand Mansion, with the group of volunteers, a man advanced a few steps forward, and he introduced himself:

- Hello. I'm the Headwaiter of the Toscana restaurant. We would also like to offer our help. All the waiters of the Toscana restaurant will be at your disposal on the day of the party, to serve lunch and dishes to the guests. And I will guarantee myself an impeccable service.

Lawyer Sloan Wilfrid exclaimed:

- That's a generous help, Monsieur. Thank you, thank you very much!

The Headwaiter of the Toscana Restaurant bowed his head respectfully:

- It's the least we can do, Mr. Wilfrid. If you will excuse me, I will join the Cooks, in order to know the number of dishes to be served, and how many waiters you will need.

At that moment, and in a curious voice, the Dean of Merchants asked:

- Where will the lunch and the party be held?

Mr. Bûchebois, the head of the grand Mansion replied:

- The grand Mansion has a large dining room and a large party room.

The Dean of Merchants affirmed:

- Perfect. And who will be in charge of arranging the tables and chairs?

The Gardener and the assistant Igor stepped forward. The Gardener replied:

- Me and Igor, we will take care of the arrangement of these two places. The tables and chairs are in the attic of the grand Mansion. How many men can help us bring them downstairs?

The Dean of Merchants turned toward the Gardener:

- Here are 6 men to help you carry and adjust tables and chairs.

The Gardener rolled up the sleeves of his shirt:

- Good ... very good ... that will be enough for us. And can someone help us hammer and varnish the chairs and tables? It's been a long time since we've used this furniture.

At this moment, a man emerged from the group of volunteers. Dalya was surprised to find a familiar face. Dalya's paternal uncle, Giorgi Bouvard proudly announced:

- I will take care of repairing and varnishing the furniture. I already have all the equipment I need. I will just need a place to work.

Dalya exclaimed:

- Thank you, Uncle Giorgi! Thank you for your help!

The old man blushed:

- It will be with great pleasure, Biggo! And I'm good at fixing furniture!

The Gardener turned to his assistant:

-   Igor, lead Monsieur Giorgi Bouvard to the back garage. It's spacious. And I will lead the men to the attic to bring down the tables and chairs. Mr. Giorgi, we'll bring the chairs to you first to repair and varnish them. Then, we'll bring the rest of the furniture to you.
-   Understood, Monsieur !

Immediately, the men split in two; one group headed to the attic, and the other group headed to the garage. Instantly, a small silhouette came out among the volunteers, and she asked in a soft voice:

-   And who will take care of decorating the places?

Everyone turned toward Lalla Fatim Fadl. The old woman was wearing a long light pink dress, a gray apron, and a small scarf held her beautiful white hair with shiny highlights. Lawyer Sloan Wilfrid replied in an amused voice:

-   Honestly, we didn't even think about the decoration at all.

Lalla Fatim Fadl smiled:

-   To charm the guests of this party, my flowers can help very well. The decoration is much necessary to embellish the place. And it would be a pleasure for me to contribute to this party, by offering my flowers.

Dalya hugged the old woman:

-   Thank you, Lalla Fatim! Thank you so much! Your help will be very useful to us!

The head of the grand Mansion Mr. Bûchebois came forward and he bowed to the old woman with a respectful move:

-   I can show you the party room and the dining room, Madame. If you would like to follow me.

Lalla Fatim Fadl thought aloud:

-   Certainly, Monsieur. I need to see the two places and to plan the decoration that will be installed there. And once the tables and chairs are set up, my two helpers will transport the plants from my workshop until here.

Followed by two male helpers, the old woman walked with the head of the grand Mansion, toward inside the house. Lalla Fatim Fadl asked in a curious tone:

-   I thought I heard you were of French origin, Monsieur Bûchebois?
-   Yes, Madame. I was born in the capital, Paris.

Lalla Fatim Fadl exclaimed in a fascinated tone:

-   Paris! The city of the magnificent gardens of Versailles, a pure wonder of the world! France has the most beautiful plantations and gardens on the entire continent!

The head of the grand Mansion blushed with pride, and he whispered:

- I... Thank you, Madame... please come in, come in.

When Lalla Fatim Fadl entered the grand Mansion, followed by the two assistants and Mr. Bûchebois, the Dean of Merchants continued to distribute the works:

- I imagine with a lot of guests, the lighting needs to be boosted, in order to beautify the flower decoration and the cooked dishes. Who will take care of the lamps and candles?

A man among the volunteers replied:

- I will take care of the lights in this house. But I need two people to hold the ladder and hand me the tools.

Immediately, Alfie Jaq and Maurice Gus jumped:

- We will help you!

Heading inside the grand Mansion, the man explained to Alfie and Maurice:

- First, I must walk around the house to assess the condition of the lamps and candles. Then, I will return to my workshop to bring back the ladder and the tools to be installed. It's a big house, there will be some work in the lighting.
- I'll use my father's carriage to bring your ladder here. Maurice suggested.
- Are we going to increase the lighting in the hall too? Alfie asked.
- Certainly, yes. Even in the kitchen and the hallways, to facilitate the work of waiters and Cooks. The man answered.

While the volunteer, Alfie Jaq, and Maurice Gus were discussing their work plan, the Dean of Merchants turned around:

- And the most important work; Household chores. Who takes care of it in this house?

The maid Cristelle replied, exclaiming joyfully:

- Me! Cristelle! Present!

Staring at the huge Mansion, for a few seconds, the Dean of Merchants announced:

- It's a very big house, Miss Cristelle. I present to you 4 women who volunteer to help you clean this house. I imagine you have a lot of work to do!!

Cristelle stifled an amused laugh:

- Lots of work, yes! It's very nice of you, Mesdames, to come and help me with the housework. I really do need it!

Leading the female volunteers to the grand Mansion, Cristelle announced the work plan to them:

-   Before the men set up the tables and chairs, we will clean the floor and the windows. Then, we will wash the curtains, the vases to be wiped, the carpets and the cushions to be exposed to the sun.

At one moment, a soft voice stood out among the volunteers:

-   Have you thought about music?

Everyone was surprised by this question. And to tell the truth, no one thought of including music in this event. Dalya Bouvard was surprised, first by the question, and second by the origin of this voice; it was her music Teacher Miss Haîyang, in person!

Dalya and Amira exchanged a surprised look. The presence of the Music Professor at the grand Mansion was unusual. The young woman was always serious and distant. Dalya constantly felt Miss Haîyang's stare on her, in the College. Except that Dalya still couldn't understand why Miss Haîyang was watching and following her.

That day, Miss Haîyang took a few steps forward, and she explained in a calm voice:

-   The Factory you are trying to save is the main source of income of ten Asian families. My compatriots and I will be honored to participate in this party. We can form an orchestra, made up of 8 instruments. We just need to know what kind of music you want, and where the orchestra will be placed.

Hearing this proposal, Dalya and Amira were surprised and delighted. Having heard Miss Haîyang play in music class, Dalya and Amira were certain that the music played on the day of the party, will simply be magnificent.

Lawyer Sloan Wilfrid exclaimed happily:

-   Music for a Thanksgiving party is a great idea! It will make lunch more joyful, and it will relax the guests. Thank you for your offer, Madame.

Turning toward a person, Sloan Wilfrid asked:

-   Miss Amira Mounier, please guide Madame to the party room, where the orchestra will play. And for the kind of music, I'll join you in a few minutes.

Amira Mounier replied:

-   Right away, Mr. Wilfrid. It's this way, Professor Haîyang. The party room is very large, I can help you set up the orchestra and the instruments. As soon as you decide on the place, I will arrange the chairs and the wooden music stands for you to place the melodies papers.

Before Professor Haîyang would leave for the grand Mansion, Dalya interrupted her in an intimidated voice:

-   Thank you very much for your offer, Professor Haîyang. It's a really generous gesture.

And for once, Professor Haîyang's serious face changed. The young woman smiled tenderly:

- To save the Factory, this party must succeed. And the music will contribute to it.

When Amira Mounier and the Music Professor left them, the Dean of Merchants turned to the rest of the present people, and he announced proudly:

- Demoiselles, Messieurs ... the party is in preparation! I think everything will be ready for Thanksg...

When suddenly, two small silhouettes interrupted the Dean of Merchants, and they clung to the tall man's legs. The little twins jumped:

- And us do what? And us? And us?
- Us help too! Us do what? And us?

An amused laugh invaded everyone. The Dean of Merchants bowed in front of the little twins, and he smiled tenderly at them:

- It's very nice of you, Demoiselles Ari and Adi, to want to participate and help. There is a lot of work to do, to prepare for this party. And people will need to refresh and to eat. Can you serve lemonade and sandwiches to all workers? This is a very easy task for you and useful for the workers!

Ari and Adi exchanged a look and a happy smile. The idea of serving lemonade and sandwiches to all workers was brilliant. The sooner said the sooner done, the little twins ran to the kitchen of the grand Mansion. An assistant Cook continually prepared lemonade, and sandwiches of lettuce and pâté. Ari took care of carrying the small glasses and the lemonade in a basket, and Adi took care of carrying the sandwiches in a backpack. And during the entire period of the preparation for this party, the little twins were happy and active, going around the grand Mansion, serving all the workers, fresh lemonade, and sandwiches.

At one point, the Dean of Merchants thought aloud:

- I think we covered all the parts of this party. The cooking, the household chores, the furniture, the lighting, the decoration, the music. At this rate of work, I think we'll be ready for the Thanksgiving party.

At this moment, the young Lyor Laszlo announced in a serious tone:

- However, we have one real problem. The Thanksgiving party is in 3 weeks. I've tried every excuse to avoid my father, but he insists on filing the Factory dissolution to Court, tomorrow Monday, first thing in the morning.

The accountant Mr. Jacob Mounier thought aloud:

- If the dissolution of the Factory is filed tomorrow Monday to Court, it will be too late to save the Factory. The party and fundraising will be useless then. You must absolutely delay filing this document to Court ... by at least 3 weeks!

Lawyer Sloan Wilfrid asked the young Lyor Laszlo, in a worried voice:

- Your father Ernest Laszlo needs your signature to file the dissolution of the Factory to Court. Can you leave the city of Georgetown, for the next 3 weeks? Lyor, you must absolutely disappear from this town, at least for 3 wee...

When suddenly, an old man interrupted the conversation, with a furious tone:

- I should have been invited to this meeting!

All surprised eyes turned to the entrance of the grand Mansion. And everyone was shocked by the presence of a familiar face. The Lawyer Master Victor Barold, in person, came to the grand Mansion!

As he advanced toward the group of people gathered, Master Barold exclaimed in an angry tone:

- So just like that, you're planning a scheme against Ernest Laszlo, without including me?!

Lawyer Sloan Wilfrid displayed a nervous smile:

- I'm sorry, Master Barold. I forgot to let you know. I didn't think such a matter would interest you.

The Lawyer Master Victor Barold affirmed in a strong voice:

- Anything that can break a nerve of Ernest Laszlo, interests me!

A wave of laughs invaded the present people. Lawyer Sloan Wilfrid pulled himself together and he asked in a serious tone:

- We have a big worry, Master Barold. We need at least 3 weeks to organize the Thanksgiving party, raise funds, and invest them in the Factory, to prevent its closing. Lyor Laszlo will be forced to sign and file the dissolution of the Factory tomorrow. Can you offer us 3 more weeks?

With a defiant smile, Master Victor Barold replied in a confident tone:

- I can offer you 5 more weeks.

In front of this announcement, all the present people were joyfully surprised by this news. Master Barold was a man of his word. To this offer, the accountant Mr. Jacob Mounier informed the people gathered:

- With 5 more weeks, we can raise even more funds. More time, more possibilities.

Master Victor Barold confirmed his offer:

- And you will have your 5 weeks!

Although intimidated by the strong character of the old man, Dalya took a few steps forward:

- Thank you for your help, Master Bar...

Except that the old man interrupted her quickly:

- Oh, but I correct you right away, Mademoiselle Dalya Bouvard. I'm not helping you out of kindness.

Turning toward a man, Master Barold ordered in a menacing tone:

- Sloan Wilfrid! I want to be seated at the best lunch table, I want 2 take-out turkeys, and I want all menu dishes delivered to my house the night of the party.

Everyone laughed heartily, unable to contain themselves. Lawyer Sloan Wilfrid affirmed in a serious and decided tone:

- Very well understood, Master Barold! The best table and the best turkeys, for you! And I will deliver the dishes myself, to your home!

Master Barold ordered a young man:

- Lyor Laszlo, follow me! We must go back to downtown, to visit some old acquaintances, and get you these 5 weeks.

Lyor Laszlo jumped:

- At your command, Master Barold!

A few minutes later. Inside the grand Mansion.

When the Lawyer Sloan Wilfrid entered the hall of the house, he was followed by the accountant, Mr. Jacob Mounier. The grand Mansion was busy and vibrant. Men were bringing down the chairs from the floor above, women were carrying long curtains to the living room, the little twins were carrying refreshments out of the kitchen, the head of the grand Mansion Mr. Bûchebois was receiving the latest instructions from the Dean of Merchants. Dalya joined her friend Amira in helping their Music Teacher set up chairs in a corner of the party room.

For a long minute, Lawyer Sloan Wilfrid watched all the volunteer workers. Within minutes, the party was organized, and everyone had a job to do. The accountant Mr. Jacob Mounier exclaimed in astonishment:

- A big party is getting prepared in the grand Mansion!

As he watched young women carrying plates and cutlery to the dining room, Sloan Wilfrid thought aloud:

- At first, we thought we would invite about 100 people. But with the help of all these workers, maybe we can organize a bigger party. We can invite even more people. And collect more money!

The accountant Mr. Jacob Mounier answered by leafing through a file:

- Our guest list includes all the Businessmen and Bankers in this town. About 100 people. Apart from these two categories, who else can we invite?

Lawyer Sloan Wilfrid thought for a long minute:

- Who else can we invite? Who else can we invite?

Suddenly, the accountant Mr. Jacob Mounier asked:

- Why not the Ambassadors?

Lawyer Sloan Wilfrid turned back to the accountant. Mr. Jacob Mounier continued:

- Mr. Charleston whom I work for, I remember several years ago, he had requested financial assistance from the Ambassador of a Country, in order to invest in his business, in return for a price reduction of the product to his Country. And Dumbarton Oaks Park is a place that brings together ...

Suddenly, Lawyer Sloan Wilfrid jumped:

- Embassies! That's a brilliant idea, Monsieur Jacob! A brilliant idea!

The accountant Mr. Jacob Mounier blushed:

- We need all possible ideas. This is a big amount of money to collect.

Lawyer Sloan Wilfrid walked toward the Library of the grand Mansion:

- Monsieur Jacob Mounier, follow me! We have names to add to this guest list!

On this day of Sunday, the city of Georgetown lived a special autumn, different from the previous ones. In the grand Mansion, not only a great splendid feast was getting prepared ... a determined defense was also getting prepared.

And just like the Excelbox affirmed ... the modest little Alley N°106, inhabited by employees, workers, and craftsmen ... Dear readers, by the little Alley N°106, amazed you will be!

Chapter 57

The Thanksgiving Menu

Monday, November 6th, 1893.

The day was long for Dalya Bouvard and Amira Mounier. They were eager to finish their courses at the College, in order to return and help at the grand Mansion. The volunteers worked hard there to prepare for the feast.

Dalya and her friend Amira were each carrying several wooden music stands, which the Music Professor asked them to place in the party room at the grand Mansion. On the road of Dumbarton Oaks Park, Amira thought aloud:

- Professor Haîyang chose the place to set up the Orchestra, near the windows overlooking the large garden. We should ask that the curtains of the windows be wide open, to allow the musicians a better view of the melody papers.

Dalya smiled:

- You are right, yes. I will ask Alfie and Maurice for a better lighting of the lamps near the Orchestra.

Arriving at the entrance gates of the grand Mansion, Amira continued to think:

- Can we place two small tables near the musicians? They may need refreshments or something to eat.

Dalya entered the hall of the grand Mansion, answering:

- Certainly, yes! The Orchestra will play for hours. I'm going to ask the Gardener to leave me two small tab...

Suddenly, a great noise was heard in the hall of the grand Mansion. Dalya and Amira put the wooden music stands in a corner and they exchanged a worried look.

- What's going on? It looks like a quarrel.
- Yes, and it's coming from the kitchen. Let's check.

Upon entering the kitchen of the grand Mansion, Dalya and Amira discovered an intense scene. A dozen Cooks seemed to be quarreling, they were talking simultaneously.

- I recommend cabbage gratins with béchamel sauce.
- It's ridiculous, it's not Easter!
- We can roast the turkeys with the mustard and honey sauce.
- Mustard is not liked by everyone!
- Spinach and melted cheese quiches!

- Out of the question to have the smell of spinach in this kitchen!
- And for my pastry then? I need a kitchen of my own!
- Turkeys stuffed with mushrooms?! Who invented this horror?
- Why not my pizzas and my pasta with tomato sauce and herbs?
- It is not with pizzas and pasta that we will succeed in collecting this money!
- Are you ridiculing my cooking? How dare you?!
- I propose entirely French dishes! It is the best gastronomy!
- In your opinion, yes! Why not entirely Italian dishes?
- The idea of spicy duck pâté is ridiculous!
- Carrot and lentil soup?! Really?! Is this the only recipe you found?!

The Lawyer Sloan Wilfrid was standing in the middle of the Cooks and their quarrel. He tried to calm the Cooks, but no one heard him:

- Gentlemen, gentlemen! We absolutely must agree on the menu today! We must decide quickly, in order to gather the ingredients and decide on the cutlery. Gentlemen! A little calm, please!

The accountant Mr. Jacob Mounier noticed the presence of Dalya and Amira. He approached them, and he informed them:

- It's the same repeated scene, since this morning. The Cooks still haven't decided the Thanksgiving lunch menu.

Dalya asked in a curious tone:

- But, it's a simple lunch. Can't we cook stuffed turkeys, baked vegetables, Cramberry sauces, and pumpkin pies? It's the usual Thanksgiving menu.

The accountant Mr. Jacob Mounier explained to her:

- A party menu may seem insignificant and not so important. Except that the Cuisine can create conflict, just like solving problems. For this party, the dishes served will have to charm the guests and convince them to invest their money.

Amira Mounier understood her father's idea:

- So then, you need an original and unusual menu to charm the guests. Turkeys, baked vegetables, and pumpkin pies are common dishes.

Dalya Bouvard observed the still quarreling Cooks, while murmuring in a worried tone:

- The Cooks don't seem to agree on a single plate.

Lawyer Sloan Wilfrid raised his voice, trying to direct the Cooks' conversation:

- Gentlemen! Gentlemen! How about we start with the salads first? Do you have any new and simple recipes?

The quarrel between the Cooks resumed:

- There's nothing better than a cherry tomato salad with tuna!
- It's ideal for summer yes, but tomatoes and tuna in the fall months, it's too cold!
- How about a fig salad with goat cheese and honey?
- If there are any figs left in the market! The fig season ended in October.
- I propose a fresh salmon and avocado salad, it's simple to make.
- Yes, but the avocados darken quickly, how are you going to keep them fresh?
- So, mushrooms cooked with Provencal herbs!
- A hot salad?! Really?! Is this your best idea? It's ridiculous!
- I recommend roasted peppers, with tomato sauce. It's exquisite!
- It's a main dish, not a salad!

Dalya and Amira stood motionless at the kitchen door, watching the Cooks' quarrel with worried eyes. The accountant Mr. Jacob Mounier murmured:

- It is unlikely that this menu will be decided today.

Amid loud voices and disagreements, Lawyer Sloan Wilfrid tried to come up with another idea to solve the problem:

- Why not start with the desserts? we can present various dis...

Lawyer Sloan Wilfrid was interrupted by the escalating Cooks' quarrel.

- A salad of shrimps and seafood, with corn and cer...
- No way we cook fish! The smell will spread to other dishes!
- My recipe for cold pasta with dried fruit is the best!
- In your restaurant only! I wonder how many customers they order it.
- How dare you criticize my recipe?!
- I suggest cabbage with mayonnaise sauce and eggs.
- All your dishes are with mayonnaise sauce. Don't you have other sauces to use?
- It is an insult!! My sauce is the best in the entire region!!

At one moment, in the midst of the quarrel and the loud voices, a man and an old woman entered the kitchen of the grand Mansion. The man was in his thirties, he was wearing a large coat, winter boots, and on his head a crocheted hat, in many colors. Immediately, Dalya recognized him and she came close to him:

- Good evening, Dadès !

Dalya was surprised that the Royal Georgetown College Concierge showed up at the grand Mansion. The man answered with a smile and a foreign accent:

- Good evening, Lalla Dalya. Me here with my mother. This is Lalla Tafernout.

The old woman who accompanied the Concierge was very small, very chubby, a serene and calm smile imprinted on her face. And despite her advanced age, the old woman seemed to have a strong personality. She was wearing a long green outfit with pretty embroidery, a beige crochet shawl over her shoulders, a large white scarf that hid all her hair. The old woman had beautiful dark green tattoos on her face; strange signs on her forehead and her chin.

Dalya smiled politely at her:

- Good evening, Lalla Tafernout. Welcome to the grand Mansion.

The old woman didn't say a word; she smiled happily and bowed her head. The Concierge Dadès explained:

- We here to help in the kitchen. My mother is excellent Cook.

Dalya answered in a moved voice:

- That's really nice of you, Dadès. Thank you very much for your help, Lalla Tafernout.

It is true that Dalya greatly appreciated the Concierge Dadès, he was always kind and helpful. And that day, Dalya was surprised by the visit of the Concierge Dadès and his mother. They appeared to be modest people, and despite that, they offered to help. Dalya was touched by this generosity.

Except that, at this precise moment, the quarrel between the Cooks escalated. Lawyer Sloan Wilfrid, the accountant Mr. Jacob Mounier, and his daughter Amira Mounier, they all tried to calm down the Cooks, but no one was able to make themselves heard. Everyone was talking at the same time and loudly.

Dalya tried to call Lawyer Sloan Wilfrid, to introduce him to the new volunteers. She screamed in a loud voice:

- Mr. Wilfrid... I... one moment, please... there is... Mr. Wilfrid...

The kitchen was so noisy that Dalya's voice couldn't even be heard. At one moment, the mother of the Concierge Dadès, Lalla Tafernout advanced a few steps forward, and she emitted a piercing and strong sound; a youyou sound. And immediately, all the voices went quiet, and the kitchen became silent. All eyes turned to the old woman, with the strange tattoos and clothes. Immediately, Dalya took advantage of this silence and this attention, she announced:

- Mr. Wilfrid, this is Dadès, the school Concierge. And she is his mother Lalla Tafernout. They came to help in the cooking of Thanksgiving lunch.

Lawyer Sloan Wilfrid greeted all the volunteers to this party, with the same joyful smile and the same grateful tone:

- Good evening, Monsieur. Good evening, Madame. Thank you for your presence and your help.

The old woman ordered her son, in a foreign language:

- ترجم لهم. نحن هنا لتحضير غداء الحفل كاملا.

The Concierge Dadès turned around and he explained:

- Mother does not speak language of here. Mother only speaks Arabic. She speaks, I translate. We here to cook entire lunch of party.

At this precise moment, a wave of laughs invaded all the Cooks.

- No but it's a joke! An old woman wants to decide on the menu for this party!
- She should teach us how to cook, while she's at it!
- Will this old woman cook better than us Chefs? Really?
- Wouldn't she be more useful to help with the decoration of the flowers?
- She must have gotten the wrong doors!
- Thank you, but we don't need culinary advice from an unknown old woman!
- She doesn't seem to know how to cook.
- She can help us boil eggs or stir onions.

Dalya was embarrassed by the Cooks' mocking remarks and laughter toward the old woman. Dalya sincerely hoped that the old woman did not understand their words. The Lawyer Sloan Wilfrid shot the Cooks with a cold look:

- Gentlemen, any help offered to us is welcomed! This old woman didn't come all the way to the grand Mansion to be laughed at!

The Cooks hardly suppressed their amused laughter. And although the Concierge Dadès and his mother were foreigners, barely speaking the language of the Country, Dadès and his mother seemed to have understood the mocking laughs of the other Cooks.

At one moment, the old woman took a confident step toward the table in the middle of the kitchen. Her son Dadès followed her, and he placed a big straw basket on the kitchen table. The old woman opened the basket and she took out dishes wrapped in napkins. She placed unusual and splendid kitchen objects on the table; the plates were in painted ceramic, the spoons in wood, and the white napkins were embroidered in several colors.

With calm and meticulous moves, the old woman filled the small plates with strange foods that she took from her straw basket. She was arranging the food on the plates, in a very unusual order. For some long minutes, in an imposed silence, everyone in the kitchen watched the old woman arranging the dishes. There were about fifteen small plates filled with different foods.

When she finished, the old woman asked her son:

ـ قل لهم أن يتذوقوا هذه الأكل.

The Concierge Dadès explained:

- Mother asks you to taste these dishes.

Everyone present exchanged confused and hesitant looks. Nobody knew this woman, her clothes and her tattoos on her face were strange, the ceramic plates and the wooden spoons were strange, her name Lalla Tafernout was strange. It is therefore certain that the dishes offered will also be quite strange.

Not wishing to appear rude, Lawyer Sloan Wilfrid was the first to taste the dishes proposed. He took a wooden spoon, and he smiled:

- It's very generous of you, Madame, to have come here, to propose your dishes to us.

As the Lawyer tasted the old woman's dishes, the smile faded away from his face. At the end of his tasting, Sloan Wilfrid looked confused. Putting down his spoon, Lawyer Sloan Wilfrid ordered in a serious voice:

- Gentlemen Cooks. Please taste these dishes.

With hesitant looks and forced movements, all the Cooks came close to the kitchen table. They observed the dishes and the strange kitchen utensils. Dalya and Amira were curious, they too approached, to better see the dishes. All the Cooks used the wooden spoons, and they tasted the proposed dishes. And as strange as it may seem, all the Cooks lost their mocking smiles, confusion and shock appeared on all faces, at the first tasted bites. A heavy and serious silence settled in the kitchen of the grand Mansion.

The first to pull himself together and break the silence was Lawyer Sloan Wilfrid. He spoke to the Concierge Dadès:

- Can you explain the cooked meals to us, please?

Dadès the Concierge turned to his mother and he translated this request to her. Lalla Tafernout advanced toward the kitchen table, and she indicated the dishes:

ـ بلادي المملكة المغربية، وهذه أكل مغربية تقليدية

ـ في السلطات، هذا زعلوك، باذنجان مع الطماطم والتوابل. هذه تكتوكة، فلفل مع الطماطم والتوابل

ـ هذه قرعة معسلة بالقرفة. وهذه السبانخ بالثوم والحامض والزيتون

Dadès translated his mother's explanations:

- Our Country is the Kingdom of Morocco, and this is traditional Moroccan Cuisine. In salads, this is Zaalouk, eggplant with tomato and spices. This is Tektouka, peppers with tomato and spices. This is Graa Maassla, caramelized pumpkin with cinnamon. This is spinach with garlic lemon and olives.

The Cooks tasted, the Concierge and his mother explained the dishes, and the Lawyer Sloan Wilfrid listened attentively to the explanations, while observing the dishes with an examining stare.

Lalla Tafernout continued to explain:

في الأطباق الرئيسية، لدينا كسكس بالخضر والسميدة. وعدة أنواع من الطاجين المغربي

ـطاجين حلو باللحم والفواكه الجافة. طاجين الدجاج بالبصلة معسلة. طاجين سوسي بالخضر

طاجين الكفتة بالبيض والطماطم

ـهذه بسطيلة بالسمك وفواكه البحر. وهذه تسمى بريوات، ممكن مالحة أو حلوة. وهذه شوربة
حريرة

ـفي الحلويات، لدينا كعب غزال ومحنشة، مع شاي بالنعناع

Her son Dadès enthusiastically translated:

- In main dishes, we have couscous with vegetables and semolina. And several types of
  Moroccan Tagine. Sweet meat Tagine with dried fruits. Chicken Tagine with caramelized
  onions. Tagine Soussi of vegetables. And minced meat Tagine with eggs and tomatoes.
  This is Fish and Seafood Pastilla. This is called Briouates, it can be sweet or salty. This is
  Harira Soup. In the pastry, we have cornes de gazelle, and Mehencha, with mint tea.

Without hesitation, Dalya and Amira also tasted the dishes. At the first bite, Dalya and Amira
exchanged a surprised look. They finally understood the confused reactions of the present
people. The dishes proposed weren't just good … they were incredibly delicious! The sweet
meat melted in your mouth, the semolina with vegetables was succulent, the seafoods were
exquisite, the pastry was simply magical!

At one moment, Lalla Tafernout pointed to a strange bread, which no one tasted. A round
flatbread, still warm, a little thin. The old woman took a piece of bread, she spread it with
butter, and she offered it to the Lawyer Sloan Wilfrid, displaying a polite smile:

ـ هذا الخبز يسمى تفرنوت، الذي عليه سميت. نتذوقه مع زبدة الزعتر

Her son Dadès also smiled:

- This is Tafernout bread, from where my mother's first name, Lalla Tafernout. We taste it
  with Thyme Butter.

The Thyme Butter Bread was so delicious, the Lawyer Sloan Wilfrid ate it in small bites and
slowly. Lalla Tafernout distributed pieces of Thyme Butter Bread to everyone in the kitchen.
It was only Thyme, bread, and butter, but everyone seemed amazed and dazzled by the taste.

Lalla Tafernout also explained other details:

ـ هذه الصحن من فخار وبنقش مغربي. الملعقة الخشبية من عود الخيزران. المناديل بطرز مغربي.
هذا الأثاث صنعة بلادي وتراث أجدادي، هو رمز الأصالة وفخر بلادي المغرب

Her son Dadès continued to translate:

- These plates are in ceramic, with Moroccan engravings. The spoon is made of bamboo wood. The napkins are embroidered with Moroccan motifs. This is the craftsmanship of our Country and the heritage of our ancestors; it is the symbol of the originality and the pride of our Country Morocco.

After several minutes, when all the dishes were tasted, when all the explanations were given, and when all the words were translated, the old woman Lalla Tafernout indicated with a hand gesture, all the dishes and the objects presented on the kitchen table, and she affirmed with a sincere smile:

- Proudly Made in Morocco!

These are the only words of the local language that the old woman pronounced. Lalla Tafernout's accent wasn't perfect, but her words were very clear.

Instantly, Lawyer Sloan Wilfrid turned toward all the Cooks present, and he asked in an authoritative voice:

- Gentlemen … can anyone do better than what has been presented to us?

The Cooks exchanged silent glances. A minute of silence invaded the kitchen of the grand Mansion. No Cook dared to laugh, or make fun, or even say a word, they all displayed a surprised, silent and above all disarmed face. After thinking for one second, the Lawyer Sloan Wilfrid addressed the Concierge Dadès, in a serious voice:

- Translate to your mother, please. The guests of this party will be Businessmen, Bankers, Politicians, and Ambassadors. This lunch is our main asset to charm the guests and to raise the necessary funds, in order to save the Cotton Factory. Lalla Tafernout, do you think you can convince them with your Cuisine?

At this moment, the old woman understood perfectly well the words of the Lawyer Sloan Wilfrid. Even before receiving the translation from her son, Lalla Tafernout announced with a determined smile:

ـ أقسم أنه لن يرجع صحن واحد ممتلئ.

I swear not a single plate will return full.

Sloan Wilfrid needed no translation to understand Lalla Tafernout's promise. The Lawyer and the old woman exchanged a determined and an understood smile.

Immediately, Lawyer Sloan Wilfrid announced his decision:

- Thanksgiving's lunch will be … Moroccan!

The days that followed were busy in the kitchen of the grand Mansion. It is true that the strange old woman was of an advanced age, of very short stature, and did not speak the language of the Country. Except that, Lalla Tafernout led the activity in the kitchen, in a military way.

The Concierge Dadès translated all his mother's instructions. Lalla Tafernout decided on the entire menu for this lunch, including the traditional turkey for this feast. The Cook of the grand Mansion, Mr. Ferrero Lutché ensured that the old woman had all the ingredients and food she needed. All the Cooks and helpers followed Lalla Tafernout's directives and orders; she guided them in the cooking and the preparation of the dishes.

Lawyer Sloan Wilfrid insisted on including Moroccan handcrafts objects. This is how the engraved ceramic plates, the wooden spoons, and the embroidered napkins were used, in addition to the usual table service.

Lalla Tafernout promised that not one single plate will return full.

Promise of a Moroccan woman.

Chapter 58

The training

Tuesday, November 7th, 1893.

The activity in the grand Mansion was lively. There were workers everywhere. Men moving furniture, women cleaning windows, Cooks preparing ingredients, helpers fixing chairs in the garage, young people setting decorations in living rooms, carts of products and materials coming in and out. The grand Mansion was preparing to host a big event.

The help Cook Océanie had taken out all the forks and knives, and she had spread them out on the big table in the dining room. Océanie instructed her aides on how to wipe properly:

-   Hold the fork with two fingers, like this, and pass the napkin all the way. Then, lay it down like this, so as not to stain it.

When Océanie finished her explanations, the aides picked up the napkins and cutlery, and they imitated Océanie's moves. At one moment, Dalya Bouvard approached Océanie:

-   The Cook Mr. Ferrero Lutché wanted to know where the Paprika spice mix is. He can't find it.

The help Cook Océanie picked up another fork to wipe:

-   The Paprika is stored in a jar, on the upper right shelf, in the pantry. And remind the Cook, please, not to use a lot. The last time, the dish was inedible!

Dalya stifled an amused laugh. And before leaving Océanie to bring the message back to the Cook, Dalya noticed the various forks and knives, in various shapes and sizes. Dalya was curious:

-   This is the first time I've seen a two-pronged fork. It's weird. Océanie, why do we need all this weird cutlery?

Without stopping to wipe the fork, Océanie explained to her:

-   The two-pronged fork is specially designed for cheese, desserts, and for picking fruit from our plate. It's a prestigious party, it requires prestigious cutlery, even if sometimes strange.
-   These are very funny cutlery. Dalya laughed before leaving for the kitchen.

Océanie continued to wipe the cutlery and correct the moves of her aides. When suddenly, a strange idea invaded the mind of Océanie, to the point that the young girl jumped. She ordered in a shaken tone to her aides:

-   Keep wiping cutlery. Place them like I showed you. I'll be back in a minute!!

It didn't take long for Océanie to find the head of the grand Mansion. Mr. Bûchebois was guiding two aides, to fix decorations on the edge of the windows of the living room.

- A little to the right… more… more… yes, that's good!

The help Cook Océanie approached the Manager, and she asked in a worried voice:

- Mr. Bûchebois, I have a question. Who is hosting this party?

The head of the grand Mansion replied instantly:

- It's a funny question … the Heiress of the grand Mansion, Mademoiselle Dalya Bouvard, of course!

Océanie continued:

- And who will be seated at the head table at lunch with the Ambassadors?

Mr. Bûchebois quickly replied to Océanie, before continuing to guide the two aides:

- It's Mademoiselle Dalya Bouvard, of course! … raise the decoration up a bit… yes… just a little… it's perfect! now, follow this pattern, and fix these decorations the same on the other windows.

Except that Océanie's concern increased. The help Cook held the head of the grand Mansion by the arm, to have his full attention:

- Mr. Bûchebois… Mr. Bûchebois!… Mademoiselle Dalya Bouvard has just asked me what is the point of having several strange cutleries on the lunch table! She didn't know what the two-pronged fork was for!

At this precise moment, the head of the grand Mansion, Mr. Bûchebois finally turned toward Océanie, looking stunned:

- Goodness … we must form her!

Océanie confirmed with a worried air:

- Yes! And we must form her very very quickly! I'll get her immediately!

A few minutes later, Dalya entered the Library, followed by her friend Amira. The two girls thought they were called to help with the preparation of the party. Except that the serious faces of Océanie and the Head of the grand Mansion, worried Dalya:

- What's going on? Is there a problem?

Clearing his throat, the head of the grand Mansion addressed Dalya in a respectful tone:

- Mademoiselle … during the Thanksgiving party, there will be prestigious guests. And since you are the designated Heiress, you must have lunch with the guests.

Dalya still didn't understand the problem. The help Cook Océanie continued with a kind and somewhat hesitant smile:

- ... and therefore, Mademoiselle, given that this party is very important, it would be very useful if ... if you learned to master all the cutlery on the table.

Exchanging a surprised look with her friend Amira, Dalya thought aloud:

- Master the strange forks and knives?

Amira Mounier approved this idea, she exclaimed:

- They are right, Dalya! We didn't think of that before. There will be some very prestigious guests at your lunch table. It is absolutely necessary that you know which cutlery to use.

Dalya replied instantly:

- Alright... yes, of course... I must know how to use all the cutlery, even the strangest ones. I'll learn anything that won't make me a laughing stock. But... how am I going to learn?

The head of the grand Mansion indicated to her the table in the Library, which he had already transformed into a lunch table:

- It would be my honor to train you in table etiquette, Mademoiselle.

When Dalya and Amira approached the table, they discovered about twenty objects that were placed with millimeter precision and order. Dalya worried:

- I... I must remember everything? Before this party?

And being always present to support her friend, Amira Mounier took a small notebook out of her pocket and she affirmed in a determined voice:

- Don't worry, Dalya! Try to memorize everything you can, and I will write down everything Mr. Bûchebois explains. At lunch, on the day of the party, I will be sitting next to you. And with this notebook open on my lap, I can guide you!

Océanie jumped:

- That's a great idea, Miss Amira! No one will notice.

Dalya and Amira sat down in front of the table, and Mr. Bûchebois announced the start of the training:

- So, Mesdemoiselles, let's start the table etiquette!

Chapter 59

The contribution of the Royal Georgetown College

Friday, November 10th, 1893.

Dalya Bouvard was overwhelmed with work at the grand Mansion and classes at the Royal Georgetown College. And yet, Dalya was happy with the rapid progress of the preparations for the party. Her friend Amira was happy too, she was helping Dalya in classes at the College, in preparing for the party, and also in training Dalya for the table etiquette.

That day, in the school Library, Dalya and her friend Amira were sitting, writing silently, each focused on her work. At this hour, the Library was empty, all the students were gathered for lunch in the College canteen.

When suddenly, a familiar voice approached the two students:

- Good afternoon, Mesdemoiselles. Did you finish your lunch so early?

Dalya and Amira looked up at the Director's Secretary, Miss Uplerine Amana. She was wearing a magnificent green dress that embellished her caramel-colored skin. Miss Uplerine was holding books in her hands, and she had stopped at the table where the two students were. Dalya smiled at her:

- We preferred to skip lunch today. We have a lot of work to finish.

With a quick glance, Miss Uplerine Amana observed the multiple papers and envelopes, on the table of the two students, and she asked in a curious tone:

- Invitations … you are writing invitations?

Although she was an intimidating woman, Dalya had complete trust in Miss Uplerine. After several strange helps from this woman, Dalya appreciated Miss Uplerine very much. Dalya then decided to inform her:

- Yes, Miss Uplerine. We are having a Thanksgiving party at the grand Mansion. It's a fundraiser, to help a Factory stay open. The Lawyer Mr. Sloan Wilfrid and the father of my friend Mr. Jacob Mounier, they have prepared guests' lists. And we have 300 invitations to write.

Strangely, Miss Uplerine did not seem surprised by this news. It seems that no secret is well-kept in the city of Georgetown. The tall woman asked:

- 300 invitations to write. It is a work of several hours. How many are you at?

Dalya and Amira exchanged a nervous laugh. Dalya answered in a small voice:

\- We ... we are only at 6. We try to well write the invitations.

At this moment, Amira sighed:

\- Just by reading my writing, the guests will think it's a kindergarten party!

Dalya and Amira stifled an amused and a worried laugh at the same time. They had to write the invitations well and quickly. Dalya and Amira were working hard. Except that between classes at the College, preparations for the party at the grand Mansion, and training for the table etiquette, Dalya and Amira didn't have one free minute. The invitations seemed almost impossible to complete in time.

After a little second of thinking, Miss Uplerine asked politely:

\- Mesdemoiselles ... May I see these guests' lists?

With a spontaneous move, Dalya handed her the papers; thinking that Miss Uplerine was curious to know the guests for this party. Except that, strangely, Miss Uplerine didn't even look at the papers Dalya handed her. The tall woman placed the papers on top of the books she was carrying in her hand. The Director's Secretary Miss Uplerine was a very strange and unpredictable woman, Dalya felt it from her first day in this school. With a sincere smile, Miss Uplerine Amana ordered Dalya and Amira:

\- Go have lunch in the canteen, Mesdemoiselles. There's a delicious crème brûlée for dessert today.

Dalya and Amira exchanged a hesitant look. Dalya asked:

\- What about our guests' lists, Miss Uplerine?

Amira was as confused as her friend:

\- We still have hours of work ahead of us!

At this moment, Miss Uplerine Amana bowed before the two students, and she whispered to them:

\- Tomorrow at 5 PM, come see me at my office. Your 300 invitations will be ready!

And without giving the two students time to understand what was happening, the Director's Secretary Miss Uplerine left them and she went toward another section of the Library, murmuring:

\- This will be my little contribution.

Watching Miss Uplerine walk away from them, Dalya and Amira barely repressed their surprise. After a long minute of confusion, Dalya recovered from what had just happened:

\- Miss ... Miss Uplerine Amana... she's going to write 300 invitations, in one day, for us!

Miss Uplerine Amana's help was a touching and generous gesture. Dalya didn't have time to thank her, she just observed the silhouette of the tall woman until she disappeared in the section of the Library.

When suddenly, Amira Mounier pulled herself together from her confusion; she quickly picked up her notebooks and her bag, and she ran toward the exit of the Library, without even waiting for her friend. Dalya exclaimed:

- But where are you going? Why are you running?

Amira Mounier screamed joyfully as she ran:

- Crème brûlée ! Crème brûlée ! Crème brûlée !

Dalya laughed heartily, slowly gathering up her things in her bag. She was well aware that she couldn't catch up her friend Amira who was already far ahead from her.

Walking toward the canteen, and turning down a corridor, Dalya met a familiar silhouette. It was impossible not to recognize the man who always wore an elegant checked suit. Professor Canfield was carrying several books in his hands, and he seemed to be heading toward the Library. As soon as he noticed Dalya, Professor Canfield smiled at her:

- Good afternoon, Mademoiselle Dalya. It's always a pleasure to meet you! And I presume you are leaving the Library at this instant.

Apparently, Professor Canfield knew her better than anyone. Dalya laughed:

- Yes, Professor. I was in the Library with my friend Amira. She walked ahead of me to the canteen.

Professor Canfield smiled:

- Yes, I did meet your friend Miss Amira Mounier who was running toward the canteen. I think she wanted to catch up on the crème brûlée, before it ended. And I advise you to quickly join your friend in the canteen. The crème brûlée is exquisite today!

With an amused laugh, Dalya replied:

- Yes, Professor.

At this moment, and before leaving each in his direction, curiosity caught up with Professor Canfield. He stopped in the middle of the corridor, and he turned to Dalya:

- Mademoiselle ... just a moment please.

Dalya stopped. Professor Canfield approached her, and he asked in a hesitant voice:

- There's ... there's a pretty strange rumor going around the city of Georgetown these last few days. This rumor concerns a little girl who is planning a party at the grand Mansion, in order to raise money and save a Factory from closing. Is it true?

Dalya felt her cheeks blush a little:

- That's right, Professor. It's about the Cotton Factory, which includes thousands of jobs, and is part of the BalthEnterprise Holding.

A surprised and astonished smile appeared on Professor Canfield's face:

- Well ... it's brave and kind to help the employees of this Factory, Mademoiselle. I didn't expect less from you.

From the first day he was in charge of the education and teaching of this little girl, Professor Canfield never ceased to be impressed by her. Dalya was delighted to inform the Professor about this event:

- The Lawyer, Mr. Sloan Wilfrid will invite several Businessmen, Bankers, Politicians and even Ambassadors, in order to collect the money necessary to keep this Factory open. And about 40 people have been working for days preparing for this party at the grand Mansion. There are Cooks, greengrocers, aides to arrange decorations and furniture, cleaners, musicians, an electrician for lighting. They are all volunteers. I hope this party will be successful!

Professor Canfield smiled:

- It will be a real success, I'm sure of that, Mademoiselle!
- Thank you, Professor, we are working on it!
- I'll let you join your friend in the canteen. Very good afternoon, Mademoiselle!

Except that before leaving, a tiny detail caught the attention of Professor Canfield. He turned to Dalya for a second time:

- Pardon my curiosity, Mademoiselle. Did I hear you say that Ambassadors will be invited to this party?

Dalya stopped for the second time, and she answered his question:

- Yes, Professor. Lawyer Mr. Sloan Wilfrid thinks the Ambassadors can help us by investing in the Factory.

At that precise moment, Professor Canfield thought aloud:

- Ambassadors ... Ambassadors ...

When suddenly, a strange and unpredictable idea invaded Professor Canfield's mind. In a serious voice, Professor Canfield announced to Dalya:

- Mademoiselle, I think you will taste the crème brûlée another day.

Dalya observed the Professor with a curious and confused look. She didn't understand his sentence and even less the idea he had in mind. However, having complete confidence in her tutor, since her first day in this College, Dalya followed all the directives of Professor Canfield, without ever asking any questions.

Heading toward a corridor other than the Library where he was supposed to go, Professor Canfield ordered his student, with a determined smile:

- Please follow me to my office. We have a lot of work, and not a lot of time!
- Yes, Professor.

This time, curiosity invaded the little Dalya Bouvard. What work was Professor Canfield talking about? Why did he change his way to go to his office? What is this strange idea the Professor had in mind?

Without hesitation, the little Dalya Bouvard followed Professor Canfield to his office. The crème brûlée will wait for another day. But the answers to your questions will soon come.

Chapter 60

The dress

Saturday November 11th, 1893.

Despite the busy season at the Law firm, Sloan Wilfrid visited the grand Mansion almost daily. He spoke with the employees and volunteer workers, in order to follow the preparation of the party. And although the amount of money to be collected was immense, Lawyer Sloan Wilfrid was determined to make the party a success and save the Cotton Factory.

Entering the hall of the grand Mansion, Lawyer Sloan Wilfrid found a familiar face.

- Good morning, Mr. Bûchebois. How are the preparations going on today?

The head of the grand Mansion was carrying several white tablecloths, and he was heading toward the dining room:

- Good morning, Mr. Wilfrid. The work is going well. Today, the old woman, Lalla Tafernout will cook all the dishes on the menu for the first time. To set the cooking time and the ingredients. Lalla Tafernout will distribute the preparation of the dishes to the Cooks and the helpers. Regarding the tables and chairs, the workers are still working on them. The furniture will be varnished and installed within a few days. The decorations are in the final phase. The lighting will be finalized next week. There is still some work to be done, but preparation is underway.

Lawyer Sloan Wilfrid smiled proudly:

- Excellent work, Mr. Bûchebois!

The head of the grand Mansion also replied proudly:

- Thank you, Mr. Wilfrid. It is thanks to all the volunteers. The employees of the grand Mansion alone would never have managed to prepare this big party, in such a short time.

Sloan Wilfrid took off his coat and he laid it on an empty chair.

- They are brave people; their help came at the right time. This event is of supreme importance, Mr. Bûchebois. Everything must be perfect!

Mr. Bûchebois affirmed with a confident tone:

- And it will be, Mr. Wilfrid. I personally take care of all the details. Would you like a coffee, Monsieur?

Lawyer Sloan Wilfrid observed a few aides hanging decorations around the living room windows:

- You are already busy, Mr. Bûchebois. Continue your work. I'm going to serve myself some coffee, and I will check the party room.
- Understood, Monsieur.

Before Sloan Wilfrid headed to the kitchen to get himself some coffee, two small silhouettes came down the hall stairs, screaming happily:

- Frite!! Frite!! Frite!! Frite!!

Lawyer Sloan Wilfrid smiled as he greeted the little twins Ari and Adi:

- Good morning, Mesdemoiselles! How pretty you are in these dresses!

Arriving at the hall, the little twins spun around like spinning tops. They were happy to wear large pink and white dresses, with patterns of flowers and sequins, and on their heads a crown of flowers and pearls. Ari and Adi paraded proudly in front of the Lawyer:

- Yes, we zolies!! Look at our dresses!! Look our crowns!!
- We princesses!! istelle gave us these dresses, for the party!!

Sloan Wilfrid knelt down to take a good look at the dresses the little twins were wearing:

- I admit that with these dresses, you will easily divert all eyes in this party! and I love these flower crowns, it suits you very well!

The little twins exclaimed in a joyful tone:

- Yes!! Crowns because we princesses!! These are our pretty dresses for the party!!
- And Dindin is also going to wear a pretty dress!! Dindin will be pretty too!! Very zolie!!

Watching the little twins spinning like spinning tops, happy with their dresses, Sloan Wilfrid let out an amused laugh. When suddenly, an idea abruptly appeared in the Lawyer's head. He whispered:

- Dindin will be pretty too… Dindin will be pre…

Suddenly, Sloan Wilfrid hugged the little twins very tightly:

- Ari, Adi! You are geniuses! Thank you, thank you, thank you!!

The little twins didn't know why the Lawyer was hugging them, or why he was thanking them. Still, Ari and Adi laughed heartily:

- We genius princesses!!
- And us wear the prettiest dresses of the party!!

Immediately, Sloan Wilfrid took up his coat again, and he hurried out of the grand Mansion. One thing was missing from the party that was getting prepared. And thanks to the little twins Ari and Adi, the Lawyer realized it, just in time!

Several minutes later, Sloan Wilfrid stopped his car in front of a specific place; Mrs. Lancel's Haute Couture Boutique.

When the Lawyer entered, a tall silhouette greeted him in a high-pitched voice:

- Welcome Master Wilfrid! I am delighted to see you today, in my shop!

Mrs. Lancel was a tall woman, of advanced age, a chubby silhouette, and always elegant in long brightly colored dresses. Mrs. Lancel always arranged her hair in a perfect chignon, and she assiduously wore a large necklace of white pearls.

Lawyer Sloan Wilfrid greeted the elegant woman with a respectful move:

- And it's always a pleasure to visit you, Mrs. Lancel.

The elegant woman asked:

- To what do we owe the honor of your presence, Master? Would you like a suit? Or a coat? We have a splendid collection for men this Fall.

Lawyer Sloan Wilfrid approached the elegant woman, and he whispered in a serious voice:

- Thank you, Mrs. Lancel. But I came today for something quite different. Have you heard of a big party coming up soon?

Mrs. Lancel answered in a low voice:

- Of course! The entire city knows about it, Master Wilfrid. I admit that after knowing the reasons for this fundraiser, I was touched by the kindness and courage of Mademoiselle Dalya Bouvard!

Lawyer Sloan Wilfrid smiled:

- She's a brave girl. And today, she needs your help, more than ever!

Mrs. Lancel needed no more words to guess the Lawyer's request:

- Mademoiselle Dalya Bouvard needs a dress for this party.

The Lawyer continued in a serious voice:

- Exact! But not just any dress. This party is of vital importance; the lives of thousands of families will depend on it. And the guests are some of the most prestigious in this city. We absolutely must charm them and convince them to invest in this Factory. Dalya Bouvard must have an original and breathtaking dress.

For a long minute, Mrs. Lancel observed the dresses presented in her shop, while thinking aloud:

- An original and breathtaking dress ... an original and breathtaking dress ... my dresses are sublime, of course, but I only follow fashion. Mademoiselle Dalya must stand out with an original dress; she must look magnificent to charm the guests.

Mrs. Lancel's Haute Couture Boutique was the best in all of Georgetown city. Her dresses and suits were the finest and most elegant. Except that, for this party, the Lawyer Sloan Wilfrid asked for a more than beautiful dress. And Mrs. Lancel understood this request. At a moment, Mrs. Lancel approached her office table, and she pulled out a dozen papers from a folder. A strange idea invaded Mrs. Lancel's mind, she murmured:

- I wonder if ... Master Wilfrid, what do you think of these sketches?

The second Sloan Wilfrid looked at the papers presented to him; a surprised smile appeared on his face:

- These are ... these are magnificent dresses! Really magnificent!

Mrs. Lancel explained to him:

- The dresses drawn on these sketches are quite original. This is the usual cut of a party dress. However, the details are new and revisited. The dress is made up of two pieces; a simple and light first dress below, and a second dress above with a more worked fabric, decorated with pearls and refined patterns. The dress is embellished with a richly adorned belt. The seam is in the form of a tripled ribbon and woven in white and gold silk thread. All the details and ornaments are worked by hand.

It is true that Lawyer Sloan Wilfrid was a man who was always elegant in his suits, and refined in his clothing choices. He had a taste for fashion. Observing the sketches of drawings, Sloan Wilfrid did not hide his amazement:

- These are very new details. Fabrics adorned with pearls is a sublime idea. The belt refines the waist and embellishes the dress. I have never seen such dresses!

Mrs. Lancel informed him:

- These are sketches of dresses by a young dressmaker. She is from a foreign Country... Morocco.

Immediately, the Lawyer Sloan Wilfrid exclaimed in an amused and surprised tone:

- Morocco ... really?! the Thanksgiving lunch menu is made by a woman of the same origin. And after tasting her dishes, I can tell you that the Cuisine of this Country has easily surpassed all the other cuisines. Certainly, Morocco is gifted, not only for the Cuisine, but also for the Couture.

In a confident voice, Mrs. Lancel affirmed:

- Master Wilfrid, this style of dress is exactly what you need. The young dressmaker left these sketches in my office a few days ago. I was thinking of recruiting her next week. I have never seen such original and sublime dresses. I admit that it is the work of a true craftsman.

It took only half a second for Lawyer Sloan Wilfrid to decide:

- Mrs. Lancel, do whatever is necessary! I place this dress under your responsibility!

At this moment, a proud and determined smile appeared on Mrs. Lancel's face:

- It would be a great honor for me, Master Wilfrid ... not only to prepare Mademoiselle's dress, but also to contribute to this party, and save the jobs of this Factory. I will personally take care of the dress, the hairstyle, and the accessories. On the day of the party, Mademoiselle Dalya Bouvard will be magnificent, and she will have a breathtaking dress. You have my word!

Lawyer Sloan Wilfrid thanked the elegant woman, and he left the shop with peace of mind. He had complete trust in the work and the word of Mrs. Lancel. As soon as the shop door closed, Mrs. Lancel turned to her employees and she ordered:

- Mesdemoiselles ... stop all your work, now. We have an urgent and special order. The entire workshop will work on it. Miss rose, clear the work table. Miss Claudine, bring me the new fabric and thread samples. Miss Eva, pull out the party dress patterns. I need my sketchbook and a cup of coffee. Can someone find Monsieur Karl, the hairdresser? Tell him to come see me here at the shop, it's urgent business. Miss Daisy, turn on the extra lights. Mesdemoiselles ... a lot of work awaits us!

Instantly, the Haute Couture Boutique activated at the orders of Mrs. Lancel. Turning to a young girl, Mrs. Lancel asked her:

- Miss Julie ... do you remember the young dressmaker from Morocco, the one who left her sketchbook a few days ago? She wrote an address where we can reach her. Put your coat on, and search for her, right now! Don't come back without her!

The young girl answered:

- Understood, Mrs. Lancel!

Barely an hour later, two young girls entered the Haute Couture Boutique. The employee, Miss Julie, immediately went to her boss:

- Mrs. Lancel, I have brought with me the dressmaker you requested.

A young girl appeared behind the employee. She seemed a discreet character, she was small, with a slender figure, light brown hair, a mole on her left cheek. She was wearing a simple light beige coat, and a nice brown hat. Looking at her, no one could have guessed that this foreign and discreet young girl made sublime and magnificent dresses.

Immediately, Mrs. Lancel stood up and she greeted the young Moroccan dressmaker with a delighted smile.

During the days that followed, Mrs. Lancel's Haute Couture Boutique was closed to visitors, and all orders were postponed. Except that inside the shop, the activity was overflowing and very busy. Usually, a dress would get ready in 2 months. But this special order was urgent and it had to be ready in 12 days.

Mrs. Lancel put her entire workshop at the disposal of the new Moroccan dressmaker. All the employees worked day and night on this dress; some took care of the embroidery of the fabrics, others took care of the belt to embellish, and some took care of the ribbons to weave.

In the Haute Couture Boutique, the employees, including even the boss Mrs. Lancel, they all worked hard, day and night. A magnificent dress was getting prepared.

Chapter 61

Body aches

At the end of the afternoon, Dalya went back up to her bedroom. As soon as she opened the door, Dalya immediately sat down on the large armchair in front of the fireplace. The Snow Panther was still following the little girl, like a shadow. Séraphine entered the bedroom, and stretched out on the armchair opposite to Dalya, observing her with a calm and attentive stare.

- It was an exhausting day, Séraphine!

As strange as it may seem, Dalya Bouvard got used to talking to the snow Panther, as if it were her best friend. And strangely, the Snow Panther understood Dalya's words perfectly well, and even participated in the conversations, emitting meows according to the subject discussed.

Dalya took off her jacket, and she continued:

- Look at my arms and my hands! I feel body aches!

Séraphine observed Dalya with an interested look. Dalya explained to her:

- Today was the last Gym class before the Thanksgiving holiday. I was hoping to have a calm and relaxing breathing exercise … except that I had to do the same usual training… the 3 moves; block, repel, defend.

The Snow Panther listened attentively to everything Dalya was telling her:

- Professor Tudi is very kind and encouraging and patient … but I have been practicing these same 3 moves for 3 months … every day … all day long. I don't understand the usefulness of this training. We just repeat these 3 moves. Always block, repel, and defend.

The Snow Panther mewed, and Dalya understood it:

- You want to know why I don't ask Professor Tudi for a new training… I'm very lucky to study at the Royal Georgetown College. I don't dare to ask for new trainings from Professor Tudi, and new lessons from Professor Canfield… I don't want to appear capricious or difficult.

At a moment, Dalya relaxed in her armchair, and she sighed:

- I'm exhausted, Séraphine. I feel body aches from my workouts. And my day is not over yet, I must help the employees of the grand Mansion, in the preparation for the party. I must take care of my little twin sisters, and put them to bed. And I must finish an assignment due tomorrow.

While Dalya Bouvard closed her eyes for a minute, laid back and exhausted on the chair, the Snow Panther got up and headed for the bathroom. Returning to Dalya, Séraphine placed a small object on the little girl's legs, and emitted an encouraging meow. When Dalya opened her eyes, she found that the Snow Panther brought her a bath towel. Instantly, Dalya laughed:

- A towel? ... Do you recommend a cold shower for my body aches, Séraphine? Are you sure about your idea?

Strangely, the Snow Panther smiled. Dalya caressed the head of this strange animal.

- I admit that a cold shower will calm my body aches, and help me finish the day's work. Thank you for this idea, Séraphine!

Dalya Bouvard followed the Snow Panther's advice. And Séraphine was delighted to help the little girl calm her body aches.

Chapter 62

Delivering the invitations

Tuesday November 14th, 1893. In the grand Mansion.

The Lawyers Sloan Wilfrid and Lyor Laszlo, Dalya Bouvard, Amira Mounier, and her father the accountant Mr. Jacob Mounier, the employees of the grand Mansion ... everyone was gathered in the living room of the grand Mansion. In the middle of a serious silence, all eyes were focused on a pile of envelopes placed on the small table in the living room.

The Director's Secretary, Miss Uplerine Amana had done a remarkable job; as promised, she delivered the 300 invitation envelopes, on the day and time promised. The writing was elegant and clear. Dalya was grateful for Miss Uplerine Amana's help.

Lawyer Sloan Wilfrid was the first to break the silence in the living room of the grand Mansion:

- Now the 300 invitation envelopes are ready. Who will distribute them?

All throats tightened. Planning a big party was one thing. Delivering invitations to prestigious guests was quite another thing.

The accountant and father of Amira, Mr. Jacob Mounier stood up and he advanced toward the table of envelopes, announcing in a confident voice:

- I will take the 67 Bankers' and Financiers' invitation envelopes. I will ask for a day off from my work, in order to deliver them all, in one day.

When Mr. Jacob Mounier sat down in his place, the young Lyor Laszlo stood up:

- I will take the 52 Congressmen envelopes. There's a General Assembly at Congress in 2 days. I think they will all be there.

When Lyor Laszlo sat down, Lawyer Sloan Wilfrid stood up too:

- And I will take the 89 envelopes of the Businessmen. I've already written down the list of their office addresses. I will distribute the envelopes myself.

Sloan Wilfrid returned to his chair. At that moment, Dalya asked:

- There are 92 envelopes left. The Embassies. Do we have to deliver them at the reception desks?

Lyor Laszlo sighed in a worried tone:

-   The Embassies' receptions receive hundreds of other invitations. Our envelope will certainly not be visible.

Sloan Wilfrid thought aloud, looking at the pile of the envelopes left:

-   Inviting Ambassadors to this party isn't as easy as I thought.

Amira Mounier wondered:

-   So ... how to distribute these 92 envelopes?

Everyone in the living room fell into a worried silence. The Ambassadors were the most prestigious and also the most important guests at this party. Their presence and contribution would be important in saving the Factory. The Lawyers, the accountant, the employees of the grand Mansion, Dalya and her friend Amira, everyone was thinking about finding a way to deliver these 92 invitations. Suddenly a soft voice announced:

-   I'll take care of it!

Everyone turned to the origin of the voice. It was the flower seller, who volunteered to decorate the party rooms at the grand Mansion. Lalla Fatim Fadl was wearing a modest green coat, and a light pink scarf held back her white hair.

Immediately, Dalya stood up to greet her:

-   Lalla Fatim Fadl ... Welcome. Come in, please.

As she walked into the living room, Lalla Fatim Fadl repeated her offer in a confident voice:

-   I am sorry to intrude, I overheard your conversation at the living room door. I offer my help; I will take care of the 92 envelopes of the Ambassadors.

Everyone exchanged a surprised look. Lawyer Sloan Wilfrid was as confused and surprised as everyone else:

-   The 92 envelopes? You wish to distribute the 92 invitations of the Ambassadors?

Lalla Fatim smiled with a serene calm:

-   I don't just wish ... I will deliver the invitations into the Ambassadors' own hands.

An astonished silence invaded the living room. Lawyer Sloan Wilfrid cleared his throat:

-   But, Madame ... no one here is capable of delivering these invitations to the Ambassadors' own hands.

Lalla Fatim Fadl finished the sentence and the idea:

-   ... and you think a modest old woman like me, would be incapable to do it too.

Lawyer Sloan Wilfrid immediately replied in a respectful tone:

- I mean no disrespect to you, Madame! But ... but the maximum that can be reached is the reception desks of the Embassies. Delivering the invitations to the Ambassadors' own hands ... it's almost impossible!

Dalya approached the old woman, and she explained to her in a worried tone:

- Lalla Fatim, these are the most important invitations to deliver. And the presence of the Ambassadors at this party, is important to save the Factory.

Immediately, Lalla Fatim Fadl caressed Dalya's cheek, and she replied with a determined voice:

- Moonlight ... I promise you that these invitations will be delivered to the Ambassadors' own hands!

Turning toward the Lawyer, Lalla Fatim Fadl smiled with an amused air:

- And Mr. Sloan Wilfrid ... never underestimate the size of a help. Doesn't the immense armored door simply open with a small key?

At this precise moment, Dalya Bouvard was struck by lightning. Her friend Amira Mounier jumped up from her chair. The two girls exchanged a shocked look. They had heard this same sentence before, in the 3rd clue of the Excelbox. Dalya and Amira spent long hours trying to understand this sentence, without succeeding. Until that day...

And you too, Dear readers, soon you will understand the sentence of the old flower seller, Lalla Fatim Fadl. Patience, patience ... the Excelbox is never wrong. The immense armored door ... will open simply with a small key!

A few minutes later, and a few kilometers further. At the beginning of the evening, calm and silence reigned in the modest Alley n°106. But not for long.

When the flower seller Lalla Fatim Fadl returned to her house, she met a few steps from her door, a group of little children, girls and boys. They were all sitting on the ground on cardboard boxes, playing little marbles' game on the sidewalk. Lalla Fatim Fadl approached them, and she asked in a curious voice:

- Who is winning the game?

A little boy replied proudly:

- Me, Lalla Fatim!!

The other boys and girls exclaimed defiantly:

- It's not over yet!
- We're only in the first round!
- Wait until I crush your little marbles!!

The old flower seller Lalla Fatim Fadl stifled an amused laugh:

- Everyone will win their game one day, my little ones. Be patient.

The children were focused in their game of little marbles on the sidewalk. At a moment, Lalla Fatim Fadl asked them with a soft voice:

- My little ones ... I need a favor.

Straightaway, all the children stopped their game immediately, and they all stood up in a jump:

- Yes, Lalla Fatim!
- Right away!
- How can we help you, Lalla?
- At your command, Lalla!

The old woman smiled at the obedience and kindness of the neighborhood children. She addressed them in a serious tone:

- I need you to ask all the women in this Alley to come see me at my house. I have an important mission to entrust to them.

The children didn't need to be repeated a second time. They dispersed immediately, and they ran quickly, knocking at all the doors of the neighborhood, screaming:

- Aunt!! Lalla Fatim needs you!!
- Mom!! Grandmother!! Lalla Fatim needs both of you!!
- Put down your sewing fabric, Sister!! Lalla Fatim is waiting for you!!
- Cousin!! turn off the stove, Lalla Fatim needs you!!

The next morning, something very strange happened in the city of Georgetown.

At the Japanese Embassy.

Early in the morning, the maid came into the bedroom, and she gently pulled back the window curtains, inviting the first rays of sunshine inside. A silhouette slowly sat back on the bed. The maid turned around and she bowed her head respectfully:

- Good morning, Mr. Ambassador. How was your night?

The Japanese Ambassador was a short man, very svelte, with white hair and very lively little eyes. He seemed to be a calm man, and of great character. Turning to his bedside table, the grand man drank a glass of water, and he exclaimed:

- My best night sleep in days! I slept for hours without interruption!

The maid approached the bed, and she smiled:

- I take it that the nighttime herbal tea I prepared for you helped you sleep well?

The Japanese Ambassador seemed very happy:

- A real miracle! And I thank you for it, Miss Marie!

The maid bowed:

- I am very glad that this remedy suits you, Mr. Ambassador. I will make sure to prepare it for you every evening. Your breakfast will be ready in a moment. In the dining room, as usual?
- Yes, please. Thank you, Miss Marie.

Before the maid would leave the bedroom, she took a small envelope from her pocket and she handed it to the grand man with a polite move:

- Mr. Ambassador … this is for you.

The grand man took the envelope and he opened it with a curious air. At a moment, the Ambassador seemed surprised:

- A party… at the grand Mansion?

The maid approached the Ambassador and she explained to him:

- Yes, Mr. Ambassador. A big party will be organized on Thanksgiving Day, at the grand Mansion. Several Businessmen, Bankers, Financiers, Politicians, and other Ambassadors are invited. From what I heard, there will be an important business opportunity to discuss at this party.

The Japanese Ambassador stared at the invitation in his hands for a long second. Of all the explanations that Miss Marie gave him, only 3 words caught the attention of the Ambassador of Japan; important business opportunity.

With a discreet movement, Miss Marie stepped back and she left the room of the Ambassador of Japan. A proud smile appeared on the face of the maid, Miss Marie.

At the French Embassy.

Mrs. Clémence had worked as a hairdresser at the French Embassy for several years. All the employees granted her special respect and attention. Small, chubby, over sixty years old, Mrs. Clémence was a sweet, kind and always smiling woman. When Mrs. Clémence knocked at the bedroom door, a voice answered:

- Come in.

Mrs. Clémence opened the door, and she bowed her head.

- Good morning, Madame Ambassador.

A tall figure was sitting in front of her makeup dresser. The Ambassador of France was a woman of an intimidating character, and of remarkable beauty, despite her advanced age. On this beautiful morning, the grand woman was still wearing her long dressing nightrobe, she was putting on makeup in front of the mirror of her makeup dresser, and her long gray hairs were falling down her back. The Ambassador turned to greet her employee:

- Good morning, Mrs. Clémence. I was waiting for you.

Mrs. Clémence approached the grand woman, she put her big bag on a small empty table, and she asked:

- What do you wish for today, Madame Ambassador?

The grand woman finished putting a day cream on her face, and she replied:

- A high impeccable bun, please. I have an important meeting today. I will be the only woman in a room full of about 30 men. And so, I must look as intimidating as possible!

The hairdresser Mrs. Clémence knew all the needs and tastes of her employer, since several years of work:

- Understood, Madame Ambassador.

Mrs. Clémence took out her special hairbrushes and at the same time a small envelope, which she placed on the grand woman's makeup dresser:

- When Madame Ambassador has a free moment to read this...

Immediately, the Ambassador took the envelope and she opened it:

- I always have a free moment for my favorite hairdresser! ... What is it?

Mrs. Clémence brushed the grand woman's long hairs, while she attentively read the contents of the envelope. After a moment, the grand woman exclaimed in a surprised tone:

- An invitation to a party at the grand Mansion? I thought no one lived in this house.

Mrs. Clémence continued to brush the long hairs and she informed her:

- The grand Mansion is still open, Madame Ambassador. A party will be organized there, and all the High Society of Georgetown city, is invited. The host is a charming little girl. She is the Heiress designated by Late Mr. Governor, in his Will.

The Ambassador of France looked at the invitation card, and she thought aloud:

- Dear Iskander Balthazar. He was a great man, honest and true. I really appreciated his humanity and his intelligence. If relations between the United States and France are so solid today, it is partly thanks to him. He has always been a great ally of France. I admit ... we owe him a lot.

Mrs. Clémence confirmed:

- The Late Mr. Iskander Balthazar was a great man. All the people he met attest to his qualities.

Reading the invitation, a second time, the Ambassador seemed to have made up her mind about this party. And at this precise moment, the hairdresser Mrs. Clémence smiled proudly.

At one point, picking up two small objects, the Ambassador asked her employee:

- In your opinion, Mrs. Clémence ... which lipstick for today? Beige or pink?

The hairdresser Mrs. Clémence answered without hesitation:

- To intimidate 30 men at once ... red cherry lipstick, Madame Ambassador!

The two women exchanged an accomplice smile.

At the Hungarian Embassy.

Breakfast in the dining room was ready. Scrambled eggs, caramelized sausages, chocolate croissants, various cheeses, orange juice, and raisin bread. Miss Alice adjusted the arrangement of plates and cutlery to the millimeter. When the dining room door opened, Miss Alice bowed.

- Good morning, Mr. Ambassador!

The man was in his sixties, he was wearing a very elegant tie suit, a large mustache and a bald head gave him an imposing air, full cheeks, a big belly, and a light gait. He entered and he immediately sat down at the table:

- Good morning, Miss Alice.

Instantly, the young woman served him a cup of coffee with milk. The Ambassador observed the dishes presented in front of him, with happy and delighted eyes:

- That's a copious breakfast, Miss Alice!

Miss Alice has been the Hungarian Ambassador's private Cook for some years now. The grand man was certainly of a strong character, honest, polite, hardworking, dynamic, and with one only fault; a big big appetite. Miss Alice can confirm that cooking for this man was equal cooking for 3 men. And his big appetite was especially strong early in the morning. Miss Alice smiled:

- I've prepared some Hungarian sausages for you, Mr. Ambassador. As you like them.

Letting out a childish laugh, the Ambassador helped himself to the plate of sausages first, even before tasting his coffee. Miss Alice handed him the basket of raisin bread. And with a discreet move, she placed a small envelope near the grand man's cup of coffee:

- This may interest you, Mr. Ambassador.

The grand man replied with a busy air:

- Really? What is it? … pass me the scrambled eggs, please. Did you add cheese to it?

Miss Alice obeyed and she served him the scrambled eggs on his plate:

- Certainly, Mr. Ambassador! I added grated Cheddar cheese to it.

At the first bite, the Ambassador was conquered:

- It's… it's very very delicious, Miss Alice… very very delicious!
- I'm glad you like it, Mr. Ambassador.

Miss Alice stepped back and she stood motionless near the dining table, patiently waiting for the Ambassador to finish his breakfast. After a moment of silence and tasting, the grand man took his coffee, and he noticed the small envelope placed near his cup:

- … you said I might be interested?

This was the moment Miss Alice had been waiting for. She approached the dining table, and she explained to the grand man:

- This is an invitation to a party at the grand Mansion. On Thanksgiving Day. Several distinguished people will attend. The entire city has been talking about this party for days.

Immediately, the Hungarian Ambassador put down the invitation, without continuing to read it:

- A party at the grand Mansion? On Thanksgiving Day? … no thank you! It will surely be a party with tiny amuse-bouche and miniature appetizers. The last party I attended, I almost passed out hungry! No, no, thank you! I prefer my hearty Thanksgiving meal here at my house!

At that moment Miss Alice poured some orange juice for the grand man, and she replied in a natural voice:

- I heard that more than 10 Cooks and 6 helpers will manage the lunch for this party. The greengrocer, from whom I regularly get supplies, informed me that the grand Mansion has ordered enormous quantities of products and ingredients. I assume that the dishes will be very generous. And apparently the menu is made up of dishes of foreign origin.

The Hungarian Ambassador helped himself to the little croissants, and he seemed surprised by the news from his Cook:

- A foreign menu for Thanksgiving?! ...really?! ...this is the first time I've heard of a foreign menu for an American party. Are you sure you heard correctly, Miss Alice?

The Cook Miss Alice approached the grand man, and she whispered with a serious tone, as if to divulge an important secret:

- Mr. Ambassador ... one of the Cooks informed me that it was a woman from a Country, Morocco, who took care of the menu. I obtained, after several attempts, the list of dishes that will be served at this party. There will be caramelized cinnamon pumpkin salad, garlic and olives spinach salad. In the main dishes, there will be vegetables with semolina, sweet meat dishes, chicken with lemon. A puff pastry filled with fish and seafood. And for desserts, there will be br...

At a moment, the Hungarian Ambassador interrupted Miss Alice:

- What time will the party start?

At the British Embassy.

After putting on his coat and hat, the Ambassador of the United Kingdom took his cane, he left his residence, and he walked toward the car parked in front of the Embassy. The Chauffeur opened the car door, bowing his head respectfully.

- Good morning, Mr. Ambassador!

The grand man approached the car, and he replied with a smile:

- Good morning, Mr. Martin. It looks like a busy day. I have many appointments today. Let's start!
- Understood, Mr. Ambassador.

The Ambassador sat in the back seat of the car, and the Chauffeur sat in the front seat.

The two men were almost of the same advanced age. The Chauffeur Mr. Martin was always clean-shaven, wearing a neatly pressed uniform, and impeccable white gloves. He took great care not only of his appearance, but also of his work car. Every morning, for more than 15 years, the Chauffeur would wash the car, before the start of his day. Courteous and very discreet, the Chauffeur had earned the respect and esteem of the Ambassador over the years.

Before the Chauffeur would start the car, he gave his employer an object:

- Here are today's newspapers, Mr. Ambassador.

With a spontaneous move, the grand man took the newspapers and he asked his Chauffeur in a curious voice:

- Did you find the missing word of yesterday, Mr. Martin?

For more than 15 years, the Ambassador and the Chauffeur shared not only the service car, but also the pleasure of the crossword game. The two men helped each other to solve the grid printed each day in the morning paper, while on their way to appointments. And that day, the Chauffeur answered proudly:

- Gardening tool, hoe with two irons, 10 letters' word ... Serfouette. I looked it up in a book last night, for almost an hour, Mr. Ambassador.

The Ambassador thought aloud:

- Hoe with two irons ... Serfouette ... Serfouette ... 10 letters, 10 boxes ... yes, you are right Mr. Martin! Very right!

The Chauffeur smiled and he continued his driving. When the Ambassador opened the newspaper, he found an envelope inside:

- Oh ... What is this?

The Chauffeur watched the grand man through his rear-view mirror. He waited patiently for the Ambassador to read the contents of the letter. After a few seconds, the Chauffeur informed his employer:

- It's an invitation to a Thanksgiving party, Mr. Ambassador. It takes place at the grand Mansion. My wife works there as a volunteer, since few days now, she helps them in the household. Apparently, all High Society people are invited to it.

The Ambassador put the envelope in the seat next to him, and he picked up his newspaper again:

- I hate social parties. I am tired of these hypocrites and arrogant nobles. It's exhausting having to smile for hours.

The British Ambassador was a hard-to-convince man. He needed solid arguments to attend this party. And given that this event was important to save the Cotton Factory and its jobs, the Chauffeur needed at all costs, to find an argument to convince the British Ambassador.

At one moment, after several minutes and several kilometers of driving, the Ambassador sighed:

- Today's crossword puzzle is very difficult! I haven't found a single word yet!

Suddenly, the Chauffeur had an idea. He asked in a respectful voice:

- Mr. Ambassador ... can I make you an offer, if you don't mind?

Without lifting his stare from the newspaper, the Ambassador replied:

- Certainly.

The Chauffeur announced:

-   If I guess today's entire crossword puzzle grid ... can you attend this party, for at least a few minutes, Mr. Ambassador?

Instantly, the British Ambassador let out an amused laugh:

-   If you guess the entire grid, I will attend the entire party, not just a few minutes! Today's grid seems impossible to solve. I couldn't find a single word. Are you sure of your offer, Mr. Martin?

At this precise moment, a determined smile appeared on the face of the Chauffeur Mr. Martin.

And meanwhile ... in a modest house in the Alley No. 106, an old woman, a modest flower seller, was sitting busy sewing a cloth. At one point, Lalla Fatim Fadl let out a confident amused little laugh.

Chapter 63

A special invitation

Thursday, November 16th, 1893. In the grand Mansion.

This afternoon, when the clock in her room struck 4 PM, Dalya Bouvard closed her homework books and she stood up. After several minutes in front of her closet, and several outfits tried on, Dalya decided to wear a long light pink dress, a light blue coat, a small hat with a pink flower, white winter gloves, and white shoes. Carefully slipping an envelope into her pocket, Dalya left her bedroom.

In the hall of the grand Mansion, Dalya found the help Cook Océanie. The employee was carrying small towels to the living room. As soon as she saw Dalya, Océanie exclaimed:

- You are very elegant, Mademoiselle! This light blue coat suits you perfectly!

Dalya smiled:

- Thank you, Océanie. I will bring an invitation of the Thanksgiving party, to the French Neighbors Les Poirier. I hope they can attend.
- Surely, Mademoiselle. The entire city wants to attend this party.

When Dalya Bouvard left the grand Mansion, and she resumed her way, the employee Océanie approached the window of the living room, and she observed the silhouette of the little girl walking slowly. And for the first time in a long time, Océanie felt a strange feeling of anxiety and worry.

The help Cook Océanie was well aware that Dalya was very fond of the old woman neighbor Mrs. Marianne Poirier, and the housekeeper Mrs. Glorina. Except that, since several months, Océanie gradually noticed the unusual moves, and clothing efforts of the little Dalya Bouvard.

That day, Océanie watched Dalya leaving the grand Mansion to deliver herself, a special invitation. At one moment, the Snow Panther approached Océanie, and the animal placed its paws on the edges of the window, to better look at the silhouette of the little Dalya Bouvard leaving the grand Mansion.

After long seconds of silence, Océanie caressed the Snow Panther's head, and she thought aloud, while watching the little girl through the windows:

- I don't know why, but I'm worried about Mademoiselle Dalya. I have a bad feeling.

The Snow Panther understood Océanie's concern. Séraphine let out an anxious meow as well. The help Cook Océanie murmured in a worried voice:

- I hope I'm wrong, Séraphine. I really hope I'm wrong.

Chapter 64

High heels

Saturday November 18th, 1893.

Thanksgiving Day was approaching faster than expected. Preparations were in the final stages. The party and the dining rooms were well arranged and decorated. The silverware was perfectly placed. Waiters were cleaning and retouching their outfits. The Cooks waited patiently for the start signal of cooking. The grand Mansion was ready to host the biggest party in the city of Georgetown.

In the living room of the grand Mansion, Lawyer Sloan Wilfrid was holding Dalya by the hands:

-   And one two three ... one two three ... good, very good ... one two ... aie ... carry on Mademoiselle ... one two three ... one ... aie ... you're getting better ... one two ... aie aie ... one two ...

Lawyer Sloan Wilfrid was determined to use every means possible to make this party a success and raise as much money as possible. And in order to conquer the prestigious guests, Dalya had to dance and charm the High Society of Georgetown city. And it wasn't such a simple thing ...

Being gifted, Sloan Wilfrid insisted on teaching Dalya the art of dancing. Unfortunately, as hard-working and driven as Dalya was, dancing was not her forte at all. She was stepping on the Lawyer Sloan Wilfrid's feet; with the high heels he made her wear.

Dalya asked pleadingly:

-   Can I take off the high heels? They are difficult to wear. I can't even walk in them, let alone dance. Can I wear flat shoes? Ballet flats?

Lawyer Sloan Wilfrid kept Dalya dancing:

-   Sorry Mademoiselle, but you will be wearing a party dress, high heels are a must. Go on, don't worry about my feet ... one two three ... one two tr... aie ... you'll get there ... one two three ... one two tr... aie ...

While Sloan Wilfrid and Dalya Bouvard danced, the young Lyor Laszlo was sitting comfortably in an armchair, reading a newspaper, and enjoying a coffee. And although he seemed focused on his reading, Lyor Laszlo was smiling and enjoying the torture of his mentor Sloan Wilfrid's feet.

A chair further away, Amira Mounier was sitting, with a few books and notebooks open on her lap. Amira was determined to help her best friend Dalya at this party. She was writing down all the moves that Dalya will have to perform during the party lunch. And while Dalya was learning to dance, Amira made her revise the table etiquette notes, asking her questions.

- What is the exact location of the cutlery?

Her feet guided by Lawyer Sloan Wilfrid, Dalya Bouvard turned slowly, and she answered her friend Amira:

- The forks are at my left. Spoons and knives are at my right.

Amira smiled:

- Correct!

Lawyer Sloan Wilfrid ordered Dalya:

- Raise your head Mademoiselle ... good ... carry on ... one two three ... and one two three ... aie ... one two three ... aie ... slowly ... and one two three ...

Amira Mounier asked:

- How should you hold the fork and the knife?

Dalya thought:

- I hold my fork in my right hand when I don't need a knife. If the food needs to be cut, I hold the fork in my left hand, and the knife in my right hand.

Amira turned over the page of her notes:

- Correct!

Lawyer Sloan Wilfrid raised Dalya's arm a little:

- Put your hand on your host's shoulder, like this ... it will help you keep your balance ... slowly ... here you go ... follow my rhythm ... and one two three ... aie ... it's okay ... carry on ... aie ... and one two three ... one two tr... aie aie...

Lyor Laszlo sighed as he flipped the page of his newspaper. He seemed bored. Yet, Amira Mounier and Sloan Wilfrid were all the more determined to help Dalya Bouvard.

- How should you eat spaghetti?

While dancing slowly, Dalya answered slowly too:

- I use the fork with my right hand ... no, my left hand ... I spin the fork over the pasta 3 turns. I cut the rest with a knife in my left hand. And I eat the spaghetti in one bite?

Amira Mounier corrected her:

- The knife is on your right ... and we turn the fork on the pasta only 2 turns.

Lawyer Sloan Wilfrid asked:

- Set your back straight ... chin up ... aie ... spin to my rhythm ... that's it ... go on ... aie ... one two three ... softly aie ... one two tr... aie aie ...

Amira Mounier continued:

- What is the location of the glass for the water, and the glass for the juice?

Dalya hesitated to answer:

- The water is ... the water glass is on my left ... and the juice glass is ... is on my right.

Amira corrected in a thoughtful voice:

- It's the other way around ... the water glass is on the right, and the juice glass is on the left.

Lawyer Sloan Wilfrid kept Dalya dancing:

- One two aie ... it's getting better ... one two tr... aie...aie... it's ok ... and one two tr...aie...

Amira continued:

- How to eat the soup?

Dalya whispered:

- The spoon is on my left ... and I eat the soup from the side near the bowl.

Amira hesitated to correct:

- It's... It's wrong. The spoon is on your right. And you eat the soup from the far side of the bowl.

At that moment, with a natural move, Lawyer Sloan Wilfrid turned left. Except that instead of keeping pace with the Lawyer, Dalya turned opposite, to the right. And suddenly, in a second, Dalya tripped over Sloan Wilfrid's feet and she landed on the floor.

A silence invaded the living room of the grand Mansion. All eyes observed Dalya Bouvard with an empathetic air. Her friend Amira Mounier closed her notebooks with a slow move, and the Lawyer Sloan Wilfrid rubbed his tired eyes. Dalya remained on the floor, not daring to move or to get up. Her throat was tight, her cheeks were blushing, her lips were pale, Dalya was shaking ... and it wasn't because of her fall.

At one moment, Dalya Bouvard asked in an anxious voice:

- If I make the slightest misstep, we won't have the money, and the Cotton Factory will close. Thousands of jobs will be lost because of me, isn't that right?

Lawyer Sloan Wilfrid and Amira Mounier exchanged worried looks. No one dared to answer Dalya's question. Except Lyor Laszlo:

- Technically, yes!

Turning quickly, Lawyer Sloan Wilfrid looked at him with an angry stare. Lyor defended himself in a natural voice, folding his newspaper:

- She asked a question.

Lawyer Sloan Wilfrid replied in an upset voice:

- And you didn't have to answer it, Lyor! There is no need to add more stress to it than that!

Amira approached Dalya, and she tried to reassure her friend:

- You have made a lot of progress already, Dalya. Don't worry about the lunch, I'll be sitting next to you, and I'll have my notebook on my lap. You will just have to follow my mov...

Except that in a second, Dalya's throat constricted, her heart was racing, her cheeks were out of breath, Dalya was having trouble breathing, and she was choking. Amira understood what was happening, she exclaimed in an alarmed tone:

- Dalya is having a panic attack! She needs air!

Immediately, Lawyer Sloan Wilfrid picked Dalya up and he led her to the living room's window. Opening the window, and still holding Dalya, Sloan Wilfrid ordered her in a caring tone, hardly hiding his concern:

- Breathe ... slowly ... close your eyes ... that's good ... slowly ... breathe ...

Amira poured water into a glass and she helped Dalya drink it. Without daring to say another word, Amira Mounier and Sloan Wilfrid exchanged a worried look. Dalya stood by the living room's window, struggling to breathe in the cool air. The party that will take place in the next few days was a Challenge as difficult and impossible as the 4th Question of the Excelbox.

And even if he seemed calm, the young Lyor Laszlo observed with concern, the difficulty of Dalya Bouvard to breathe.

After several long minutes, Dalya resumed her normal breathing, and her heart slowed down. A breeze of cold air caressed her face and chilled her cheeks. Lawyer Sloan Wilfrid broke the silence, addressing Dalya with a confident tone:

- It is true that this party is important for thousands of people. However, the responsibility for its success does not rest solely on you, Mademoiselle Dalya. Several people will contribute and work to make this party a success. The Cooks, the waiters, the cleaners, the helpers, the employees of the grand Mansion, your friend Amira, and her father the accountant, Lyor and me ... everyone will take part in it! Everyone will give their best, in order to convince the guests to invest in this Factory. It will be a group work!

Dalya listened intently to Sloan Wilfrid's words, and his words had a calming effect on her anxiety. Sloan Wilfrid continued in a caring voice:

- And even if the amount of money to be collected seems almost impossible, even if the Challenge seems unachievable, all the employees of the Factory are already grateful to you for trying to save their jobs. Trying is always always better than giving up!

Amira Mounier who was standing near Dalya, she confirmed the words of Sloan Wilfrid:

- It's true. Trying is always always better than giving up!

Dalya straightened up and she turned toward Lawyer Sloan Wilfrid and her friend Amira. The anxiety was still present, the Challenge still seemed impossible, and the chance of success was very minimal ... except that at that moment, Dalya felt less alone, while facing this Challenge. Lawyer Sloan Wilfrid looked at the little Dalya Bouvard, and he affirmed in a determined tone:

- At the Thanksgiving party, do your best. And everything will be alright!

Amira Mounier hugged her friend, and she affirmed:

- We will all be near you during the party, Dalya. A little wink from you, and everyone will help you correct your misstep. Don't worry, you won't be alone!

Dalya smiled and she whispered in an emotional tone:

- Thank you ... thank you.

After getting past that panic attack, Lawyer Sloan Wilfrid smiled encouragingly:

- Mesdemoiselles, let's resume our lessons! And this time, maybe without high heels, just in socks. My feet have endured enough for today!

Dalya and Amira let out an amused laugh. Lyor Laszlo went back to reading his newspaper. Sloan Wilfrid pulled Dalya closer to the center of the living room. Amira opened her notebooks. And the dance lessons and the table etiquette, resumed.

Chapter 65

Bets are open

Tuesday, November 21st, 1893.

In a luxurious living room, several men of High Society were gathered. It seemed like an important meeting. All faces seemed worried, and appeared serious.

- The Cotton Factory was supposed to be closed this week, Ernest Laszlo!

A man stared at the Lawyer with an angry look. And by his elegant suit and luxurious wooden cane, the man appeared to be a wealthy Noble. He continued with the same angry voice:

- We had a deal, Ernest Laszlo! The Cotton Factory was to be closed and demolished at the end of this month. It was expected that I would buy this land at a derisory price!

The Lawyer replied in a calm tone:

- And our deal is still ongoing, Monsieur. It's the legal proceedings to declare the Factory bankrupt, that are holding us back.

A man was sitting on an opposite armchair, he was cleaning his luxurious gold watch with a small handkerchief, and he thought aloud:

- It's quite strange. The legal procedure never exceeds 1 week. Why is the judge reluctant to declare the Cotton Factory bankrupt? Are the papers not complete?

The Lawyer Ernest Laszlo himself, did not understand why the judge was delaying this case. This same judge had yet handled thousands of similar cases before, and in less time.

The Late Governor's nephew, Mr. Ferdinand Edelmen whispered in a worried tone:

- There's been a rumor going around Georgetown city, these past days. Apparently, there will be a fundraiser, being organized for the Cotton Factory.

At this news, the Lawyer Ernest Laszlo jumped from his chair:

- This is a ridiculous idea!! I checked myself the statement of accounts and the losses of this Factory, it is impossible to keep it open, not even for one more month!!

Another man asked in a mocking voice:

- So, if I understand correctly ... it's these poor employees who decide how our affairs are managed, now?

All the men present in this living room, knew about the party which was being organized to save the Cotton Factory. If there's one thing rich Nobles can't stand; it's that poor employees interfere in their business.

The situation was different for each group of people. The rich Nobles wanted to close, demolish, and sell the Factory land, at a derisory price. The modest workers wanted to raise funds to keep the Factory open and running.

At one point, the Lawyer Ernest Laszlo exclaimed in a furious tone:

- It's all the fault of that little vermin, that little Heiress! I'm sure it was her idea to throw a party to raise funds. I'll have a word with that little vermin, to stop this party!

Suddenly, a man's voice was heard in the living room:

- Let her try.

A man listened to the conversations of this meeting, from the beginning. A slim silhouette, impeccable blond hair, a perfect black-tie suit; he was a Government employee. The same man who had the idea of imprisoning Antman Bouvard, to force his daughter Dalya to give up the inheritance. The Government employee watched the rain throughout the living room windows. And without turning around, the Government employee thought aloud:

- Let her try. One, it is impossible for them to raise the amount of money necessary to keep the Cotton Factory open. They need more than 1 million dollars, and very urgent. It's good to dream, but one must be realistic, all the same. These poor workers are naive, they have no expertise in management and finance. They think 1 million dollars will be easily raised and donated.

The rich Nobles exchanged a serious look. The arguments of the Government employee were quite correct. It was not a small amount of money, it is more than 1 million dollars needed, and in a very short time.

The Government employee continued:

- And two, when this little girl will fail to save the Factory, she will lose the support and the admiration of these poor workers. Everyone will finally understand that she's not that special, she's just a little vegetable seller. She will destroy her popularity herself, without any help from us. So then ... let her try.

The Lawyer Ernest Laszlo, the nephew of the Late Governor Ferdinand Edelmen, the rich Nobles ... they all relaxed on their chairs. A long minute of silence and thinking reigned in the luxurious living room. The Government employee brought up an idea that no one had thought of before; the little Dalya Bouvard was doomed, and it is better to let her try and fail. At this precise moment, a confident look and a sure smile appeared on all the faces of the rich Nobles present, in this luxurious living room.

Dear readers ... Mesdames and Messieurs ... a defense was being organized in the city of Georgetown. Modest volunteers were working hard, day and night to organize a party, to raise an impossible amount of money, and to save a Factory. Meanwhile, rich Nobles more experienced in business, were determined to close down the Factory.

Who do you think will win? ... The modest workers or the rich Nobles?

Dear readers, bets are open ... and the battle will begin!

Chapter 66

The day of the party

Thursday, November 23rd, 1893. The morning of Thanksgiving.

The Lawyer Sloan Wilfrid got up early that day. It was an important and crucial day. He forced himself to eat his breakfast. Always calm by nature, Sloan Wilfrid was nevertheless anxious and stressed on this last Thursday of November.

Adjusting his bow tie around his neck, Lawyer Sloan Wilfrid stared at himself in his bedroom mirror. The event was serious, and the guests will be most distinguished, Sloan Wilfrid had to be very elegant. He wore a very chic black suit, an impeccable white shirt, a dark gray coat, shiny black shoes, and white gloves.

After adjusting his hat one last time, Lawyer Sloan Wilfrid left his house. At the doorstep, Sloan Wilfrid paused for a moment. Early this morning, the street was already lively, passers-by were walking rapidly, the air was fresh, the sky was clear of all cloud, and the sun was gradually asserting itself. It was a beautiful day of celebration. Sloan Wilfrid took a long breath; he looked up at the sky and he prayed:

- We need a helping hand today!

And as strange as it was, as if the sky heard Sloan Wilfrid's request, a group of birds flew across the sky and landed on the stairs of his house. Brave and cheerful little birds. Sloan Wilfrid smiled, he felt encouraged to face this long long day.

Several minutes later, Sloan Wilfrid arrived at the grand Mansion. The house was lively. Hundred workers marched quickly in all directions, preparing to welcome the biggest party in the city of Georgetown.

As he got out of the car, Sloan Wilfrid met a familiar face, the Gardener.

- Good morning, Mr. Rosenwald. It's a busy day, I imagine?

The Gardener was coming out of the garage, and he was heading toward the entrance of the grand Mansion, his arms were loaded with 2 chairs. The Gardener continued on his way, while informing the Lawyer:

- Good morning, Mr. Wilfrid. Yes, a busy day! All the volunteers are present. We are adding the finishing touches to the party room and the dining room. I bring the extra chairs.

The Lawyer smiled:

\-   Good ... very good!

Sloan Wilfrid discovered that the hall of the grand Mansion was almost a roundabout. As soon as he got inside, the Gardener took the chairs to the dining room. The help Cook Océanie came out of the kitchen, and without even noticing the presence of the Lawyer, she walked toward the dining room, followed by many assistants:

\-   We need to start placing silverware and plates. And two of you will do the napkin folding. Hurry up Mesdames ... hurry up!

The employee Igor came in through the front door, and he nearly bumped into Lawyer Sloan Wilfrid:

\-   Sorry Monsieur ... I didn't see you. I must bring the chairs to Mr. Gardener. But where has he disappeared to? He didn't tell me where to place off these chai…

Suddenly the voice of the Gardener was heard:

\-   Igor, over here! How many chairs did you get? I still need 6 chairs. Do you need help?

Igor followed the Gardener inside the dining room. A second later, the head of the grand Mansion appeared in the hall.

\-   Good morning, Mr. Wilfrid.

Lawyer Sloan Wilfrid turned around and he asked the head of the grand Mansion:

\-   Good morning, Mr. Bûchebois. How are the preparations going on?

The head of the grand Mansion handed a pile of towels to a helper and he ordered her:

\-   Bring those towels to Cristelle, please. She is in the living room. Thank you.

Turning toward the Lawyer, the head of the grand Mansion proudly announced:

\-   We are all busy, but we will be ready at the exact time, Mr. Wilfrid. The party and dining rooms are finalized. The waiters are dressing in their uniforms, at this very moment. Océanie takes care of setting the tables. Cristelle is in charge of doing a final touch of cleaning. The Cooks are all busy. Everything will be perfect, Mr. Wilfrid.
\-   Excellent ... Excellent!

When the head of the grand Mansion returned to the kitchen, Lawyer Sloan Wilfrid observed for a long minute, the bustling activity inside the Mansion, and he thought aloud, with a proud, surprised smile:

\-   An immense party, for prestigious guests, organized with the participation of volunteers only. Who would have believed it ... who would have believed it.

At that moment, a familiar silhouette entered the hall of the grand Mansion. Sloan Wilfrid turned around and he greeted her with a cheerful smile:

\- Welcome Mrs. Lancel! Come in, please! Thank you for coming here, today.

The elegant woman, owner of the Haute Couture Boutique, was wearing an elegant long fur coat, above her very chic black dress. A necklace of white pearls occupied her neck. And a perfect bun adorned her hair.

\- Good morning, Master Wilfrid! It is a pleasure to bring my contribution today.

Mrs. Lancel was followed by several people. The elegant woman proudly announced:

\- Master Wilfrid, I present to you the hairdresser, the jeweler, the make-up artist. And here is … the dress!

Lawyer Sloan Wilfrid walked toward two young girls who held in their hands a garment, perfectly and completely wrapped in a white silk sheet, it seemed to be a precious garment. Mrs. Lancel asked a young girl to approach:

\- Master Wilfrid, I present to you the young dressmaker who designed this dress. She comes from Morocco. She is very talented, and it was a real pleasure working with her.

Lawyer Sloan Wilfrid and the young Moroccan dressmaker greeted each other with a smile. Mrs. Lancel looked for a particular person among the people passing through the hallways:

\- Where is Mademoiselle Dalya Bouvard?

Before Sloan Wilfrid would answer this question, two small silhouettes appeared in the hall of the grand Mansion, and they exclaimed joyfully:

\- Dindin in her room! Dindin takes a shower!
\- Dindin with her friend Mia! In her room!

The little twins were wearing gorgeous party dresses, with patterns of pink flowers and green leaves. Their light brown hair was neatly arranged, with flower crowns on their heads. Little twins Ari and Adi had been wearing their party dresses since dawn that day. The employee Océanie ordered them not to stain the dresses before the party. The little twins Ari and Adi showed their dresses to everyone, turning like spinning tops:

\- Frite! Look at our zolies dresses! We flowers!
\- We dance at party with zolies dresses! We pretty flowers!

Lawyer Sloan Wilfrid let out an amused laugh:

\- And you will be the most beautiful flowers of this party, Mesdemoiselles. I guarantee it!

Immediately, Lawyer Sloan Wilfrid turned to the elegant woman:

\- Mrs. Lancel, I present to you Mesdemoiselles Ari and Adi. They are the little twin sisters of Mademoiselle Dalya Bouvard. They too live at the grand Mansion.

Mrs. Lancel bowed and she greeted the little girls with a kind smile:

-   It's nice to meet you, Mesdemoiselles. And I confirm, you are very pretty in your dresses!

Ari and Adi replied with a happy laugh:

-   Mici! Mici!

Lawyer Sloan Wilfrid knelt in front of the little twins:

-   Ari... Adi... can you show Mrs. Lancel the way to your big sister Dindin's bedroom?

With one voice, the little twins jumped up:

-   Yes! This way! Dindin over here!
-   Come come! Dindin room over here!

Mrs. Lancel's team followed the little twins toward the stairs, going up to the upper floor. The little twins Ari and Adi proudly showed the way. And before Mrs. Lancel would go up the stairs, Lawyer Sloan Wilfrid approached her and he whispered to her in a serious voice:

-   Mrs. Lancel ... she must be a breathtaking beauty, today!

With a determined smile, Mrs. Lancel answered without hesitation:

-   ...And I will deliver a breathtaking beauty, today!

Chapter 67

Party time

Midday.

The grand Mansion was ready for the event. The first guests were starting to come and the party room was filling up more and more.

For this great occasion, Amira's father, Mr. Jacob Mounier wore a charming black suit, with a pretty bow tie. Approaching a man, Mr. Jacob Mounier smiled:

- Good afternoon, Mr. Wilfrid!

The Lawyer finished his cup of coffee, and he replied to the accountant with a grateful smile:

- Good afternoon, Mr. Jacob. Thank you for being here with us, today. Your help will be priceless to us!

The accountant blushed, and he whispered to the Lawyer:

- It is a real pleasure to contribute to this fundraiser, Mr. Wilfrid! I inform you that I delivered myself the 67 invitations, of which I was in charge. The group you see over there...these are the Bankers and Financiers to whom I hand delivered the invitations. They are all present today, except for 2 people who are traveling outside the city of Georgetown.

Lawyer Sloan Wilfrid observed the group indicated by the accountant:

- Excellent work, Mr. Jacob! I'm counting on you to write down the amounts of money we'll raise today?
- Certainly, Mr. Wilfrid!

While the group of Bankers and Financiers received refreshments, the Lawyer Sloan Wilfrid and the accountant Mr. Jacob Mounier were joined by the young Lyor Laszlo. Usually, Lyor Laszlo was often in a crumpled suit, and looking tired after many nights in the office. Except on that day, Lyor Laszlo was elegant in a neat black suit, and a perfect white shirt.

Lawyer Sloan Wilfrid smiled at his apprentice:

- You are very elegant today, Lyor. And you look good.

Lyor Laszlo greeted the two men, with a nod and an amused smile:

- I had 5 coffees this morning to look good and look awake.

Adjusting his bow tie, Lyor Laszlo affirmed:

- All 52 Congressmen are present here, today. Guess who convinced them to come to this party? Congressman Yolan McKlain himself!! When he learned the purpose of this party, saving the Cotton Factory, Congressman Yolan McKlain insisted on accompanying me and delivering the invitations himself, to all the offices of the other Congressmen.

Lawyer Sloan Wilfrid replied, finishing his coffee:

- That's excellent, Lyor! We badly need the support of Congressmen today.

The accountant Mr. Jacob Mounier asked hesitantly:

- May I greet Congressman Yolan McKlain? If you do not mind. He is a great man; I have always admired his personality and his greatness.

Lyor Laszlo smiled:

- Sure. I will introduce you to him, later.

More and more guests were entering the party room. And unsurprisingly, a few familiar faces showed up, too, at the party in the grand Mansion. The nephew and niece of the Late Mr. Governor, Ferdinand Edelmen and Mrs. Honoré Edelmen, the Lawyer Mr. Ernest Laszlo, and several rich Nobles. Who invited them? Nobody. Who was delighted with their presence? Nobody. Who needed their help? Nobody.

The entire city of Georgetown knew about this party at the grand Mansion. And since the Edelmen family, the Lawyer Ernest Laszlo, and the rich Nobles, they all held a hatred for Dalya Bouvard, they all showed up at this party, without even being invited, for the sole and clear goal ... to defeat the plan of saving the Cotton Factory!

As soon as they entered the party room, Lawyer Sloan Wilfrid ordered in a worried tone:

- Lyor ... you absolutely must keep an eye on the Edelmen family and those rich Nobles! They are definitely here to crash this party. We don't need trouble today. At the slightest concern or suspicious movement, you warn me.

Lyor Laszlo understood the order:

- I am watching them!

Suddenly, the accountant Mr. Jacob Mounier exclaimed when a man entered the party room:

- It's Mr. Hershey, himself!

Lawyer Sloan Wilfrid turned around and he explained:

- Yes, in flesh and bones! Mr. Hershey was in our town to visit a friend. When he heard about this party, he asked to accompany his friend. All the businessmen of Georgetown responded to the invitation, just to meet Mr. Hershey. I admit ... he did us a great service!

The young Lyor Laszlo observed Mr. Hershey from afar, with an admiring look:

- He is one of the greatest businessmen in the Country. His chocolate Factory is a success. It's a stroke of luck that he is present at this party!

Lawyer Sloan Wilfrid smiled, while observing the party room getting filled more and more. The accountant, Mr. Jacob Mounier thought and he counted aloud:

- There are 65 Bankers and Financiers ... 52 Congressmen and 2 Secretaries of State ... 89 Businessmen ... 4 other Businessmen, including Mr. Hershey ... so in total there are 212 guests. Apart from the Edelmen family, the Lawyer Mr. Ernest Laszlo, and the few men who accompany them. All the people who have received an invitation are present.

With a serious voice, Lawyer Sloan Wilfrid replied:

- All ... except the 92 Ambassadors. They were our most prestigious guests. Their presence would have helped us raise more funds. With these 212 guests; Bankers, Businessmen, and Congressmen, we can collect 20 % of the amount wanted ... about $ 240,000. But that won't be enough to keep the Cotton Factory open any longer. It remains far from our goal of 1 million and 200 thousand dollars.

Lyor Laszlo and the accountant Mr. Jacob Mounier exchanged a worried look. Lawyer Sloan Wilfrid was right; the presence of the Ambassadors was decisive to this party.

The clock showed 12:30 PM, almost 30 minutes late after the time of the invitation. Suddenly, a voice rose among the present guests. The arrogant laughter of the Late Mr. Governor's nephew, Mr. Ferdinand Edelmen, was heard throughout the party room:

- Well... I thought this party would be full of new people to meet! I already know every face in this room. I'm very disappointed it's not a remarkable party as advertised.

Lawyer Sloan Wilfrid's concern was confirmed. Almost all the present guests hoped to meet the prestigious Ambassadors. Inviting all the Ambassadors to a Thanksgiving party was a surprising idea, but still impossible!

The Late Mr. Governor's niece, Mrs. Honoré Edelmen stood up from her armchair and she put on her luxurious fur coat, affirming in an annoyed voice:

- We would have done better to spend this party at our house. Ernest Laszlo, would you drive us home, please.

The Lawyer Ernest Laszlo displayed a haughty and victorious smile. Observing the few hundred guests only, the Lawyer Ernest Laszlo was relieved that this party was over before it even started.

The accountant Mr. Mounier Jacob whispered in a stressed voice:

- Mr. Wilfrid ... what should we do now? The guests are about to leave the party!

The young Lyor Laszlo was also worried:

-   The Congressmen are bored ... the Bankers are putting on their coats ... the Businessmen are getting impatient. What shall we do now?

With a paralyzed look, Lawyer Sloan Wilfrid had no idea in his mind. He remained motionless, he didn't know what to do and what to say to retain these few hundred guests, and save this party. For the first time in a long time, Lawyer Sloan Wilfrid felt helpless.

The Lawyer Ernest Laszlo walked toward the exit of the party room, and he announced in a loud and arrogant tone:

-   I admit that it was quite useless to have come all the way here. We have overrated this party way too much. I will inform the chauffeur to prepare the ca...

Suddenly...a strange noise was heard in the party room...a noise that turned all the heads of the few present guests...a noise that paralyzed everyone...a strange noise that emanated from outside the grand Mansion.

All the people present turned around to understand the origin of this noise. Lawyer Sloan Wilfrid and the young Lyor Laszlo looked as confused as everyone else:

-   What's going on?
-   Where is this noise coming from?

At this moment, the accountant Mr. Jacob Mounier pulled the Lawyer Sloan Wilfrid by the arm, with an insistent move, and he brought him close to a window of the party room:

-   Mr. Wilfrid, it's the sound of car horns! Look at the cars coming!

A long, endless line of luxurious cars entered the grand Mansion. Immediately, the young Lyor Laszlo noticed a detail, he exclaimed:

-   All the cars are black, with yellow car numbers. These are the official cars of the Ambassadors!

Observing the long line of cars, Lawyer Sloan Wilfrid let out a relieved and surprised laugh all the same:

-   The Ambassadors! Mighty Lalla Fatim Fadl! She succeeded! An old woman selling flowers at the market managed to deliver the invitations to the Ambassadors and get them to come to this party! I absolutely must know how she pulled it off!

The young Lyor Laszlo could hardly believe his eyes:

-   But how did she do it?! It was really impossible! She is only a flower seller... and she managed to get the Ambassadors to come to this party! The 92 Ambassadors responded to the invitation!

The accountant Mr. Jacob Mounier let out an amused laugh and he too was astonished by this last-minute surprise. Immediately, the accountant Mr. Jacob Mounier took a small notebook and a pencil out of his pocket, and he thought in a joyful voice:

-   My work begins now. I must write down all the names of the Ambassadors, and all the other guests, in order to better manage the fundraising. Apparently, all the people invited are present at this party!

Car horns sounded more and more clearly. The guests present in the party room, observed with curiosity, through the windows, the next prestigious guests entering. Several people sat back in their chairs. Bankers and Financiers adjusted their ties. The Congressmen exchanged informations on the Ambassadors to better approach them. The Businessmen were more than happy and eager to meet the next guests.

All the people present in the party room were delighted by the presence of the Ambassadors. Except a few people; the Lawyer Mr. Ernest Laszlo, the Edelmen family and the few rich Nobles accompanying them, they exchanged a tense and worried look.

At one moment, the head of the grand Mansion, Mr. Bûchebois entered the party room, and he announced the first name, in a loud and proud voice:

-   Mesdames and Messieurs … Mr. Ambassador of Germany!

The few minutes that followed were astonishing. The prestigious guests entered the party room one after the other. Lawyer Sloan Wilfrid and the young Lyor Laszlo listened attentively and with great happiness to Mr. Bûchebois' announcements:

-   Mr. Ambassador of Hungary … Mr. Ambassador of Japan …

The accountant Mr. Jacob Mounier wrote down the names of the prestigious entering guests in his little notebook, murmuring in a sincerely happy voice:

-   It's unbelievable … really unbelievable!

Dear readers … the old woman flower seller, Lalla Fatim Fadl was right … Never underestimate the size of a help! … And the strange Excelbox box was also right … the immense armored door opens simply with a small key!

Chapter 68

The preparation of Dalya Bouvard

In the party room.

The accountant Mr. Jacob Mounier announced in a proud voice:

- All the guests in our list are present.

Lawyer Sloan Wilfrid observed the guests with a serious stare, thinking aloud:

- I admit, it is a real miracle to have succeeded in bringing together all these guests today. Except that our cause is not won yet, we still must convince all these people to participate in our fundraiser.

The young Lyor Laszlo agreed with his mentor Sloan Wilfrid:

- Yes, it is not won yet. The Challenge begins now!

The two Lawyers and the accountant observed the filled party room, with determined eyes. The guests were present. The employees and volunteer workers were ready. Only one person was missing to start the party ... Dalya Bouvard.

On the upper floor, in a bedroom.

Through the windows of her bedroom, Dalya Bouvard and her friend Amira Mounier watched the long convoy of black luxurious cars, parking at the entrance.

Amira Mounier wore a pretty light green dress, with flower patterns in green and white. And for this occasion, Amira abandoned her usual long braids; she arranged her long light brown hair in an elegant ponytail.

Watching the prestigious guests entering the grand Mansion, Amira Mounier smiled:

- They are all present!

Dalya's throat tightened; she answered in a trembling voice:

- They are all present.

Being friends long enough now, Amira Mounier guessed in a second the anxiety and fear of her friend Dalya. The event was important, and the stakes of the party were serious. Amira held tightly Dalya's hands, and she affirmed to her with a confident tone:

- Everything will be alright, Dalya. Breathe.

At this moment, Mrs. Lancel, the owner of the Haute Couture Boutique, approached the two girls, and she announced:

- Mademoiselle Dalya Bouvard, it's time to get ready.

Dalya was wearing her bathrobe, her light brown hair was dried and wrapped around several rollers. Dalya turned around and she followed Mrs. Lancel with a trembling but determined step. This party must succeed at all costs, despite the anxiety and the fear of the little girl.

In the minutes that followed, Dalya got ready in her bedroom, with the help of her friend Amira Mounier, Mrs. Lancel, and her entire team.

The Moroccan dressmaker and the 2 helpers took the dress out of its silk wrapper, and they laid the dress delicately and slowly on the bed. Equipped with needles, threads and scissors, the young Moroccan dressmaker checked for the 115th time, all the tiny details of this precious dress.

The hairdresser took out his brushes and tools, and he spread them out on a table. The make-up artist lined up brushes, assortments of powders and creams, on another table. The jeweler put white gloves back in his hands, and with a thin fabric he meticulously wiped off precious and shiny jewelry.

The entire team got to work, including Dalya's friend. Amira Mounier sat down on an armchair, she took a notebook out of her little bag, and she reviewed her written notes. Amira Mounier had learned by heart all the advice on etiquette and the art of the table, which Dalya will need during this party. She was determined to help her friend Dalya, to avoid any missteps.

And while Dalya Bouvard was putting on her dress, surrounded by the team of craftsmen, the owner of the Haute Couture Boutique, Mrs. Lancel settled down on an armchair right in front, and she observed the little girl with a focused stare, in order to correct all the details of her appearance.

It is true that Dalya Bouvard has always been a pretty little girl. Except that, her real beauty was shy and often hidden under work clothes, big hats, boy's overalls, and gardening boots. On this important day, it was necessary to give confidence to this beauty to reveal itself and shine with all its splendor.

After a few minutes of work, Mrs. Lancel stood up, and she gave her last instructions to the craftsmen:

- The train of the dress needs to be lengthened further. These two strands of hair need to be curled. A little more rosy blush, please. Bring the shoes, please. The gloves to be lengthened a little more.

At one moment, and after several minutes of preparation, Mrs. Lancel took a few steps back and she stared at the little girl with an examining gaze. All the craftsmen moved behind Mrs. Lancel, and they observed their work. A few long seconds of intense silence invaded the bedroom. When finally, Mrs. Lancel turned toward her team, and she smiled proudly:

- Mesdames, Messieurs ... it's a great work! It's a great great work!

The Moroccan dressmaker and her 2 helpers, the hairdresser, the makeup artist, they all displayed a proud and happy smile, in front of the little girl. Mrs. Lancel turned toward the last craftsman:

- Mr. Jeweler, it's your turn.

An old gentleman remained seated on an armchair, patiently awaiting his turn, during the preparation. The jeweler stood up and he approached the little girl. Wearing white gloves in his hand, the jeweler delicately put earrings on the little girl's ears, and he slowly placed a tiara on her hair, with the help of the hairdresser. Then, the jeweler took several steps back in order to observe the accuracy of the jewels placed on the little girl. The jeweler's smile indicated that his work was done.

Immediately, Mrs. Lancel advanced toward Dalya:

- And now, the final touch.

Mrs. Lancel took a small crystal bottle, she circled around Dalya Bouvard, sprinkling her with an exquisite perfume. When she finished her gesture, Mrs. Lancel announced:

- Mademoiselle, you are ready.

All the people present in the bedroom watched the little girl with a look proud of their work, and a look amazed by her beauty finally revealed. Amira Mounier stood next to the craftsmen, and she stared at her best friend. And although Amira couldn't say a word, her stare was clearly amazed.

When Dalya Bouvard finally approached the large mirror in her bedroom, she discovered what she truly was, for the first time ever in her life.

The little girl stared at the mirror in front of her, for long seconds. A serious silence invaded the bedroom; no one dared to interrupt the little girl who was looking at herself in the mirror.

Dalya Bouvard discovered a magnificent creature in front of her. Brilliant sapphire blue eyes, embellished foxy spots freckles, a light rosy skin, long light brown hair arranged in long free curls, a splendid royal blue party dress with shiny golden patterns, an original and sublime tiara on her head, yellow gold earrings embellished her neck.

The little girl who always wore boys' clothes; blue overalls, a white shirt, black boots. And the hair always tied in a badly arranged bun, and hidden by a large cap. This little girl was no more.

For the first time ever in her life, Dalya Bouvard discovered that she is ... beautiful.

After a long minute of silence, Dalya turned toward Mrs. Lancel and her team. And despite a trembling voice, Dalya was able to say a few words:

-   Thank you ... I ... thank you so much for your help today ... and I ... thank you for transforming me and making me so... so...

Mrs. Lancel dared to interrupt her:

-   We did not transform you, Mademoiselle. We have only brought out your shy beauty, hidden since a long time.

Moved and with a tight throat, Dalya Bouvard smiled, with tears in her eyes:

-   Thank you ... I ... I ... thank you.

All the craftsmen smiled proudly, and they all seemed to agree with Mrs. Lancel. The little girl was truly beautiful, since a long time, without knowing it.

Mrs. Lancel continued to address Dalya Bouvard in a kind tone:

-   It is us who should thank you. You were not concerned by the closing of the Cotton Factory. And yet, today you must meet prestigious and influential people, in order to convince them to save this Factory. This is a brave and noble gesture, coming from you. And everyone will remember that.

At this precise moment, Mrs. Lancel bowed in reverence in front of the little girl, and she spoke words, for the first time, with a confident voice:

-   Thank you ... Lady Dalya Bouvard.

Instantly, all the craftsmen surrounding the little girl bowed before her, and they affirmed with one voice:

-   Lady Dalya Bouvard.

Amira Mounier displayed an admiring smile; and she could not restrain her tears. From the first day they met at school, Amira Mounier understood that her friend Dalya Bouvard was a special girl. And with a sure move, Amira Mounier made a beautiful bow, and she affirmed:

-   Lady Dalya Bouvard.

Dalya Bouvard was touched and moved by these gestures of respect and this title. With a trembling heart, Dalya smiled and she whispered:

-   Thank you ... thank you very much.

It was time to show up at the party room, and meet the guests. Dalya Bouvard turned around and she left her room, followed by her friend Amira Mounier, Mrs. Lancel, and the entire team of craftsmen.

At the end of the corridor, before the stairs, the Gardener of the grand Mansion Mr. Weil Rosenwald was waiting for Dalya Bouvard to escort her downstairs. The Gardener wore an elegant and modest suit. As soon as he saw her, the Gardener seemed surprised and happy by the new appearance of Dalya Bouvard. The Gardener smiled at her, a thoughtful and proud smile.

The Gardener was the first to call her Lady, and he was quite happy to have been the first to guess that this little girl was very special. And that day, in the corridor, before the steps of the stairs, the Gardener bowed his head and he offered his arm:

- Lady Dalya Bouvard.

The little girl leaned on the Gardener's arm, and she smiled, while going down the stairs of the grand Mansion.

The little girl who slept on the floor, in a corner of the kitchen... the little girl who sold fruits and vegetables at the market... the little girl who made bags to sell, in order to help her family... the little girl who suffered insults and physical abuse from her mother... the little girl who suffered the mistreatment and selfishness of her father... the little girl who was humiliated and ridiculed at school, in the market, at the Law firm... the little girl that almost everyone underestimated and despised... the little girl who constantly received threats, slaps, knocks, hurtful words, and injustices.

She is no longer a little girl, but a young girl from now on. She has grown and blossomed, without anyone realizing it. This little girl has become ... Lady Dalya Bouvard.

In the hall of the grand Mansion.

In the hall, Lawyer Sloan Wilfrid was reunited with the employees of the grand Mansion:

- The account is fixed. We have 312 guests. Luckily, we added extra tables and chairs. The party will proceed as planned. In an hour, after the introductions, lunch will be served. Afterwards, guests will be escorted back to the party room for refreshments.

The head of the grand Mansion, Mr. Bûchebois confirmed:

- Understood, Mr. Wilfrid. At the scheduled time, we will begin to serve the dishes.

The Cook Mr. Ferrero Lutché proudly announced:

- The dishes are in finishing, at this very moment!

Igor announced in a dynamic voice:

-   All servers are ready.

Lawyer Sloan Wilfrid ordered:

-   Be sure to serve all tables. Fill the glasses with juice, regularly!

Cristelle and Océanie exclaimed with one voice:

-   We will take care of it personally, Monsieur!
-   Yes! We will go around the tables, with 3 helpers. All juice glasses will be refilled regularly!

Lawyer Sloan Wilfrid insisted on the employees of the grand Mansion:

-   Good… very good… you've all done a great job so far. Continue! Make sure the service is impeccable. Make sure the waiters don't trip and walk slo...

When suddenly, the Lawyer Sloan Wilfrid and the employees of the grand Mansion froze in front of the hall stairs. The Gardener came down proudly, offering his arm to a magnificent young girl. They were followed by Mrs. Lancel, a team of craftsmen and Amira Mounier.

All eyes and open-mouths turned toward the magnificent young girl holding the Gardener's arm. The head of the grand Mansion and the Cook exchanged a bewildered smile. Igor wondered aloud if it was really her. Océanie and Cristelle barely stifled a scream of admiration. Lawyer Sloan Wilfrid observed in amazement as the young girl descended the stairs. And for the first time in a long time, Sloan Wilfrid was surprised at the point of losing his words and becoming mute.

When she arrived at the hall, Dalya Bouvard was the center of all eyes. It is true that no one had ever seen her in this allure before. The young girl blushed, feeling uneasy in front of all this attention.

When Mrs. Lancel and her entire team were gathered in the hall of the grand Mansion, Mrs. Lancel spoke to the Lawyer, displaying a happy and proud smile:

-   I always honor my promises, Master Sloan Wilfrid. As promised, I delivered a breathtaking beauty!

Lawyer Sloan Wilfrid approached Dalya Bouvard; he observed her dress, her jewels, and her hairstyle, with an admiring and astonished stare, thinking aloud:

-   The dress is splendid. The jewelry is original. The hairstyle is very beautiful. It's... it's... you are splendid ... simply splendid!

Dalya Bouvard lifted her dress a little, and she murmured with a hesitant voice:

-   I... I couldn't wear high heels. It's hard to walk with, and I'm afraid to step on the feet of a prestigious guest, and offend him.

Lawyer Sloan Wilfrid noticed that Dalya was wearing pretty golden and transparent ballerina shoes, he smiled at her:

- The dress is big enough, no one will see your ballerina shoes.

And in front of everyone in the hall, Lawyer Sloan Wilfrid addressed Dalya, in a serious and sincere voice:

- Please know that regardless of the outcome of this party, it is a great honor for me to serve and watch over you...

For the first time since their meeting, Lawyer Sloan Wilfrid bowed in reverence in front of the young girl, and he affirmed with a confident tone:

- ...Lady Dalya Bouvard!

And instantly, with a natural and spontaneous gesture, the head of the grand Mansion Mr. Bûchebois, the Cook Mr. Ferrero Lutché, Igor, Océanie and Cristelle... all the employees of the grand Mansion bowed in reverence before the young girl, and they affirmed with one voice:

- Lady Dalya Bouvard!

Dalya Bouvard couldn't hide her emotion. She was touched by the respectful gesture of the Lawyer and the employees of the grand Mansion.

At one moment, Sloan Wilfrid offered his arm to Dalya:

- Are you ready, Lady?

Dalya leaned on his arm, and she smiled at him. With a brave and determined step, Dalya Bouvard advanced toward the party room. Holding the arm of the Lawyer Sloan Wilfrid, she was followed by the employees of the grand Mansion, by her best friend Amira Mounier, by the owner of the Haute Couture Boutique Mrs. Lancel and the entire team of craftsmen. Dalya Bouvard felt confident, followed by several people ... followed by the people.

Chapter 69

The introductions

In the party room. 1:10 PM.

When Dalya Bouvard and Lawyer Sloan Wilfrid entered the party room, moves and conversations froze. All eyes watched the young girl with a curious look, everyone wondered who she was.

Lawyer Sloan Wilfrid guided Dalya Bouvard to introduce her to the prestigious guests, starting with the Ambassadors. And as expected, just as there were people to help Dalya in this party, there were also people determined to make it fail. With an arrogant voice, the niece of the Late Mr. Governor, Mrs. Honoré Edelmen let out an amused laugh:

- Well... I'm curious to know how a little vegetable seller at the market, will address the Ambassadors. It promises to be a very funny show!

A wave of laughter invaded the Edelmen family, the Lawyer Ernest Laszlo, and the rich Nobles who surrounded them. At that precise moment, the Lawyer Sloan Wilfrid stopped paralyzed halfway, not daring to take another step. Being busy with the party menu and the guests' list, Sloan Wilfrid had completely forgotten to form Dalya in the art of conversation, and how to present herself to distinguished people. This little detail, however important, completely escaped the mind of the young man. For a long second, anxiety entirely paralyzed the Lawyer Sloan Wilfrid.

With a determined gesture, Dalya squeezed Sloan Wilfrid's arm, indicating him to move forward, she whispered to him:

- I am ready, Mr. Sloan Wilfrid. Trust me.

Lawyer Sloan Wilfrid observed Dalya with a hesitant look. And finally, the Lawyer decided to trust the young girl, and to advance toward the first man in front of them. Sloan Wilfrid bowed his head respectfully, and he announced in a trembling voice:

- Mr. Ambassador of Germany ... I present to you Lady Dalya Bouvard. Heiress of the Late Mr. Governor Iskander Balthazar.

At that moment, all eyes and ears were focused on Dalya Bouvard, waiting for the misstep of the little vegetable seller, and the start of a scandalous evening. With a natural calm and grace, Dalya Bouvard smiled at the Ambassador and she addressed him directly, with a small voice:

- Ich fühle mich durch Ihre Anwesenheit geehrt, Herr Botschafter. Und ich hoffe, Sie genießen diese Party. *(I am honored by your presence, Mr. Ambassador. And I hope you will enjoy this party)*

Immediately, a wave of astonishment and exclamations rose in the party room. The Lawyer Sloan Wilfrid couldn't believe his ears, the Edelmen family froze in their seats, everyone present exchanged a surprised look. Indeed, her accent wasn't perfect, but Dalya Bouvard pronounced her words in a confident and sure tone.

The German Ambassador seemed surprised and charmed by the young girl's courteous gesture. He kissed Dalya's hand, responding with a smile:

- The honor is mine, Lady Dalya Bouvard.

Lawyer Sloan Wilfrid continued the introductions, confused, and surprised by Dalya's attitude. Stopping in front of a new guest, Sloan Wilfrid bowed his head:

- Mr. Ambassador of Japan ... I present to you Lady Dalya Bouvard.

And with the same confident smile, Dalya bowed her head and she addressed the Japanese Ambassador:

- Taishi, go shusseki arigatōgozaimashita. Soshite, watashi wa anata ga kono pātī o tanoshinde kureru koto o negatte imasu. *(I thank you very much for your presence, Mr. Ambassador. And I hope you will enjoy this party)*

The Japanese Ambassador was not the only one surprised by the young girl's words. The Lawyer Ernest Laszlo exploded angrily:

- But it's impossible!! How? How did she manage to speak Japanese? She's a vegetable seller at the market?! This is insane!!

Dalya Bouvard continued:

- Soshite watashi no hatsuon erā o yurushitekudasai. *(And please forgive my pronunciation errors)*

At that moment, the Lawyer Sloan Wilfrid could no longer contain his happiness, his astonishment, and his spirit of revenge. Turning back to the Lawyer Ernest Laszlo and the Edelmen family, the Lawyer Sloan Wilfrid made sure to drive the nail into the wound, and he affirmed in a clear loud voice, repressing with difficulty his joyful laugh:

- It's real ... she speaks Japanese!

Naturally and always calm, the Japanese Ambassador couldn't hold back a little amused giggle. He approached the young girl and he whispered to her:

- Thank you for your invitation, Lady Dalya Bouvard. And don't worry; your pronunciation is very graceful.

Dalya felt her cheeks blush, she was delighted to succeed in welcoming the prestigious guests. The next Ambassadors were men dressed in clothes quite distinct from the other guests; a man wore an elegant white outfit, a little red hat, and yellow shoes. The other man wore an elegant white outfit, with a large black cape and a scarf on his head.

Lawyer Sloan Wilfrid bowed respectfully to the two men:

- Mr. Ambassador of Morocco … Mr. Ambassador of Saudi Arabia … I have the honor to introduce to you Lady Dalya Bouvard.

The Arab countries were among the wealthiest guests of this party, and their support would be very beneficial for the Cotton Factory. If German and Japanese were difficult languages, Arabic was an entire other story. And if Dalya did not provide the same welcome as with the other diplomats, the Ambassadors of these two countries risked being offended.

All eyes then were curious to know how Dalya Bouvard will handle it. Taking a deep breath, Dalya approached the two men, and she smiled nervously at them:

- نتشرف بحضور المملكة المغربية و المملكة العربية السعودية لهذا ال ... ال ...

(We are honored by the presence of the Kingdom of Morocco, and the Kingdom of Saudi Arabia at this … this…)

When suddenly, Dalya Bouvard froze in her place. She was missing a word. Her brain stopped working, her throat tightened, her cheeks blushed, Dalya stressed. Beside her, the Lawyer Sloan Wilfrid began to worry. The Late Mr. Governor's nephew, Ferdinand Edelmen laughed in an arrogant voice:

- And diplomatic incident!!

Dalya trembled as she tried to search with all her energy, for the missing word in her mind:

- لهذا ال ... ال ...

(At this... at this...)

At this moment, and with a gesture full of kindness and empathy, the Ambassador of Morocco bowed and he whispered to her:

-لهذا الحفل

(At this party)

Dalya Bouvard jumped, and she continued in a more confident and sure voice:

- لهذا الحفل ... ونتمنى أن تقضوا وقتا طيبا و ممتعا هذا اليوم

(At this party... and we hope you will have a great time today)

At the end of her words, Dalya looked breathless and pale. She was relieved to have finished her sentence, except that she feared she had offended the Arab diplomats because she stumbled over a word. The Ambassadors of Morocco and Saudi Arabia exchanged an accomplice look and smile. The Ambassador of Saudi Arabia replied in a respectful voice:

ـ الشرف لنا آنسة دالية ... ونشكرك على حسن الضيافة

(The honor is ours, Lady Dalya. And we thank you for your hospitality)

The Ambassador of Morocco smiled at Dalya:

ـ لهجتك العربية متقنة ... نشكرك على جهدك آنسة دالية

(Your Arabic accent is good. We thank you for your effort, Lady Dalya)

Dalya smiled nervously:

ـ شكرا حضرات السادة

(Thank you Gentlemen)

When Dalya Bouvard and Lawyer Sloan Wilfrid walked away from the two Ambassadors, Sloan Wilfrid immediately whispered to Dalya in a relieved voice:

- I didn't understand what you said, but the two Ambassadors smiled. Therefore, they are not offended. We came close to a diplomatic incident, and we survived it!

Dalya was delighted that she was doing more or less well. Approaching a grand woman, the Lawyer Sloan Wilfrid bowed his head:

- Madame Ambassador of France. It is an honor to see you with us today. I present to you Lady...

The grand woman interrupted Lawyer Sloan Wilfrid, with a strong intimidating voice:

- Dalya Bouvard ... the Heiress of the Late Mr. Governor Iskander Balthazar.

If Dalya was able to win the sympathy of other diplomats with a few sentences in foreign languages, it will take much more than that to impress the Ambassador of France. A few days earlier, Lawyer Sloan Wilfrid had explained to Dalya that the French Ambassador was a powerful, daring, and intimidating woman. In order to rally the Ambassadors of other countries, the opinion of France weighed heavily. It was necessary to convince and charm at all costs the Ambassador of France.

The grand woman observed Dalya Bouvard with a curious look. And as expected, Dalya Bouvard gathered all her strength; she spoke with a calm voice and a good French accent:

- Je suis ravie et honorée de votre présence, Madame l'Ambassadeur. Je vous en remercie infiniment. Je porte une grande estime pour votre pays, la France. Et j'esp...

(I am delighted and honored by your presence, Madame Ambassador. I thank you very much. I have great esteem for your Country, France. And I hop...

When suddenly, the grand woman interrupted her:

- I smell a scent. A strange scent. A strong perfume...

Everyone exchanged confused and anxious looks. The Ambassador of France was a woman of great intimidating character. Dalya smiled nervously and she replied with a little voice:

- I ... I am wearing the perfume Noire Gabrielle. I admit, yes, it is a strong perfume. However, it is a Perfume that gives me confidence, when I need it.

There was a long second of serious, tense silence. Lawyer Sloan Wilfrid trembled with all his bones. Dalya Bouvard turned all pale, she regretted having worn perfume that was too strong. The men surrounding the French Ambassador held their breath. The Late Governor's niece and nephew understood that the French Ambassador was irritated by this too strong perfume. The rich Nobles displayed an arrogant smile. The Lawyer Ernest Laszlo seemed happy with Dalya Bouvard's misstep.

When finally, the Ambassador of France took a few steps toward Dalya Bouvard, and she whispered to her:

- I inform you that the Perfume Noire Gabrielle is of French origin. And it's an excellent choice to have an extra dose of confidence. We are then two women who understand each other. And ... next time, in addition to this Perfume, I recommend a cherry red lipstick!

Dalya Bouvard was surprised by this answer. And she wasn't the only one, everyone exchanged looks and surprised exclamations. Lawyer Sloan Wilfrid didn't believe his ears or eyes. Is it possible that Dalya Bouvard conquered the Ambassador of France, simply thanks to a French Perfume? ... Apparently, that's what had just happened.

With a happy smile, Dalya Bouvard replied with a respectful reverence:

- Thank you for your advice, Madame Ambassador. And I thank you very much for your presence at this party. It is a great honor for me to meet you, Madame Ambassador.

The intimidating Ambassador of France bowed her head slightly, and she displayed a kind smile:

- We thank you for your invitation, Lady Dalya Bouvard. And it is a great pleasure to meet the Heiress of the Late Mr. Governor Iskander Balthazar.

The rest of the introductions went as gracefully as the first ones. The naturalness and spontaneity of Dalya Bouvard conquered the prestigious guests.

And by the way, nobody understood how Dalya Bouvard managed to speak several foreign languages. Nobody understood how…except one man.

Since the beginning of the introductions in the party room, Professor Jullien Canfield was standing in front of Dalya; he followed her closely as she spoke her words. A few times, when Dalya hesitated at a word, she guessed it from Professor Canfield's lips, and she immediately continued.

Several days ago, at school, when Dalya informed him about the presence of the Ambassadors at the grand Mansion's party, Professor Canfield quickly guessed that his student would need to charm and seduce the prestigious guests. And over several days of practice, Professor Canfield helped Dalya memorize a few sentences in several languages. Short sentences certainly … but enough to charm the prestigious guests, and open immense armored doors!

Chapter 70

Meeting the Congressmen and the Businessmen

1:40 PM.

Lawyer Sloan Wilfrid did not believe in this stroke of luck; the meeting of Dalya Bouvard and the Ambassadors, went so easily and so naturally. As he walked away from the prestigious guests, Lawyer Sloan Wilfrid whispered to Dalya in a happy and proud voice:

- You did a great great job!! The idea of sentences in foreign languages saved us!! All the Ambassadors are charmed by you, Bravo Dalya!! Keep it up, and the party will be more successful than we could have imagined!!
- Thank you, Monsieur.

Dalya Bouvard was relieved and happy to have passed the introductions to the Ambassadors, especially after several days of practice with Professor Canfield at school. Lawyer Sloan Wilfrid continued to whisper to Dalya, this time in a serious voice:

- The Ambassadors were the most difficult to meet. Now, you must welcome Congressmen, Bankers, Financiers, and Businessmen. Continue in the same natural way as with the Ambassadors. Raise your chin. Stand up straight. Take a long breath. Exhale. Smile. Let's go!

The guests of this party were not all strangers to Dalya Bouvard. Approaching a large group of politicians, Dalya immediately recognized a familiar face.

- Lady Dalya Bouvard! It's always a pleasure to meet you!

Congressman Yolan McKlain greeted Dalya Bouvard with a bow and a sincere smile. And as usual, the Congressman wore an elegant and refined suit, his big belly and his large size, gave him an imposing look. And despite being a man of great character and intimidating, Congressman Yolan McKlain was a fair and upright man. He had saved Dalya Bouvard from the schemes of the Lawyer Ernest Laszlo, several times.

Dalya smiled at him:

- Good afternoon, Monsieur. The pleasure of meeting you, is all mine. I am glad you accepted my invitation to this party. Thank you very much. Your help is invaluable to us.

Immediately, Lawyer Sloan Wilfrid bowed his head respectfully to the Politician:

- We are all grateful to you, Congressman Yolan McKlain. It is thanks to you that all the Congressmen are here today. We couldn't have convinced them to come here without your help. Thank you ... thank you so very much!

The Congressman answered in a serious voice:

- It's the least I can do to help you. The Cotton Factory employs thousands of workers. Its closing will have serious consequences on unemployment and on the activity of our Georgetown city. It is the main source of income of thousands of families. And in addition, the Late Mr. Governor Iskander Balthazar was a respectable man and mediator, he was appreciated by all politicians. No Congressmen dared to refuse your invitation.

At one point, the Congressman observed the other politicians, and he continued in a lighter tone:

- And honestly... I am happy to find all my fellow Congressmen in the same party. We often disagree in politics; the meetings always take place in offices. I am glad that for once a Thanksgiving lunch brought us together.

A few steps further on, addressing his colleague from a different party, Congressman Yolan McKlain exclaimed in an amused voice:

- We are meeting only for this lunch, Charles, aren't we? Next week, I am blocking your Finance Bill! You have been warned!

His fellow Congressman from a different party replied with an amused laugh:

- Understood! The truce is only for today's lunch. Wait until you find out what I am preparing for you next week! Your Tax Bill, forget it!

Instantly, an amused laugh invaded the group of politicians. And with all the stress and anxiety of the party, Dalya Bouvard and Lawyer Sloan Wilfrid needed a laugh too. It did them good.

Lawyer Sloan Wilfrid continued to introduce Dalya to Congressmen, Businessmen, Bankers, and Financiers. Armed with a smile and grateful words, Dalya Bouvard shook hands and she welcomed everyone present in the party room of the grand Mansion.

Chapter 71

The Poirier family

1:56 PM.

After several minutes, the introductions to the guests ended. Lawyer Sloan Wilfrid and Dalya Bouvard greeted most of the people in the party room. And after several smiles, several greetings, and several bows, it was quite clear that the guests liked the organized party, and they especially liked the host, Dalya Bouvard.

At one moment, the Lawyer Sloan Wilfrid left Dalya, and he walked over to greet some old Financier friends. Meanwhile, waiters weaved between guests to offer drinks. Suddenly, Dalya Bouvard noticed familiar faces a few steps away from her; the French neighbors, the Poirier family.

Approaching the silhouettes, Dalya Bouvard was even more stressed than approaching the Ambassadors and the other prestigious guests. The Poirier family was important to the young girl. The great woman Mrs. Marianne Poirier was seated on an armchair, wearing a very refined long emerald green dress, a fur shawl covered her shoulders, and a jeweled brooch embellished her white hair. The great woman greeted the guests, tilting her head slightly and smiling. Standing by her side was her son Richard Poirier, he was chatting with a guest man. Richard Poirier was attractive in his black tuxedo suit and satin bow tie.

When Dalya approached Mrs. Marianne Poirier, she greeted her with a joyful smile:

- Good afternoon, Madame. I'm so glad you could come to this party! I hope you will like it!

The great woman's eyes clearly displayed fascination and surprise, while observing the young girl's new allure. Dalya Bouvard approached her and she explained to her:

- This dress is a creation of a young dressmaker, coming from Morocco.

Mrs. Marianne Poirier smiled, while caressing the young girl's long curly hair. And although it was difficult for the great woman to speak because of her illness, Mrs. Marianne Poirier whispered very clear words:

- You are … very … very beautiful.

Dalya Bouvard was touched by Mrs. Marianne Poirier's remark. She thanked her with a shy smile, and she hugged the great woman. When she straightened up, Dalya greeted the great woman's son, in a nervous and intimidated voice, as always:

- Good afternoon. Thank you for coming today.

And as strange as it was, when Richard Poirier stopped his conversation with the man, and he turned toward Dalya, he seemed to have lost his words. Richard Poirier observed Dalya with a look of surprise and amazement at her new appearance. The young man discovered for the first time since ever, the magnificent long hair of Dalya Bouvard, her embellished foxy spots freckles, her shiny sapphire eyes, her proud neck, her slender waist dressed in a splendid dress... Richard Poirier was paralyzed in front of Dalya Bouvard's beauty. The young man was not expecting this appearance at all, he murmured in a confused tone:

- We ... yes ... Good evening ... Good afternoon ... it's a ... it's very nice to... to ...

Feeling Richard Poirier's amazed stare on her, and the young man's difficulty in pronouncing a correct sentence, Dalya Bouvard was happy deep inside. She hoped to please Richard Poirier, and she was delighted to have succeeded. Mrs. Marianne Poirier understood her son Richard's confusion, and Dalya Bouvard's blushed cheeks. Richard Poirier was trying with all his might to pull himself together:

- It's... it's very nice to... to...

Suddenly, an intruding voice completed Richard Poirier's sentence:

- ...to invite us to this party. I admit it's cute. I did not expect the house employees to be able to organize anything without a Master of the place.

Dalya Bouvard turned to discover a young girl of great beauty. The intruder was in her early twenties, a few years older than Dalya. Green eyes, very blond hair, a very slender waist, a naturally haughty smile. She wore a yellow dress, with shiny patterns. Dalya did not know who was this young girl, who interrupted her conversation with Richard Poirier. And yet, Dalya was polite, and she greeted her:

- Welcome to the grand Mansion. I'm glad you like the party. The employees and volunteers worked for da...

The young girl ignored Dalya, and she turned toward Richard Poirier:

- So, she's the vegetable seller you told me about? I didn't think she was civilized. I'm amazed she learned High Society manners so quickly.

The words of this intruder were as hurtful as the silent attitude of Richard Poirier. As soon as this young girl appeared, Dalya noticed that Richard Poirier became mute, his stare became cold, and his attitude became icy.

The intruder introduced herself to Dalya, with a naturally haughty voice:

- I am Lina Hill. Daughter of the Ambassador of Lebanon, granddaughter of the ex-president of Lebanon ... and fiancée of Richard Poirier.

At this precise moment, Dalya Bouvard became paralyzed:

- Fi ... Fiancée ... of ...

Richard Poirier drank his glass in one slow sip, avoiding eye contact with Dalya. The intruder spontaneously clung to the young man's arm, and she continued Dalya's sentence, with a haughty smile:

- Fiancée of Richard Poirier.

Dalya Bouvard's heart ... stopped.

Chapter 72

The shock

A few steps further from Dalya Bouvard, at the door of the party room, the employees of the grand Mansion carefully followed the course of the party. When the intruder introduced herself as Richard Poirier's fiancée, the help Cook Océanie froze and she exclaimed in a petrified voice:

- Fiancée?! Good Lord, her heart is broken!

At that moment, the maid Cristelle noticed Dalya's strange attitude:

- Why does Mademoiselle look shocked? She seems to have received a slap.

The Gardener worried:

- What's going on?

Curiosity attracted the head of the grand Mansion, Mr. Bûchebois:

- Mademoiselle turned pale, in a second. What is happening to her?

It was at this moment that Océanie turned toward the other employees, and she explained to them in a trembling voice:

- It's that … it's that … Mademoiselle liked Richard Poirier. And... and he's engaged.

This news fell like a thunder on the employees of the grand Mansion. Cristelle could not contain her shock:

- She liked him? But he looks like a vampire!

The employees of the grand Mansion exchanged a confused look. The Cook asked:

- Richard Poirier?! Are you sure, Océanie? How do you know she liked him?

In a trembling and hesitant voice, Océanie replied:

- I… I was observing her when she used to visit the French neighbors. Mademoiselle was careful to wear her prettiest dresses, and she looked after her appearance. She always blushed when I pronounced the young man's name. It is true that Mademoiselle greatly appreciated the great woman Mrs. Marianne Poirier and the housekeeper Mrs. Glorina. But... Mademoiselle had a particular attention to... to Richard Poirier.

Astonishment appeared on the faces of the employees of the grand Mansion; no one was aware of this news. With a worried look, all the employees of the grand Mansion observed Dalya Bouvard who had become pale and paralyzed.

The housekeeper of the French neighbors, Mrs. Glorina was standing near the employees of the grand Mansion, at the threshold of the door of the party room. Mrs. Glorina had overheard the entire conversation of the employees of the grand Mansion. Instantly, Mrs. Glorina leaned against the wall; she felt that her feet no longer held her. With a confused and shocked look, Mrs. Glorina observed Dalya Bouvard, while murmuring:

- But... he... I was sure that he... no it's not possible... he... he...

Immediately, the help Cook of the grand Mansion Océanie turned toward the housekeeper of the French neighbors Mrs. Glorina and she asked her with an insistent voice:

- Mrs. Glorina... how come Richard Poirier already has a fiancée?! Were you aware of that? How long have they been engaged? Is it serious? Is it official?

In a second, all the employees of the grand Mansion turned toward the old woman, to have more explanations on the matter. The housekeeper Mrs. Glorina choked, her throat constricted, her cheeks flushed red. With a trembling voice, Mrs. Glorina replied:

- I... it's just... I heard a rumor a few months ago... but it wasn't confirmed. Lina Hill is the daughter of the Ambassador of Lebanon; she comes from a very Noble and very rich family. But... but it was only a rumor. I didn't think Richard would be so serious about this Lina. I was however sure that Richard Poirier appreciated Mademoiselle. I was sure of that! ... I... Good Lord ... I feel sorry for... poor Mademoiselle... poor Mademoiselle...

Shock and confusion overcame the employees of the grand Mansion and the housekeeper Mrs. Glorina. At the threshold of the door of the party room, no one dared to move, no one dared to say a word. All worried eyes were focused on Dalya Bouvard.

Chapter 73

In a second

In the party room.

Long painful seconds passed away. Richard Poirier used all his strength to avoid Dalya Bouvard's eyes. The young man remained silent, with a cold allure, a marble face, tasting his drink, while observing the other guests of the party. Richard Poirier completely ignored the presence of Dalya, right in front of him.

His mother, Mrs. Marianne Poirier had lost her smile in a second. And although it was difficult for her to speak, the confusion and surprise clearly showed on Mrs. Marianne Poirier's face. Apparently, the mother Mrs. Marianne learned of the engagement of her son Richard, at this very moment.

Only the intruder seemed happy and serene. With her arm clinging to her fiancé Richard Poirier, Lina Hill continued to speak haughtily:

- My father ... the Ambassador of Lebanon, was very surprised by this invitation. Usually, only the Nobles and the High Society, organize this kind of refined and luxurious parties. Honestly, I didn't think to attend. I changed my mind when I found out that my fiancé Richard Poirier will be there. My father the Ambassador of Lebanon loves discussing politics with my fiancé. And I imagine that will be the only topic of conversation at this party. I am quite surprised that several Ambassadors are present, by the way.

And during all these long painful seconds, a single word was looping in Dalya Bouvard's head. Fiancée... Fiancée... Fiancée... Richard Poirier's fiancée.

Struck down, Dalya Bouvard remained motionless in front of Richard Poirier and his fiancée. And as painful as it is to describe, Dalya had difficulty breathing, her throat was tight, her cheeks were pale, her lips trembled, her legs weakened, her stomach tightened, and a burn invaded her heart. Dalya didn't know what to say or what to do. In front of this shock, Dalya stood paralyzed.

A few steps away from Dalya, the Lawyer Sloan Wilfrid was chatting with a guest. When in a brief spontaneous glance, Sloan Wilfrid realized that something was wrong with Dalya Bouvard. Immediately, the Lawyer Sloan Wilfrid cut short his conversation with the guest, and he walked over to Dalya. And at the same precise moment, Amira Mounier who was discussing with her father, she noticed the strange immobility of her friend Dalya. Amira returned the notebook to her father, and she walked over to Dalya.

Except that before the Lawyer Sloan Wilfrid or Amira Mounier approached her, in a second, Dalya Bouvard decided to leave the party room, with a hasty step, under the surprised and confused looks of all the guests.

In the hall of the grand Mansion.

Dalya Bouvard hurriedly crossed the hall of the grand Mansion. When she entered the Library, Dalya collapsed in the first chair she found. Her throat tight, Dalya found it hard to breathe and to think. Her cheeks went pale, her lips trembled, and an intense pain invaded her lungs. Sitting alone in the Library, Dalya Bouvard was in shock. Her tears flowed nonstop.

The employees of the grand Mansion stood paralyzed in the hall. No one dared to say a word, and no one dared to make a move, or even enter the Library. All the employees were forced to listen to the girl's tears, without being able to intervene.

At one moment, the Gardener broke the heavy silence in the hall. He said out loud, what the other employees were really thinking:

- This young girl tries by all means to save a Factory and thousands of jobs... and this idiot breaks her heart.

Suddenly, the Gardener turned and he walked furiously toward the party room:

- This idiot deserves a punch in the face!

Immediately, and with a spontaneous and quick move, all the employees of the grand Mansion cut the way to the Gardener and they tried to stop him from advancing. Except that being a tall and strong man, it was difficult to block the Gardener. The Cook held him back by pulling his jacket:

- Calm down! Calmati! Calmati!

Cristelle and Océanie pushed the Gardener's stomach with all their might:

- You cannot enter in this state!
- There are Ambassadors and prestigious guests!

Igor pulled him by his left arm and the Manager Mr. Bûchebois pulled him by his right arm:

- Breathe! Breathe!
- Rosenwald! Calm down! Please!

And despite the efforts of the employees, the Gardener fought and he slowly but surely made his way toward the entrance of the party room.

Suddenly, a man entered the hall. In front of the fight scene of the grand Mansion's employees, the Lawyer Sloan Wilfrid exclaimed in a worried tone:

- But what is going on here?

In the Library of the grand Mansion.

Alone, Dalya's entire body was trembling. Her throat was choking, her lips were tingling, her tears were abundant, and a burning sensation was becoming more and more intense in her heart. This news was the last thing she expected to hear. Dalya Bouvard had been stabbed. And it hurt her very very badly.

Suddenly, in the midst of the painful silence of the Library of the grand Mansion, a hand was extended to the young girl. Dalya looked up at this extended hand.

In the hall of the grand Mansion.

The employees explained what had upset and forced Dalya to leave the party room, abruptly and hurriedly. Her friend Amira Mounier exclaimed in a shocked voice:

- But this is not possible! Dalya never spoke to me about him! She always tells me everything! She never spoke to me about him!

Lawyer Sloan Wilfrid was also stunned by the news:

- Richard Poirier? Really?! Are you sure? Since when do you think she liked him?

The help Cook Océanie answered in a trembling voice:

- I discovered it by pure chance, a few months ago, while observing Mademoiselle. But I think that she liked Richard Poirier since she moved to the annex house, with her family, three years ago.

A grave silence invaded the hall of the grand Mansion. At one point, Sloan Wilfrid addressed Océanie in a serious tone:

- I must have known about this! You should have told me right away, Océanie!

In a trembling voice, Océanie apologized:

- I'm sorry, Mr. Wilfrid. I didn't think this matter could be so serious and so important as that. It was just a detail...

Sloan Wilfrid insisted:

- Everything about the Heiress of Iskander Balthazar is serious and important! Every detail of her life is serious and important!

All employees of the grand Mansion agreed with the Lawyer. No detail of the life of the young Heiress should be underestimated. Océanie bit her lip for not taking this matter more seriously.

Lawyer Sloan Wilfrid took a deep breath, he pulled himself together, and he asked in a calmer tone:

- Where is she now?

The head of the grand Mansion Mr. Bûchebois answered in a sad voice:

- In the Library, Monsieur. Alone.

Cristelle said in a sad voice:

- She seemed shocked by this news. She didn't expect it at all.

The Gardener barely restrained his anger:

- This idiot gave her a hard slap.

Amira Mounier was worried about her friend:

- I don't think Dalya will be able to continue attending this party.

The Cook asked in a curious tone:

- What are we going to do, now?

Lawyer Sloan Wilfrid thought aloud:

- Dalya Bouvard was our best asset to convince these guests, and to raise funds. I knew this party would not be easy to pull off. But I was far from imagining that such a worry will occur. I don't know what to do. How can we explain the absence of Dalya Bouvard? She is the host of this party. We have a room full of prestigious guests wai…

Suddenly … the door to the Library opened, and two people came out. Dalya Bouvard was leaning on a man's arm.

The employees of the grand Mansion, Lawyer Sloan Wilfrid, and Amira Mounier, they all froze in their places, silent and surprised, watching the two people, with curious eyes. No one dared to ask for explanations or to make a move.

In a total and imposed silence, Dalya and the man crossed the hall of the grand Mansion, and they headed with a confident step, toward the party room. The young girl had a strangely calm face; her tears were dried; her lips were still a little pale.

Entering the party room, Dalya and the man walked to the center, and they stopped, facing each other. All conversations went silent, all eyes turned toward these two people, all minds were asking questions, curious about what was happening.

Immediately, guessing the intention of Dalya and the man, the musicians resumed their instruments, and the orchestra played music. The notes emanating from the instruments resonated through the party room, and it imposed a sublime silence.

Passing his hand along Dalya's lower back, the man brought her closer to him, with a slow gesture. He took the young girl's right hand, and he stood straight in front of her.

And for the first time ever, Dalya and the man dared to look each other straight in the eye. And as strange as it was, an unusual confidence invaded these two people.

At a moment, the man smiled:

-    Ready ... Lady Dalya Bouvard?

The young girl's cheeks blushed involuntarily. And in a second, Dalya Bouvard was guided in the dance, by the steps of ... Lyor Laszlo.

Life is strange sometimes. It happens that our destiny changes ... in a second.

Chapter 74

The reactions

The employees of the grand Mansion.

Naturally, all eyes were on Dalya Bouvard and the young Lawyer Lyor Laszlo who were dancing in the middle of the party room. And a strange feeling invaded the place.

The employees of the grand Mansion stood at the threshold of the door of the party room. And like all the guests, the employees watched the two young people dancing. The head of the grand Mansion Mr. Bûchebois and the Cook Mr. Ferrero Lutché exchanged an emotional smile:

- She's back to the party! è tornata alla festa!
- Yes, she saved the party!

Craning his neck to get a better view of the scene, Igor asked:

- So, it's all good, isn't it? The party continues?

The Gardener thought aloud, watching the young girl from afar:

- She returned to the party, despite the slap she received. She dried her tears, and she pulled herself together to complete her mission. If that's not courage!

All the employees agreed with the Gardener on this point. It takes a lot of courage to be hurt, and still finish your job.

And while the employees of the grand Mansion had their eyes focused on the young girl, Océanie observed a completely different person. At one point, the help Cook Océanie approached the maid Cristelle, and she whispered to her:

- You won't believe what's happening now!

The maid Cristelle exclaimed in a relieved voice:

- Mademoiselle is dancing! She went back to the party! Even though that idiot broke her hea...

Océanie pulled Cristelle from her hand, and she insisted:

- No, I'm not talking about Mademoiselle! Watch who she is dancing with! Watch what is happening!

Cristelle examined the young Lawyer Lyor Laszlo for a long second:

- Yes, I admit I didn't think Lyor Laszlo could save the party. He dances well, by the way. And for once, he is very elegant in his su...

Océanie grew impatient:

- Cristelle!! Watch his eyes!!

At that precise moment, Cristelle noticed something strange in the eyes of the young Lyor Laszlo. Cristelle finally understood what Océanie was trying to tell her. And not believing her eyes, Cristelle whispered:

- But... wait a second... it's not possible... that look... him?... but it's ...

Océanie affirmed with a convinced tone:

- Cristelle ... it's real, I'm sure of that!

The two women exchanged a shocked and accomplice smile. The help Cook Océanie and the maid Cristelle discovered something very precious ... thanks to a look.

Congressmen and Businessmen.

Surrounded by several men, Congressman Yolan McKlain watched the young girl dance. For a moment, he thought aloud:

- She is a charming young girl. Since the first day she was named Heiress of Late Mr. Governor Iskander Balthazar, this young girl hasn't stopped impressing us.

Businessman Mr. Milton Hershey approached the Congressman, and he gave his opinion:

- I heard about this young girl. Apparently, she is intelligent, hardworking, and endowed with a great sense of empathy and responsibility. As I knew the Late Mr. Governor, Iskander Balthazar did not choose her randomly.

Congressman McKlain followed Dalya with an attentive stare, repeating in a confident voice:

- She is certainly not chosen randomly ... certainly not chosen randomly!

As he finished his glass of juice, Businessman Mr. Milton Hershey smiled:

- This young girl is brave, too. I admit, it takes a good deal of will to bring together all these Noble and prestigious guests, in order to convince them to invest in the Cotton Factory. I noticed that all the Embassies are present.

At this remark, Congressman McKlain whispered to him in an amused tone:

- The President himself couldn't gather all the Ambassadors in one party! For these Diplomats to put aside their different politics, and meet in one place, it's a feat! I absolutely must know how it was done!

The Congressmen and Businessmen watched the dancing young girl in the middle of the party room. With an admiring look and with an impressed smile, all the men were amazed by the young Dalya Bouvard ... almost all the men.

Richard Poirier.

In a corner of the party room, there was a young man with a calm allure. Except that, despite his cold appearance, Richard Poirier felt a fire burning in his throat, and a fever invading him. He attentively observed Dalya Bouvard dancing with the young Lawyer Lyor Laszlo.

And strangely, Richard Poirier could not understand why a feeling of anger suddenly invaded him. Richard Poirier had a beautiful fiancée, of Noble lineage, from a very rich family, given an excellent Bourgeois education... Lina Hill was beautiful, rich, well educated, and perfect. However, observing Dalya Bouvard dancing with another man, Richard Poirier was forced to make a considerable effort to hide his anger. The young man squeezed the glass of juice in his hand with all his strength, to the point of almost breaking it. His throat choked, his heart raced, and his body was invaded by an uncontrollable fever. Richard Poirier felt an unusual anger.

Lawyer Sloan Wilfrid.

Like all the guests present, the Lawyer Sloan Wilfrid observed the two young people dancing. Sloan Wilfrid was confused by what was unfolding in front of him.

Since the Will of the Late Mr. Governor, Lyor Laszlo was always passive and indifferent in everything that concerned the young Heiress. Sloan Wilfrid often had great difficulty convincing Lyor Laszlo to help Dalya. Not to mention that Lyor Laszlo was always unpleasant and always rude to Dalya Bouvard.

And now, on this day, the young Lyor Laszlo intervened to save the party. Sloan Wilfrid's brain was eagerly trying to find out why Lyor Laszlo changed his attitude.

A man approached the Lawyer and he greeted him:

- Good afternoon, Master Wilfrid!

The Lawyer replied in a joyful tone:

- Good afternoon, Professor Canfield!

Watching the two young people dance, alone in the middle of the party room, Professor Canfield whispered:

- Your apprentice...

Lawyer Sloan Wilfrid replied in a proud voice:

- Your student...

Suddenly and abruptly, the mind of the Lawyer Sloan Wilfrid was invaded by an insane completely crazy idea. All of a sudden, Lawyer Sloan Wilfrid smiled. And as you know him so well by now, Lawyer Sloan Wilfrid never hesitated in front of an idea, no matter how crazy and insane it was.

Observing the two young people dancing in the middle of the place, the Lawyer Sloan Wilfrid addressed his neighbor, in a confident tone:

- Professor Canfield ... it seems to me that from now on, we will work a great deal together, you and I.

And as strange as it was, Lawyer Sloan Wilfrid wasn't the only one with this crazy idea in mind. Attentively observing the two young people dancing, the Professor answered to the offer without hesitation:

- I will be more than happy to, Master Wilfrid.

The two men exchanged the same accomplice smile, and the same crazy idea in mind. And the Lawyer Sloan Wilfrid and Professor Canfield weren't the only people making an important decision on this Thanksgiving party.

The Ambassadors.

Tasting his juice, and watching the two people dance, the Japanese Ambassador thought aloud:

- A vegetable seller and an apprentice Lawyer... both are trying to save a Factory, and thousands of families. It is a beautiful union.

The Ambassador of France affirmed with a confident tone:

- Indeed, yes. It's a beautiful union.

After a long minute of thinking, the Ambassador of France turned toward the other Ambassadors. And endowed with a strong voice and a great personality, the Ambassador of France announced:

- Gentlemen ... I have been informed that this party was organized entirely by volunteers, who contributed with their time, their products, and their services, in order to offer us this splendid party. Sincerely, I think that the effort that has been put into this party deserves to save the Cotton Factory.

Immediately, all the Ambassadors approached the grand woman. The German Ambassador asked:

- How can we help this Factory?

At this moment, a man dared to intervene:

- With all due respect, Excellencies ... may I offer my humble answer to this question? My name is Jacob Mounier, I am an accountant, and I have studied the Cotton Factory file and numbers.

The British Ambassador replied:

- Certainly, Monsieur. Explain to us, please.

Under the attentive eyes of the Ambassadors, the accountant Mr. Jacob Mounier advanced forward:

- The Cotton Factory has several production secti...

When suddenly, an arrogant voice interrupted the accountant's explanations:

- Ambassadors have no right to intervene in the economic affairs of the host Country! Your only role is to represent your Countries, in political affairs only!

All eyes turned toward the Lawyer Mr. Ernest Laszlo. He stood straight, a defiant and haughty allure. Mr. Ernest Laszlo continued:

- Messieurs ... I inform you that your presence here is a mistake. The power of the Ambassadors stops in the Consulates' places only!

In front of these words, the Ambassadors were shocked that a Lawyer, as recognized and famous as he was, addressed them with such insolence. And although all the Ambassadors were furious and shocked by the Lawyer's words, the French Ambassador took over, and she waved to all the Ambassadors not to intervene. Among all the Ambassadors present, there was only one person capable of putting the Lawyer back in his place.

The Ambassador of France took a few steps toward the Lawyer Mr. Ernest Laszlo. If the grand woman was naturally intimidating ... imagine her angry.

The Lawyer Ernest Laszlo insisted in an arrogant voice:

- Your power and responsibility are clearly limited in the soil of our Country! It is out of the question for Ambassadors to intervene in the economic affairs of ou...

The French Ambassador interrupted him with an icy voice:

- And you are the one who's going to teach us our work, Ernest Laszlo?

The Lawyer Ernest Laszlo was certainly not going to be intimidated by an Ambassador, let alone a woman, regardless of her status:

- Madame, you have no rig...

The Ambassador moved even closer to the Lawyer, and she looked him straight in the eyes:

- Before lecturing us on our rights and responsibilities, before telling us how to do our job, I remind you that you are addressing the Ambassadors of the Countries that support the United States of America in the most important global decisions. Therefore ... choose your words very very carefully, Ernest Laszlo!

The Lawyer noticed that all the Ambassadors were looking at him furiously. Ernest Laszlo's arrogance made him forget who he was talking to. The French Ambassador continued in a threatening tone:

- You are neither in size nor in the power to dictate us on our work. Turn around and get out of my sight! Right now!

The Lawyer never believed that he would be fired this way, by anyone. With a pale face, and muttering incomprehensible words, the Lawyer Ernest Laszlo turned and walked away from the group of Ambassadors.

Finding her natural voice, the Ambassador of France addressed a man:

- Mr. Jacob Mounier ... continue your explanations, please.

The conversation resumed its normal course between the accountant and the Ambassadors. Several Businessmen and Bankers joined in the discussion.

It was important to explain to the guests the situation of the Cotton Factory, and the plan for its rescue, in order to convince them to invest in it. And knowing better than everyone the file of this Factory, the accountant Mr. Jacob Mounier explained to the guests the situation of the Factory and how to contribute, in order to save it from closing. Although his legs were shaking, and he was intimidated by all these great personalities, the accountant Mr. Jacob Mounier ardently and sincerely defended the cause of the Cotton Factory.

It must be admitted that the presence of the great Businessman Mr. Milton Hershey, contributed greatly to this cause. Mr. Milton Hershey's chocolate Factory was a success story in Business and Industry. After listening carefully to the accountant Mr. Jacob Mounier's explanations and numbers, Mr. Milton Hershey did not hesitate to give his opinion; he approved the Factory's rescue plan, and he even added two other solutions to speed up production. Mr. Hershey had great notoriety and expertise in Factory management.

Several minutes later, all the guests received complete informations about the Cotton Factory, on the intended rescue plan, and on the contributions to be made to save the thousands of jobs.

At one moment, the Ambassador of Germany and the Ambassador of Japan, decided with one voice:

- We agree to participate!

The Ambassador of Morocco and the Ambassador of Saudi Arabia exchanged an accomplice look, and they agreed to contribute to the rescue of this Factory.

As he finished his juice, the British Ambassador thought in a loud voice:

- It seems to me that all the Ambassadors present are ready to make their contribution. Except that … except that, I have a little confusion. In the Will of the Late Mr. Governor Iskander Balthazar, it is stated that a young man Lyor Laszlo is solely responsible for the management of the BalthEnterprise Holding, of which the Cotton Factory is part of. However… it seems to me that it is his father who holds the reins of this Holding, and he acts as the sole decision maker.

The Hungarian Ambassador confirmed this confusion:

- It's true. Who is the decision maker then? The father or the son? If we invest in this Factory, this situation must be clarified!

The Ambassador of France observed for a long second the Lawyer Ernest Laszlo, who was standing a few steps away from the Ambassadors. Ernest Laszlo seemed furious at the course of the events. The French Ambassador turned toward the other diplomats, and she affirmed in a determined tone:

- Gentlemen Ambassadors … it would be a pleasure for me to fix this confusion, once and for all!

All the other Ambassadors smiled and were reassured. The French Ambassador was a woman who never failed her word.

Dalya Bouvard and Lyor Laszlo.

The music played by the Orchestra embellished the party room, and captivated the spirits. All eyes were attentively observing the two young people dancing. The Governor's Heiress and the young Lawyer danced gracefully and naturally, without any missteps.

At one point, at the end of their dance, Dalya Bouvard and Lyor Laszlo stopped. Immediately, admiring applause rose throughout the party room. Noticing all the stares toward them, Dalya Bouvard blushed, and Lyor Laszlo looked embarrassed. Before parting ways and returning to the guests, Lyor Laszlo said to Dalya:

- Thank you.

Dalya looked confused; she didn't understand why he was thanking her. Lyor Laszlo smiled at her:

- Thank you for not having crushed my feet, during our dance.

At this moment, as strange and improbable as it may seem … Dalya Bouvard smiled.

Chapter 75

Thanksgiving lunch

2:25 PM. Lunch time. In the hall of the grand Mansion.

This party had to succeed at all costs. What was at stake was crucial; saving thousands of jobs. Therefore, the Lawyer Sloan Wilfrid was watching over all the details of the party, and he was directing all the volunteers. The guests were led to the huge dining room, where the tables were perfectly set and embellished. The Orchestra moved toward the dining room, to continue to charm the guests with soft music. In the hall of the grand Mansion, Lawyer Sloan Wilfrid addressed the waiters:

- Messieurs ... The service must be perfect. Juice glasses should not empty. Fill the plates fully. Walk slowly, adjust your uniform, and smile. Charm the stomachs of these guests, and we will have won this party!

Immediately, the servers executed the orders; they formed a long line in front of the kitchen of the grand Mansion, and they waited their turn to serve the dishes in the dining room.

Lawyer Sloan Wilfrid walked into the kitchen of the grand Mansion. A small silhouette with tattoos on her face stood out among the dozens of Cooks and helpers; the old Moroccan Cook Lalla Tafernout. Lawyer Sloan Wilfrid smiled politely at her:

- Lalla Tafernout ... it's up to you now! Good luck!

The old Moroccan Cook did not speak the language of the Country, but she understood perfectly well the encouragement of the Lawyer Sloan Wilfrid. Lalla Tafernout replied with a calm and above all confident smile. Immediately, the old Moroccan Cook turned to the Cooks and the helpers, and she provided them with a model to follow for the dressing of the dishes. Lalla Tafernout took care herself of all the details and the final touches of the plates, before the waiters took them away.

Lawyer Sloan Wilfrid came out of the kitchen, and he ordered the head of the grand Mansion, in a serious voice:

- Monsieur Bûchebois ... the chair of the French neighbor Mrs. Marianne Poirier, will remain in its place, next to the Ambassador of France. The two grand women are longtime friends. On the other hand, the chairs of Richard Poirier and his fiancée, you must m...

Mr. Bûchebois continued this sentence:

- Move them to the opposite side of the dining room.

Lawyer Wilfrid confirmed:

- Exact! very very far from Dalya Bouvard!

The head of the grand Mansion entered the dining room, with a hasty step, in order to fix this last-minute change.

Lawyer Sloan Wilfrid instructed Dalya's best friend, Amira Mounier:

- Miss Amira … don't leave Dalya for a second! She was brave to continue this party, after the shock of Richard Poirier. But it is absolutely necessary to protect her, to help her and stay close to her for the rest of this day.

With a determined voice, Amira Mounier was ready to support her only and best friend:

- Understood Monsieur! I'm not leaving her!

In the dining room.

Lunch began.

The waiters entered the dining room, in perfect coordination, and they presented the dishes to the guests. Instantly, and as expected, astonishment appeared on all the faces of the guests. In addition to the luxurious dinner service, there were engraved ceramic plates, wooden spoons, embroidered napkins in several colors. And the contents of the dishes seemed as delicious as original. At the first bites, the guests were bewitched.

The employees of the grand Mansion were all busy. Standing in a corner of the dining room, Mr. Bûchebois watched with a focused stare the progress of the lunch, he corrected the slightest detail. The help Cook Océanie and the maid Cristelle went around the tables to serve the juices. Assistant Igor joined the waiters in serving lunch. The Cook Mr. Ferrero Lutché stood at the entrance of the dining room, in order to carefully check all the entering plates. Even the Gardener Mr. Rosenwald joined his colleagues, he adjusted the uniforms and ties of the waiters, at the entrance of the dining room.

Dalya Bouvard sat down at the table with several Ambassadors; France, the United Kingdom, Morocco, Saudi Arabia, Japan, as well as her best friend Amira Mounier, and the French neighbor Mrs. Marianne Poirier. And as agreed, Amira Mounier sat close to Dalya, in order to help her with the table etiquette.

The French neighbor Mrs. Marianne Poirier sat next to the Ambassador of France; apparently the two women were great friends since a long time. Mrs. Marianne Poirier not being able to speak abundantly, she brought a small notebook and she wrote down her sentences in it. The Ambassador of France seemed to like Mrs. Marianne Poirier very much. The two women were laughing and whispering throughout the entire lunch.

As requested, the head of the grand Mansion moved the chair of Richard Poirier and his fiancée, to a table well well far from Dalya Bouvard, on the opposite side of the dining room.

And strangely, throughout the entire lunch, Richard Poirier and his fiancée remained mute, silent, and cold. They didn't appear to be a newly engaged, happy couple.

Meanwhile, Dalya Bouvard used all her strength and all the energy of her body to focus on this lunch. On Dalya's left, there was the Ambassador of the United Kingdom, and on her right, there was the Ambassador of Morocco.

Although he was reluctant at first to attend this party, the British Ambassador was surprised at enjoying this lunch, and spending a good time. He discussed at length with Dalya Bouvard, several subjects; the latest Political news, the Late Mr. Governor Iskander Balthazar who was a great friend of the Ambassador, and the Cotton Factory. At a moment, Dalya Bouvard and the British Ambassador discovered a shared passion: the game of guessing words. The British Ambassador was a great, calm, serene, intellectual man, and a pleasant company for Dalya Bouvard.

On Dalya's right, there was the Ambassador of Morocco. As soon as the guests were served lunch, the Ambassador of Morocco was pleasantly surprised to find the dishes of his Country in this lunch. The Ambassador of Morocco proudly explained the names and contents of his Country's dishes to the guests at his table. The Ambassador of Saudi Arabia was seated next to his Moroccan homologue, he also explained the cultural differences between Arab Countries and the West.

Dalya Bouvard used all the appropriate cutlery, and she copied exactly all the moves of her friend Amira Mounier, who sat across from her. Amira Mounier was installed between the Ambassador of Saudi Arabia and the Ambassador of Japan. Throughout lunch, Amira was fascinated to discover the Arab culture on her right, and the Asian culture on her left. In a courteous voice, Amira asked hundreds of questions, sometimes to her right, sometimes to her left. The Saudi Ambassador and the Japanese Ambassador answered proudly.

At a nearby table, Dalya's twin little sisters, Ari and Adi, sat near the Hungarian Ambassador. And one must admit that the little twins and the Hungarian Ambassador had one thing in common; a big big appetite. Lunch was delicious and exquisite; the little twins and the Hungarian Ambassador lived a real moment of happiness and a pleasure of tasting. At one point, the Hungarian Ambassador filled himself the plates of the little twins.

At another table near Dalya, Lawyer Sloan Wilfrid was chatting at length with Congressman Yolan McKlain. While the young Lyor Laszlo and the accountant Mr. Jacob Mounier listened attentively to the advice of the great Businessman Mr. Milton Hershey.

Thanksgiving lunch went much better than expected. And as she had promised, the old Moroccan Cook Lalla Tafernout was proud and happy to observe the empty plates coming out of the dining room. The original menu bewitched all the guests.

The employees of the grand Mansion, the volunteers, the Cooks, the helpers, the waiters, they all worked hard to make this party a success, and to be able to save the Cotton Factory.

Dear readers, it is true that the Late Mr. Governor Iskander Balthazar was no longer here to defend his Cotton Factory ... nevertheless, rest assured, Iskander Balthazar left behind an army that will defend and preserve his legacy!

Chapter 76

A success ... at a price

Several hours later. The end of the Thanksgiving party. 7 PM.

The moment everyone has been waiting for, has finally arrived. In the hall of the grand Mansion, all the employees, the volunteers, the Cooks, the waiters, Lawyer Sloan Wilfrid, Dalya Bouvard, and her friend Amira Mounier, they were all gathered. Everyone held their breath, in a tense and impatient silence. All eyes were focused on one man; the accountant Mr. Jacob Mounier. During the entire party, the accountant Mr. Jacob Mounier was responsible for noting and collecting all the contributions and donations from the guests.

Days and nights of work, hundreds of volunteers generously offering their time, their services, and their products. The time to know the result of their work has finally arrived. Lawyer Sloan Wilfrid grew impatient:

- So?

Surrounded by volunteers and employees, the accountant Mr. Jacob Mounier clearly felt all the curious eyes focused on him. The accountant revised the total donations for the 48th time. Finally, the accountant Mr. Jacob Mounier looked up at the Lawyer Sloan Wilfrid, and he announced with a trembling voice:

- We... we didn't... we didn't get the amount we wanted.

This announcement was a hard knock to all the volunteers and employees gathered in the hall of the grand Mansion. They had all worked hard to organize and make this party a success. They were hoping for good news. Everyone was disappointed and crushed by this announcement. Lawyer Sloan Wilfrid thought aloud:

- We all knew that the amount of 1 million and 200 thousand dollars would not be easy to obtain. Even with the presence of the prestigious guests. Ambassadors have been generous, Congressmen have offered all their support, Businessmen have contributed as best as they could. But the amount wanted was immense to collect, especially in such a short time!

For days, everyone had been living on a glimmer of hope, and praying for a miracle. And at that moment, in the hall of the grand Mansion, hope collided with reality. All employees and workers were disappointed. Lawyer Sloan Wilfrid forced himself to smile, he still tried to hide his disappointment, and he affirmed in an emotional voice:

- You have all done a remarkable and exceptional job, you should be proud of it. We will use the amount collected, and we will try to negotiate with the Banks for additional loa...

Suddenly, the accountant Mr. Jacob Mounier interrupted the Lawyer:

\- We surpassed it!

Confusion reigned in the hall of the grand Mansion. All the volunteers and employees watched the accountant with a confused look. Lawyer Sloan Wilfrid asked him:

\- What? I don't understand what you w...

For the 2nd time, the accountant Mr. Jacob Mounier interrupted the Lawyer, with an amused and trembling laugh:

\- We have surpassed the wanted amount!

It took several long seconds for volunteers and employees to understand this news. For the 3rd time, the accountant Mr. Jacob Mounier screamed out with all his might, and he repeated:

\- WE HAVE SURPASSED THE WANTED AMOUNT! WE RAISED MORE THAN 1 MILLION AND 200 THOUSAND DOLLARS! WE HAVE SURPASSED THE WANTED AMOUNT!

Suddenly, a wave of joy screams invaded the hall of the grand Mansion. The Cooks jumped, the maids hugged, the waiters laughed, the employees of the grand Mansion congratulated each other. No one could contain their joy and surprise.

Lawyer Sloan Wilfrid approached the accountant, and he insisted:

\- Are you sure? How many have we collected? Have you checked all the numbers? Are you sure? What is the exact amount?

The accountant laughed wholeheartedly, showing his little notebook with a trembling gesture:

\- We have collected 1 million and 265 thousand dollars!! I checked this number 50 times!!

This news was surprising and shocking. Lawyer Sloan Wilfrid laughed as he hugged the accountant:

\- We made it!! We made it!! It was impossible, but we made it!!

In front of the effort that has been made to achieve this Thanksgiving party, all the prestigious guests were more than generous. And in order to preserve thousands of jobs and the main source of income of thousands of families, all the guests contributed without hesitation.

After weeks of stress and pressure, the hall of the grand Mansion became noisy with joy and screams of happiness. All the volunteers and employees laughed, relieved and proud of this great success. A success ... at a price.

A little silhouette was standing discreetly in a corner of the hall of the grand Mansion. Watching the employees and volunteers laugh happily, Dalya Bouvard smiled. The young girl's smile was sincere, but it was a broken smile.

While everyone was kissing and congratulating each other, Dalya Bouvard discreetly retired and she went up the hall stairs alone, toward her bedroom.

At this moment, the employees of the grand Mansion, her friend Amira Mounier, and the Lawyer Sloan Wilfrid, they observed the young girl going up the stairs, alone. Their laughs and joy faded as they watched the heartbroken young girl, walking away alone, toward her bedroom. No one dared to follow her, no one had words to comfort her, no one could help her. The employees of the grand Mansion, Amira Mounier, and the Lawyer Sloan Wilfrid, they were happy to have succeeded in saving the Cotton Factory. And they were also sad for the young girl, heartbroken.

In her room, Dalya Bouvard sat down on the floor, alone in front of the fireplace, and she released the tears that she had been holding back for hours. In one minute, her tears wet entirely her party dress. Dalya felt her lungs constrict. A pain was getting more and more intense on the left side of her chest, his heart was burning. Her throat was choking. Her cheeks blushed. The fever rose to her forehead. And her tears wouldn't stop. Dalya Bouvard cried all the tears in her body.

A silhouette entered the bedroom. The Snow Panther had remained quietly in the upper floor of the grand Mansion, until the end of the party and the leaving of the guests.

And as natural as it was, the Snow Panther felt perfectly well the young girl's pain. The Snow Panther could do nothing to relieve her protégé. While Dalya Bouvard was sitting on the floor, motionless in front of the fireplace, crying continuously, the Snow Panther lay down on the floor near the young girl. Séraphine just silently observed Dalya Bouvard, crying the tears of her body.

Life is quite strange sometimes ... the evening when Dalya Bouvard saves thousands of jobs, and she makes thousands of families happy ... is the same evening when her heart is broken into a thousand pieces.

Dalya Bouvard had sincere feelings for Richard Poirier. She really liked him, from the first day she met him. But ... did Richard Poirier ever had feelings for Dalya? ... no one knows the answer to this question. Neither Dalya, nor even the Author writing this story.

Chapter 77

A stupid decision

In the house of the French neighbors, the Poirier.

At the end of the party in the grand Mansion, the return home of the Poirier family happened in a heavy and dense silence. The great woman Mrs. Marianne Poirier seemed very upset. Her smile faded away, she looked tense and cold. And for the great woman to be angry, which was quite rare ... something serious must have happened, that night.

The housekeeper Mrs. Glorina, sitting next to Mrs. Marianne in the car, she looked sad and crushed. Always cheerful and smiling by nature, this is the first time in a long time that Mrs. Glorina felt deep sadness. With a sad face and pale lips, Mrs. Glorina stared at the tissue she was holding in her hands, and she seemed lost in her sadness.

You wouldn't have thought that just a few minutes ago, the two women were attending a joyful and successful party.

Sitting opposite to the two women, Richard Poirier noticed his mother's angry air and Mrs. Glorina's sadness. A small idea formed in Richard's mind about what would have affected the mood of the two women. Except that, with all the strength of his mind, Richard Poirier tried to occupy his thoughts with something else, thinking about the work meeting he had, the next morning at the Government.

The arrival at the Poirier family's house seemed to last an eternity, under this heavy silence. When the car stopped, Richard Poirier got out of the car first, and he turned to offer a helping hand to his mother. And getting ready to get out of the car, Mrs. Marianne Poirier observed her son's hand for a few long seconds. Then, with a firm move, Mrs. Marianne Poirier leaned with one hand on her cane, and with the other hand on the armrest of the car door, and she got out of the car alone. Richard remained shocked for a few moments by his mother's cold move. For his mother to refuse his help, she must be very upset at him.

The housekeeper Mrs. Glorina got out of the car, mute and dejected; she seemed to be under shock of a serious event. She followed Mrs. Marianne inside the house. The two women left Richard Poirier behind them, without addressing a word or even a glance to him.

Several minutes later, Richard Poirier entered his mother's room. The great woman was sitting on an armchair, she seemed calm, but still upset. In her mauve velvet nightrobe, Mrs. Marianne was occupied in her thoughts. Richard sat down in a chair near his mother, and he asked in a courteous tone:

-    You look upset, Mother ... what's going on?

Mrs. Marianne did not move. Her serious stare was focused on the night landscape throughout the windows of her bedroom. Richard insisted on knowing:

- Something has upset you. May I know what it is?

At this moment, Mrs. Marianne took a piece of paper with an annoyed move, and she wrote a few words. Giving the paper to her son, Mrs. Marianne looked him in the eyes for the first time since the end of the party at the grand Mansion. And although the great woman didn't say a word, her eyes were clearly very very angry. When Richard took the paper, he read:

It was a stupid decision Richard!
You have lost a diamond forever!

Richard was stunned by what he read. He tried to defend himself:

- Mother, my decision was well thought out, since a long time. Lina is the best choice th…

Suddenly, Mrs. Marianne Poirier banged her fist abruptly on the table, so hard that the teapot spilled. The great woman stood up quickly, she walked closer to the large windows of her room, turning her back on her son.

Richard Poirier had never seen his mother in such a state. He would never have believed that his engagement decision would cause his mother's anger. And rereading the 2nd sentence written by his mother, Richard Poirier felt a little twinge in his heart, despite all the arguments he had in mind about his noble rich beautiful Bourgeoise fiancée.

The great woman Mrs. Marianne Poirier had her back turned, Richard understood that his mother did not want to extend this conversation any further. In a tense silence, Richard stood up and he left his mother's room, without another word.

Chapter 78

Sick

3 days later. Sunday, November 26th, 1893.

The entire city of Georgetown was celebrating this success, and the reopening of the Cotton Factory. All employees and their families were happy and relieved. In these last days of November, the air was fresh, the blue sky was clear, the sun was shining joyfully, the people were lively and happy. Joy and relief invaded Georgetown city. Except in one place.

In the kitchen of the grand Mansion.

A sad and painful silence hovered over the grand Mansion, since the end of the Thanksgiving party. That day, at lunchtime, the employees were all gathered around the kitchen table. Lunch was served and it looked delicious. Yet, no employee had the appetite to eat. They were all turning their forks, looking sad and somber.

After several minutes, the Gardener was the first to break the silence. He put his fork down on the table with an angry and brusque move:

- He's an idiot! He deserves a punch in the face, for what he did! He's a real idiot!

The Cook Mr. Ferrero Lutché murmured words in an angry tone:

- Idiot! Stupido! Si merita uno schiaffo!

The help Cook Océanie thought in a loud and sad voice:

- She didn't deserve this disappointment. She saved thousands of families! She really didn't deserve to have her heart broken!

Assistant Igor leaned back on his chair:

- It was a very successful and joyful party, all the same. It's really too bad it ended badly for her.

The maid Cristelle asked in a worried voice:

- We must help her! We must do something!

The head of the grand Mansion Mr. Bûchebois answered in a sad voice:

- I am afraid there is nothing we can do to help her.

On the upper floor of the grand Mansion, Amira Mounier ran with all the strength of her legs, in the corridors. She jumped down the steps of the hall stairs, she opened the doors with a brusque move. When Amira Mounier arrived in the kitchen of the grand Mansion, she screamed breathlessly:

- BRING A DOCTOR!! RIGHT NOW!!

Immediately, the employees of the grand Mansion, sitting around the lunch table, they all stood up at once.

Several minutes later.

In the corridor, outside a bedroom, the employees of the grand Mansion and Amira Mounier, were impatiently waiting for news. They all looked anxious and worried.

At a moment, the Doctor and the Lawyer Sloan Wilfrid came out of Dalya Bouvard's room. Everyone observed the Doctor, eager for his answer. And seeing the serious and tense face of the Doctor, everyone understood that the situation was grave. The Doctor announced in a serious voice:

- It seems that Mademoiselle Dalya Bouvard has not eaten for several days. Her body is weakened. She cried incessantly, which caused dryness in her eyes, and a severe headache. At this rate, she is likely to be in grave condition.

All the employees of the grand Mansion exchanged worried looks. Lawyer Sloan Wilfrid asked:

- What can we do to help her, Doctor?

The Doctor replied:

- I gave her a sleeping pill, to put her to sleep. She needs to stop crying, at least for a few hours. You must force her to eat. I recommend preparing hot soups for her, it will be easier to swallow. And warming herbal teas, with honey and ginger, it would also be beneficial. Her body needs to be warmed up during her recovery period. I will be back to check on her, in 2 days.

Assistant Igor accompanied the Doctor to the car. Standing in the corridor outside the bedroom, Lawyer Sloan Wilfrid looked worried:

- I underestimated the incident that happened on the Thanksgiving party. Richard Poirier, who showed up with his fiancée, was a hard slap to Dalya Bouvard. She's not doing well at all!!

After a moment of thinking, Lawyer Sloan Wilfrid looked up at the people gathered in the corridor, and he ordered them in a serious tone:

- You heard the Doctor's instructions!

And immediately, everyone knew what to do. The Cook Mr. Ferrero Lutché affirmed:

- Yes, Monsieur. Soup and warming herbal teas. I will take care of that, as of tonight!

The Gardener replied:

- I will take care of filling the wood of her chimney!

The head of the grand Mansion asked Océanie and Cristelle:

- Mademoiselle Dalya Bouvard must take hot baths, every day.

Océanie and Cristelle replied simultaneously:

- Understood, Monsieur!
- We will take care of it!

Amira Mounier decided:

- I will inform my father that I will spend the next nights here, at the grand Mansion. I will stay close to her, and I too will help you.

Lawyer Sloan Wilfrid insisted:

- You all must keep an eye on her and watch over her, day and night. Don't leave her for a second. Dalya Bouvard needs all of us. We must help her heal.

In a second, the employees of the grand Mansion and Amira Mounier spread to perform their roles. They were all ready and determined to take care of Dalya Bouvard, and help her heal.

In the hall of the grand Mansion, the help Cook Océanie knelt in front of Dalya's little twin sisters, and she explained to them in a kind voice:

- Your big sister Dalya is a little sick. That's why you shouldn't disturb her for the next few days. She needs to sleep and rest.

Instantly, Ari and Adi replied seriously:

- We zentilles, we don't make noises.
- We not disturb Dindin.

The help Cook Océanie hugged the little twins before leading them to their bedroom.

The same day, in the house of the French neighbors, the Poirier.

As usual, Richard Poirier was working in his office. He had many papers to correct, and many references to search for. When he was interrupted by the housekeeper Mrs. Glorina at the door of his office. The old woman entered with a silent step, and she placed a tray of tea on a table.

- Thank you, Mrs. Glorina.

For several days, the great woman Mrs. Marianne Poirier and the housekeeper Mrs. Glorina had not spoken a word to Richard Poirier. The home of the French Poirier family sank into a tense silence. Mrs. Marianne refused to take her meals with her son, and she completely ignored him. Mrs. Glorina only answered Richard with nods, and she avoided looking him in the face. Richard Poirier did not understand the attitude of the two women toward him. After all, she was just a vegetable and fruit seller at the market.

Richard continued editing his report. When suddenly, he noticed the presence of Mrs. Glorina in front of his office table. And for the first time in several days, Mrs. Glorina looked at Richard, straight in the eyes. The old woman looked worried; her voice trembled:

- I saw the Doctor's car ... coming out of the grand Mansion, this morning.

At this news, Richard Poirier froze in his move. And although he had used all his strength to hide his surprise, Richard turned pale in a second. He didn't need more words to understand what was happening at the grand Mansion. Mrs. Glorina, still standing in front of him, she continued in a serious and upset tone:

- It is true that she is only a vegetable and fruit seller at the market. However, never in all my life have I ever met a more noble heart and such humble politeness. Of all the things she has done and of all the things she will still do ... everyone can assure you that this young girl is one of a kind. She is a diamond!

A cold feeling invaded Richard Poirier at this precise moment. In all her years of service, the housekeeper Mrs. Glorina had never addressed Richard Poirier in such a tone. And the old woman's words were as piercing as they were true. The housekeeper Mrs. Glorina pronounced the same word that his mother Mrs. Marianne Poirier used; a diamond.

Richard didn't dare to move or say a word; he didn't dare to defend his decision of being engaged to the noble rich beautiful Bourgeoise. Richard Poirier remained motionless and mute.

Mrs. Glorina turned around to leave the office. And before closing the door, Mrs. Glorina wanted to confirm one last thing to Richard Poirier:

- ... And you lost her.

Chapter 79

The 4th clue

Saturday, December 2nd, 1893. In the grand Mansion.

Dalya Bouvard's condition did not improve. She spent all her days in her room, lying on the bed, watching the days go by from the windows. Her appetite decreased. Her body was weakening. Her sadness grew heavier. And her silence intensified.

In the kitchen of the grand Mansion, the employees were all confused and helpless. Amira Mounier worried about her friend:

-   The 4th Challenge is in 10 days. Dalya is required to answer it. She must get back in good shape, to correctly answer the 4th Question. It's been several days since she hasn't been able to even get up from her bed.

The Cook Mr. Ferrero Lutché sat down on a chair, looking exhausted:

-   I cooked for her, all her favorite dishes. I cooked for her the best soups and gratins. I baked the most delicious cakes for her. Nothing cheers her up. I don't know what else to cook.

The Gardener leaned against a kitchen wall and he thought aloud:

-   She hasn't left her bedroom since several days. She is getting weaker and weaker. She can't go on like this.

The head of the grand Mansion Mr. Bûchebois replied:

-   Yet, we have tried everything. Soups, herbal teas, baths. Nothing works.

Leaning back on her chair, the help Cook Océanie wondered aloud:

-   We brought her the best Doctor in town. Is there anyone who can help her?

At that precise moment, a crazy idea crossed the mind of the maid Cristelle:

-   Or ... is there something that can help her?

Everyone looked at Cristelle with a curious and confused air. Immediately, the maid Cristelle left the kitchen of the grand Mansion, with a rapid step. A few seconds later, Cristelle returned breathless, and she placed a small box on the table in the middle of the kitchen:

-   The Excelbox will help us!

Immediately, all the employees and Amira Mounier were surprised by this gesture. Cristelle affirmed with certainty:

- If no person can help Mademoiselle Dalya Bouvard, then this strange box will help her!

Amira Mounier exclaimed:

- Dalya told me that this box always provided her with solutions to the most impossible situations! It's very strange, but Dalya had total confidence in this box!

A determined smile appeared on the face of the maid Cristelle:

- So… I will ask for the 4th clue!

The help Cook Océanie asked in a curious tone:

- One second, one second … this box answers only to the writing of Mademoiselle Dalya Bouvard. How are we going to ask for a clue?

With a proud move, Cristelle took out a piece of paper from her pocket:

- The other day, while cleaning her desk, I found this piece of paper, with this question: what is the 4th clue? … Maybe Mademoiselle forgot to use this piece of paper, or maybe she thought she'd ask for that clue later. Anyway, I will use her paper and her writing, to ask for the 4th clue!

The assistant Igor exclaimed in a surprised voice:

- That's luck!

Immediately, the head of the grand Mansion exclaimed:

- That's cheating!

Cristelle answered without hesitation:

- It's just a little cheat! And besides, it's for a good cause!

With a quick move, the head of the grand Mansion stood up and he firmly opposed it:

- But that's insane! This is cheating! Only Mademoiselle Dalya Bouvard must ask this box for the clues! We have no right to use this box!

Except that, Cristelle defended her idea firmly too:

- Mademoiselle can't even get out of bed! We'll ask for a clue instead. And this box will provide us with a solution or a remedy to help Mademoiselle!

All the employees of the grand Mansion completely agreed with Cristelle. Amira Mounier supported the idea of the maid Cristelle:

- Monsieur Bûchebois ... if Dalya does not answer the 4th Question, her life will go back to the way it was before. She will leave school and she will return to the market. We must help her.

The Cook Mr. Ferrero Lutché thought aloud:

- She saved thousands of jobs; it's our turn to save her now!

The Gardener affirmed with a thoughtful tone:

- Cristelle is right. We will ask only for a clue to help Mademoiselle feel better and be able to answer the 4th Question. She needs a helping hand.

Océanie answered in a moved voice:

- Mademoiselle needs us.

At this moment, Cristelle had one last argument to convince Mr. Bûchebois of her idea. With a defiant tone, Cristelle affirmed:

- Richard Poirier will not win! The idiot who put her in this state, he will not win!

A tense silence invaded the kitchen. All eyes turned toward the head of the grand Mansion. Mr. Bûchebois was a very straightforward man, and his honesty was hard to convince. However, the situation was grave and serious. After a few long seconds of thinking, Mr. Bûchebois decided. He stared at the employees with a menacing look:

- This will be the first and the last time, one of you uses this box. Is that clear? I warn you all! The first and the last time!!

Although the threats of the head of the grand Mansion were very real, a determined and happy smile appeared on all faces.

Immediately, everyone approached the strange box. With a trembling but determined hand, the maid Cristelle placed the piece of paper on the opening of the box.

What is the 4th clue?

Quickly, the paper disappeared inside the box. The Excelbox activated. An impressive light emanated from the strange box, and it invaded the kitchen of the grand Mansion. Everyone jumped and moved back. The Excelbox's help was requested, and the strange box responded.

When the box turned off and calmed down, the maid Cristelle approached it with a hesitant step. Even unlit, the strange box was magnificent and fascinating. Slowly, Cristelle pulled out the little piece of paper emitted by the Excelbox.

Breathe. Exhale. Gather all your wounds, and heal.

The 1000 pieces can avail.

To survive the outside, look inside.

The employees of the grand Mansion and Amira Mounier, they all came close to Cristelle. And from that precise moment, all the brains worked to decipher the clue.

The Cook Mr. Ferrero Lutché exclaimed, his eyes wide open:

- It seems like a tricky clue to figure out.

Assistant Igor wondered:

- But how did Mademoiselle manage to understand the clues of this box? And all alone, too! I don't even understand the first sentence!

Amira Mounier replied:

- Dalya almost never understood the clue at the first reading. Often, it took her days and weeks to understand the clue.

The Gardener rubbed his head:

- It's not clear at all.

The help Cook Océanie was disappointed:

- I thought the clue would be easy to understand. We needed a remedy to help Mademoiselle. And quickly!

The maid Cristelle thought aloud:

- If Mademoiselle trusted this box, then we too should trust this box. The remedy is surely in this clue. We may need to use a book from the Library to understa…

Suddenly, the head of the grand Mansion exclaimed:

- It's the puzzle!

All the gathered people went silent, and they observed the grand man. Mr. Bûchebois took the 4th clue from Cristelle's hands, and he read it in a focused voice:

- The first sentence is unclear. But the second sentence … the 1000 pieces … the 1000 pieces … it is the puzzle!

Suddenly, the clue was becoming clearer to everyone. The maid Cristelle was surprised:

- Monsieur Bûchebois … are you talking about the game of the Late Mr. Governor? the 1000 pieces' game he used to spread on his big desk?

The help Cook Océanie remembered:

- Mr. Governor prevented us from approaching the table, so as not to lose a piece. Are you sure the clue is about the puzzle game?

Amira Mounier thought:

- The Excelbox advises us to use this game to help Dalya? How will this game help her feel better? It's quite strange.

The Gardener and Igor announced with one voice:

- Igor and I have put the Late Mr. Governor's things away in the attic.
- Yes, all of his belongings and personal items are stored in boxes upstairs.

For a few long seconds, everyone watched the head of the grand Mansion. Mr. Bûchebois re-read the piece of paper of the 4th clue, more than 10 times. And the only and the same idea occurred to him. When finally, Mr. Bûchebois announced:

- I don't know how or why … but the clue indicates us to the Late Mr. Governor's puzzle. I'm sure of that!

All employees and Amira Mounier, were ready and determined to help Dalya Bouvard. The Cook Mr. Ferrero Lutché ordered:

- Mesdames, Messieurs … To the attic!

A few minutes later.

In the attic of the grand Mansion, everyone actively searched for a specific box; small size, in precious wood, with golden patterns. After several minutes, the Cook let out a scream of fear because of a spider, the help Cook Océanie fell on her back because of her giggles at the Cook's scream of fear, the Gardener bumped his head at an open cupboard, the maid Cristelle hurt her finger closing a box, Amira Mounier sneezed exactly 117 times because of the dust, the assistant Igor knocked his knee at a chair, and … suddenly, the head of the grand Mansion Mr. Bûchebois exclaimed:

- Found it!

Immediately, everyone surrounded the old box of the Late Mr. Governor. And although nobody understood how and why this puzzle game could help Dalya Bouvard, the employees and Amira Mounier, they were all happy to have understood what the clue indicated to them, and happy to have found this box.

While leaving the attic, and going down the stairs toward the hall of the grand Mansion, the maid Cristelle thought aloud:

- We managed to decipher the clue in a few minutes. What if we falsified Mademoiselle's handwriting, and we asked the 4th Question directly. All of us, we can answ...
- CRIIIIIIIIISTELLE !!!!!!! The head of the grand Mansion screamed in a threatening tone.

The same day. Saturday, December 2nd, 1893. The night.

Since a few days, Dalya Bouvard stopped crying, she had no more tears in her body to pour. The hot soups that the Cook prepared for her, did her good. Océanie and Cristelle insisted that she finishes her entire meals. The hot and fragrant baths warmed her body. Herbal teas of honey and ginger lengthened her naps. All the employees of the grand Mansion watched over her, in a caring and considerate way. Lawyer Sloan Wilfrid visited her almost daily, to bring her the day's newspapers himself and to check on her. Her friend Amira Mounier spent her days near her, reading her favorite books, trying to entertain her. The Snow Panther didn't leave Dalya for a second.

And yet ... Dalya Bouvard was heartbroken, she had trouble getting up from her sadness and getting up from her bed.

Dalya spent all her days, lying down in bed, in a painful silence, looking confused, searching in vain for answers to her questions. Her lungs were tightened, and she felt uneasiness with every breath. Since the end of the Thanksgiving party, Dalya Bouvard had been locked up in her room, morning and night, mute and silent, watching the sky change throughout the large windows of her room. Because the feeling of being rejected is painful. Dalya Bouvard felt despised, humiliated, broken, as if she was worth nothing at all.

That night, as usual, Dalya Bouvard was lying down on her bed. Silent and lost in her thoughts. At a moment, someone broke the silence in the bedroom. The maid Cristelle came in, holding a tray in her hand, and smiling tenderly:

- Good evening, Mademoiselle! I bring you your dinner. The Cook has prepared delicious pasta for you, with an exquisite tomato sauce, and minced meat. And since you love cheese, he put a lot of it. You will definitely like tonight's dinner!

Dalya forced herself to smile at her, without having the strength or the energy to speak a word. The maid Cristelle put the dinner tray on the bedside table, near Dalya.

Stepping back a few steps away from the bed, Cristelle took a small box out of her pocket and she placed it on Dalya's work desk. With an encouraging smile, Cristelle announced:

- This is for you, Mademoiselle. You might be interested.

Dalya's stare remained focused on the large windows of her bedroom. She didn't even hear the maid Cristelle's words, and even less noticed the box placed on her desk. Since several days, Dalya Bouvard had lost motivation and interest in everything.

With slow hesitant steps, Cristelle discreetly withdrew. At the door of the bedroom, all the employees of the grand Mansion observed from afar the young girl lying down on the bed, motionless and weak, since several days. Her friend Amira Mounier whispered:

- Do you think this puzzle game will help her rise up again?

No one understood why the strange box indicated them to this puzzle game. And no one was sure how this puzzle game could help a young girl feel better and recover from her sadness. Only the Excelbox held the answers to these questions.

.

Chapter 80

Just a puzzle

The day after. Sunday, December 3rd, 1893.

This December day was going to be freezing. The sky was completely gray. No bird ventured outside. The rain was abundant. And the cold of winter invaded the city of Georgetown.

The grand Mansion had sunk into a forced sadness since several days. Dalya Bouvard's condition was not improving; she spent days, lying down on her bed, silent and lost in her thoughts, she had lost her taste for everything. The employees of the grand Mansion, her best friend Amira Mounier, and even the Lawyer Sloan Wilfrid, they were exhausted and out of ideas; they had tried all the tricks and all the remedies, they had even dared to cheat and ask the strange box for a clue. But in vain.

This afternoon, all the employees were gathered in the kitchen. No one dared to smile or speak. They were all busy with their work, in a cold and sad silence.

Suddenly, footsteps were heard entering the kitchen. And when the employees turned around, they were shocked to find a little silhouette at the kitchen door; Dalya Bouvard, herself! The young girl left her room for the first time in several days. She still looked tired and weak, but she got out of her bed anyway and she left her room!

The employees remained shocked and motionless in their moves. Dalya Bouvard asked with a small voice and a shy smile:

- I ... I would like to work on the large table, in the Library. May I have a piece of cake, please?

Instantly, and with a single move, all the employees of the grand Mansion jumped up from their chairs, and they answered with joy and astonishment:

- Immediately, Mademoiselle!
- I'm going to turn on the lights and the fireplace in the Library!
- I will bring the wood immediately!
- I bring you a warm blanket for your feet!
- Would you like a hot chocolate with it?
- Do you want to add caramel to your cake?

In a second, the kitchen of the grand Mansion lit up. Everyone hurried and moved quickly. The Cook prepared the hot chocolate, Océanie arranged the tray and a plate of cake, the Gardener went out to turn on the lights and the fireplace, Igor went out to get the wood, Cristelle went to a room to bring a blanket.

No one believed their eyes; Dalya Bouvard left her room. Finally!

As everyone was happily running around the kitchen, the head of the grand Mansion noticed a small object; Dalya Bouvard held in her hand the box of puzzles that the employees searched for in the attic, the day before. At this moment, the head of the grand Mansion approached Dalya, and he smiled at her:

- I will bring the big table closer to the fireplace, for you, Mademoiselle. Right away.

Tuesday, December 5th, 1893.

- A ... puzzle game? Really?

The Lawyer Sloan Wilfrid observed Dalya Bouvard discreetly, at the doorstep of the Library of the grand Mansion. 2 days prior, when the young girl left her room to ask for cake, Lawyer Sloan Wilfrid was notified of Dalya's condition. And despite being a busy day at the Lawyer's office, Sloan Wilfrid still visited the grand Mansion, to check on the young girl.

The Lawyer Sloan Wilfrid muttered in a confused tone:

- A puzzle game...a puzzle game helped her rise up again. Where did you find this game?

Still at the doorstep of the Library, the head of the grand Mansion explained to him:

- It is a puzzle game that belonged to the Late Mr. Governor. We searched for it in the attic, in his personal belongings. The Governor always asked us to set up a large table for him in the Library, especially for this game. He made sure to spread out all the 1000 pieces of the puzzle on the large table.

Lawyer Sloan Wilfrid was beginning to understand what was going on:

- So... Dalya Bouvard needed a large table to put together the 1000 pieces of the puzzle. That's why she left her room, and she's here in the Library.

The head of the grand Mansion, Mr. Bûchebois affirmed:

- That's right, Monsieur. The puzzle game forced her out of her bed, out of her room, and out of her isolation. Mademoiselle stays all day in the Library. She takes her meals here, she reads books, and above all she finishes this puzzle game.

Lawyer Sloan Wilfrid thought aloud, while watching the girl from afar:

- She seems very focused on this game.

The head of the grand Mansion continued:

- I don't know why or how; the Late Mr. Governor was also obsessed with this game. He used to spend an entire week in the Library, in order to collect the 1000 pieces of the puzzle. Mademoiselle is obsessed with it too.

2 days before, when the maid Cristelle placed the box of the puzzle game on her desk, Dalya took no interest in it. She was tired and lost in her sadness. After hours of silence, when she sat up on her bed to eat her dinner, Dalya noticed the box placed on her desk.

At first, the young girl was not interested to know what the box contained. Except that, toward the end of her dinner, curiosity invaded her. And for the first time in days, Dalya got out of her bed, and she sat down in front of her desk. For a few seconds, Dalya stared at the luxurious wooden box, with its golden patterns.

And as soon as opened, the contents of this box conquered Dalya Bouvard's mind.

It only took a few seconds for Dalya to understand the game. On the back of the box there was a pasted picture of the magnificent United States Capitol building. And inside the box, there were 1000 small pieces, which had to be put together, in order to obtain the perfect image of the Capitol.

The game required immense and complete concentration of the brain. And as strange as it was unexplained, the puzzle game bewitched the mind, occupied the brain, calmed the doubts, rested the fears, soothed the pains, and it offered oxygen to the brain. Strange and unexplained, the puzzle game did a lot of good to Governor Iskander Balthazar ... and apparently Dalya Bouvard too.

Quietly closing the Library door, Lawyer Sloan Wilfrid asked:

- Mr. Bûchebois, do you think she is ready to answer the 4th Challenge?

At this moment, the head of the grand Mansion seemed worried:

- Honestly, Monsieur ... I don't know. It is true that she came out of her isolation and her room. On the other hand, she is too silent, she is too calm. She often remains alone. She looks sad and broken. Which is normal, after receiving a shock. Mademoiselle needs more time to heal.

Lawyer Sloan Wilfrid was also worried:

- Except that, she doesn't have enough time. The 4th Challenge is in a week.

Walking toward the exit of the grand Mansion, Mr. Bûchebois asked:

- What more can we do to help Mademoiselle?

At the exit door, Lawyer Sloan Wilfrid sighed with a worried tone:

- Keep watching over her until she feels better. That's all we can do to help her.

Chapter 81

The attack

Tuesday, December 5th, 1893.

The same day, in a small Alley on the West side of Georgetown city. After several minutes of walking, the young Tudi finally arrived at a door. She checked that no one was following her, then she entered.

And apparently, the young Tudi was expected. In the square garden at the center of the house, the great Master Fong Ka-Ho was sitting on a thick carpet, surrounded by Miss Haîyang and General Shang. The three people waited patiently and in a calm silence. A cold winter breeze passed regularly, caressing the branches and leaves.

The young Tudi greeted the 3 people with a bow, before sitting down.

For several days, the young Tudi went to the grand Mansion, discreetly and secretly, to acquire news of Dalya Bouvard. And luckily, the grand Mansion had transparent and big windows; Tudi could easily read people's lips and see what was going on inside the grand Mansion.

And just like many days before, Tudi reported the smallest details she found at the grand Mansion:

- Mademoiselle no longer stays in her room. She spends her days in the Library, working on a game that belonged to the Late Mr. Governor.

General Shang exclaimed in a confused air:

- A game?

The young Tudi was sure of her informations:

- It's a Puzzle game, 1000 pieces to gather. It was indicated in the 4th clue. It was the employees of the grand Mansion who asked for this clue, and the box provided it to them. Mr... Mr. Bûchebois, the head of the grand Mansion, he is the one who found the meaning of the clue and the puzzle game.

Miss Haîyang understood the usefulness of this game:

- The puzzle occupies the mind, it calms anxiety, it entertains from negative ideas. If the box recommended this puzzle game, it's because it's effective.

The great Master Fong Ka-Ho asked:

- And how is she?

The young Tudi answered with a somewhat hesitant voice:

- The puzzle game helped her ... somehow. She ... she came out of her room. But ...

Instantly, the great Master finished the sentence:

- But she didn't come out yet of her sadness.

Young Tudi explained the situation:

- Mademoiselle spends her days at the Library, alone. All the employees of the grand Mansion watch over her, day and night. She eats much more than before; she takes naps in the afternoons. She receives visits from her school friend and the Lawyer. Except that ... except that, she is still weak. Her recovery is very slow. She is too quiet, and often lost in her thoughts. She seems to have lost her motivation. She has trouble to rise up again.

Miss Haîyang and General Shang exchanged worried looks. On receiving this news, the great Master Fong Ka-Ho decided with a sure voice:

- In this case, we must intervene and help her.

All eyes were curious, and they turned toward the great Master. General Shang asked:

- How can we help her, Master?

The old man smiled:

- We will use her pain to help her rise up again.

No one understood the words of the great Master, nor the idea he had in mind. With a worried voice, the young Tudi dared to say:

- The 4th Challenge is only a few days away, Master...

And without a second of doubt, the old man replied:

- And she will be ready!

At that moment, the great Master ordered:

- Shang, Tudi ... get ready for the attack, tomorrow night. Haîyang ... notify our new ally. He must understand our role.

Although no one understood the idea of the great Master Fong Ka-Ho, Miss Haîyang, General Shang, and the young Tudi, they answered with one voice:

- At your command, Master.

Wednesday, December 6th, 1893.

It seemed like a peaceful and calm night in the grand Mansion. In the Library, Dalya was focused reading a book, lying down on an armchair in front of the brightly lit fireplace. The Snow Panther was half asleep on a rug near Dalya.

When the head of the grand Mansion entered:

- I am bringing you tea with ginger, lemon, and honey. I added some oatmeal cookies.

Dalya sat up in her armchair:

- Thank you, Mr. Bûchebois.

By placing the tray on a table near Dalya, Mr. Bûchebois asked her in a caring tone:

- Would you like something else, Mademoiselle?
- No, Monsieur. Thank you for the cookies. I'll finish a few chapters of this book, and I'll go back to sleep in my room.

The Manager added 2 woods to the fireplace:

- I will be in the kitchen, Mademoiselle. If you need anything, let me know.

Dalya thanked him with a smile, before lying back on the armchair and continuing her reading. Mr. Bûchebois closed the Library door, and he headed toward the kitchen. He had to write the shopping list for the next day. The head of the grand Mansion made himself a hot herbal tea, and he settled down at the kitchen table to write the list. All the other employees had finished their work, and each were in their room.

At one moment, a smell infiltrated the kitchen of the grand Mansion. A mixture of herbs and lavender. The head of the grand Mansion thought aloud:

- It's a strange smell. Where is … this … this … smell … com…

Suddenly, the head of the grand Mansion fell into a deep sleep, sitting at the kitchen table, a pencil still in his hand.

The smell infiltrated the employees' rooms. The help Cook Océanie was folding the baby's clothes; she fell asleep on her big armchair. The maid Cristelle was reading a cookbook, she fell asleep on the bed. The Gardener was cleaning his shoes; he fell asleep on his chair. Assistant Igor was counting his salary money; he fell asleep in front of his table. The Cook was sewing a hole in his apron; he fell asleep on his chair. All the employees fell into a deep, undisturbed sleep.

At one moment, in the Library of the grand Mansion, the Snow Panther stood up with a sudden and rapid move. The Panther's senses were highly developed and intense. Séraphine sensed that something strange and abnormal was happening in the grand Mansion.

Lying on the armchair, Dalya felt the Panther's jump.

- Is everything alright, Séraphine?

The Snow Panther ignored the young girl, and stared at the door of the Library, convinced that someone would enter. Dalya thought the animal's behavior was very strange. Except that, before continuing her reading, Dalya heard the door of the Library open.

In total silence, 3 people entered the Library of the grand Mansion. The 3 people wore black outfits, and black masks hid their faces. Without any further details, the 3 people were impossible to recognize.

In a second, the Snow Panther released her claws, her canines appeared, her paws strengthened, her fur spiked, and her sapphire eyes lit up. At the entering of these 3 people, the Snow Panther felt a danger. Séraphine preceded the young girl, and she was ready to defend her.

Dalya stood up quickly, worried and surprised by this intrusion:

- Who are you? How did you get here? What do you want?

The 3 people remained motionless and silent. Dalya did not understand what was happening, and who these masked people were. Fear and anxiety invaded Dalya, she had never seen masked people entering the grand Mansion, at such a late hour, and above all without being introduced by an employee of the grand Mansion.

The Snow Panther moved in front of Dalya to defend her. Séraphine let out a growl, the animal was in a position to fight. The Panther's protective attitude only increased Dalya's fear and anxiety. Thousands of questions invaded the young girl's mind; who are these masked people? Why are they at the grand Mansion? Are they thieves? Why are they masked? How did they get here? What do they want?

One of the masked persons advanced a few steps toward Dalya, and he said:

- Wǒmen bùshì lái shānghài tā de. Wǒmen lái zhèlǐ shì wèile shìfàng tā de lìliàng, bāngzhù tā zhàn qǐlái. Wǒmen yāoqiú nín ràng wǒmen cǎiqǔ xíngdòng, ér bùshì gānyù.

(We are not here to hurt her. We are here to unleash her strength, and to help her rise up again. We ask you to please let us act, and not interfere).

The masked person's voice indicated that he was an old man. Dalya didn't understand what he had said, it was a foreign language. Except that ... one would have thought that the masked old man was not speaking to Dalya Bouvard ... but to the Snow Panther! And strangely, it seems that the Snow Panther understood perfectly well the words of the masked old man.

Instantly, the Snow Panther calmed down; her claws and canines withdrew, her paws let loose, and her fur soothed down. With a slow movement, the Snow Panther moved away from Dalya Bouvard, and she sat down near the fireplace in the Library.

Immediately, the 3 people bowed their heads in reverence, in front of the Snow Panther. It was a very strange and unusual gesture. Dalya couldn't understand the words of the masked old man, the reverence of the 3 people in front of the Panther, and even less the attitude of the Snow Panther who moved away from her. For a long time, the Snow Panther had been Dalya's shadow; she followed her everywhere and always remained close to her. Except tonight. The Snow Panther sat down a few steps away from Dalya. And with an intense and focused stare, the Snow Panther watched the young girl.

Dalya found herself alone in front of 3 masked people. In a trembling voice, Dalya asked the same questions again:

- Who are you? What do you want?

Immediately, the 3 masked people advanced and they surrounded Dalya Bouvard. The young girl's heart trembled. She repeated:

- What do you wa...

Dalya didn't finish her sentence because she was hit on the back. Her legs gave out, Dalya fell. The 3 people remained standing and motionless. With a quick movement, Dalya stood up and she tried to escape by running toward the Library door. Except that, a knock to her legs struck her down. The 3 people surrounded Dalya again. When she stood up, Dalya tried to understand what was happening:

- Who are y...

Dalya received a knock on the stomach, she fell back. Lying on the floor, Dalya screamed:

- SÉRAPHINE! HELP ME! SÉRAPHINE!

Except that, strangely, the Snow Panther did not move. Séraphine remained motionless, watching Dalya Bouvard receive knocks from masked intruders, without intervening or defending her. The Snow Panther had defended Dalya many times; against the Lawyer Ernest Laszlo, against the nephew Ferdinand Edelmen, and even against her own mother Augustine Bouvard. Except that night. The Snow Panther followed the attack on Dalya Bouvard, with an intense stare, and without intervening.

Dalya stood up and she addressed the old masked man:

- Listen to me! If you are looking for money, here at the grand Mansion ... there is no...

A knock to the back struck Dalya down. The knocks became more and more painful, rapid, and unpredictable. Dalya was surrounded by the 3 people; she couldn't see the knocks she received.

- I DON'T UNDERSTAND WHAT YOU WAN...

A knock to the ankles struck Dalya down. As soon as she stood up, Dalya screamed for help:

- CRISTELLE!! BUCHEBOIS!! ROSENW…

None of the employees of the grand Mansion heard her screams, and that was very strange.

As soon as she stood up, Dalya received a knock on the cheek which made her turn around and fall. Out of breath, Dalya remained on the floor for some long seconds, surrounded by the 3 people. She didn't understand what these people wanted from her. She didn't know why the employees of the grand Mansion didn't hear her screams. She didn't know why the Snow Panther watched her being attacked, without intervening. Her legs and arms ached, her back was broken, her cheeks puffy, her lips pale. After receiving several hard knocks, Dalya no longer had the strength to stand up. Tears streamed down her cheeks.

At this precise moment, the masked old man spoke to Dalya, in a foreign accent and a strong voice:

- Block. Repel. Defend.

Dalya was surprised and shocked to hear these 3 words. These were the same instructions that her Gymnastics Teacher repeated to her, during her lessons at the College Gymnasium. The young Professor Tudi taught Dalya precise moves linked to each word. However, Dalya did not understand why the masked old man pronounced these words, and how the repetitive moves of a Gymnastics lesson could be useful to her.

Dalya stood up, and she faced the old masked man:

- Why are you telling me these wo...

Before Dalya could finish her sentence, she received a knock on her cheek from the masked person to her right. Except that … with a spontaneous move, Dalya raised her arm quickly to block the knock coming toward her, and she pushed away the masked person's hand.

Dalya made spontaneous moves, without even thinking about it. These were the same movements that the young Professor Tudi taught her during the last 3 months of class. Dalya remembered these movements thanks to the 3 words spoken by the masked old man. Each word corresponded to a precise move; raise your arm to block an attack, repel the movement of the attack, and move your arm forward to defend yourself.

Brusquely, before Dalya could make the 3rd move of defense, she received a knock on the back, from the masked person at her left. Dalya fell to the floor.

The masked old man repeated:

- Block. Repel. Defend.

In a second, Dalya understood that the repetitive moves she learned in her Gymnastics class could save her life and help her defend herself against these 3 people. How and why, Dalya will seek the answers to these questions later. For now, she had to get out of this situation and deflect the attacks of these 3 intruders.

396

Dalya stood up, and as expected, she received a knock on her legs from the masked person at her left. With a spontaneous move, Dalya firmly blocked the attack with her leg, she pushed the masked person's leg away, and she was about to advance and defend herself ... when a knock on her shoulder from the person at her right, struck her down.

One of the masked people said in a foreign language:

-   Tā hěn màn, zhǔrén. *(She is slow, Master)*

Dalya didn't understand these words, nor to whom they were addressed, but she confirmed that the 2nd masked person was a young man. So, there was an old man and a young man, among the 3 intruders who were attacking her. And they were all of foreign origin.

Dalya felt great pain in her limbs, and she had difficulty breathing. The repetitive knocks she received, were getting harder and stronger. Dalya remained lying down and crushed on the floor, for a moment. When suddenly, the masked old man knelt in front of her, and he said in a calm and icy voice:

-   You deserved to be mistreated by your father.

These words pierced Dalya Bouvard like a slap in the face. No one has ever dared to say such a thing to her. Never has anyone been so mean and so cruel, saying these words to her.

Dalya felt an unease invade her, despite the pain in her legs and arms. Quickly, Dalya stood up. As soon as she stood on her legs, a punch rushed at her, from the person at her right. Quickly, Dalya firmly blocked the intruder's hand, and she pushed the intruder to her right several steps away.

Feeling an attack coming from her left, Dalya turned just in time to block the intruder's leg, and push him away. But before defending herself and pushing the person on her left, Dalya received a knock on her stomach, which made her fall back. Although Dalya acted quickly, she was not fast and strong enough against the attacks of the 3 masked people.

The masked old man knelt in front of her for the 2nd time, and he said to her:

-   You deserved to be beaten by your mother.

A wave of heat invaded Dalya. She felt her sweaty forehead, her cheeks turn red, her lips pale, her breathing quickened. And it wasn't because of the pain of the knocks and attacks, but because of the masked old man's cruel words.

What Dalya Bouvard endured from her own mother was unjust, cruel, and despicable. Years of suffering, abuse, and injustice. Hearing these words, Dalya was upset.

Getting up, Dalya avoided an attack from her left, she blocked a punch and she pushed the masked young man away with a strong move. In a second, Dalya blocked an attack at her right, pinning the intruder's leg, and she pushed him away from her. Sensing a coming attack,

Dalya turned to her left to block it. Except that, she received a knock on her legs from her right, and she fell back.

Pain, fatigue, despair. Dalya Bouvard crashed to the floor, looking dejected and exhausted. She was tired of defending herself, repelling attacks and knocks from intruders.

With a slow move, the masked old man knelt in front of her for the 3rd time, and he said to her:

-   You deserved to be rejected by Richard Poirier.

Dalya Bouvard's heart tightened. Of all the cruel and nasty words she received, this remark was the most hurtful. Her parents' abuse was one thing. But the rejection of Richard Poirier was entirely something else.

And at that precise moment, an unusual thing happened in the Library of the grand Mansion.

Meanness, mistreatment, humiliation, rejection … these pains can weaken you, or can strengthen you. The choice is yours.

And that night, Dalya Bouvard chose. With a slow and sure movement, Dalya Bouvard stood up. She bent her legs, she raised her hands to protect her face, she positioned herself in front of the 3 intruders, and she waited for the next attack. The young girl's eyes revealed neither pain nor sadness nor fatigue. Dalya Bouvard's sapphire blue eyes displayed ... anger.

And as always, the Snow Panther felt the young girl's anger; Séraphine straightened up to better follow what was going to happen.

The 3 masked people also noticed a change in the young girl's attitude, they exchanged an accomplice look. The masked old man was sure he had struck a sensible chord in the young girl. And he had finally achieved his goal; using pain and anger to help her rise up again.

Long seconds of intense silence invaded the Library of the grand Mansion. When finally, the masked old man whispered:

-   Tā zhǔnbèi wèi zìjǐ biànhù. (She is ready to defend herself).

Immediately, with rapid and abrupt moves, the 3 intruders attacked Dalya Bouvard. Knocks and attacks multiplied one after the other. And with confident and strong moves, Dalya Bouvard avoided the knocks by blocking the movements of the 3 intruders, by pushing away their attacks, and by defending herself.

The attacks of the 3 intruders became more and more rapid and violent. And Dalya Bouvard's defense grew stronger and stronger. Her senses awakened, her body grew stronger, her gaze intensified, her legs and hands hardened, and her moves became more and more precise.

At one instant, and within a second, Dalya blocked the punch of the 1st masked person, and she pushed it away with a strong move, to the point that the person took several steps back. Dalya turned in time to block a kick aimed at her legs, she narrowly dodged it, and she pushed away the 2nd masked person with a punch, which knocked him back away several steps. And instantly, Dalya dodged the knock on the back of the 3rd person, and she pushed it away with a powerful move, to the point that the 3rd person stumbled and fell to the floor. Suddenly, the 3rd masked person who fell to the floor, emitted a woman's scream. Dalya finally understood who her attackers were; an old man, a young man, and a young girl.

And for the first time since the beginning of this intrusion, Dalya did not fall to the floor. She had repelled all the attacks, and she had pushed the 3 intruders away. Despite the pain of the knocks received, despite the pain of the cruel words, Dalya Bouvard rose up and defended herself. And at this precise moment, a strange sensation invaded Dalya Bouvard's body; an invincible and determined inner force.

The old man smiled proudly behind his mask, when he spoke his words:

- Xiànzài, tā zhànle qǐlái! *(Now, she rose up!)*

The other two people exchanged a proud and happy look. Dalya couldn't understand their language, and even less their proud and happy looks. She had just repelled all their attacks and knocked down one of the intruders, why were they proud?

In a much more confident voice than before, and still standing on her guard in fear of a coming attack, Dalya asked:

- Who are you? Why are you here? What do you want from me? Why are you attacking me?

The masked old man answered all these questions with just one sentence:

- You deserve to be Nature's Chosen One.

Instantly, and with a respectful gesture, the 3 masked people bowed in reverence in front of Dalya Bouvard. The young girl was shocked and confused by this gesture. A minute ago, these 3 intruders were attacking her, and now they are bowing before her.

And it was only then, that the Snow Panther decided to came close to Dalya. The animal had followed the attack of the intruders, from the beginning, without intervening or defending the young girl. When the Snow Panther approached Dalya, Séraphine let out an unusual roar; one would have thought that the Snow Panther was happy, too, as much as the 3 intruders.

The masked old man and the Snow Panther exchanged an accomplice look. Apparently, the man and the Panther understood each other without the need for words.

Dalya grew impatient; she didn't understand the accomplice smiles, the reverence gestures, and even less the attitude of the Snow Panther and the 3 intruders:

- For the last time, I demand to know who you are, and why you are here!!

Without pronouncing another word, and just like lightning, the 3 intruders disappeared from the Library of the grand Mansion, through the front door. Dalya had no time to catch them up.

As soon as her attackers disappeared, Dalya collapsed into the nearest armchair; her legs no longer held her, fatigue invaded her, and the pain of the knocks caught up with her. The Snow Panther approached Dalya, and caressed her hands reddened from the beatings. Strangely, the Snow Panther was smiling and was proud of the young girl.

Chapter 82

Gymnastics classes

The same night.

Outside the grand Mansion, more precisely behind the windows of the Library, two silhouettes had followed the entire scene of the attack on Dalya Bouvard, from the beginning. When the 3 intruders disappeared, and when Dalya collapsed on the floor, Miss Haîyang explained in a proud voice:

- She has assimilated all the movements learned in the intensive Gymnastics classes. She repelled all the attacks. It was not easy, especially against 3 skilled people. However, she defended herself well.

Turning toward a man, Miss Haîyang smiled:

- Dalya Bouvard rose up again.

Through the windows of the grand Mansion's Library, Professor Canfield observed Dalya, sitting on the floor, and surrounded by the Snow Panther. It is true that the scene of the attack was brutal and intense. However, after watching the young girl's rise up, her movements to block the attacks, and her determination to defend herself against the 3 intruders, Professor Canfield was surprised and as proud as Miss Haîyang.

After a long minute of silence and thinking, Professor Canfield turned toward Miss Haîyang, and he asked her in a serious tone:

- You must watch over her, you must protect her!

Without a second of hesitation, Miss Haîyang replied in a determined voice:

- I will protect her with my life!

Dear readers… you are certainly wondering why Professor Canfield was outside the grand Mansion on the night of the attack on Dalya Bouvard.

12 months ago. Monday, January 2nd, 1893. At the Royal Georgetown College. A few minutes before the start of classes.

Miss Haîyang was observing the activity in the school yard, through the large windows on the 2nd floor. The school yard was filled with students, reuniting after a long absence, laughing, and discussing their holidays. And although Miss Haîyang seemed to follow the activity in the school yard, her mind was entirely preoccupied with something else. She was patiently waiting for someone to come.

A few minutes passed, Professor Canfield appeared in the hallway and he walked to his office. Stylish as always, Professor Canfield wore a checkered suit in navy blue, matched with a white shirt and blue tie. He carried in his hand several large folders that seemed to be heavy. As soon as he opened the door to his office, Professor Canfield dropped the stack of folders on his desk.

- Good morning, Professor Canfield. Do you have a moment, please?

The man greeted her with his usual cheerful smile:

- Good morning, Professor Haîyang! Sure... sure... come in!

Professor Canfield opened one of his files, letting out a happy laugh:

- It's a busy day... hundreds of schedules to distribute!!

Miss Haîyang advanced toward the office table:

- It's a very complicated job to create all these schedules, I imagine.

Professor Canfield laughed:

- Oh yes!! I couldn't have done it without Professor Wyatt's help. He loves organizing them, I don't know how or why!! It's child's game for Professor Wyatt, and a headache for me!!

Miss Haîyang smiled. Professor Canfield turned toward her and he asked her:

- What can I do for you, Professor?

The young woman cleared her throat:

- I wanted to know the schedule of Mademoiselle Dalya Bouvard, this semester, if you allow it?

Professor Canfield searched for a file for a few seconds:

- I think I have put her schedule... somewhere... here... and here it is!

After giving Miss Haîyang the paper, Professor Canfield informed her in a proud tone:

- This little girl has made remarkable progress! And this semester, I enrolled her in 2 additional courses, so that she can catch up at the same level as the other students. She will follow your music class, just like before. In total, she will have 10 classes this semester. I think she will succeed in them all.

Professor Canfield continued to arrange the files on his desk:

- I admit, I am very proud of her! Her delay did not prevent her from being a good student.

Miss Haîyang scanned the student's schedule paper with a focused air. After a few moments of thinking, Miss Haîyang announced in a serious tone:

- Professor Canfield ... I think Mademoiselle Dalya Bouvard's schedule needs to be changed.

The man moved some files to a cupboard, and he replied with an amused laugh:

- Believe me; I would have loved to enroll her in all the courses at her level. But I fear an overwork for her brain.

Although Professor Canfield was right, Miss Haîyang had received clear orders, and she had to carry them out. The young woman insisted:

- Professor Canfield... it is imperative that Mademoiselle's schedule changes.

Professor Canfield took some papers from a file and he checked them briefly, answering in a spontaneous tone:

- I agree with you, Miss Haîyang. But she is already quite busy. All her weekdays are full. She will already be very busy with 10 classes. One more class for her is simply impossible.

Faced with this impasse, Miss Haîyang had no other choice. She advanced a few steps toward the man, and she announced in a grave tone:

- Professor Canfield ... Dalya Bouvard must take one special class. It is a question of life or death!

At that moment, Professor Canfield was surprised by the words he heard. He stopped in his move and he turned toward the young woman, with a shocked air. Professor Canfield thought he had misheard, he asked again in an amused tone:

- A question of ... what? ... Are you joking, Miss Haîyang?

And seeing the serious and worried face of Miss Haîyang, Professor Canfield understood that the young woman was not joking. The man's curiosity awoke:

- Dalya Bouvard? ... Why a matter of life and death? ... What's going on?

Miss Haîyang replied in a serious voice:

- Professor Canfield, what I'm about to tell you, must not leave this office. I am sorry to have to include you in this matter, but I have no other choice. I received clear orders, Professor. And I need your help and cooperation!

Professor Canfield didn't understand all of Miss Haîyang's words, but he understood that the matter was more serious than he thought. Since a long time, Professor Canfield had the greatest respect and complete trust in Miss Haîyang. And since the Will, Professor Canfield was determined to protect and watch over Dalya Bouvard, the Heiress of Iskander Balthazar.

After a few seconds of serious silence, Professor Canfield walked toward his office door, and he closed it:

- I am listening, Miss Haîyang.

Some minutes later, Professor Canfield sat down in the nearest chair he could find. His legs no longer held him, his brain was in shock, his throat constricted. Being of a cheerful and calm nature, Professor Canfield was stunned, for the first time since ever.

What Miss Haîyang had told him, was hard to believe and to understand. The young woman sat down on an armchair in front of the Professor. A long moment of silence and confusion settled in the office. At one point, Professor Canfield muttered in a confused tone:

- It's... but she just a little girl... it's... Irea Senderlson? Iskander Balthazar's wife? Are you sure? ... it's incredible ... I never would have believed that such a thing would happen ... I understand better now, why Iskander Balthazar chose Dalya Bouvard ... I understand better now ...

After a long minute, Professor Canfield recovered hardly from his shock, and he turned to Miss Haîyang:

- How can I help Dalya Bouvard?

At that moment, Miss Haîyang handed a paper to Professor Canfield, answering his question:

- Her schedule needs to be changed.

And this is how, Dear readers, Professor Canfield contributed to Dalya Bouvard's training, by enrolling her in only 2 classes. The intensive Gymnastics courses helped and prepared Dalya Bouvard to stand up again and defend herself.

Chapter 83

Just a bad dream

The next morning, Thursday, December 7th, 1893. In the kitchen of the grand Mansion.

- Last night?

The Cook, Mr. Ferrero Lutché exclaimed in a surprised air, for the 2nd time. He was stirring a cooking soup, while listening intently to the conversation going on in the kitchen. Dalya replied in a sure voice:

- Yes, last night, here at the grand Mansion. 3 individuals entered and they attacked me in the Library.

All the employees of the grand Mansion exchanged a confused and shocked look. The Manager Mr. Bûchebois was surprised by Dalya's story:

- But ... Mademoiselle, I myself make sure that all the doors and windows are closed. How could they have entered and left the grand Mansion?

Dalya thought aloud:

- I don't know how or from where they entered. I was in the Library, and suddenly I found them in front of me. And when they disappeared, I couldn't follow them.

The Gardener put down his bag of tools, and he asked in a curious tone:

- And do you know who they are? Have you seen them before?
- No, they wore black masks. But from their voices, I understood that they were an old man, a young man, and a young girl. They spoke a foreign language.

The maid Cristelle continued to fold the napkins, with a slow and astonished move:

- It's strange. We never had this kind of incident at the grand Mansion before.

After Dalya informed them of the 3 intruders and the attack she endured, the employees had a hard time believing this scene. Dalya asked the employees:

- I remember screaming your names for help. Didn't you hear anything?

The help Cook Océanie put the plates on the table:

- I didn't hear anything, Mademoiselle. Last night, I was so tired that I slept on my armchair folding the baby's clothes. I realized it only this morning.

Assistant Igor let out an amused laugh:

- It's strange, me too! I fell asleep in front of my table. It never happened to me to sleep so early and so quickly.

The Gardener affirmed:

- Last night, I fell in a deep sleep; I slept on my chair. But I had spent the entire day working in the garden.

The head of the grand Mansion and the Cook exchanged a look:

- It must be because of fatigue and the winter cold. I slept for several hours, sitting in front of the kitchen table. I have body aches this morning.

- Me too! Anche io! Ho dormito on my armchair.

The maid Cristelle replied in a serious voice:

- Sorry Mademoiselle. But we didn't hear anything.

For all the employees to fall into the same deep and undisturbed sleep, Dalya thought that was very strange. And it wasn't the only unusual thing. At one moment, the assistant Igor exclaimed in a curious tone:

- And during the attack, the Panther Séraphine did not defend you?

When Dalya told them about the attitude of the Snow Panther during the attack of the 3 intruders, the employees of the grand Mansion did not believe their ears. The Gardener was the first to respond:

- It's hard to imagine that the Panther didn't react to the intrusion of 3 masked people at the grand Mansion. The Panther chases small snakes and even mice. Séraphine does not allow anyone to enter the grand Mansion. She would have defended you against strangers.

The help Cook Océanie was confused about a detail:

- And ... and you think the Panther understood the foreign language of the intruder?

The maid Cristelle murmured in a surprised tone:

- I can't even manage to get the Panther out of a living room, in the native language of this Country. So, for the Panther to understand a foreign language?! That's strange!

Left without answers to these questions, Dalya began to doubt herself. It is true that looking back, all the doubts of the employees were correct, and the story of Dalya Bouvard was hard to believe.

At one point, the Cook announced in a thoughtful voice:

- Mademoiselle, it's certainly the ginger that gave you hallucinations. I've put a lot of it in your herbal teas, these past few days.

The head of the grand Mansion said in a respectful voice:

- It must have been a bad dream, Mademoiselle. Just a bad dream.

A few minutes later, crossing the hall of the grand Mansion, Dalya thought seriously:

- Even if the employees were asleep, they would have heard my screams. And the attitude of the Panther is strange; Séraphine protects my little sisters against spiders. So, to stand still in front of masked intruders, it's an unusual thing.

Entering the Library of the grand Mansion, Dalya continued to think:

- It's very strange that the intruders didn't attack the employees, they only attacked me. And they didn't steal anything from the grand Mansion, it's weird. I admit that Mr. Bûchebois may be right; it was just a bad drea...

Suddenly, Dalya tripped over an object on the floor of the Library. When she took it in her hands, Dalya discovered a pretty little hair pin in the shape of a cherry blossom. Dalya wondered:

- It's a pretty brooch. But who does it belong to? The employees Océanie and Cristelle don't wear jewelry. My friend Amira can't stand jewelry. My little sisters wear only plastic jewelry. I've seen this brooch somewhere before, but I don't remember. Who owns it? Who dropped this brooch on the floor of the Libr...

Suddenly, Dalya jumped:

- When I knocked down the masked intruder, a young girl's scream was heard!! This cherry blossom brooch belongs to ... it belongs to the masked intruder who attacked me!! So, it wasn't a bad dream!! I didn't dream or hallucinate things because of the ginger in my tea!! I was indeed attacked by 3 masked intruders!!

In her hands, Dalya Bouvard held the proof that she was attacked by 3 intruders, in the Library of the grand Mansion. And she was more than determined to find out who this brooch belonged to.

Chapter 84

Unexplained events

Friday, December 8th, 1893. In the morning, at the front door of the Royal Georgetown College.

Alfie Jaq jumped:

- I have a brilliant idea!

His friend Maurice Gus sighed:

- No, that's a very bad idea!

Amira Mounier was curious to know:

- What idea?

Alfie explained with a motivated voice:

- We could wait for this Richard Poirier, at the door of his work, and throw onions at him.

Maurice sighed again:

- And for the 10th time, I'm telling you that's a very bad idea!

Alfie didn't lose his enthusiasm:

- We throw tomatoes at him, then?

At this moment, Maurice replied in a firm tone:

- Throwing anything at him, is out of the question!

Alfie was not short of ideas to avenge his friend Dalya Bouvard. Barely a second of silence and thinking later, Alfie exclaimed again:

- We can push Richard Poirier on the stairs of the Parliament entrance. There are about fifty steps; he will lose all his bones when he reaches the last step.

The idea was diabolical and clever. Amira Mounier hardly held back her laugh. But Maurice tried to reason his friend:

- I too want to give a good slap to this idiot. But he works in the Government. If we touch him, we'll be caught by the police.

Amira Mounier was of the same opinion:

- Maurice is right. You can't do anything against Richard Poirier, he's a high-ranking employee, you risk big trouble. And believe me, you're not the only ones wanting revenge. All the employees of the grand Mansion, the Lawyer Mr. Sloan Wilfrid, and even the flower seller Lalla Fatim Fadl, everyone hates this Richard Poirier.

Alfie forced himself to calm his thoughts of revenge. He asked in a worried voice:

- And how is she?

Amira Mounier, Alfie Jaq, and Maurice Gus, they met almost every morning in front of the door of the Royal Georgetown College, to exchange news of their friend Dalya. And Amira Mounier informed them of all the details concerning Dalya:

- She has come out of her room, and she spends her days in the Library. All the employees of the grand Mansion watch over her, day and night. She finishes her meals, and she takes regular naps. But she is too quiet, and often wandering in her mind. She's better than before, that's for sure. However, I believe she needs more time and rest.

Maurice affirmed:

- I'm sure she will rise up again. Dalya is a fighter!

Alfie agreed:

- Yes, she has always been strong!

Amira continued:

- On the other hand, I haven't yet dared to ask her questions about this Richard, or even approach the subject with her. Dalya never spoke to me about him.

Maurice replied in a serious voice:

- It's better to wait until she recovers, to find out more about this idiot.

Alfie jumped joyfully:

- Anyway, we already know one thing about him; his workplace! Our friend Charles is an excellent stone shooter. He can aim at him from afar, and throw onions straight to his brain. Our friend Charles will not refuse to help us!

Maurice lost his patience:

- You will be in big big trouble!! I have warned you!! Let's calm down!!

At this moment, a silhouette approached the 3 friends, and Amira Mounier exclaimed with a happy smile:

- Good morning, Dalya! What a nice surprise!

It was a beautiful sunny day in the city of Georgetown. But despite the shining sun, an icy cold blew in all the streets. The maid Cristelle made Dalya dress well and wear a large scarf and winter gloves. The Gardener offered to drive Dalya by car, but she wanted to walk to stretch her legs.

Alfie and Maurice were also surprised to see Dalya that day. She hasn't left the grand Mansion for weeks.

- Hello Dalya!! It's nice to see you today!!
- Yes!! We are happy to see you!!

Dalya smiled at her friends:

- I thought I'd get some fresh air today, and come to College to get my holiday homework.

Alfie lifted his face up to capture more sunlight:

- You did well to go out, we have a beautiful sun today.

Maurice readjusted his coat:

- And we also have a cold that awakens!

Dalya displayed an amused smile. Apparently, some things still haven't changed. Alfie is still always comfortable in winter, and Maurice is still always shivering in this season.

No one dared to ask Dalya questions about Richard Poirier, or approach the subject with her. Alfie, Maurice, and Amira were aware that their friend had just come out of her isolation. They didn't want to bother her with questions and be intrusive.

Alfie and Maurice picked up their bags of newspapers and shoe shining:

- Well, it's time for us to continue our way. We have work today.
- Yes, the cafes will be full this time. The gentlemen need newspapers and their shoes to be polished.

At one point, before parting ways, Alfie, Maurice, and Amira exchanged an accomplice look. And suddenly, abruptly, and simultaneously, the 3 friends hugged Dalya.

- We were worried about you!
- We are relieved that you feel better!
- We are glad you finally came out!

Dalya was very touched by her friends' gesture. She whispered in a moved voice:

- Thank you for caring about me. You are the best friends in the world. On the other hand, it would be nice to release me now, I have trouble breathing.

With a happy and relieved giggle, the 3 friends released Dalya. When Alfie and Maurice turned and disappeared around a street corner, and before going inside the College, Dalya turned toward her friend, and she announced to her in a serious voice:

- I was attacked at the grand Mansion 2 days ago, by masked intruders.

The news shocked Amira, to the point that she screamed out of surprise:

- Attacked at the grand Mansion? By... by masked intruders?

While entering the College, Dalya informed her friend of all the details of this attack, the attitude of the Snow Panther, how the employees did not believe her, and that she thought it was just a bad dream. Arriving in a hallway, Dalya took a small object out of her pocket:

- I found this brooch on the floor of the Library. This is proof that I did not dream, and that the attack indeed happened. Do you know who this brooch belongs to? Have you ever seen it somewhere? The person who wore it was a young girl, thin, short, and of foreign origin. Do you have any idea who this brooch belongs to?

Amira thought for a second:

- No, I've never seen it before.

Dalya put the brooch back in her pocket, and she thought aloud:

- I'm sure I've seen this brooch somewhere before, but I can't remember where. I absolutely must find the owner of this brooch. I need to understand why these 3 intruders attacked me, and who they are.

In a determined tone, Amira answered without hesitation:

- We'll find the owner of this brooch! I'll help you find it!

Before joining the Philosophy classroom, Amira had to go to the restroom to adjust her hair in braids, and Dalya accompanied her. In front of the restroom mirror, Amira thought aloud, while brushing her hair:

- The attitude of the Snow Panther is really unusual. I understand why the employees didn't believe you. Once, Séraphine pushed a spider away from the table where I was working. So, for the Panther to remain motionless in front of 3 intruders attacking you ... I admit, it's hard to believe.

Dalya took advantage of this moment in the restroom, to take off one of her sweaters. The maid Cristelle forced her to wear 3 sweaters and a coat, fearing that Dalya would catch a cold. And the College was already warm, Dalya was feeling hot. Taking off her sweater, Dalya replied:

- I too admit, at a moment, I thought I had just a bad dream. But after finding this brooch in the Library, I'm sure it belongs to the masked person I knocked down.

Amira finished a braid, and she turned to her friend:

- Anyway, I see they hurt you. You have bruises on your arms.

Wearing only a tank top, Dalya packed her sweater in her bag:

- No, these bruises are not from the attack. But from the Gymnastics class.

At this moment, Amira stopped in her move:

- What class?

Dalya replied spontaneously:

- Gymnastics class. I have these bruises from this class. At first, the exercises were easy. But since the start of the school year in September, these last 3 months, the exercises have been more and more intense, and the bruises are more and more numerous. I have body aches after every class.

Suddenly, Amira let go of her hair, and she approached Dalya. Amira seemed confused by what she was hearing and especially by what she observed:

- Dalya ... your back and your arms are full of bruises. You have bruises from the Gymnastics class?

Dalya explained to her friend:

- Yes, it is a very physical and painful class. It took me weeks to master the knocks on the Punchingball. And I admit that it is difficult to repel the attack knocks. I had to learn for months the movements of block, repel, defend. And by the way, these are the moves that helped me against the 3 intruders at the grand Mansion.

Amira forced herself to ask in a natural voice:

- And ... and what are the trainings you do with the Professor, in this Gymnastics class?

Dalya answered the question:

- I have trained for 1 month on hand knocks, 1 month on leg knocks, and 1 month on defense positions. At each class, we do 1 hour of relaxation and breathing, 1 hour of stretching and warming up, 2 hours of kicking in the air, 2 hours in front of the Punchingball, and 3 hours of face-to-face exercises with the Professor.

As Dalya explained her class, Amira seemed more and more surprised by what she was discovering. Dalya didn't understand why her friend was shocked.

- What's going on Amira?

In a serious and grave voice, Amira was forced to inform her friend:

- Dalya ... the Gymnastics class consists of running and jumping. That's all we do in this course.

This news shocked Dalya, to the point that she remained motionless and speechless. Amira continued in a serious tone:

- Punchingball? Hand knocks? Attack knocks? Defense positions? Movements to block, repel, defend? ... Dalya, what class are you taking?! No one has ever been injured in Gymnastics class. Your entire body is covered in bruises and scars. But what are they making you do?

At this precise moment, doubt invaded Dalya:

- You ... you just run and jump? That's all? So, you don't wear gloves, helmets, and a chest protector?

Amira exclaimed:

- Never! All the students in this school follow this same course of Gymnastics; running a distance, and jumping. That's all we do in this course. I've never heard of Punchingball or attack moves or defense positions. Are they preparing you for a war or what?!

A confused and intense silence invaded the girls' restroom. Amira Mounier observed the bruises and scars on her friend's body with a worried look. And Dalya Bouvard had thousands of questions in her head. At one point, Amira Mounier affirmed in a serious tone:

- Dalya ... I don't want to worry you ... but, weird things are happening around you. The attack you endured at the grand Mansion, and the Gymnastics class. It's ... it's weird.

Dalya put on her sweater and coat, thinking aloud:

- I totally agree with you Amira. And that worries me more and more! Since my name was pronounced in this Will, unexplained events are happening around me. The attack at the grand Mansion, the strange Gymnastics class, the attitude of the Snow Panther toward the 3 intruders. I must find the answers to these unexplained events!

The two friends exchanged a worried look, but above all determined to find answers.

Chapter 85

The reins of BalthEnterprise

Friday, December 8th, 1893. The afternoon, in the Lawyer's office.

When Sloan Wilfrid entered the office, his Secretary caught up with him in the corridor, and she whispered to him in a serious voice:

- Master Wilfrid ... it happened today.

Lawyer Sloan Wilfrid was eagerly awaiting this news. A smile appeared on his face, he whispered:

- Finally! It's not too soon. We have been waiting for this decision for several weeks. I take it there was another disagreement?

The Secretary took the Lawyer's coat, and she informed him:

- Yes, just an hour ago. Mr. Ernest Laszlo and his son Lyor were not of the same opinion about the Transport Company. Lyor refused to sign the paper for the sale of the Company's buildings. Mr. Ernest Laszlo had enough of Lyor's questions and disobedience; he fired him from the firm.

It was not really a surprise for the employees of the Law firm. Since the Antman Bouvard affair, when Ernest Laszlo lost in Court against Lyor, there was more and more tension between the father and his son. And after the Thanksgiving party, precisely since the Cotton Factory was saved thanks to the funds raised, disagreements and clashes between father and son, became more and more frequent in the Law firm.

It must be admitted that Lyor Laszlo had become less easy to force and to manipulate; he demanded to see reports and numbers, he looked for other alternatives, and he refused to sign his father's orders, without asking questions.

In the corridor, Lawyer Sloan Wilfrid asked:

- Where is Lyor now?

The Secretary took the Lawyer's gloves and she informed him:

- He is at his office, gathering his things.

When Sloan Wilfrid entered the office, he immediately sensed his apprentice's anger and frustration. Lyor Laszlo was gathering his files in a corner of his Library. He worked in a heavy, tense silence.

The Lawyer Sloan Wilfrid expected Lyor Laszlo to be fired sooner or later. It was an obvious thing, especially after all the past events. Sloan Wilfrid approached Lyor's desk, and he said in a sympathetic voice:

- I learned what happened today. The Secretary informed me of your father's decision.

The young Lyor Laszlo remained silent, putting away a few books in a box. He didn't even look at his mentor Sloan Wilfrid; he didn't say a word. His lips were pale, repressing his anger. His hands were shaking as he packed his things into the boxes. Sloan Wilfrid perfectly understood Lyor Laszlo's frustration:

- I'm sorry things didn't turn out the way you wanted, Lyor. I know how much you wanted to work here, with your father.

With a brusque move, Lyor placed a box on the floor, and he replied in a crushed voice:

- I have just passed my Bar exam 2 months ago, and my career is already over!

At that moment, a strange smile appeared on the lips of the Lawyer Sloan Wilfrid:

- Sorry to disappoint you Lyor, but your career as a Lawyer will start this very afternoon!

With a confused and furious look, the young Lyor Laszlo observed his mentor:

- Wilfrid, you are joking?! I'm fired from my dad's office! I'm fired from the most prestigious Law firm on the East coast. My career is over; my reputation is over. Who will recruit me?!

It turns out, Dear readers, that several conversations happened behind the scenes and in all discretion, during the previous days.

With a proud smile, Sloan Wilfrid was delighted to answer Lyor's question:

- The BalthEnterprise Holding is recruiting you.

It was a simple announcement, a simple sentence. However, Lyor Laszlo did not understand what that meant. Lawyer Sloan Wilfrid had kept this secret for several weeks, and he was more than happy to finally inform Lyor. Sitting down in an armchair in front of the desk, Sloan Wilfrid announced to him:

- During the Thanksgiving party, the Ambassadors and the Businessmen contributed to the fundraising to save the Cotton Factory... on one condition. Do you know which one?

Lyor Laszlo was surprised by this statement:

- I didn't know that investors had a condition to their contribution.

Lawyer Sloan Wilfrid explained:

- During this party, I was called by the Ambassador of France. She is a woman with great strength of character. She informed me that all the investors were willing to contribute to the fundraising ... on one condition; that you are the sole Managing Lawyer of BalthEnterprise Holding.

Lyor Laszlo had to sit down, because his legs no longer held him:

- Why this condition?

Lawyer Sloan Wilfrid continued:

- In the Will, the Late Mr. Governor Iskander Balthazar chose you to lead the Holding. However, everyone observed your father who freely made the decisions concerning the Holding. Naturally, everyone was confused by this situation. There had to be only one leading Lawyer of BalthEnterprise Holding, the one whose name was written in the Will. And the Ambassador of France was very clear and firm on this condition.

Now, Lyor Laszlo's office was filled with a surprised silence, instead of an angry silence. Lyor seemed to be stunned by what was happening:

- Why didn't you tell me about this condition before?

Repressing an amused chuckle, Sloan Wilfrid answered this question:

- As I know you, Lyor ... I knew that I would not be able to convince you to leave your father's firm to manage the Holding. So, I waited for your dad to fire you.

Lyor Laszlo was forced to admit that Sloan Wilfrid was quite right in this idea. Since the reading of the Will, Lyor Laszlo did not want the Holding's responsibility. All Lyor wanted was a simple low-key career as a Lawyer in his father's firm, and nothing would have convinced him to leave that firm ... unless he was fired.

At that moment, Sloan Wilfrid continued in a serious tone:

- Believe me, Lyor ... you don't belong here in this firm. Behind the shadow of your father, you will never progress.

And for the 2nd time, Lyor Laszlo had to admit that Sloan Wilfrid was right. Under the shadow of his father, Lyor will never progress. Conflicts of ideas became more and more frequent, the style of management was divergent, Ernest Laszlo desired total obedience without questions, and Lyor Laszlo could no longer sign the papers naively.

Sloan Wilfrid offered a few seconds of silence to his apprentice Lyor, in order to assimilate this latest news. After a moment, Lyor Laszlo exclaimed:

- It's ... BalthEnterprise is an immense fortune. It is a huge Holding that includes hundreds of companies and properties. I can't handle it alone!

Immediately, Sloan Wilfrid reassured him:

-   You will not be alone in managing this fortune. All the Managers of the Holding appreciate your way of management which aligns with that of the Late Mr. Governor Iskander Balthazar. You want to develop the factories and renovate them, instead of selling them and getting rid of them. All the Managers are ready and determined to work with you.

As expected, Lyor Laszlo doubted his abilities:

-   I studied the management of a company, but not the management of a huge Holding. It's much more complicated than it sounds. I don't know anything about the management of a Holding! I won't succeed!

And as expected, Sloan Wilfrid defended his plan:

-   Lyor, I confirm that you have enough practical experience to manage the Holding. Certainly, it will take you a few months to master reports, numbers, and decision-making techniques. But you already have the basics and management skills. You learn quickly, you listen to all opinions, you look for solutions and you ask questions. You will succeed in managing the BalthEnterprise Holding, I'm sure of that!

Lyor Laszlo was moved and touched by his mentor Sloan Wilfrid's affirmation. Having guided him for several years in his legal studies and his work at the firm, Sloan Wilfrid knew Lyor better than himself.

Sloan Wilfrid relaxed in his chair:

-   And the last surprise I have for you today … you will have a new mentor who will help you manage the Holding.

Lyor Laszlo was curious. Sloan Wilfrid announced with a proud smile:

-   Master Victor Barold!

As he straightened up on his chair, Lyor was surprised. After having worked with the old Lawyer for several months to prepare Antman Bouvard's defense file, Lyor Laszlo vowed great admiration for Master Victor Barold. Sloan Wilfrid informed Lyor:

-   With his expertise and knowledge, Master Barold will be an invaluable help to you. He will be your adviser from now on.

At one point, Sloan Wilfrid couldn't hold back his amused laugh:

-   I didn't need to convince him for this job, Master Barold accepts without hesitation, anything that can make your father furious. Master Barold has already settled into his office at BalthEnterprise Headquarters, several days ago. He recruited a courier just to deliver the croissants to him, every day of the week. The Managers of the Holding were so happy to recruit Master Barold, they installed a small kitchen adjacent to his office, and they hired a Chef just for him.

The old Lawyer's manners were eccentric and bizarre, but everyone recognized that Master Victor Barold was the best Lawyer in the entire Country.

Several contradictory feelings invaded Lyor Laszlo's mind; the impatience to work with Master Barold and to learn from his expertise, the anxiety of managing the huge BalthEnterprise Holding, the curiosity of a new job, the fear of not being up to the task, the anger of been fired for no valid reason from his father's firm.

Except that, it seems that the career of the young Lyor Laszlo has already been decided behind the scenes, since several weeks, without him being aware. At this moment, Lyor Laszlo was short of excuses, pretexts, and reluctance. Apparently, Lyor Laszlo had no choice but to take on the job assigned to him by the Late Mr. Governor, in his Will.

Lawyer Sloan Wilfrid stood up from his chair, and he announced in a confident voice:

- Your office is ready, Lyor. The Managers and Master Barold are waiting for you at the Holding's Headquarters. I must inform Madame the Ambassador of France, that you will join the Holding officially, as of today. Everyone has been waiting for this news impatiently, since several weeks.

Offering his hand to greet his apprentice, Lawyer Sloan Wilfrid smiled proudly:

- Lyor Laszlo … Congratulations on your firing from your father's firm. And Congratulations on your new job, as Managing Lawyer of BalthEnterprise Holding!

With a trembling gesture, and out of words, Lyor Laszlo stood up, and he greeted by hand, Sloan Wilfrid.

Chapter 86

Determined to help

Saturday, December 9th, 1893. The afternoon, at the grand Mansion.

There were more than 2 weeks left before the Christmas holiday. However, the grand Mansion already wore its finest decorations. A huge Christmas tree was installed in the Library. Magnificent ornaments came out of their boxes and embellished the tree. The Christmas flowers were hung on all the doors and windows. The fireplaces were adorned with fir leaves and silk bows.

When the Lawyer Sloan Wilfrid entered the hall of the grand Mansion, he was surprised by the splendor of the decorations. The head of the grand Mansion greeted him:

-   Welcome, Master Wilfrid.

Looking up at the magnificent chandelier recently hung in the hall, the Lawyer exclaimed:

-   You've surpassed yourself in the Christmas decoration this time, Monsieur Bûchebois.

The Manager of the grand Mansion smiled:

-   Thank you, Master Wilfrid. We installed the Christmas decoration early this year, in order to help Mademoiselle Dalya Bouvard de-stress and feel better.

Lawyer Sloan Wilfrid took off his gloves:

-   That's a great idea, Mr. Bûchebois! Christmas decorations revive the spirit.

The Lawyer visited the grand Mansion almost every day. He insisted on knowing every detail about Dalya Bouvard.

-   Does she finish her meals? Does she still take the ginger teas? Does she sleep well at night?

The head of the grand Mansion informed him assiduously:

-   Yes, Master Wilfrid. Mademoiselle is doing better and better. We serve her herbal teas with honey and ginger, every afternoon. Océanie and Cristelle watch over her. The Gardener and Igor take care of the fireplaces, every day.

At one moment, a smell invaded the hall of the grand Mansion. And before the Lawyer Sloan Wilfrid could even ask the question, a small silhouette emerged from the kitchen and appeared in the hall. The Lawyer greeted her:

-   Good afternoon, Miss Amira Mounier. It's always a pleasure to see you.

Amira Mounier smiled:

- Good afternoon, Mr. Wilfrid.

Since weeks, Amira Mounier had been visiting her friend Dalya at the grand Mansion, almost every day. Amira brought to her friend; homework, books, school news, anything that could cheer up her friend Dalya.

Lawyer Sloan Wilfrid noticed the plate of apple and cinnamon cookies Amira was carrying, he exclaimed with an amused air:

- I see that the grand Mansion is seriously preparing for the Christmas holiday.

Amira Mounier explained to him:

- These are Dalya's favorite cookies. And since she has regained her appetite, the Cook prepares all her favorite dishes. For tonight, there's a spinach and cheese gratin in the oven, salmon with fine herbs on the pan, and a chocolate mousse with raspberry.

Lawyer Sloan Wilfrid laughed:

- It's a feast! I now understand the delicious smell emanating from the kitchen!

The head of the grand Mansion answered in an attentive tone:

- We are all trying to help Mademoiselle Dalya, as best as we can.

Lawyer Sloan Wilfrid understood the reason for the magnificent Christmas decorations, and the extensive menu. He was grateful to the employees of the grand Mansion and to Amira Mounier, for having worked hard to help Dalya recover. Except that despite all these efforts, Sloan Wilfrid was worried:

- Dalya Bouvard is a brave young girl. She endured many hardships this year; the blackmail of Ernest Laszlo, the arrest of her father, the physical abuse of her mother, the anxiety of the trial, the pressure to save the Cotton Factory, and the Richard Poirier slap. It was a hectic and difficult year for her. I wonder if ... I wonder if she will be ready for the next 4th Challen...

Instantly, Amira Mounier interrupted the Lawyer, in a determined voice:

- But of course, Dalya will be ready for the 4th Challenge! You have my word on that, Mr. Wilfrid! Besides, I am spending the weekend here at the grand Mansion, with her. We will study the clues that this strange box provided. We will camp in the Library until we find an answer!

The head of the grand Mansion affirmed in a serious tone:

- All employees are aware of the 4th Challenge which will take place in the next few days. We are all working so that Mademoiselle Dalya lacks nothing and is comfortable.

Lawyer Sloan Wilfrid smiled. Apparently, Dalya Bouvard was in very good hands.

In the Library of the grand Mansion, Dalya was sitting at her usual desk. She was writing on a paper, when she was interrupted by the entrance of 2 silhouettes.

- I am always sure to find you in this Library, Mademoiselle Dalya.

Dalya greeted the Lawyer with a smile:

- Good afternoon, Mr. Wilfrid.

Sloan Wilfrid walked toward her:

- And I am glad to see you are feeling better, Mademoiselle.

Dalya was touched by everyone's attention and care for her, including Lawyer Sloan Wilfrid.

When Amira Mounier placed a plate on the desk in front of Dalya, she exclaimed:

- And here are your favorite cookies. Océanie will bring us hot chocolate, in few minutes. And the dinner being prepared for tonight is delicious!

Lawyer Sloan Wilfrid let out an amused laugh:

- I confirm. The smell emanating from the kitchen is exquisite!

Dalya suggested:

- It would be my pleasure if you would join us for dinner tonight, Mr. Wilfrid.

Adjusting his tie, Sloan Wilfrid smiled:

- Thank you for your invitation, Mademoiselle. But that will be for next time. I'm expected for dinner tonight at Congressman Yolan McKlain's house. I came today only to inquire about your health, and also to announce good news.

The two young girls were curious. Lawyer Sloan Wilfrid continued:

- Lyor Laszlo has officially taken over the reins of BalthEnterprise Holding. He moved into the offices of the Holding's Headquarters, yesterday afternoon. He will be guided by Master Victor Barold, who has accepted the position of Advisor in the Holding. All BalthEnterprise Managers are happy and ready to support Lyor Laszlo.

Dalya and Amira exchanged a happy laugh. Amira exclaimed:

- Lyor is always of an upset temper, but he is much nicer than his father.

Dalya was relieved by this news:

- At least Lyor won't close the factories on a whim, like his father.

Lawyer Sloan Wilfrid confirmed this idea:

- It's true. In addition to being an excellent Lawyer, Lyor Laszlo is honest and upright. He looks for all possible solutions, and he listens to all opinions before taking decisions. Lyor will have at its disposal the expertise and advices of the Lawyer Master Barold. BalthEnterprise Holding is in good hands.

Having witnessed the scenes of humiliation that Lyor suffered from his father Ernest in the Law firm, Dalya was certain that Lyor Laszlo would be more productive and at ease in his new position at the Holding.

At one point, Sloan Wilfrid added a log of wood to the lit fireplace:

- Now, Mesdemoiselles, I must leave you, and I wish you a very good evening!

The two young girls greeted the Lawyer with a smile. And before Sloan Wilfrid would close the door of the Library, he turned around discreetly one last time to observe the two young girls. Dalya handed a paper to her friend:

- Here are the clues that I have received. I have a feeling that the 4th Challenge will be a question, and the answer will have to be a single word.

Amira Mounier was more than determined to help her best friend. Reading the paper, Amira thought ardently and aloud:

- So, we must find the meaning of these clues, and what connects them to the 4th Challenge. Except that ... it's weird, there are many words and even an entire sentence repeated in all the clues. Breathe ... Exhale ... breathing advice, but why? ...To survive the outside, look inside. What does the Excelbox mean by outside and inside?

Dalya tasted a biscuit, wondering in a curious voice:

- The Excelbox wants me to search for something inside... but search for what? Inside what? The grand Mansion? The Library? My bedroom? The attic? Inside what? And what should I look for?

Amira took a blank paper, and she announced in a determined voice:

- First, we will write down all the possible answers to these clues. Then, we will eliminate the vague answers. And next, we will look up the synonyms of the words in the Library. Maybe the outside...

Dalya understood the idea of her friend:

- Maybe the outside and the inside mean something other than places!

While the two young girls worked hard to decipher the clues, Lawyer Sloan Wilfrid discreetly closed the door of the Library. And he left the grand Mansion, with a smile on his face. Apparently, many people were determined to help Dalya Bouvard.

Chapter 87

Océanie and Dalya

Sunday, December 10th, 1893. In the grand Mansion.

Dalya Bouvard and her friend Amira Mounier slept all weekend in the Library of the grand Mansion, in order to understand the clues of the Excelbox. They looked for all possible answers and ideas, they searched through all the existing books, they used all their neurons in their brains ... without managing to understand the 4 clues of the 4th Challenge.

Monday, December 11th, 1893. The night, in the grand Mansion.

It seemed like a calm, silent night. The full moon shone brightly. A breeze of cold air blew from time to time.

The maid Cristelle entered the kitchen of the grand Mansion, and she asked:

- Océanie ... can you bring the dinner tray to Mademoiselle? I must sweep the hall carpet. Igor can't move a pot of earth without scattering it all over the place!

Immediately, Océanie left the dishes to dry, and she arranged the tray for the young girl's dinner. A few minutes later, the help Cook Océanie knocked on the bedroom door, before entering inside, the dinner tray in her hands. Dalya was sitting alone, on an armchair in front of the fireplace, looking busy reading for the thousandth time the clues of the 4th Challenge.

When Océanie placed the tray on a table near her, Dalya smiled at her:

- Thank you for bringing me my dinner, Océanie.

In a caring voice, Océanie replied:

- Monsieur the Cook added cheese to the pasta, just the way you like it.

Dalya was not hungry. The pressure of the 4th Challenge which will take place the next day, took away her appetite, even though pasta with cheese and tomato sauce was her favorite dish. Océanie understood the young girl's anxiety about the next day's Challenge:

- You can't sleep on an empty stomach, Mademoiselle. You need to eat to be in great shape tomorrow.

With a slow and tired move, Dalya straightened up on her chair and she picked up her fork. After the 2nd fork of pasta, Dalya exclaimed:

- The sauce is delicious. And the cheese is exquisite.

Océanie put a few logs in the fireplace, and she smiled:

-   Monsieur the Cook will be happy if you finish your plate.

Under the strict orders of Lawyer Sloan Wilfrid, all the employees insisted on Dalya to finish her meals. And Dalya had no strength to refuse or to argue. A few minutes later, Dalya had finished eating her dinner, all of it.

-   Would you like anything else, Mademoiselle?
-   No, thank you Océanie. I'm going to bed in a moment.
-   Good night, Mademoiselle.
-   Good night, Océanie.

Dalya continued reading the clues. Océanie picked up the tray, and she was about to leave the bedroom. Suddenly, Océanie stopped in her move.

Since several weeks, Océanie had refrained from talking about an important thing. She didn't dare to speak about it, neither to the employees of the grand Mansion, nor to the Lawyer Sloan Wilfrid, nor to anyone. Océanie was impatiently waiting for Dalya Bouvard to regain her strength and feel better, in order to talk to her about it.

The help Cook Océanie didn't know how the 4th Challenge would go, the next day. She didn't know if she was going to see Dalya Bouvard again in the next few days. Therefore, not having enough time in front of her, Océanie had to talk to Dalya Bouvard about it that very evening!

At that moment, with slow steps, Océanie turned around and she approached Dalya. Still holding the dinner tray in her hands, Océanie hesitated to find her words:

-   There ... there is something that ... that you need to know, Mademoiselle.

Dalya realized that Océanie wanted to talk to her, but she hesitated. Dalya encouraged her:

-   What's going on, Océanie? Do sit down.

Immediately, Océanie put the empty tray on the table, and she sat down on the armchair opposite Dalya.

-   Mademoiselle ... I am sorry to sound intrusive and indiscreet. But it's been weeks that I have been holding back from telling you about it. Several months ago, one evening, you said something very true to me. And I allow myself to remind you of it, to you too, today.

Dalya Bouvard observed the young woman with a worried and curious look. The help Cook Océanie affirmed with a confident voice:

-   He doesn't deserve you, Mademoiselle.

Neither the employees of the grand Mansion, nor the Lawyer Sloan Wilfrid, nor her friends Amira Mounier, Alfie Jaq, or Maurice Gus ... no one dared to approach the subject of Richard Poirier, with Dalya Bouvard. And the young girl didn't dare to talk to anyone about it. Until that evening.

Dalya remembered that one day, several months ago, she tried to comfort Océanie who was suffering from a great depression. Dalya had said this sentence to her; he does not deserve you. Except that, the young girl was far from imagining that these same words will be addressed to her, one day. And because Océanie suffered almost the same ordeal, no one could understand and relieve Dalya better than her.

With a crushed and trembling voice, Dalya asked Océanie:

-   He doesn't deserve me ... because I'm just a vegetable seller at the market? It's because I'm not rich enough, not pretty enough, not educated enough, not from a Noble and Bourgeoise family like his fiancée? That's why he didn't choose me, isn't i...

Suddenly, Océanie interrupted Dalya in a strong and firm tone:

-   No, Mademoiselle !! I correct your idea immediately !! Richard Poirier doesn't deserve you, because he is miser ... and you are generous !!

Océanie's words were strange and difficult to understand for Dalya Bouvard. The young girl observed the help Cook with a confused look. Océanie seemed sure and certain of what she was saying, she repeated with a strong conviction:

-   He doesn't deserve you ... he is miser ... and you are generous!

That's all the help Cook Océanie wanted to say that night, and that was more than enough. Although Dalya Bouvard did not understand her words, she was grateful for all the encouragements and the cares of many people; including the help Cook Océanie.

For days and weeks, Dalya had been trying to understand why Richard Poirier rejected her and he didn't choose her. Except that sometimes the answers to our questions are revealed over time. So, Dear readers ... patience, patience.

It is true that we cannot avoid rejection, and we cannot control the healing. However, you must remember one important thing, Dear readers ... pain always has a limited time. And the wound always ends up closing. And as the Excelbox said it so well; breathe ... exhale ... gather all your wounds, and heal.

In this story and in reality, Dalya Bouvard really hoped to have a chance with Richard Poirier. She sincerely liked him. And even if she was rejected and despised, the poor little vegetable seller will rise up again and she will smile a second time!

Rising up again after a fall is a choice. Courage is a choice. Perseverance is a choice. Patience is a choice. And the 4th Challenge that will follow ... is certainly a choice!

And before we end this December night, the next few words are destined for one reader only. The real Richard Poirier will read these words one day. And just as the Author of this story begged to be granted 10 minutes, Richard Poirier will in turn beg to be granted 10 minutes.

Promise of James Arendorf.

Chapter 88

The Challenge

Tuesday, December 12th, 1893.

Generally, birthdays are happy days, spent around a delicious cake, discovering several gifts, and surrounded by happy laughs. Except for Dalya Bouvard.

On each day of her birthday, Dalya must answer a Question asked by a strange box, the Excelbox. Passing these tests is a requirement in the Will of the Late Mr. Governor Iskander Balthazar, in order to inherit his colossal fortune. Thus, every December 12th, the answer to the Question will determine the future of Dalya Bouvard. Either she will come close to the inheritance, which will save her family from poverty. Or, she will go back to selling vegetables and fruits at the market. Therefore, it is quite useless to describe the pressure, the heavy burden, and the fear of failure that invaded Dalya Bouvard, each December 12th.

In the evening, at 8 PM. In the grand Mansion.

The tension and the anxiety of this day invaded not only Dalya Bouvard, but other people as well. Lawyer Sloan Wilfrid couldn't focus on his files at the firm. That day, the mind of Sloan Wilfrid was preoccupied not only by this 4th Challenge, but also by the state of Dalya Bouvard.

As soon as he arrived at the grand Mansion, the Lawyer Sloan Wilfrid was greeted by the Manager Mr. Bûchebois. Immediately, Sloan Wilfrid asked him:

- How is she?

During the previous days, all the employees of the grand Mansion worked hard, day and night, to help Dalya Bouvard feel better and heal. But their efforts weren't enough. The head of the grand Mansion replied in a worried voice:

- She hasn't eaten much today. It is surely due to the stress of the Challenge which will take place tonight. She stayed in her room all day. She is too quiet, and often lost in her thoughts. She is still weak.

Lawyer Sloan Wilfrid took off his coat, and he understood:

- So ... she's not ready to answer the 4th Challenge tonight.

The head of the grand Mansion and Lawyer Sloan Wilfrid exchanged a worried look.

Upstairs, in front of a bedroom, Lawyer Sloan Wilfrid forced himself to smile and to look natural. He knocked on the door, before entering:

- Good evening, Mademoiselle.

Dalya Bouvard was sitting on an armchair, silent and motionless, watching the flames in the fireplace with a lost stare. The Snow Panther was lying down on the floor at the girl's feet. And as always, Séraphine perfectly felt the sadness of Dalya Bouvard. The Snow Panther looked worried for the young girl.

Dalya answered in a small voice, and a forced smile:

- Good evening, Mr. Wilfrid.

Worry invaded more and more Sloan Wilfrid. Since few years, and more precisely since the announcement of the Will, Sloan Wilfrid had always watched over, defended, and protected Dalya Bouvard. Except that day, the Lawyer was unable to help the young girl to come out of her sadness and to overcome her weakness.

When he sat down in the chair across from her, Sloan Wilfrid asked in a caring voice:

- I imagine that you have studied the clues that will allow you to answer the Challenge tonight. Do you have any idea what the 4th Question might be?

Dalya Bouvard remained silent for a long second. For several days, everyone, including the Lawyer Sloan Wilfrid, noticed that the young girl had changed; Dalya was quieter and more reserved, less dynamic and active. It was as if Dalya Bouvard lost a glow inside of her.

After a long second of silence, Dalya looked at the Lawyer Sloan Wilfrid, and she replied:

- I can no longer continue in these Challenges. I have no more energy.

Lawyer Sloan Wilfrid fully understood the young girl. This year has been eventful, difficult, and very painful to overcome, for Dalya Bouvard. The detention of her father, the blackmail of Lawyer Ernest Laszlo, the physical abuse of her mother, the mocking of the entire school, the anxiety of the trial, the pressure to save the Cotton Factory, the intensive preparation of the Thanksgiving party, the Richard Poirier slap ... and also what the Lawyer Sloan Wilfrid didn't know; the intensive and strange Gymnastics classes, the attack of the 3 masked intruders in the Library of the grand Mansion.

On the evening of the 4th Challenge, Dalya Bouvard was exhausted and empty.

8:35 PM.

For a few minutes, Dalya Bouvard and Sloan Wilfrid remained silent, sitting in the armchairs, staring at the flames in the fireplace. Dalya Bouvard had no more energy, neither to move, nor to speak, and even less to think about the 4th Challenge which will take place in a few hours. Dalya Bouvard lost her motivation and dynamism.

And the Lawyer Sloan Wilfrid had no words to say to encourage and comfort the young girl. That night, Sloan Wilfrid didn't know what to do or what to say. Silence and confusion invaded the Lawyer, the young girl, and the Snow Panther.

At one moment, strange noises were heard outside the grand Mansion. The Snow Panther, lying down by the fireplace, slowly straightened up and approached the bedroom windows. Séraphine lengthened her head to better see the origin of the strange noises, outside of the grand Mansion.

Curiosity invaded him, the Lawyer Sloan Wilfrid stood up too, and he approached the windows of the bedroom. Discovering the origin of the strange noises, Sloan Wilfrid seemed surprised:

- You should come see what's going on outside, Mademoiselle.

With the little energy she had left, and not wishing to appear rude, Dalya stood up and she approached the windows of her bedroom. The strange noises heard outside, were the sound of footsteps. At the entrance gate to the garden, there were thousands of people entering the grand Mansion. Men, women, old people, little ones, modest people, walking in a long line, and entering the grand Mansion.

Dalya exclaimed in a curious voice:

- Who are these people?

Lawyer Sloan Wilfrid recognized several faces, and he understood what was going on:

- They are the employees of the Cotton Factory, and their families.

Dalya still didn't understand the reason for the presence of these thousands of people at the grand Mansion. The Cotton Factory was saved many days earlier. The case is over. The Factory problem is solved.

- Why did they come to the grand Mansion, tonight?
- They are here for you, Mademoiselle.

At this precise moment, Dalya fell silent, observing the long line of people, entering the grand Mansion. Lawyer Sloan Wilfrid smiled as he observes the modest people:

- You have helped them to save the Cotton Factory, to keep their jobs, and their main source of income. You have defended them, while the others wanted to close the Factory and kick them out. You have supported them in a difficult time of their lives. So, tonight … all the Factory workers and their families, they have walked until the grand Mansion, for you, Mademoiselle. Their presence is their way of supporting you, today, in an important time of your life.

Dalya was amazed and touched by the presence of these thousands of people.

- They are all here ... for me?

Lawyer Sloan Wilfrid found his words and he finally knew what to say to encourage Dalya Bouvard:

- Mademoiselle ... I understand that you no longer have the energy to continue these Challenges. I understand that it is becoming more and more difficult and painful to succeed. Except that ... you must continue.

  You must continue for these thousands of employees of the Cotton Factory and their families, present for you tonight, at the grand Mansion. You must continue for the thousands of other employees of the other factories of the BalthEnterprise Holding. You must continue for this Inheritance coveted by the vultures, and which will be mercilessly liquidated. Thousands of lives are at risk.

  You must continue for the Governor Iskander Balthazar who believed in you and gave you a chance.

  You must continue for your family, and your little twin sisters Ari and Adi. You must continue for all the employees of the grand Mansion. You must continue for your friends Amira Mounier, Alfie Jaq, and Maurice Gus.

  You must continue for all the people who believe in you, and in your success. You must also continue for all the people who believe in your failure.

  And above all ... above all ... you must continue for yourself, Mademoiselle Dalya Bouvard!

9:07 PM.

With an encouraging smile, Lawyer Sloan Wilfrid greeted Dalya Bouvard, and he left her room, to offer her a few minutes of rest and thinking, before the start of the 4th Challenge.

Lawyer Sloan Wilfrid's words looped through the girl's mind. And he was quite right; despite the difficulties, the fatigue, and the obstacles, Dalya Bouvard had to continue in these Challenges. For her, and for thousands of other people.

For a long minute, Dalya watched through the windows of her room, the thousands of people entering the grand Mansion. Suddenly, the Snow Panther approached Dalya, she held her by her shirt, and gently directed her toward the small desk, where the strange box was placed.

The Snow Panther was a strangely intelligent and fascinating animal. Dalya understood what the Snow Panther was asking of her.

- I still have a 5th and last clue to ask, before the Challenge.

The Snow Panther displayed an encouraging smile. The strange box offered 5 clues, to help answer the Question, on the day of the birthday. Until this night, Dalya Bouvard had only asked for 4 clues. She had one more left.

Slowly and tiredly, Dalya Bouvard sat down in front of her desk, facing the strange box. The Excelbox was shining in all its glory. The small rectangular opening on the edge was always open, welcoming doubts and questions. The transparent and oval glass cage was gracefully straightened, welded by 4 cylinders in the shape of a vine plant. The clock inside was also fascinating and unusual, showing days and months. The big and small needles were close of only a few hours.

Spontaneously, without really thinking about it, Dalya wrote her question on a small piece of paper.

What is the 5ᵗʰ clue?

The Excelbox was always happy and eager to answer the young girl's doubts, anxieties, worries and questions. Immediately, the Excelbox swallowed the small piece of paper, an impressive light sprang from the strange box, and an answer was offered to the young girl. Dalya picked up the paper, and she read:

Breathe. Exhale. And now you rise up.
To survive the outside, look inside.

At that precise moment, Dalya Bouvard closed her eyes. Sitting in front of the Excelbox, Dalya Bouvard carried out the instructions of this strange box, without thinking and without trying to understand.

Eyes closed, Dalya Bouvard slowly inhaled a long breath, she slowly exhaled a long breath. Then, Dalya Bouvard opened her eyes ... and she rose up.

9:22 PM.

Despite the 5 clues offered by the Excelbox were incomprehensible, despite the 4ᵗʰ Question was a mystery, despite the fatigue and weakness, Dalya Bouvard gathered the little energy she still had, and she left her room, followed by the Snow Panther.

When she reached the end of the corridor on the upper floor, and about to descend the stairs, Dalya stopped abruptly. Thousands of people waited patiently on the stairs, in the hall, and at the entrance of the grand Mansion. Men, women, old people, adults, children.

As soon as Dalya Bouvard appeared, all the whispering stopped, and all eyes turned toward her. For a second, a total silence invaded the grand Mansion.

When Dalya Bouvard moved to walk down the stairs, suddenly thousands of people applauded warmly. Dalya Bouvard descended the stairs slowly, surprised and moved, under warm applauses and encouraging smiles.

Descending the stairs, Dalya recognized several familiar faces; the volunteers who helped in the preparation of the party, the employees of the Cotton Factory and their families, some Managers of the BalthEnterprise Holding, the waiters of the Toscana restaurant, the dressmaker Mrs. Lancel and her craftsmen, the Moroccan Cook Lalla Tafernout and her son the Concierge Dadès, the women of the Alley N°106 who delivered the invitations to the Ambassadors, the Dean of Merchants Mr. Kenan Einsenberg, and the flower seller Lalla Fatim Fadl ... they all applauded, with a sincere smile.

Arriving in the hall, Dalya noticed the employees of the grand Mansion in a corner. Mr. Bûchebois, the Cook Mr. Ferrero, Cristelle, Igor, Océanie and her baby, the Gardener, they all applauded intensely. Dalya's paternal Uncle, Giorgi Bouvard was smiling proudly, and he was holding the little twins, each in one hand. And like everyone else, Ari and Adi joyfully applauded their big sister Dalya.

At the entrance of the grand Mansion, Professor Canfield was easily recognizable by his checkered suit. Professor Canfield and Professor Haîyang applauded and smiled proudly. The Library assistant Miss Guendolyn and Dalya's best friend, Amira Mounier, they applauded, without succeeding to hold back their tears. Dalya's friends, Alfie Jaq and Maurice Gus cheered ardently and louder than everyone.

At the door of the living room where the Challenge will take place, Dalya was surprised to see familiar faces. Congressman Yolan McKlain joined everyone present, and he applauded with an encouraging and determined smile. The Lawyer Master Victor Barold was also present; he applauded intensely, and he prayed for the success of Dalya Bouvard, in order to continue his revenge on the Lawyer Ernest Laszlo.

Lawyer Sloan Wilfrid was surprised by the unexpected presence of these thousands of people that night at the grand Mansion. And above all, Sloan Wilfrid was relieved and happy that Dalya had come out of her room, and that she decided to continue the Challenges. With a thoughtful gesture, Lawyer Sloan Wilfrid smiled and applauded.

As of now, the career and the future of the young Lyor Laszlo, were connected to BalthEnterprise Holding, and therefore to the success of Dalya Bouvard. With a discreet smile, Lyor Laszlo joined everyone, and he applauded discreetly.

At one moment, and for a long minute, Dalya Bouvard stood motionless, in the middle of the hall, she observed the thousands of people around her ... on the stairs, in the hall, at the front door, at the living room door ... thousands of people were smiling and applauding. Nobody needed to say a word. The warm applauses and the encouraging smiles were enough. Dalya Bouvard was moved by the applauses, the smiles, and the presence of all these people, that night, at the grand Mansion. This gesture, however small it seems, filled Dalya Bouvard with a strange feeling ... a strange strength.

10:07 PM.

In the living room of the grand Mansion, when Dalya Bouvard placed the strange box on a table, silence reigned throughout the house. All curious and impatient eyes observed the Excelbox. It is true that the strange box fascinated and intimidated, no one understood how it worked, but everyone obeyed to it.

The few seats in the living room of the grand Mansion were occupied by Congressman Yolan McKlain, Lawyers Sloan Wilfrid and Lyor Laszlo, the Edelmen family and their ally Lawyer Ernest Laszlo, Professor Canfield and Amira Mounier, Uncle Giorgi Bouvard and the little twins Ari and Adi. The living room door remained wide open; the thousands of other people attentively followed all the details of this 4th Challenge. In the hall, the stairs, and at the entrance of the grand Mansion, the thousands of people held their breath, and they waited patiently.

It is useless to remind the attitude of the Edelmen family and the Lawyer Ernest Laszlo, that night. No applauses of course, haughty looks, arrogant allures, despised smiles. The niece Mrs. Honoré Edelmen and the nephew Mr. Ferdinand Edelmen didn't even stood up to greet Congressman Yolan McKlain. And the Lawyer Ernest Laszlo didn't dare to pronounce a word in the presence of the Congressman.

Lawyer Sloan Wilfrid stood up, he faced everyone present, and he announced:

- Mesdames and Messieurs. The 4th Challenge required in the Will of the Late Mr. Governor Iskander Balthazar … begins!

Turning toward Dalya Bouvard, Lawyer Sloan Wilfrid whispered to her:

- Good luck!

Dalya Bouvard answered with a calm and serene smile. Strangely, and without being able to explain how and why, the presence of these thousands of people soothed Dalya Bouvard's fear and anxiety. And for the first time since ever, Dalya felt calm and confident, before knowing the Question of a Challenge.

With a spontaneous gesture, Dalya Bouvard wrote her request:

What is the 4th Question?

The Excelbox waited 12 long months to get this request. As soon as the small piece of paper was placed on the rectangular opening, the strange box swallowed it inside, and emitted an impressive light. And immediately, a little paper came out of the strange box. Dalya Bouvard took it, and she read aloud:

The first helps to start,

The second helps to ahead walk,

The third helps through cross.

The fourth ... found inside, helps to rise up.

My 4ᵗʰ Question is

In one word, what is it?

A serious and grave silence invaded the entire grand Mansion. The Congressman straightened up on his chair. The niece and the nephew Edelmen were anxious. Ernest Laszlo became pale. Sloan Wilfrid and Lyor Laszlo exchanged worried looks. Amira Mounier clearly felt her throat choke. Professor Canfield looked confused. Uncle Giorgi Bouvard trembled.

And Dalya Bouvard ... she smiled.

As unusual as it may seem... at this precise moment... as soon as the statement of the Challenge was pronounced... Dalya Bouvard knew the answer to the 4ᵗʰ Challenge, in a second!

- I know the answer to the 4ᵗʰ Question.

Dalya Bouvard's announcement surprised everyone present. And above all, the speed and the confident calm of this announcement. In the first 3 Challenges, it took Dalya Bouvard several minutes of thinking to find the answer. Except this time.

And as usual, Dalya stood in front of the present people, and she explained her answer.

- I received 5 clues, supposed to help me find the answer to the 4ᵗʰ Question.

The 1ˢᵗ clue: Breathe. Exhale. Wait. To survive the outside, look inside. I asked for this clue after my father was detained. And without really thinking, I followed the Excelbox's instructions, I breathed in, I exhaled, and I waited. Patience is all the Excelbox advised me to do. From this clue, I learned the strength it takes to be patient in the painful times of our lives.

The 2nd clue: Breathe. Exhale. Confront. To survive the outside, look inside. This clue was given to me the day before my father's trial. And again, the Excelbox advised me to inhale, exhale and confront. From this clue, I learned that at some point in our life, we must have the strength to fight and confront the difficult Challenges.

The 3rd clue: The immense armored door opens simply with a small key. By the 106, amazed you will be. To survive the outside, look inside. After the intention to close the Cotton Factory, I asked the Excelbox for help. The amount of money to be raised was immense, the people to invite were impossible to reach, and there were thousands of jobs at risk. However, and as the Excelbox has affirmed, the Alley N°106 amazed us, and we managed to save the Cotton Factory. From this clue, I learned the real strength of mutual aid and solidarity.

The 4th clue: Breathe. Exhale. Gather all your wounds, and heal. The 1000 pieces can avail. To survive the outside, look inside. I don't know why the Excelbox insisted so much on the breathing, but I followed its instructions. And I admit that in difficult times, this simple gesture of breathing and exhaling can save our life. I also don't know why the Excelbox indicated Governor Iskander Balthazar's 1000 Piece Puzzle. But... it occupied my mind, and forced me to get out of my bed and out of my sadness. And just as the Excelbox has ordered, I gathered my wounds, and healed. From this clue, I learned the strength it takes to heal ourselves.

The 5th clue: Breathe. Exhale. And now you rise up. To survive the outside, look inside. From this clue, and because of a strange incident with 3 intruders at the Library of the grand Mansion, I learned that I had deep inside me ... the strength to rise up again.

The Excelbox repeated the same sentence in all 5 clues. To survive the outside, look inside. I learned that to survive difficult times and hardships, we must seek the necessary strength, within ourselves.

Observing the people present in the living room, the thousands of people at the entrance door and in the hall, Dalya Bouvard continued:

- To answer the Excelbox's Question ... Courage helps to start, Perseverance helps to ahead walk, Patience helps through cross. The Strength ... found inside, the strength helps to rise up.

And instantly, Dalya Bouvard wrote her answer to the 4th Question, on a small piece of paper:

Strength

Dear readers ... what if, just for once, you too followed the advice of the Excelbox? ... Breathe, exhale, be patient in difficult times. Breathe, exhale, confront the difficult Challenges. Breathe, exhale, gather all your wounds, and heal. Breathe, exhale, and now ... rise up!

And above all, Dear readers ... look no further. To survive the outside, you will find inside yourself ... an invincible strength!

Promise of the Excelbox.

11:15 PM.

The grand Mansion was invaded by an intense silence. All eyes were focused on the young girl and the strange box.

With a serene gesture, Dalya Bouvard approached the Excelbox, and she introduced her answer. At that precise moment, everyone present held their breath, and they waited for the judgment of the Excelbox. A single word from this strange box ... will influence the fate of thousands of people.

And Dear readers, before ending this day, there is one last piece of information to clarify ... just as the Excelbox has asked; the Author of this story can proudly confirm ... Dalya Bouvard rose up!

Dépôt légal : 2022MO3477
Cover design & Print by ALPHA PRINT
www.alphaprintmaroc.com